"Ten."
Barbousse announced grimly.
"Nine . . . Eight . . . Seven . . ."

Brim had to fight the controls with all his concentration. *Come on Barbousse!*

"Four . . . three . . . two . . . one . . . Torpedoes running, Cap'm!"

In the wink of an eye, dark spindles flashed out from beneath *Starfury*'s bridge and headed squarely for the battleship. Instantly, Brim threw in full military power, pulled the nose up and rolled out into a violent jink. But he was moments too late.

With unbelievable concussion and sound, the whole forward tip of *Starfury*'s starboard pontoon disappeared in a tremendous blast of radiant energy. Her hull jumped and quivered for a long moment as Brim fought to bring the ship back under control.

Then, without warning, they were again blasted off course—this time by an even more stupendous explosion. And the whole Universe seemed to light up by the birth of some hellacious new star . . .

Also by Bill Baldwin

THE TROPHY
THE HELMSMAN
GALACTIC CONVOY

THE MERCENARIES

BILL BALDWIN

WARNER BOOKS

A Time Warner Company

WARNER BOOKS EDITION

Copyright © 1991 by Merl Baldwin
All rights reserved.

Questar is a registered trademark of Warner Books, Inc.

Cover illustration by John Berkey
Cover design by Don Puckey

Warner Books, Inc.
666 Fifth Avenue
New York, N.Y. 10103

A Time Warner Company

Printed in the United States of America

First Printing: June, 1991

10 9 8 7 6 5 4 3 2 1

CHAPTER 1

Bromwich, 52009

Commander Wilf Brim, I.F., scanned a mass of polychrome data cascading over his four readout consoles—then checked the panel clock. "It's time, Number One," he said, nodding to Lieutenant Nadia Tissaurd at the CoHelmsman's station beside him. "Let's pipe it on the blower."

"Aye, Captain," Tissaurd replied; a deft pass of her index finger triggered the starship's intercom. "Hands to lift-off stations," she announced, her voice resounding into every cubic iral of the big starship. "Hands to lift-off stations. Stand by mooring and fender beams!"

Abruptly, the bridge filled with noises of imminent departure: running footfalls, airtight doors slamming, the cadenced babble of thirty different checklists. Brim settled into his recliner with a full measure of excitement. Beneath his boots, I.F.S. *Starfury*'s deck trembled to the steady beat of six Admiralty A876 gravity generators running at fast idle in long pontoons at either side of the main hull. Above it all, he sensed (more than heard) the treble rush of steering engines as Engineering Officer Strana' Zaftrak carried out her last-moment checklist at the Systems Console behind him. No need for worry there. The Sodeskayan woman was thorough.

A scraping thud announced the brow had been swayed back

1

to the edge of the gravity pool; anyone aboard now was on his way to the space trials—whether that was what he intended or not.

"Hands stand by for internal gravity," Tissaurd announced on the blower. A woman in her early forties from the Lampsen Provinces with laughing eyes, jet-black hair, and a compact figure, her matter-of-fact competency had been an asset since the day she signed on as First Lieutenant—only metacycles following Brim's own arrival as Commanding Officer. With the million-odd tasks to be accomplished before the new ship was commissioned, her kind of cheerful willingness had been doubly appreciated. Besides, she was sexy in her own way.

Once more Brim verified the flow of information over his console, then swallowed hard and nodded to Zaftrak's furry visage in a display. "Switch it, Strana'," he ordered quietly.

The Sodeskayan winked and passed a delicate, six-fingered hand over the gravity console beside her, changing sixteen flashing red indicators to steady blue—and savaging Brim's stomach in an avalanche of nausea as gravity cycled from planetary to the ship's artificial gradient. During twenty-nine years in space he had never become inured to the change, especially if it happened abruptly.

When his vision cleared, he shunted one of his displays to the PoolMaster in a control cupola on the rim of the gravity pool, twenty-five irals beneath *Starfury*'s levitated hull. "Single up the moorings, if you please, Master Scirri," he ordered.

"Singling up moorings," replied Scirri's bearded face from the display. He had narrow lips, a sharp nose, and the humorless, close-set eyes of a sharpshooter. He was the best PoolMaster at Sherrington's.

Through the Hyperscreens—normally transparent crystalline windows that simulated conventional vision at Hyperspeeds— Brim watched a network of greenish mooring beams wink out one by one. Presently, the ship was tethered by a single set of four springs projected from the corners of the gravity pool, flaring up and abating as *Starfury* moved to the wind.

Outside, the weather was moderating—at last. Bromwich city (indeed all of Rhodor's boreal hemisphere) had been stormy that winter. But at present, the air was clean and crisp over squalid, whitecapped Glammarian Bight. Brim looked out across the ship's snub-nosed prow, drinking in the pair of graceful ebony pontoons that jutted almost fifty irals beyond. From the tip of each, two 406-mmi disruptors continued forward for another seventy-five irals. Once exclusively reserved for use on the largest battleships, twelve of these deadly and brutally efficient ship-killing mechanisms could now be mounted on light cruisers like *Starfury*—but only by dint of recent technology, developed not a moment too soon. A sad, fragile peace that doggedly persisted among the Galactic dominions reminded Brim of the thin winter dayshine outside: it still managed a pallid light, but all the heat had long ago escaped. Even as he sat in his Helmsman's seat, the old enemy was constructing new, deep-space fortifications in a score of locations. War was about to break out all over the galaxy, and with a sadly depleted Imperial Fleet, only *Starfury* and the sister ships that would follow her from the Sherrington Works held any genuine promise for a bleak-looking future. . . .

The bridge had grown quiet now, every console manned and active. "Ship's buttoned up, Captain," Tissaurd reported with a grin. "All hands are at stations and pretaxi checklists are done," she said. "Ready to proceed. . . ."

"Good work, Nadia," Brim replied. He touched the COMM panel at his right hand. "Bromwich Ground," he sent, "Fleet K5054 requests immediate G-pool departure."

"K5054: affirmative. Cleared immediate G-pool departure."

"K5054," Brim acknowledged. Then, into the display: "Master Scirri, stand by springs!" He checked fore and aft through the Hyperscreens—all clear. *Starfury* had a quartering wind on her starboard bow. No particular problem, but it never hurt to be careful. . . . Narrowing his eyes, he waited for the proper balance of wind and mooring beams, before "Let go port springs!"

"All clear port, Captain," the bearded PoolMaster reported from his console.

The crosswind meant that Brim would have to go ahead on the back spring and get the stern to swing out to port. He touched his power console. Immediately two narrow amethyst damper rays warmed the palm of his hand, each controlled three of the ship's six gravity generators on its respective side. Nudging the starboard glow forward without altering its color, he called up only enough power to move the ship. "Let go the forrard spring!" he barked.

"All clear forrard, Captain," Scirri acknowledged.

Starfury's deck throbbed steadily to the increased beat of her Admiralty A876s; a mug of cvceese' rattled on a nearby console.

"Stow that mug," Brim snapped quietly.

"Aye, Captain," came someone's embarrassed reply. The mug disappeared immediately.

Brim regarded the spring tightening below. Too much strain and the poolside projectors would override—letting *Starfury* skid downwind into a sleek destroyer moored on the next gravity pool. Unthinkable! He trained a second display aft, watching his gravity generators turn the view to shimmering haze, then remembered to breathe as afternoon light began to blank the blue glow of stationary repulsion units at the bottom of the pool. The stern was beginning to swing out, angling away while the solitary spring took the starship's slow thrust like a great leash.

Starfury was soon skewed across the gravity pool at about ten degrees, with the PoolMaster's cupola hidden beneath the port pontoon. Brim drew the starboard damper ray back to idle. "Let go aft spring!" he ordered.

"All clear aft, Captain!"

At the precise moment the last spring beam disappeared, Brim moved both damper rays forward together. With only a moment's hesitation the big starship eased off her gravity pool and out over the strand, hovering a regulation twenty-five irals above the unique, three-element footprint she pushed into the surface of the dirty water thumping and foaming beneath her hulls. "Bromwich Ground," Brim sent, "K5054 requests taxi instructions."

"K5054: cross one seven left without delay and hold at locus six five."

"K5054," Brim acknowledged. He glanced off to starboard. A trio of Sherrington F.7/30 attack ships was running up at the landward termination of takeoff vector Seventeen Right, clouds of mist and spume mounting into the pale blue sky behind them.

They'd have to salute *Starfury*, of course. "Ready to take the honors, Lieutenant?" he prompted Morris at the COMM console.

"Ready, Captain,"

Presently, old-fashioned characters flashed across his KA'PPA display, "MAY STARS LIGHT ALL THY PATHS."

He looked up in time to see glowing KA'PPA rings shimmer out from *Starfury*'s high beacon—the message would arrive instantaneously throughout the Universe, though all but the three F.7s would ignore it: "AND THY PATHS, STAR TRAVELERS." Gradually moving both damper rays forward, he hurried across their path, then slowed and came to a hover with HOLD buoy number sixty-five off the tip of *Starfury*'s port pontoon. Moments afterward, the malevolent-looking F.7s thundered past in close formation, trailing three lofty cascades of spray that doused *Starfury*'s Hyperscreens like a waterfall before they abruptly subsided about a c'lenyt out on the bight, where the three ships soared gracefully into the sky.

Brim grinned to himself. Cheeky rascals, those young Helmsmen, just about as cheeky as he'd been himself twenty-five years ago in his native Carescria—especially when he thought he had a faster ship. They clearly hadn't heard of *Starfury*'s dazzling acceleration—yet. He relaxed in his recliner and listened to Tissaurd and Zaftrak completing their lift-off checklist.

"Transponders and 'home' indicator?" Tissaurd asked.

"On," Zaftrak responded.

"Fullstop cell?"

"Powered."

"Warning lights?"

"On."

"Engineer's check?"

"Complete."

"Antiskid?"

"Skid is on."

"Speed brake?"

"Forward."

"Stabilizer trim—delete the gravity gradient, if you please."

"Gradient null."

"Course indicators?"

"Set and checked."

"Lift-off check is complete, Captain," Tissaurd reported.

"Very well, Nadia," Brim responded, then used the next brief moments to make his own audits of the starship's systems, finishing only moments before Ground Control came back on line. "K5054: taxi into position, hold one seven right," the controller sent. "Contact Bromwich Tower. Good day."

"Into position and hold, 5054. Good day," Brim acknowledged, easing forward again to follow a series of bobbing markers until a ruby light gleamed out of the distance. Then he put the helm over, turned into the wind, and centered the glimmer in a small circle projected on the Hyperscreen from his console. "Bromwich Tower: K5054 in position and holding. . . ."

"K5054 is cleared for lift-off," the Tower sent. "Wind three one five at two seven gusts four seven."

"Cleared for lift-off, K5054," Brim acknowledged. He flicked the blower. "All hands stand by for lift-off," he warned the crew, then glanced over his shoulder.

Zaftrak was holding her left hand up, thumb in the air. *Starfury* was ready.

In all his years at a helm, Brim had never outgrown the wild, almost-physical thrill of lift-off. "I'll have full military power, Strana'," he said.

"One hundred percent military," Zaftrak replied.

"Steering engine's amidships," Tissaurd added—the last item on *Starfury*'s preflight checklist.

Taking a deep breath, Brim stood on the gravity brakes and cautiously moved both damper rays forward until they passed from amethyst to blue, then to green . . . yellow . . . orange . . . finally to flashing red. The deep rumbling of the gravity generators changed voice to a thunderous bellow that shook *Starfury*'s whole spaceframe and resonated deafeningly through the Hyperscreens as if the big ship were centered in the midst of some gigantic explosion. Astern, a long strip of the Bight had suddenly flattened into a madly flowing millrace that ended in a towering cloud of spray and ice particles soaring at least a c'lenyt into the pale winter sky.

"Six lights are on, Captain," Zaftrak called above the noise, "you've got one fifteen thrust!"

Brim cleared his flight path visually, made another pass over his readouts. "Here we go!" he shouted, then released the brakès. . . .

Instantly, the big starship began to move forward—completely unlike generations of predecessors that took what seemed to be eternities at full power before they would even respond to their steering engines. In only moments *Starfury* was trailing lofty cascades of spray and plunging smoothly across the water at tremendous velocity. The enormous quantities of power available did little to interfere with the ship's naturally delicate, quick, and positive response to control manipulations. After a moment, her bows lifted slightly to the mighty beat of the generators, then fell again while speed increased through 165 c'lenyts per meta-cycle. At about 170, Brim eased back on the controls overcoming a slight tendency to nose down farther, then as she accelerated through 180, he lifted the bow and let the ship's weight transfer to the gravs, applying about a third rudder to check a normal swing to port during lift-off. A moment later she separated from her shadow and began climbing smoothly over the Sherrington Works on the way to the ultimate freedom of her native element: deep interstellar space.

"K5054 is at one thousand and climbing," Brim reported.

"K5054: turn port fifteen to join two thirty radial outbound blue, contact Blue District Departure Control," Sherrington Tower advised while *Starfury* bounced through light turbulence.

"K5054: turning port fifteen to two thirty radial outbound blue. Good day," Brim replied.

"Best o' luck on the trials, Commander."

"Thanks, Control, we can always use it."

As he trimmed the ship's head toward the assigned departure radial, Brim glanced down at fifteen Starfury-class warships on gravity stocks below—in various forms of completion. He'd inspected three of them the previous afternoon. Another fifteen —fitting out on bay-side gravity pools—were on HOLD status while Sherrington engineers awaited results of his prototype's space trials. He shook his head while the course indicator settled onto its new heading. Those ships down there were being put together on little more than faith alone: faith that I.F.S. *Starfury*'s original design was sound—and a sincere hope that the mistakes she did embody could be easily and economically corrected. Major modifications to a fleet of thirty-one warships could actually spell financial disaster to the credit-strapped Imperial Fleet. They would almost certainly mean that Crown Prince Onrad would be deprived of his succession. The only son of Emperor Greyffin IV and heir to the Imperial throne at Avalon, Onrad had personally ordered *Starfury*'s creation at the historic Dytasburg conference in Sodeskaya the previous year, then immediately funded thirty additional "prototypes" using discretionary development funds. He took these seemingly rash actions because he *truly* believed that war might soon engulf the "civilized" dominions of the galaxy, during a time when the once-great Imperial Fleet had been reduced to a mere shadow of its former might.

Abruptly, the COMM light blinked green. Tissaurd was in contact with Blue District Departure Control. "K5054, climbing through fifteen thousand on two thirty radial," he reported.

"K5054," Control replied. "You are cleared through three hundred c'lenyts on two thirty radial outbound blue. Advise slower traffic approximately twenty-five c'lenyts off your bow. Contact Blue Planetary Control."

"K5054 cleared through three hundred c'lenyts on two thirty radial outbound blue. Contact Blue Planetary and acknowledge slower traffic approximately twenty-five c'lenyts off bow. Good day."

"Much success with the trials, Commander."

"Thanks, District," Brim acknowledged. "We'll give them our best shot." He nodded his head. A lot of people believed in *Starfury* and the royal orders that had put her into production. But that belief was by no means universal among the diverse peoples of the Empire. Since the year 52000 when the delusory Treaty of Garak ended open warfare between Nergol Triannic's League of Dark Stars and Greyffin IV's far-flung Galactic Empire, a sinister and powerful antimilitary organization had infiltrated the Imperial Government as well as the Admiralty itself.

Known as the Congress for Intra-Galactic Accord, and almost openly funded by the League itself, it was chaired by a one-time shipmate of Brims, Commodore Puvis Amherst. The CIGAs' avowed goal was dismantling—from within—the mighty Imperial Fleet that had nearly annihilated League Admiral Kabul Anak's spaceborne armadas. All, of course, in the name of "Peace."

Unfortunately, during almost nine-odd years of false truce, the craven Amherst and his CIGAs had been all too successful at their task—at the same time their League masters secretly rebuilt war-decimated battle squadrons at a feverish pace. And now they were working on their xaxtdamned space forts. . . .

Brim had seen Onrad's courageous move raise a predictable hue and cry from CIGAs all over the Empire, but the Prince remained undeterred, indefatigable in his belief that the new ships constituted the absolute minimum counterforce necessary to insure survival of civilization. Clearly, he trusted that eventually he would be vindicated—and meanwhile, each new Starfury added to the possibility that the Empire might persevere into the second phase of a war that was coming as surely as helium follows hydrogen on the chart.

Brim's LightSpeed meter read .86 when he passed the three F.7s at nearly double their speed, leaving them tossing wildly in his graviton wake. He smiled briefly, imagining the consternation aboard the fast little ships as *Starfury* swept past them as if they were still sitting on a gravity pool.

Again, the COMM light flashed on the panel before him. "K5054 at two eighty c'lenyts on two thirty outbound and climbing," he reported.

"K5054: cleared direct to deep space and light speed. Knock 'em dead, *Starfury*!"

"Count on it," Brim answered. Then, moments later, the LightSpeed meter passed 1.0 and normal radio communications ceased.

They were fourteen Standard Days at *Starfury*'s space trials, conducted for reasons of secrecy at the gigantic—and nearly abandoned—Fleet base on Gimmas Haefdon. Gimmas had been

Brim's first duty station out of the Helmsman's Academy, nearly sixteen years previously, when he was assigned to Regula Collingswood's old T-class destroyer I.F.S. *Truculent*. Closed for nearly ten years now by CIGA-contrived "economic" concerns, the great base—covering much of the planet's land mass—would already be yielding to the corrosive effects of Gimmas's brutally frigid climate. Brim had been in contact with the trials party for nearly half a cycle when *Starfury* thundered down out of perpetually dense storm clouds over the tossing Sea of Garnatz; however, nothing could have prepared him for the barren, frozen wasteland that lay below. The base's great, ocean-spanning causeways appeared to be intact, but they were covered with snow and ice, and seemed to be no more navigable than the gray, ice-strewn sea they surmounted. Nothing moved as far as his eye could see. The planet's wearisome flatness was broken only by vast complexes of forlorn structures that looked as if they were constructed of nothing more permanent than the ice and snow that covered them.

Closer to the surface, Tissaurd pointed out vast compounds of battleship-sized gravity pools covered with drifted snow and locked in ice that must now extend all the way to the bottom of their feeder canals. In sprawling scrap yards, hundreds of discarded starships lay in slipshod rows beneath the drifted snow. Some of the hulls, by their very shapes, were obsolete. But far too many were clearly serviceable, modern starships, relegated prematurely to abandonment by industrious CIGAs—citizens of the Empire who were causing more damage to their own Fleet than all the powerful squadrons of warships Nergol Triannic had been able to effect in a fully declared war.

Within half a metacycle they were sweeping low past the colossal structures that were once the Base's Central Complex: lofty glass and metal towers so tall their exaggerated perspective gave Brim a brief feeling of vertigo as he sped past. Nearby was the enormous parade ground where he received his first medals from Crown Prince Onrad so many years ago—just before he'd been transferred to I.F.S. *Defiant*. From thirty thousand irals, the great tract appeared to be no larger than his thumbnail.

Broad—empty—avenues extended out from the deserted

complex like c'lenyts-long spokes of some gigantic wheel whose interstices were filled by jumbles of odd-shaped structures, soaring conduits, rows of ship-sized tanks, huge mushroom-shaped reactor sites, and a maze of empty tram lines. All were covered by unblemished layers of drifted snow—except, strangely, the reactor sites. Every one of these appeared to be free of snow and clearly operational. Surrounded by soaring energy-transmission towers and topped by blazing beacons, their enormous collapsium domes gleamed as if they had only just been installed. Odd, Brim considered, that so much power was necessary for a purely maintenance effort, even if one counted the enormous energy needed to protect some of the base's larger, more valuable structures. But the Admiralty never had been noted for its logic —especially in peacetime.

Near the shore, and verging a prodigious expanse of half-buried maintenance structures, two small groups of buildings fronted six active gravity pools in a tiny aggregation of cleared streets and melted snow. Five of the pools were already occupied. As Tissaud piped landing cautions throughout the hull, Brim picked out two speedy-looking V-class destroyers—those would act as chase ships during the trials. A large supply vessel in the colors of AkroKahn, the Sodeskayan space line, clearly housed shops and facilities for tuning *Starfury*'s Drive components. On the next two gravity pools, a huge repair and salvage vessel and a smaller commissary transport completed the little squadron. He shook his head. All for testing a single ship.

"Ironic, isn't it?" Tissaurd's voice broke into his thoughts.

"I was thinking 'wasteful,' myself," Brim muttered as *Starfury* bumped through turbulence over the shoreline. "But I'm sure it's ironic, too," he allowed grimly. Ahead, a five-c'lenyt-long section of ice was melting into a landing strip as he watched. Clearly, the reactors here were operating flawlessly, too.

"You bet it's ironic, Skipper," Tissaurd said firmly, "sending all these ships to provide trials facilities at one of the most significant military bases in the known Universe. The Admiralty should never have closed Gimmas in the first place. Someday, we'll be sorry we let Amherst and his CIGAs get away with it."

"A lot of us were sorry way back when it happened," Brim

replied. "I wasn't even in the service then. I got bumped in the first Reduction In Force."

"The first RIF—after the Treaty of Garak?" Tissaurd asked.

"That's the one," Brim said, banking into a course paralleling the long strip of ice mush that was now churning wildly from tremendous convection currents. "I'd been in enough action to know the Leaguers for the zukeeds they really are, so I wasn't exactly in a mood to stop fighting."

Tissaurd laughed wryly. "That must have been just about the time I graduated from the Helmsman's Academy," she said. "I suppose we cadets were more acceptable to them. We hadn't seen much of the real war."

Brim chuckled. "Well, you've certainly sullied your acceptability now, shipping out in *Starfury* the way you have," Brim observed. "The CIGA factions in the Admiralty are really upset about *Starfury*—they'll be keeping a sharp eye on anyone associated with her."

"That's what I wanted," Tissaurd replied. "You know, you've only a few Standard Years on me, Skipper—I've been around awhile myself. It was about time I declared a choice."

"A declaration, unfortunately, for Right, not Might," Brim observed, glancing into the rearview monitor. "Those CIGAs all but run the Admiralty these days." Nearly ten c'lenyts distant now, the patch of slush was now turned to water and the convection currents had already subsided. He pulled off power and rolled into a bank, hauling the big starship around in a tight curve until she lined up with the strip of gray water, already speckled with whitecaps from Gimmas's constant wind. "I'll have the landing checklist now, Number One," he said, then pushed the nose over and started for the surface.

When the last mooring beams had flashed out to *Starfury*'s optical bollards and the ship was secure on her gravity pool, Brim switched the controls to Strana' Zaftrak and winked at Tissaurd. "I think we're getting the hang of this, Number One," he quipped.

Tissaurd grinned. "Best team in the Fleet"—she chuckled,

sliding out of her seat—"and damned quickly, if I do say so myself."

"Just the same, we ought to keep on practicing for a while," Brim called over his shoulder as he looked out at the little group waiting at the entrance to the brow. Even in heated battlesuits, the few humans who had ventured into the frigid wind looked miserably cold huddled in the lee of the brow entrance.

The Bears who waited with them, however, were waving heartily at the big warship. Dressed in colorful Sodeskayan winter garb, they looked right at home in the driving snow. Sodeskaya, "Mother Planet" of the G.F.S.S. (Great Federation of Sodeskayan States), orbited a cool dwarf star named Ostra that meted out little more energy than Gimmas itself.

Brim quickly donned his heated Fleet Cloak and followed Tissaurd off the bridge, clapping Zaftrak on the shoulder as he passed. "Best damned team in the known Universe, Skipper," she called after him.

"Unknown Universe, too," Brim added from the companionway. "Don't sell us short!"

Nikolai Yanuarievich Ursis, one of Brim's oldest friends and Dean of the famous Dytasburg Academy on the G.F.S.S. planet of Zhiv'ot, met him at the end of the brow with an authentic Bear hug. Standing a quarter again as tall as Brim, he had small gray eyes of enormous intensity, dark reddish-brown fur, a long, urbane muzzle that terminated in a huge wet nose, and a grin so wide that fang jewels on either side of his mouth blazed out in the light of the doorway. Although a Polkovnik in the Sodeskayan Home Guard (and an equivalent full Captain in the Imperial Fleet), he was dressed in his civilian persona. On his head he wore a colossal egg-shaped hat of curly wool that covered his ears and added at least an iral to his already formidable height. His black, knee-length greatcoat—embellished by two rows of huge gold buttons and jasmine waist sash—was cut in the old military style with a stiff collar, embroidered cuffs, and a wide skirt. Crimson trousers bagged stylishly over his thick calf-length boots, the latter of black leather so soft that it bunched at the ankles. His hands were protected by delicately embroidered, six-fingered gloves of ophet leather. "Wilf Ansor, my old comrade!" he roared. "Grand Duke Anastas Alexyi sends regards."

"Nik!" Brim exclaimed through a happy grin, "what in the Universe are you doing here? I thought you'd be tied up in Zhiv'ot this time of year."

Ursis looked serious for a moment. "Matter of relativity, Wilf Ansor," he said soberly. "Old Dytasburg Academy will survive well enough without me for little while—but not without *Starfury*, here," he said, gazing past Brim at the ship. "I doubt Nergol Triannic would permit such academic liberty as students there presently enjoy." He scowled grimly. " 'Freedom,' they say, 'is sure possession *only* of those who can defend it.' "

"I'm glad you're here," Brim said with feeling.

The Bear grinned, this time with good humor. "You will be lot more glad to learn that I am accompanied by large contingent from Krasni-Peych you see trooping across brow toward *Starfury*. They, not I, will attempt to remedy any problems you may experience with new Reflecting Drive that gives them so much pride." He motioned toward a low building just visible through the driving snow. "Operation's headquarters," he explained. "Come. I show you where you officially sign in your ship. Then, you buy us both goblet of Admiralty's rather modest meem."

Brim nodded as the Bear led off along snowdrifted walkways toward the headquarters. "I've done my best to stock *Starfury*'s wardroom," he said, "but I'll never do even half so well as Utrillo Barbousse—remember him?"

"But who could forget Barbousse?" Ursis mused with a grin. "Truly, I have lost track of that splendid individual. Greatest of all ratings. In midst of most austere wartime shortages he could supply literally anything—as if magic." He kissed the tips of his fingers. "Logish Meem that would make Universe itself jealous."

" 'Shortage' is only a relative term to people like Barbousse," Brim interjected, "like 'impossible.' You knew he sent a message of congratulations when I took over *Starfury*, didn't you?"

"He did?" Ursis said with an interested frown. "And how did this missive arrive?"

Brim shrugged. "One of the ancient Cerendellian COMM channels. I'd never seen it used before."

Ursis smiled. "Impossible to trace, of course."

"Absolutely," Brim replied. "I tried. The last time I heard from him, he was in the Helmsman's Academy. Then after I was RIFed, I lost track of him. Something happened there, but I don't know what it was. He certainly wasn't able to finish school."

"I doubt if our one-time associate Amherst and his CIGAs had much use for ex-ratings," Ursis offered.

"Too much of a free thinker, anyhow," Brim added as they reached the building. "Whatever it was that happened to him, he disappeared. Completely."

"Somehow," Ursis mused, opening the door for Brim and stamping snow from his boots, "I have feeling we've not seen last of Mr. Barbousse. He will turn up when he can do some good; mark my words."

Brim never got a chance to answer. Before he could open his mouth, he was cut off by the familiar twang of Mark Valerian, chief designer for the Sherrington Starship Works and the virtual creator of *Starfury*.

"Brim, this is absolutely horrible!" the little man growled with a twinkle of laughter in his eye. "If I'd had any idea they'd pick an orbiting iceberg like this for the trials, I'd never have designed the xaxtdamned ship in the first place." Valerian was almost painfully slim with a sizable nose; damp, humorous eyes; and a drooping black mustache of truly prodigious size. As usual, his coat and trousers were made of soft-looking wool. These were coupled with an old-fashioned white shirt, necktie, and high, pointed boots cut in the Rhodorian style.

The Carescrian grinned happily as they shook hands. He'd seen very little of Valerian since driving the designer's M-6B to victory in the final race for the Mitchell Trophy nearly a year previously. The hiatus was no reflection on their friendship; it was purely the times. Both men had all they could do simply keeping up with responsibilities. "Don't blame me for the weather," he quipped, casting a sidelong glance at Ursis. "I certainly didn't opt for this wretched stuff. We *do*, however, have associates who are *known* for their affinity to nippy climates.''

''Who can deny the benefits of bracing wintery weather,'' Ursis sighed theatrically, his fang jewels glinting opulently. ''Look how well preserved it keeps us Bears.''

Valerian grimaced. ''Nik's got a point, Brim,'' he declared —just as they were joined by a bantam Commodore with gray-blond hair, high cheekbones, piercing gray eyes, and a most sober bearing. Beneath an open Fleet Cloak, his perfectly fashioned formal uniform looked as if it had been tailored only moments previously.

''Wilf, may I present Commodore Zorfrew Tor from the Fleet Design Bureau?'' Ursis interjected quickly, ''In command of this operation.''

Brim extended a hand. ''A pleasure, Commodore,'' he said.

Tor nodded and smiled a little. ''Yes, I'm certain it is,'' he said without so much as raising an eyebrow.

''Er, yes,'' Brim allowed.

Suddenly Tor chuckled, the quick change in his aspect like sunrise after a particularly dark night. ''Ah,'' he said with a twinkle in his eyes. ''You were *listening*.''

''Well, ah . . .'' Brim stumbled, ''yes, I was.''

''Nearly a lost art,'' Tor commented with raised eyebrows.

''What?'' Brim asked.

''*Listening*,'' Tor replied with a little grin as he glanced through the windows in the front door. ''Watch. . . .''

A moment later two civilians entered the foyer in a blast of cold air and snow. One immediately glanced over at the Commodore and smiled while he stomped snow from his boots. ''How goes it today, Doctor?'' he asked.

Tor nodded his head affably. ''Horrible,'' he said with a pleasant smile.

''Good—glad to hear it, Doctor,'' the civilian replied, opening his parka with cold-reddened hands. Then, with a friendly nod to Brim and the others, he opened the door for his partner, and the two of them hurried off along an inner corridor, deep in conversation.

The moment the door swung closed, Ursis and Valerian broke

into gales of laughter. "Happens damn near every time," the designer gasped, wiping tears from his eyes. "He got me twice before Nik here finally let me in on the big joke."

Ursis's soulful eyes rolled toward the ceiling. " 'Night and green moonlight scarcely bother miners of small emeralds,' as they say," he recited with a wry smile. "It was only after I fell victim myself—three times yesterday—that I discovered the joke. Three times!"

"Unfortunately," Tor said with a culpable look on his face, "people *do* catch on." He extended his hand a second time. "Wilf Brim," he said, "I've heard a lot about you—I followed your every move in the Mitchell races."

"Thank you, Commodore," Brim said, "but it was Mark's ships that actually won. I just sat back and drove."

"I see," Tor said with a chuckle. "Easy as that, eh?" He smiled. "Well, I shall endeavor to make you a great deal busier, Commander, during the coming space trials. And since everyone has finally arrived, I suppose it is fitting that we launch our efforts with a get-together—on board my headquarters ship, I.F.S. *Refit Enterprise*." He nodded to himself. "How does that seem, everyone?"

"Horrible," Brim quipped with a straight face

"Splendid, glad to hear it." Tor chuckled with a wink. "At Evening:two, then." He closed his Fleet Cloak. "Oh, bye the bye, Brim," he added, opening the door to a blast of arctic air, "plan to have a similar affair aboard *Starfury*, if you please. The night we complete the trials."

"I shall look forward to both events, Commodore," Brim called, winking at Ursis. They both knew from experience that before the second party took place, everyone connected with *Starfury*'s space trials would be *quite* ready for any kind of deliverance.

Later that evening, Brim found the business of simply getting away from his Captain's workstation was—in itself—no easy task. It seemed that as soon as he had battled one lengthy chore to a finish, a dozen others took its place. Because of it, the party aboard *Refit Enterprise* was well under way before he straightened the area around his workstation, donned his cold-weather gear, and set off for the main hatch. "Looks perfectly awful out there, Gromnik," he commented to the Duty Officer, a tall Sodeskayan Drive Lieutenant.

Gromnik grinned as he came to attention and saluted. "Aye, Captain," he answered. "It surely must be for those without a natural fur coat."

Brim nodded agreement, pulling the Fleet Cloak tight around his neck while he turned up the heat. Through a nearby viewport, he could see that at least only a gentle snow was falling—a far cry from earlier in the evening when FULL BLIZZARD seemed to be the sole weather mode. He was about to open the outer hatch when Tissaurd appeared around the corner.

"Skipper," she exclaimed with raised eyebrows. "I thought you'd be long gone to the party."

"I might say the same about you, too, Number One," Brim grinned, suddenly happy to see her. She had the sort of face that was charming even when mostly covered by the great collars of a Fleet Cape and a beaked officer's cap. "You're going to the party, I hope."

"With the kind of day I've put in"—Tissaurd chuckled—"I wouldn't miss Tor's get-together for a whole Universe—especially the free drinks. Local scuttlebutt has it the Commodore stocks his ship with good Logish Meem."

"I never refute scuttlebutt," Brim said, holding the hatch while she stepped onto the brow, "too often it's nearly truth." Outside, Brim could feel the crisp air bite his nostrils as he breathed. Almost without thinking, he offered his arm to her as they negotiated the slippery steel grating.

She took it with a little squeeze. "You don't think anyone at home would mind, do you?" she asked.

Brim smiled. "There *is* no one at home," he answered simply, thinking back over the many women who had drifted in and out of his life since he'd joined the Fleet; some suddenly, some over a long period of time. Even his first and dearest love, the Princess Margot Effer'wyck, not only had married someone else, she had become . . . He closed his eyes for a moment. He didn't even want to continue *that* thought.

"Caught you daydreaming, Skipper," Tissaurd said at the rim of the gravity pool.

Brim nodded and pursed his lips. "Yeah," he said, experiencing a definite visceral thrill at feeling her small, soft bulk close beside him. Shipmate or not, he laughed to himself, Tissaurd was a mighty attractive package—in any middle-aged man's book.

"That was awfully nice," she murmured as they stepped onto a heated walkway. After a moment, she released his arm. "I'll remember to keep my eyes peeled for slippery spots every time we walk someplace together," she said with a little smile.

Brim felt himself blush. "Me, too," he said awkwardly, then quickly peered up at *Starfury*'s huge snow-cloaked silhouette standing out against the darkened sky. Docking beacons swung long beams of blue light through the falling snow while dim battle lanterns bobbed and hovered over her entrance hatches. Multicolored points of light glowed and blinked through the bridge Hyperscreens, and from the high mast, KA'PPA rings radiated lazily out to the far corners of the Universe as someone in the COMM center kept touch with the reality of everyday business.

"Beautiful, isn't she?" Tissaurd said quietly, her words breaking into his thoughts.

"Beautiful, at least," he mused. Somehow, it took another Helmsman to understand the way people could relate to starships. But then, Tissaurd seemed to understand lots of things about him. That's what made them such an effective team.

"Deadly, too . . ." she added. "Strange how such a graceful shape could have been created for the sole purpose of destruction."

" 'Protection' might be a better word," Brim offered.

"A nicer word, perhaps, Skipper," Tissaurd allowed softly, "but *Starfury*'s primary purpose is still destruction, pure and simple. No matter how harmless we'd·like to make her seem. Those ungodly disruptors give her true purpose away."

Brim nodded agreement as they walked. "Yeah," he said at length, "and our purpose as well. Just like those space forts the League seems to be putting up all over the galaxy." He took a deep breath of cold air. "One begets the other, I suppose. . . ." Behind them, the graceful ship had already dwindled to a pattern of blurred lights. They continued wordlessly through the cottony solitude until *Enterprise* began to appear through the falling snow.

Brim never did have an opportunity to attend Commodore Tor's party. At the entry port, a message awaited him from *Starfury*. A top secret KA'PPA dispatch had just been received that required his personal receipt. Immediately directing Tissaurd to make his apologies, he trudged back to the ship only to discover that his urgent KA'PPA was merely notification of a state visit by one of the few influential politicians who remained untouched by the CIGAs. Nevertheless, it did require a direct personal answer, and he made it. After that he retired to his cabin for one of the few full nights of sleep he got during the trials.

Throughout the next fourteen Standard Days, some of their time was spent on dilapidated gravity pools, merely loading torpedoes, mines, and other expendable munitions. Other days passed while they accomplished simplistic harbor exercises, while still others were devoted to actual space trials and the preliminary target exercises that would prove the ship's ability to fight. There could hardly have been more desolate surroundings in which to test the ship. The colossal maintenance yard to which they were assigned was occupied by gaunt, weatherworn figures of mammoth derricks and cranes silhouetted against storm-gray skies in the grip of perpetual winter; everything was covered by uniform layers of unceasing snow that had been unsullied by the tracks of living creatures for nearly a decade. The dying star Gimmas was long since dim beyond supporting any of the sentient life forms known in the Home Galaxy. There was a gaunt dignity to the surroundings, almost as if they were some gigantic vestige of a primordial civilization that pulled up cosmic stakes and departed long before the dawn of recorded history.

The crew had little enough time for pondering their surroundings and, for most, scant inclination to poke about the stormy landscape. Eyes and thoughts were constantly turned toward the ship and their tasks within her. Valerian's creation was already coming alive as more than ninety individual temperaments shook down together, melding into the single, unique personality that would become the mature *Starfury*. This was not only true in her wardroom—where the ship's leadership made the effect even more pronounced—but among the ratings as well. Like the cells of some bantling organism, they were beginning to work in concert, dedicating their energies and intellects on one exacting goal: operation of a powerful warship whose deadly function was important to them, and the ancient nation that they called home. Their battles were in the future: in an as-yet-undeclared war. But each of the specially chosen crew understood that sometime in the near offing there would be dangerous work to do, and it would be worth doing.

During a rare hiatus from the trials, Brim checked out an elderly launch from what remained of Base Operations and flew to the deserted Eorean Starwharfs, his home for nearly three Standard Years at the beginning of his career. Touching down near an abandoned skeleton of what was once an elevated tram station, he labored through knee-deep snow beneath rows of dark Karlsson lamps, past the staring, broken windows of a half-tumbled guard station, then along nearly a c'lenyt of stone jetties and crumbling gravity pools to a small sign that had nearly disintegrated with rust. "Gravity Pool R-2134," it read. Once —nearly an eon ago as Brim reckoned time—his life in the Fleet had begun here.

For a moment his mind's eye carried back across the years to that snowy dawn when he had first laid eyes on the wedge-shaped form of starship T.83, I.F.S. *Truculent*, testing her moorings in the amber glow of repulsion generators thundering steadily within the gaping walls of this now-empty pool. Only Gimmas's perpetual wind broke the lonely stillness as it wailed 'round emaciated forms of towering cranes, rattled corrugated sheets in dilapidated sheds, moaned through the yawning mouths of broken windows, and hurried powdery snow ghosts among the run-down jetties. Out of sight somewhere, an unsecured door slammed against its frame to a totally irrational rhythm. CIGAs had destroyed Gimmas Haefdon with politics mightier than the League's most powerful disruptors.

Brim shivered in his heated Fleet Cloak. Despite the loneliness, this place—the whole colossal ruin for that matter—was far from empty. Every square iral was peopled by ghosts of one sort or another. And in the silence of the deserted complex, he could still hear the shrill whines of gravity generators spooling up before thundering into ground-shaking reality. As if it were yesterday, he recalled ice-blue tongues of free ions shooting back from open waste gates, great ships marching ponderously out onto the half-frozen bay, then soaring into the overcast, heroic comrades of all races striving together to turn the tide of a war that initially cast them in the role of underdogs. He sighed. So many of those brave men and women had paid the supreme toll, and for what? When fortunes began to reverse, Emperor Triannic quickly duped the Empire and her allies with his deceitful Treaty of Garak, then set up cowardly Puvis Amherst as chief of the CIGAs to destroy his nemesis Fleet from within.

Now, the great ships had departed, replaced by lonesome wind and a banging shutter. All that presently stood between Triannic and his dreams of conquest were the tag ends of a once-mighty war fleet, the handful of half-finished Starfuries a'building at Sherrington's, and the dogged resolution of a few remaining warriors who still believed that freedom was worth fighting for—to the death.

As afternoon shadows lengthened in the stillness, Brim grimly retraced his steps to the launch and took off into the scudding gray clouds. But instead of setting a direct return course for the Central Complex, whimsy guided him only a short distance through the darkening sky before he set down again, this time in a wide courtyard fronting a snow-covered jumble of peaked roofs and tall stone chimneys. Over the great boarded-up doorway, a weathered sign swung to the wind on rusted chains that were clearly in their last days of existence. "MERMAID TAVERN," the faded letters blazoned in the gray twilight. "ESTABLISHED 51690." Opposite, through the rusting metal gate, he could see what was once a country road, now buried irals deep in everlasting snow. On either side, tangled forms of long-dead treetops wound away in snowy perspective, mute reminders of summers now gone forever as the dimming star Gimmas continued its long march toward ultimate death.

He hadn't been here in years, but the ghost of his earliest love affair was inextricably linked to this abandoned country inn. Its once-cozy, candle-lit interior was the place of his first liaison with Her Serene Majesty, Princess Margot of the Effer'wyck Dominions and Baroness (Grand Duchess) of The Torond. A lot of snow had fallen on the old building during those intervening fifteen years, and clearly, it had served its last patron sometime previously, probably with the closing of the base. Inside, he could imagine the huge fireplaces dark and cold, with only swirling soot marks from the last fire to serve as evidence that the rooms had ever known life-giving warmth.

He stood before the derelict inn only a few cycles before something drove him away. The cold? The snow? Perhaps the lonesomeness? Whatever it was, he soon climbed back into the launch and departed shortly thereafter for the warmth and fellowship of *Starfury*'s wardroom. Certain memories were simply too painful to countenance.

As the days passed, Brim began to settle more comfortably into his role as commanding officer. It was a proprietary sort of feeling, and it became more firmly established as the ship proved herself. She was all he'd expected, and then some. Quite apart from her prodigious turn of speed, she was enormously easy to fly and maneuverable at nearly any speed. Her only major snag, if a major snag really existed, was with her new reflecting Drive units: three crystal shells grown around a central core in layers. During normal operation, all layers fired aft as a unit, with the shells contributing nearly thirty percent of the unit's total thrust. However, when short bursts of speed were necessary, the outer shells could be reversed, firing forward into a ring-shaped focusing reflector that fed back this specially modulated energy directly to the core and increased the power output by nearly fifty percent.

The process, of course, exuded tremendous heat as a byproduct, and it had to be radiated quickly lest its blistering presence damage portions of the hull; collapsiums like hullmetal had physical limits like everything else. But therein lay a problem. Even *Starfury*'s prodigious radiating surfaces were insufficient to continuously dissipate heat energy from four Wizard Cs running flat out in reflecting mode. And because of it, speed runs at absolute flank speed had to be suspended when the Drive crystals passed maximum operating temperatures, usually after no more than fifteen cycles. The situation also required a great deal more diligence at the helm, especially at high speeds. Brim had no problem managing the situation. Except when running under unusual or dangerous conditions, he flew with a sixth sense anyway. But not every Helmsman was so fortunate to be born with his perfect eyesight and coordination. The Sodeskayan engineers from Krasni-Peych would have to do something about that minor flaw before combat conditions changed it to "major."

And fix it they did, in a most amazing manner. No more than a fortnight after Strana' Zaftrak's first complaints, a new and much-more-efficient space radiator system had been fabricated and was waiting for installation when *Starfury* made landfall after her second series of disruptor trials. The starship was laid up only two days while the immense system was installed—by a much larger party of technicians than Brim had guessed were housed aboard the Sodeskayan supply vessel. But then the huge system had been fabricated in a seemingly miraculous fashion also. Besides, it worked, and that was the only important point, anyway. Years ago he had learned that unnecessary questions could be a matter of embarrassment for everyone concerned.

The morning before their last day on Gimmas, Brim found a large notice on the ship's bulletin board:

NEW ABSOLUTE VELOCITY RECORD SET
The Imperial HyperDrome
Alcott-on-Mersin, Avalon, 369/52009

Today, nearly a year after the Mitchell Trophy was
permanently retired here at the Imperial HyperDrome
near Avalon, Commander Tobias Moulding, I.F., set
a new absolute speed record over the Standard three-
light-year course at 111.97M LightSpeed. Moulding,
a member of the Imperial Fleet's High-speed Star Flight
Team, set the new record in the same Sherrington
M-6 Beta that he would have flown as backup, had
Commander Wilf Brim, then Principal Helmsman to
the Imperial Starflight Society, failed to capture the
trophy himself. Moulding's M-6B was powered this
year by a specially prepared Krasni-Peych Wizard-S
(for "sprint") Drive.

The Carescrian smiled as he read the brief bulletin. Toby
Moulding was one of his closest friends, and he was genuinely
glad the man had a chance at the record. But even more, it made
him aware of *Starfury*'s potential. During her final trials, she
reached 80.723M LightSpeed, approaching seventy-five percent
of Moulding's new absolute speed record! If Sodeskayan intelligence estimates were correct, this easily made her the speediest
warship in the galaxy.

Eventually, Brim presided over a small ceremony in the wardroom where he cleared all but a few minor Action Reports pend-
ing against the ship and her systems, then signed Sherrington's
crimson Builder's Book on page 5054. *Starfury* was now ready
for her official commissioning, which occurred promptly the
following morning. At precisely Dawn:2:00, her entire crew plus
most of the lonely base personnel assembled in the bitter cold
outside her main hatch. In a simple ceremony, Brim formally
muttered a few official platitudes concerning Emperor, Duty,
Home, and Hearth. Then Tissaurd stepped to the bow and broke
a bottle of meem against the docking cupola, after which two

burly mechanics affixed a polished brass plate to the aft bulkhead just inside her main boarding hatch:

**I.F.S. STARFURY
JOB 5054
SHERRINGTON STARSHIP WORKS
BROMWICH, RHODOR
388/52009**

With that, *Starfury* entered the Fleet lists as a fully "commissioned" warship, and Brim led her crew back to their stations by stopping at the new nameplate and burnishing it with the sleeve of his Fleet Cloak. It was a tradition he'd learned on old *Truculent*, established by his greatest commander, Regula Collingswood herself. He swore to abide by it so long as he commanded a ship—*any* ship.

Immediately after the commissioning ceremony, activities got under way for the celebration Brim scheduled for the conclusion of *Starfury*'s space trials. Tired as everyone was, the idea of a party, where everyone could let down their hair and relax for the first time in weeks, seemed to create its own energy. At least there was enough energy to clean and decorate the wardroom as well as ice down a great quantity of Logish Meem in the ship's freezers.

But once again, Brim never got to celebrate. This time, however, neither did any of *Starfury*'s crew. Less than two metacycles before the first guests were to arrive, Brim received a secret transmission from Prince Onrad himself, in his persona as Commander in Chief of the Imperial Fleet. The ship was ordered *immediately* to Bromwich where an urgent, top-secret dispatch waited for personal delivery.

Onrad's message was met with considerable grousing from the exhausted crew, including a few choice words from Brim. But within a scant twenty cycles, Strana' Zaftrak connected her four Admiralty A876 gravity generators to the mains, and *Star-*

fury was spaceborne less than a metacycle afterward, coursing across the galaxy at maximum cruise velocity for Bromwich and the Sherrington plant. As Brim set the big starship on autohelm, he shook his head. *Here we go again*, he thought.

"What's going on, Skipper?" Tissaurd queried from the CoHelmsman's recliner beside him. "Nobody told us anything back there, except that we had to leave in one *perdition* of a hurry."

"That's about all the information I got myself," Brim chuckled. "Only, mine was marked 'secret.' "

"Oh, wonderful," Tissaurd fumed. "You mean this sort of thing happens all the time?"

"Sort of comes with the territory when you have the only ship like *Starfury* in the known Universe," he said with a grin. "But I can't imagine you'll be any busier than you were when we were fitting out. There are just so many metacycles you can fit into a day."

Tissaurd nodded thoughtfully. "That's probably true," she said with a grin. "And I loved every cycle of it, too. Isn't that *awful?*"

Brim answered with a wink. *Here's hoping you still feel that way a year from now*, he thought. Life could be pretty exciting, as well as dangerous, when Prince Onrad was calling the shots. And all too often it was the latter.

CHAPTER 2

Intrigue

Once they'd secured *Starfury* at the Sherrington plant in Bromwich, Brim had hardly stepped clear of the brow when a face at the rear of the boarding room sent his mind racing far into a wartime past: gray beard, gray mustache, and ageless gray eyes sparkling with the keen wisdom and humor of a lifelong starsailor. "Baxter Calhoun!" he gasped, detouring from his original course to the message center, "what in Voot's name brings you to Bromwich?"

"Tis you that brings me here, young Brim," the man answered, extending both his hand and a steely grin. "But afore I answer any mare of your questions, laddie, we'll *both* hie along to the message center an' collect the dispatch bonnie Prince Onrad ha' sent to you. It'll save a lot of explainin' once we begin to talk."

Brim sighed in capitulation. Of course Calhoun knew about the top-secret message. He *always* knew about things like that; nothing had changed at all over the years. At the far end of middle age, the man looked every inch a proper old starsailor: his chiseled countenance was handsome in a weather-beaten way and his eyes carried the imperious look of one long accustomed to command—as well as the limitless depths of intragalactic space. He was dressed in an expensive-looking white linen suit of casual finery that appeared as if it had been tailored that very morning. Gossip had it that he was wealthy beyond all belief, and the enormous StarBlaze ring that flashed from his left hand as he pushed open the door lent powerful credence to the hearsay.

At Sherrington's message center, Brim identified himself and signed for his mysterious dispatch, which was delivered to his hand in the characteristic blue and gold plastic envelope of the Imperial Courier Corps.

"It's why we didn't simply send it to your ship, Commander," the clerk explained. "We were only permitted to store this one. It was delivered to us by hand."

Nodding thanks to the clerk, Brim frowned at Calhoun. "You know all about this, don't you?" he demanded.

"Weel," Calhoun replied with a little smile, "I've ne'er exactly seen inside yon envelope, but I probably know a wee of wha's written there." He looked at the clerk. "Is yon a secure room?" he asked, pointing to a door beside the counter.

"Aye, Mr. Calhoun," the clerk assured him, "category three at minimum."

"Hie you in there and read the message, young Brim," Calhoun said. "It wull na take you lang. I'll wait here, and afterward we'll be able to talk."

Placing the envelope under his arm, Brim entered the secure room, turned on the lights, and sealed the door, seating himself on a hard, straight-backed chair at a bare table. Thoughtfully he touched his right index finger to the plastic envelope's seal—which clearly approved of his fingerprint because it immediately opened in a puff of odorless smoke. With a growing sense of excitement, he withdrew a single sheet of light blue plastic, engraved in gold with the Royal Seal of Crown Prince Onrad, heir to the Imperial Throne at Avalon.

> The Imperial Palace,
> Avalon, 388/52009

My dear Commander Brim,
    This letter comes to you under Our personal signature as introduction to Baxter Calhoun, not that you should

need such after serving with him on I.F.S. *Defiant* during the past hostilities.

First, be aware that Calhoun is no longer a civilian, although he will be most certainly dressed as one when you first encounter him in Bromwich. He is on special assignment, serving in the Fleet under Our direct orders with the rank of Commodore, I.F. His mission: to thwart the plan of high-handed annexation Nergol Triannic has concocted against the Dominion of Fluvanna, which now includes one of the League's new deep-space fortifications.

Commodore Calhoun has devised an extraordinary plan that requires both your skill as a Helmsman and the excellent ship that you command. He will personally describe this plan and the role you will play in its early stages. It is Our desire that you provide all support within your purview as both Commander and citizen of the Empire.

Until you receive further orders from Us personally, Commander Brim, you will covertly serve under Commodore Calhoun's direct command, although your "official" documents may state otherwise.

Accept, Commander, the assurances of Our highest consideration, etc., etc.

> Onrad, Vice Admiral, I.F.,
> and Crown Prince to the Throne at Avalon

Clipped to the message was a note scrawled in a hand that matched Onrad's signature: "Brim," it read, "I can't imagine whatever got into me when I agreed to team you two lunatic Carescrians together. See if you can at least stay out of major trouble." It was signed, simply, "O."

Slouching comfortably in the hard wooden chair, Brim read the dispatch twice more and frowned. Fluvanna, a tiny domain astride the Straits of Remic, supplied Greyffin IV's Empire with nearly one hundred percent of its celecoid quartz kernels: the rare—absolutely pure—crystalline "seeds" from which Drive crystals were manufactured under tremendous temperature and pressure. Well, it wasn't as if he hadn't predicted trouble since long before Nergol Triannic usurped political power in Rogan LaKarn's Torond, once the Empire's primary source of the rare and all-important crystals. Eventually, he folded the page in half, touched his thumb to the top right-hand corner, and the message evaporated into thin air as if it had never existed.

When Brim exited the room, Calhoun was in rapt conversation with a gorgeous strawberry blonde stationed behind the message counter. From their eye contact, Brim could see that his newly appointed commander had already chalked up another conquest. The gorgeous woman was Calhoun's sort of luck. She had clearly replaced the fat, middle-aged clerk who earlier delivered Brim's own message—no doubt as his last act on the shift.

"Brim, mon," Calhoun called over his shoulder, "while you pack your duffel, Miss Phillpotts and I plan to share a spot of lunch, noo. Meet me at the main lobby in, say, two metacycles and I'll drive you to my ship."

"My duffel?" Brim asked. "Your *ship* . . . ?"

"Aye, laddie," Calhoun said. "Pack eneugh for a couple o'weeks. We'll be gone at least that lang."

"Cal!" Brim protested, "I can't leave just like that. I've got my own ship to command."

Calhoun frowned, whispered a few words to Phillpotts—who smiled delightedly—then strode across the room. "What's troublin' you, young Brim?" he asked.

"My ship, Cal," Brim answered. "I can't just walk off and leave her."

"Sez who?" Calhoun asked with a grin. "Are you under special orders that I don't know about, or should I conclude that yon shapely Tissaurd is incompetent in her job as Number One?"

"Neither," Brim said. "It's just that. . . ."

"That wha?" Calhoun insisted. "If it's not secret orders that're holdin' you back, then we'll go right away and replace Ms. Tissaurd with someone who can handle her job."

"Oh, damnit, Cal," Brim replied hotly, "Tissaurd is a fine officer. It's just that . . . I don't feel I ought to leave the ship yet."

"If that's true, young Brim," Calhoun charged, poking a

finger into the younger Carescrian's chest, "then *you* are a damned poor warship captain. What would happen to *Starfury* if—Universe forbid—you got yourself killed in action?"

Brim swallowed hard. Calhoun's point was definitely well taken. He had been running everything since his arrival at Sherrington's, long before *Starfury*'s launch. He'd given no one a chance to get along without him.

Calhoun smiled. "Tissaud can take over for a while," he said. "She looks reasonably competent."

"She is," Brim grumped. "*Very* competent."

"Then it's settled," Calhoun said phlegmatically. "We'll meet in the lobby of the Sherrington headquarters at"—he consulted his old-fashioned gold timepiece and glanced at the smiling Phillpotts—"Brightness-one and a half: in two metacycles. That ought to allow us *both* eneugh time to conduct our business."

"I'll be there," Brim assured him, and started off toward the door.

"If I'm a wee late," Calhoun called after him, "you'll understand?"

"I'll understand," Brim chuckled. It was reassuring to know that Calhoun still had his priorities straight.

Nearly three metacycles later, Calhoun strode into the lobby with a lopsided grin. "Sadly," he said, "'tis time for us to be gone from this wonderful place. I would spend considerable time learning about young Miss Phillpotts."

"'The exigencies of the Service,' is how they put it, I think," Brim offered.

"Ah yes, the exigencies," Calhoun said mournfully, opening the door. "Wull, another exigency waits for us outside." He nodded toward a small, nondescript skimmer hovering at the curb. "Poor but reliable transportation, young Brim," he said. "But it wull get us to my ship without causin' undue notice."

"Lead on, Commodore," Brim chuckled, striding through the door with his duffel bobbing at his heels. "Where you and I started out lives, waterproof boots were considered first-class transportation. Remember?" Carescria was perhaps the most beggarly province of Greyffin IV's Empire.

"True," Calhoun agreed with a wry nod. "How soon we forget. . . ."

Bromwich was located midway along a nightward-facing crescent formed by Glammarian Bight, and the Sherrington plant occupied its most borcal districts. From there, the main surface route to Cruden City paralleled the bay, running along a highly industrialized corridor. Once out of the plant, Calhoun set course directly for this artery. Brim hung on to an armrest as the light suspension reacted to Calhoun's high-speed urging over an ancient cobble-surfaced road. On either side were cheapside red-brick buildings with small windows that reminded him of Carescria. "Pick-and-shovel" workers seemed to gravitate toward such housing everywhere in the galaxy.

"First and foremost," Calhoun explained as they bounced across a narrow intersection, "you must understand one underlyin' fact. Nergol Triannic means to take the wee dominion o'Fluvanna an' her supply of celecoid quartz Drive crystal seeds—as soon as he can. He's e'en buildin' ane o' his new space forts no mare than a few thousand light-years from their capital."

Brim nodded, marveling at the light traffic for that time of day. "Onrad mentioned that in his letter," he replied. "He also said you have a strategy to thwart Triannic's plans."

"O' course I do," Calhoun replied, "as promised." He pulled into the high-speed lane, blithely ignoring a flashing MAXIMUM SAFE SPEED EXCEEDED on the instrument panel. "And I've based the whole plan on legal means, in spite o' the wild stories that circulate about my many enterprises in space."

"I'm all ears," Brim responded with a grin. Calhoun had been prime suspect for a long list of deep-space acts of piracy for years, but the courts never successfully proved the link between him and the crimes. Probably this was due to the peculiar fact that Imperial ships had never fallen victim to the attacks.

"It all has to do with the Mutual Defense Treaty Onrad put in place with Fluvanna a few years ago," Calhoun began as they passed a huge metal salvage yard, glinting in the sunlight. "That scrap of plastic he signed may turn out to be a *most* important document."

"How so?" Brim asked.

"Wull," Calhoun replied, steering toward a steep up ramp, "the way I see things, that zukeed Triannic's wanted Fluvanna for a long time now, even before the Treaty of Garak in the year 52000. He'd have gone right after it once the war was officially suspended. But when Onrad inked his Mutual Defense Treaty, the Leaguers had to take us on first. And after losing the battle of Atalanta, their squadrons were in no condition to do anything like that, even though Fluvanna never had much of a fleet."

Brim nodded grimly while the skimmer careened giddily across a deckless repulsion bridge. Hundreds of irals below, a toiling switcher dragged its string of barges toward a sprawling factory. "I haven't kept up with Fluvanna lately," he said, "but the CIGAs have certainly changed the odds with our Fleet."

"You've got that right, laddie," Calhoun growled, "though we've na lost all our teeth just yet. The Tyrant's still proceedin' with a little caution." He winked. "His latest ploy is to set up an 'incident' that wull give him a legal excuse to take military action. His CIGAs wull instantly tie up our General Parliament in endless debate aboot retaliation while he invades Fluvanna's capital at Magor, and afore we know wha's hit us, we'll hae lost our supply of Drive crystals. That wull put paid to most o' our new warship construction, an' one day he'll be able to walk into Avalon essentially unopposed."

"Unless we develop some sort of new Drive technology that doesn't start with celecoid quartz kernels," Brim interjected. They were now astride a grotesque-looking complex of thick glowing transmission conduits suspended from huge spirals that towered at least two hundred irals overhead. He remembered wondering about the structures from the air, but could make no more sense of them from the ground.

"We both know that's a few years away at best," Calhoun retorted. "Too far in the future to have much effect on the short-term events that are starting e'en as we speak. That's why we've got to make certain the Fluvannians can take care o' themselves—an' yon Leaguer space fort. *Wi'out* our Imperial Fleet."

Brim frowned, staring out the window at a long row of weathered storehouses that fronted a muddy, filth-littered canal. Each was connected to one of the mysterious transmission conduits. "Not an easy task," he said thoughtfully, "if what I've heard about their fleet is correct."

"And wha's that?" Calhoun queried.

"It's said they fly some of the oldest starships in the galaxy," Brim replied. "Real antiques."

Calhoun pursed his lips. "True enough," he said. "I've seen them—e'en flown in a few. But there's a lot mair to a fleet than that. Fluvannian crewmen rate as some o' the most professional starsailors in the galaxy. An' those auld ships are in magnificent repair."

"Could they stand up to the League's new Gantheisser killer ships?" Brim asked, staring out the window at the blur of a high-speed train thundering past in the same direction, lost in clicks as it hurtled above the roadway through the glowing coils of a helical bridge.

"Depends on wha' you mean by 'stand up,' " Calhoun answered after a little thought. "Disruptors are disruptors, after all. The Fluvannians clearly couldn't survive a toe-to-toe sluggin' match wi' a squadron of Gantheissers—or that new space fort. But if they decided on suicide, they could inflict a lot of damage afore they were ground into space dust."

"Ground-up space dust doesn't stop an invasion fleet," Brim said, wondering what Calhoun was leading up to.

"That's true enough," the other allowed. "But Starfuries could."

"Starfuries?" Brim demanded, turning to face Calhoun in surprise. "I don't understand."

"You will directly," Calhoun assured him with a smile, "because Starfuries are a major part of my plan."

Brim frowned. "Cal"—he chuckled—"I'm all ears."

"Simplest thing you could think of," Calhoun explained, "an' it even makes a bit of business sense. We'll simply transfer I.F.S. *Starfury* to the Fluvannian Nabob along with the next ten Starfuries to complete. In return, Fluvanna wull send their entire production of celecoid quartz kernels to the Empire. That way, they can defend themselves wi' the same ships we wad, and the xaxtdamned CIGAs won't hae onything to say about it.''

"You may have a spot of trouble with that one," Brim cautioned. "Starfuries are the most restricted ships in the Empire. Even if Prince Onrad could get the sale approved somehow, the Bears at Krasni-Peych would never consent. The reflecting Drive is their latest technology."

"I didn't say anything about a sale, young Brim," Calhoun chuckled. "What I mean to do is *lease* them the ships."

"All right," Brim allowed. "Maybe you could get some sort of leasing arrangement past the Bears, but who would man the ships? Damned near half the systems aboard are classified, with a NO FOREIGN NATIONALS caveat. Even our closest allies are barred from the Drive chambers and the control systems."

Calhoun smiled as he urged the little skimmer around a fast-moving lorry. "Well, there you are," he said, cutting back in front of the lumbering vehicle and careening onto an exit ramp. "You already know who would man them, then. Who else but their present crews?"

"Cal," Brim objected, "you know better than that. The Imperial Fleet Oath strictly forbids us from anything like—"

"True enow," Calhoun interrupted. "But if you weren't *in* the Fleet anymore, you simply wadn't ha' that problem, noo, wad you?"

Brim considered that for a moment, then gasped in horror. "Are you suggesting that everyone simply resigns?"

"Not permanently," Calhoun answered. "Only lang eneugh to do a wee bit of fightin'—defendin', that is." The skimmer was now speeding along the perimeter of a small private spaceport Brim had often spotted from the air.

"Voot's beard," Brim growled, "whoever heard of a temporary resignation? The CIGAs would love it. They'd never let us in again."

"How about if Greyffin IV himself guaranteed your return?"

"Greyffin IV? He knows about this?"

"To be perfectly honest, I'm not sure," Calhoun admitted, "but Onrad does, as you well know."

Brim considered that while they pulled to a hover beside a large gravity pool. He'd only regained his long-revoked Fleet commission a year previously, and many of his civilian-life recollections weren't all that comfortable. "I'm not sure anything less than an Imperial guarantee would be acceptable anywhere," he concluded at length. "I know I'd certainly have a hard time with it."

"I think I understand," Calhoun said. "I hae pretty strong feelin's myself." He put his hand gently on Brim's shoulder. "When the time comes, if our plan's right, we'll hae little trouble gettin' Greyffin to back us. Wha's important noo is to start the groundwork in Avalon. We're a lang way from settin' course for Fluvanna."

Brim climbed out of the skimmer. "I take it then that we're headed for Avalon," he said, glancing up at a large starship floating on the pool, its ebony hullmetal coated stunning white. A curious red circle glimmered just aft of its bridge Hyperscreens, enclosing what could only be an old-fashioned blue hat folded into a "tricorn" shape.

"Avalon it is, young Brim," Calhoun replied. "An' welcome to my yacht, S.S. *Patriot*," he said over the roar of the pool's repulsion generators.

Mounting a short stairway to the pool's rim, Brim shaded his eyes and took in the angular lines of Calhoun's "yacht." A curious craft; with her trilon-shaped hull she looked more like someone's idea of a very fast attack vessel, pre *Starfury*, than someone's expensive toy. And she mounted no disruptors, of course: *visible ones, at any rate*, Brim considered with a smile.

"What do you think o' her?" Calhoun shouted proudly. The repulsion generators were even louder here.

"Powerful-looking," Brim called out. He guessed she was in the neighborhood of 500 irals long with a beam of perhaps 250, and by the size of the four Drive outlets in her squared-off stern, she was probably powered by Admiralty HyperDrives of some sort. "Where'd you find her?" he asked. "She's got Imperial lines right out of the last war, but I've never seen anything like her."

Calhoun smiled proudly. "That's because I own the only three e'er built," he explained, passing Brim onto the brow with a wave of his hand.

The moment his foot touched the runners, a trio of white-cloaked starsailors at the top snapped to attention. Each was armed with a large blaster holstered on his hip.

"And you're right about the era," Calhoun continued as they moved out across the brow. "They're prototypes o' fast attack ships that were to be built on an out-o'-the-way planet called Arret—in the Rhodorian province. Your Medical Officer, Penelope Hesternal, comes from there. They make damme fine deep-space cruisers, they do. But after the Treaty of Garak, there wasn't all that much demand for new warships. And then the CIGAs declared 'em surplus. That's when I got 'em. Bought all three hulls as scrap metal." He stopped at the entry port and gazed up at the wide line of Hyperscreens fronting the bridge. The angle at which they were set gave a brooding look to the ship, like some great spaceborne creature of prey. "They'd removed all the weapons and propulsion systems, but they were scrappin' so many ships at the time I had no trouble replacin' onything."

As they approached the entry port, two of the sentries gave an Imperial Fleet salute and held it while the third blew two shrill notes from a tiny silver whistle. At that moment, a fourth white-uniformed crew member appeared inside the large airlock. Even at a distance, she was stunning.

"At ease," Calhoun said, standing aside while Brim stepped over the coaming.

Inside, the woman saluted, in a most military fashion.

Instinctively, Brim returned her salute, upon which, she met his surprised gaze with a most charming smile. She was tall and slim with high cheekbones; a sharp, attractive nose; soft eyes; small breasts; and legs that seemed to go on forever. Her black, shoulder-length hair was cut in severely coiffured bangs, and she wore two full gold stripes on the cuffs of her white cloak: a Lieutenant Commander of some sort, Brim guessed. And try as he might to maintain a professional attitude toward her, she was simply *beautiful*.

"Make you feel at home?" Calhoun chuckled proudly.

"Especially the white Fleet Cloaks," Brim equivocated, struggling to dismiss the seductive woman who still held his glance. "Almost as if I'd never left *Starfury*."

"Commander Brim, meet Lieutenant Commander Cartier," Calhoun said perfunctorily, indicating the woman with his hand. "She's *Patriot*'s Number Ane."

"Eve Cartier," the woman said, extending her hand. "An' it's quite a pleasure to meet you." Her face colored for a moment. "I've heard much aboot you from the Governor."

"Any of it good?" Brim asked.

"A wee," she chuckled in a soft voice.

"Eve," Calhoun interrupted, "I'm on my way to the bridge. Show the Commander to a stateroom so he can stow his gear, then bring him along as soon as possible. I'll hae the skipper begin his start-up checklists the moment I get there."

"Aye, Governor," Cartier said. "But you'll find the checklists done already; *Patriot*'s ready for generators on a moment's notice. All we need are your orders."

"How about that for a seasoned crew?" Calhoun asked, starting toward the far end of the airlock.

Brim nodded. Clearly, Calhoun had established a little Carescrian Admiralty, with himself as First Lord.

As the older Carescrian passed *Patriot*'s builder's plaque he stopped to polish it with the sleeve of his coat. "A wee trick I learned from a mutual friend," he called over his shoulder to Brim. Then he disappeared into a companionway.

Only cycles after Brim stowed his duffel in the most luxurious stateroom he'd ever encountered, he followed Cartier onto *Patriot*'s roomy bridge. It was laid out in the standard warship manner with twelve rows of consoles split along the ship's center line by a wide aisle. Through a tremendous expanse of Hyperscreens that wrapped completely around the bridge, he could see nearly the whole upper deck. "Nice view," he whispered to no one in particular.

"Nice view indeed," Cartier answered. "And you, Commander, are one o' the very few individuals who hae e'er been up here to see it, except for the flight crews, o' course." She smiled. "Greyffin IV was here for a wee flight, and Prince Onrad's been wi' us on numerous occasions. Regula Collingswood's been here, too—she an' Admiral Plutron."

Brim nodded, peering out at two circular plates expertly fitted into the center line of the forward deck. Each was perhaps thirty-five irals in diameter. Two more occupied the aft corners of the triangular hull. "How long does it take to remount the turrets?" he asked nonchalantly.

"Something less than three Standard Days—at the Governor's private facilities in Rhodor," Cartier answered as if it were common knowledge. "That includes the twa' twin-mounts that by noo you've guessed we can carry ventrally." She laughed quietly. "'Tis why few outsiders ever get a glimpse o' the ship from her bridge."

No need for comment on that, Brim thought. A powerful warship like this in private hands would be enough to unnerve any politician. Three could cause an absolute panic! He grinned as he caught sight of Calhoun seated at one of two raised stations behind the Helmsmans' positions. He was staring intensely at his console and uttering short phrases from time to time. By the multitude of glimmering rings diffusing outward from *Patriot*'s high KA'PPA mast, Brim guessed "The Governor" was making up for time he'd lost playing chauffeur during the morning.

At that moment, a tall, aristocratic man strode onto the bridge, took one look at Brim, and thrust out his hand. He had three stripes on the cuffs of his white Fleet Cloak. "Aha, 'tis you, young Brim—finally. We've been a long time in meetin', but I used to watch you flyin' ore barges years ago in Carescria. I knew your family afore they were killed in the war."

"Universe," Brim said, shaking the man's hand. "That's a few Standard Years ago."

"Don't I know," the man agreed, rolling his eyes.

"Probably I ought to introduce the twa' o' you afore you've become auld friends," Cartier laughed. "Captain Melbourne Byron: Commander Wilf Brim."

"*Byron*," Brim said, testing the name with his mind. "That does sound familiar, but . . ."

"I wadn't expect you'd remember," Byron said with a chuck-

THE MERCENARIES / 41

le. "'Tis been a number of years noo, and you war' in a mighty big hurry to get on wi' your life."

"You've been with Calhoun long?" Brim asked.

"A wee," Byron replied, his eyes momentarily peering far into the past. "Since his first ship." He smiled. "Which reminds me that I'd best gat to my console. The Governor is anxious to be under way. We'll talk further ower a cup o' cvceese' once we're spaceborne."

"I'll look forward to it," Brim said. He turned to Cartier. "Guess I'd better find myself a place to sit," he said. "I take it the jump seats are over there along the starboard 'screens."

"They are," Cartier answered with a look of surprise, "but nae ane's sittin' there this trip, at least to my knowledge."

"What do you mean 'no one'?" Brim asked with a grin. "I'm someone, aren't I?"

"Well, o' course you are," Cartier said with a raised eyebrow. "But. . . ." Then she frowned. "Wait a cycle. I'll bet the Governor ne'er told you, did he?"

"Told me what?"

She laughed. "That you're to replace him at the right-hand command console. Beside Captain Byron."

At that moment, Calhoun swung himself out of his console and strode toward them along the main aisle. "Come on forrard, Brim," he said with a grin. "This trip, I've nae time for gawkin' thro' the Hyperscreens. An office is a better place to prepare for sellin' m' plan. Besides," he added, clapping Brim on the shoulder, "I've been told that you'd ne'er believe we war' off the ground if you didn't watch the takeoff. So I thought I'd make things easy on you." Before Brim could answer, he was through the hatch and clattering down the companionway.

"I was wrong," Cartier chuckled. "He did tell you, after all."

"When you *said* it, you were correct," Brim mumbled, shaking his head.

"All hands to stations for lift-off!" piped over the blower. "All hands to stations for lift-off!"

Within fifteen cycles, they were headed for deep space.

* * *

Four Standard Days out from Bromwich—and less than a week from the turn of the year—Brim watched Cartier lay *Patriot* in through heavy traffic for a perfect landing on an autumnal Lake Mersin just off Avalon's sprawling Grand Terminal: civilian gateway to a thousand-odd civilizations scattered throughout the galaxy—and beyond. Swinging off toward shore, they followed three gleaming liners and an old tramp into the prodigious mooring basin of bustling canals, fanciful bridges, gravity pools, reactors, and towering goods houses that surrounded the terminal, all connected by fleets of high-speed pool trams that made the mammoth complex feasible.

Under a high overcast, the sky was never without starships of one sort or another coming and going in all directions at all altitudes. War might be looming throughout the galaxy, Brim considered, but the interlocking gears of commerce still managed to turn and mesh as if little were amiss. Trade was the very lifeblood of civilization; when it stopped, whole dominions died, as had nameless thousands during the long march of history.

General Harry Drummond of the Imperial Army met them at the terminal. An enigmatic character who appeared to rove at will among all Imperial Services—including the Foreign Diplomatic Corps—Drummond often exercised extraordinary prerogative and clearly served someone with tremendous political power as a military wild card. Small and perfectly tailored in the tan and red uniform of Greyffin IV's Imperial Expeditionary Forces, he had a long narrow face, a prominent nose, and laughing eyes with an irrepressible natural humor. "Cal . . . Brim," he said, shaking their hands, "it's good that you have come. The time is ripe."

"I kind o' thought so, Harry," Calhoun replied. Then he looked the General over critically. "An' you haen't luiked so good in years. You must be takin' care o' yourself."

"No more than usual," Drummond replied with a smile. "Maybe it's that plan of yours that gives me a bit more hope these days, Cal. You know, those xaxtdamned CIGAs have made it pretty rough on those of us who stayed loyal to the Fleet."

Calhoun grinned. "Tell that to my friend Brim here," he said. "He knows."

Drummond nodded at Brim. "I've heard," he said.

"An' I've *also* heard that you hae a most attractive chauffeur, General," Calhoun continued.

"My chauffeur?" Drummond said, his cheeks reddening slightly. "Why," he blustered, "I suppose I hadn't noticed."

Calhoun grinned. "Weel, I consider myself to be an *extraordinary* noticer. An' my sources say that she's really somethin'," he pronounced, snapping his fingers to summon his traveling case. "Maybe Brim and I ought to hae a luik at her. That way, we can make a mair honest judgment. What do you think, Wilf?"

"Sounds like a great idea to me, Commodore," Brim agreed.

"Absolutely," Calhoun mused. "An' while we do that, we'll let her drop us off at our hotel, killin' twa' birdies with ane stone. How aboot it, General?"

"Unfortunately, you'll have to wait till morning for her," Drummond chuckled. "I decided I'd drive you to your hotel myself this afternoon." Then he winked. "But yeah," he admitted, his cheeks coloring, "she *is* a knockout. You'll see in the morning." With that, he led the two Carescrians through the huge terminal to a skimmer parking lot.

Next morning, Brim regretfully climbed from his luxurious hotel bed and stretched agreeably. Starship bunks were never more than just bunks—built more for durability than comfort. After a quick shower, he dressed in the living room while scanning the media. Nergol Triannic and Grand Baron Rogan LaKarn of The Torond had just issued a joint warning to Fluvanna concerning use of the Grompton Corridor, a narrow strait through the teeming asteroid shoals of Kara'g. The fact that the strait had been swept by the thrifty Fluvannian government for nearly five hundred years clearly meant little to Gorton Ro'arn, Triannic's Minister of State Security. It was no surprise to Brim who had met the man years before during a Mitchell Trophy race. Even then, Ro'arn appeared to be a most pragmatic politician. Elsewhere, CIGAs were manning twelve, disparate, anti-Fleet demonstrations throughout the Empire. Two of the larger gatherings were being kicked off simultaneously in Avalon at that very metacycle; one was before the gates of the Imperial palace; the other at the Admiralty in Locorno Square. Both would be vociferant protests against Onrad's order for Starfury production. Brim grinned in spite of himself as he strode downstairs two at a time. If nothing else, the demonstrations proved that the Leaguers felt they had little to counter Sherrington's new warships. . . .

A chilling rain began just before Drummond's big limousine pulled up to the curb. Brim knew better than to hope that it would dampen the CIGAs' enthusiasm for their demonstrations. Zealots thrived on bad weather, it seemed.

"Morning, Wilf," Drummond said as Brim climbed into the jump seat.

"Mornin', young Brim," Calhoun said, handing over a plastic mug of steaming cvceese'. "Thought this might come in handy."

"And how," Brim said, sipping the hot, sticky-sweet liquid. Somehow, cvceese' and Fleet work seemed to go together. So did Felicity, the chauffeur. Drummond had made no exaggeration the last afternoon, at least from what he could see. Long blond hair, a profile that would gladden the heart of a pin-up artist, keen blue eyes, full lips, and a captivating smile. Her wink told Brim all he needed to know. Good for Drummond!

The rain continued without let up all the way across town, along with a brisk wind that littered the streets with a rainbow of fallen leaves. As they glided across a second ruby arch spanning the Grand Achtite Canal, two humpbacked tugs below were dragging a long string of barges toward Lake Mersin, presumably for trans-shipment to some remote part in the galaxy. Farther on, past the great domed tower of Marva, only a few damp-looking tourists had gathered in the Palazzo Edrington to look up at the Desterro Monument with its colossal spiral of sculpted flame. It was the kind of morning when sensible people avoided the out-of-doors at all costs; tourists simply didn't fit that category.

Nor CIGAs. Outside the Imperial palace, Courtland Plaza was a seething mass of malcontents marching around the Savoin gravity fountain and its onyx reflecting pool. Most carried the costly holographic placards that characterized all CIGA gatherings.

> OLD MEN DECLARE WARS;
> YOUTHS FIGHT THEM.
> STOP THE ADMIRALS!

> PONDER GALACTIC PEACE

> A WAR WORTH WAGING:
> CLOSE THE ADMIRALTY,
> ONCE AND FOR ALL!

The marchers were sheltered by bobbing shoals of hovering, multicolored umbrellas struggling to keep station against the wind. Brim nodded to himself as the limousine slowed to a crawl in the single lane that remained open to traffic. Puvis Amherst needed extravagant resources to imprint pretentious posters like that, especially since they were supplied to CIGAs all over the Empire. He also needed considerable credits to pay for the large brass band that had set up in front of the guard station in a position unquestionably calculated to produce the most difficulty for Avalon's Peace Officers.

> PEACE IS MADE BY THE HEARTS OF MEN,
> NOT WARSHIPS!
> STOP THE STARFURIES!

"Leaguer money," Drummond growled as rain streaked the windows. "Triannic knows just where to put his credits. Voot's beard, we couldn't make that much trouble in Tarrott with half the Fleet."

> **EVEN FREEDOM MAY BE PURCHASED AT
> TOO HIGH A PRICE! NO STARFURIES!**

"Or what's left of half the Fleet," Calhoun laughed wryly. "Just look at those zukeeds. I'd like to see anyone try something like this outside Triannic's palace in Tarrott."

> **PEACE WON BY COMPROMISE
> OF PRINCIPLES IS SHORT-LIVED.
> STOP ONRAD! STOP THE STARFURIES!**

"Oh, they could *try*," Drummond put in. "They'd simply be jailed for their pains."

"Or shot," Calhoun snorted.

Brim peered into the crowd, concentrating on individuals here and there. He'd seen them all before; ordinary CIGAs exhibited a certain conformity. Most were elegantly costumed, except those who favored the currently fashionable simulated tatters known among the modish as "poverty chic." All but a few appeared to be well fed, too; in fact, a significant number were overly so. They marched in little bunches, seldom more than three or four to a group, and only a few had the look of bona fide zealots. Soft-looking innocents: most were babbling and laughing impulsively—well nigh nervously—as if out for some shady childhood lark. Doubtless, few had fought to protect the privileges they enjoyed. Certainly their leader had done no fighting during the last war. Puvis Amherst was one of the most craven individuals Brim had ever encountered. Until his father

—Admiral Amherst—was able to extract him from blockade duty aboard I.F.S *Truculent*, the man had spent most of his time cowering in any available hiding place.

From time to time, the marching CIGAs made furtive glances at a thin line of determined-looking men and women who marched in an opposite direction, surrounding the whole demonstration area. Hardened-looking individuals these were, dressed in ordinary clothing—some wearing portions of old Fleet uniforms from the last war. They carried hand-lettered, amateurish placards of a much different type.

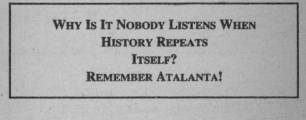

WHY IS IT NOBODY LISTENS WHEN
HISTORY REPEATS
ITSELF?
REMEMBER ATALANTA!

KEEP OUR FREEDOMS SAFE.
BACK PRINCE ONRAD!
BUILD STARFURIES!

DON'T SELL OUR CHILDREN
INTO TRIANNIC'S SLAVERY!
DOWN WITH CIGA TRAITORS!

"Glad to see those," Brim remarked, nodding through the window.

Drummond nodded. "Aren't we all?" he growled. "They've only just started to show up at these affairs." He shrugged. "It's taken a long time for the CIGAs to push people over the brink, but some of our citizens are finally waking up to what's going on. There'll be others. In the end, nobody really wants to lose his freedom.''

Continuing on, they passed Avalon's imposing Admiralty building where a second CIGA demonstration had traffic in Locorno Square tied in knots. Here again, fifteen, perhaps twenty, counterdemonstrators were carrying pro-Fleet placards.

WE ARE COMMITTED TO THE MISSION.
BACK THE FLEET!

BUILD STARFURIES!
IN DEFENSE OF OUR EMPIRE,
THERE CAN BE NO SECOND BEST!

COURAGE AND STARFURIES:
THE FLEET TEAM!

Brim smiled dourly. There weren't many of them, certainly not in comparison to the thousand-odd CIGAs who had shown up for the main demonstration. But everything had to start somewhere. The very fact that even a small segment of the population was now sufficiently aroused to take definitive and visible action in the face of overwhelming odds said a lot about the state of the Empire.

Once in the historic Beardmore Section—as always abounding in reconstruction scaffolding and derricks—Felicity slowed at two heroic marble statues of Cerenian asteroid wizards done in the classical Barrett style, turned onto ancient, tree-lined Gregory Street, and pulled to the curb before a half square of fusty old office buildings done in the flamboyant style of a bygone age. The rainy gloom made them look gray and tired, their gallant colonnades and statues out of place in these shameful days of CIGA-induced privation within the Fleet. Brim recognized the structures instantly: the old Admiralty Annex buildings. If they could only speak!

He scaled the massive front staircase while his hovering umbrella dodged this way and that in a plucky (but ineffective) struggle to outguess the chancy air currents set up by the huge stone edifice before them. With cold rain dripping from his nose, he returned a salute by four imperious-looking guards at the portico, then followed his two companions across a sculpted colonnade and into a lofty room encircled by five levels of balconies. Overhead, a vaulted ceiling holographically depicted cavalcades of historic starships that soared off toward destinations so far removed in time that some now existed only in memory.

Brim recognized many of the famous vessels at a glance: graceful I.F.S. *Valorous*, the renowned battlecruiser that cleared the Lorandal Cluster of space pirates for the first time in recorded history; S.S. *Pericole Enterprise*, a plucky little freighter that ran the deadly Qu'oodal blockade thirty times; even little I.F.S. *Idrovolante*, a classic example of Mario Castoldi's fine hand that to this very day held the speed record for starships powered by old-fashioned Agello Drive systems.

"Hey, Wilf," Drummond called out with a guffaw. "That's a great way to trip over your feet or run into a wall!"

"Oh, right," Brim said, feeling his cheeks burn as he lowered his gaze. "I always was an easy mark for old starships."

"Makes sense," Drummond chuckled. "Who else would the Admiralty put in charge of their newest Fleet iron?"

At the elevator lobby, a frosted-glass partition slid back and two pairs of eyes scrutinized each of the three before they passed into the lifts. On the seventh floor, they were stopped by three marines checking fingerprints and retinal images before they passed into a high-ceilinged hall whose length was clearly designed to foil intruders. The guard at the far end would have extra moments to activate whatever safety devices he deemed necessary before potential threats could move from one end to another. A truly ancient device, Brim considered with a smile. But effective for all that.

Once past that guard station, he found himself in a large, rectangular room like all the others he had seen in the complex over the years: row upon row of workstations, quietly humming electrical equipment, the occasional clatter of switches and keystrokes, a muffled cough or the creaking of a chair. The air was filled with odors from hot electrical equipment, whiffets of perfume, Hogge'Poa smoke indicating Bears somewhere in the area, and the all-pervading odor of mustiness from the ancient building itself. Brim's sense of history even imagined the brittle redolence of paper, though that primordial substance had been available only in museums for more than five hundred years.

"In here," Drummond said, keying open the door to a side office with his holobadge.

Brim found himself mildly shocked as he entered. Unlike the other offices he'd seen, this room was bright and airy. Tall windows with ornately rounded tops and high ceilings completely dwarfed both desks and a huge conference table that dominated the room. The latter had been carefully lined with decanters, ready for whatever libations accrued to various Admiralty dignitaries who would be briefed in the office.

"Executive office," Drummond explained to Brim's raised eyebrows. "It's also one of the best briefing rooms in the complex. I'll demonstrate soon as you've had a chance to look around. You'll want to know what the Leaguers have come up with to counter *Starfury*."

Calhoun nodded. "Aye," he said. "We'll need to know that, all right." He looked around the room appreciatively, then frowned and peered over the top of his eyeglasses. "I assume you won't hae time to personally escort us in and out for the next couple of weeks," he added.

"Your IDs ought to be here within the metacycle," Drummond countered. "I've got to get *some* army work done, after all." He nodded toward the door. "Just so you don't get too homesick for deep space, you'll find the office cvceese' brewer behind the panel outside with the usual tin for credits. There are reasonably clean mugs on the shelf. Standard rules: when you're done here, leave 'em the way you found 'em."

"The place is secure?" Calhoun asked.

"Electronically: as perfect as we can make it. Actually, it's secure as the Bears can make it. Xaxtdamn CIGAs have the same clearances as we do, but the Sodeskayans . . . well . . . they have a few extra levels all their own, so they swept the room. It's clean."

"How about the people outside?" Brim asked.

Drummond thought about that for a moment. "Most of them have higher clearances than either of you," he said. Then he frowned and pointed a finger at Brim. "What's the most reliable way you know of to tell a CIGA from an ordinary starsailor?" he demanded without warning.

Startled, Brim frowned. "I don't know, General," he said, rubbing his chin. "Unless I have some personal knowledge, or a tip from somebody I trust, there's no reliable way I can tell —at least until someone does something overt."

"That's the point, Wilf," Drummond answered with a serious look. "We can't, either. That's why we've got a good door, a good lock, and Bears to do a daily sweep. Most of the *real* security will be up to you Fleet types." Then he glanced through the door. "You're lucky, though. Cal let us re-recruit one of your old shipmates about a month ago. He's had most of the duty setting up an office here and working with the Bears."

Brim noticed Calhoun break into a wide smile. "He'll also be your new Master Chief Petty Officer when you get back to *Starfury*," he added with a wink. "Come in, Chief, while I help brother Drummond set up his League briefing."

"Aye, aye, Commodore," an oddly familiar voice replied from the hall.

Suddenly Brim caught his breath as a tall, powerfully built figure strode into the room. "Barbousse!" he shouted, a huge grin breaking across his face. "Utrillo Barbousse!"

CHAPTER 3

The Annex

Brim returned the huge man's salute, then strode across the floor to shake hands. "There were times I thought I'd never see you again, Chief," he said, fighting back a wince as his fingers were crushed in a viselike grip. "What ever became of you?"

Barbousse smiled wryly. "That's a long story, Cap'm," he said.

"Something in the neighborhood of ten years long," Brim replied, his mind rushing back in time like a whirlwind. He'd just received a transfer as First Lieutenant aboard I.F.S. *Thunderbolt*; Barbousse was off to the Helmsman's Academy; Nergol Triannic was on the run; and the future had at last begun to show some promise after nearly five years of military disasters. "Seems like a couple of lifetimes since you dropped me off at the Atalanta Terminal," he said. "Will you ever forget how we sighted our first bender?"

"Couldn't forget that, sir," Barbousse said with a faraway grin. "By accident it was. You, Polkovnik Ursis, an' me—aboard old S.S. *Providential*. She'd been abandoned close to some gas giant . . . um. . . ."

"Yeah," Brim said, pursing his lips ". . . yeah . . . Zebulon Mu! That's what it was called."

Barbousse snapped his fingers. "Right you are, sir! Zebulon

Mu. And you *just* got us out of there in the nik of time!'' His eyes looked off somewhere into a distant past. ''Those were promising days,'' he said with a shrug. ''Somehow, they simply . . . stopped. . . .''

''What happened to you at the Academy?'' Brim asked quietly.

''I lasted awhile,'' he said, taking a deep breath. ''Did pretty well, too, sir, if I do say so. But they RIFed me out, in the first Reduction . . . not long after the Treaty of Garak.'' He pursed his lips. ''I imagine you must have lost your commission in the same RIF—they were cuttin' 'way back on everything at the time.''

''You've got that right,'' Brim said. ''It seemed like everyone in the Fleet was out of work those days—all looking for those few jobs I thought I could land myself.'' He grinned wryly. ''I must have gone through a hundred of 'em, each a little worse than the last.''

Barbousse nodded. ''My life started to go that way, too,'' he said, ''but I got lucky. The Governor, er, Commodore Calhoun signed me on one of his ships. Things got considerably better afterward—and exciting.''

Brim knew enough about Calhoun to resist asking any more about *that* job.

''You worried a lot of people when you disappeared, beggin' the Cap'm's pardon,'' Barbousse continued. ''We all breathed a sigh of relief when you surfaced in Atalanta.''

The Carescrian felt his cheeks burn. After smashing up a clapped-out ED-4 (through no fault of his own), he'd fallen on such hard times he literally fled from Avalon. Shipping out as a Slops Mate on a liner, he ultimately jumped ship in the great starport of Atalanta—his friends caught up with him there. ''I learned a couple of big lessons on that trip,'' he said reflectively.

Barbousse smiled. ''I learned a few myself before I left the Fleet, sir,'' he said. ''But the most important one of all I learned at the Academy.''

''What was that?'' Brim asked. The big man was seldom conspicuously introspective.

Barbousse furrowed his brow. ''It's hard to put into words,

Cap'm," he said. "I did well at the Academy; number two in my class toward the end. But, well, even *then* I was askin' myself if I really was in the right place—doin' the right thing. And I kept coming up with 'no.' "

"Second in your class and doing the wrong thing?" Brim asked. "How could that be?"

"There's them whose lot is to be officers, Cap'm," he said, "and them that's happier bein' a rating. I'm one of the ratings, that's all."

Awestruck, Brim looked the big man directly in his face. Not many people knew themselves that well. "You were the greatest Chick in the Fleet when I knew you," he said with genuine admiration.

"Thank you, Cap'm," Barbousse said, meeting Brim's eyes with a steady gaze. "I've always tried t' do my best."

"Ah . . . when you two ancient veterans finish comparing war stories, I'm ready to begin my briefing," Drummond interrupted with a chuckle.

"Aye, sir . . . I'll cover the door, Commodore," Barbousse said, immediately restored to his normal decorum.

Brim quickly took a seat opposite Calhoun at the forward end of the table.

"About time I got the two of you back on the same ship," the elder Carescrian chuckled gleefully. "I can't think of much worse that could happen to the League."

As the room lights began to dim, Drummond looked up from his podium controls and smiled. "All right, gentlemen," he announced in a theatrical voice, "presenting Gorn-Hoff's new light cruiser prototype, the P.1065." He was immediately obscured by the three-dimensional, holographic representation of a rocky desert just before dawn—or just following sunset; it was impossible to tell. After a few moments, the distant rumble of spaceborne gravity generators overlaid the lonesome sound of wind moaning along a rocky desert floor. In the narrow band of lighter sky above the right horizon, Brim's trained eye immediately caught a distant speck of movement traveling toward him at high velocity—a starship making landfall. As the form resolved itself, he could see that the Leaguers had built their new ship in the angular silhouette of a double chevron, the smaller one nestled inside its considerably larger counterpart.

"Sorry to say that none of us are sufficiently cleared that the Bears would divulge *where* these holograms were taken"—Drummond's voice intruded over the rising thunder—"but unless I miss my guess, it's close to one of their remote test ranges in the Gelheim Sector. At any rate, the content ought to more than make up for other information we lack."

Before the angular Gorn-Hoff could pass "overhead," it gently reversed course over a pulsing crystal tower that cranked rapidly into the air from the desert floor. During straight and level flight, the ship appeared to carry yellow lights at each tip of the large chevron and a red light mounted at its apex. The latter was visible from both fore and aft. When the new cruiser changed course over the tower, however, a bright red ventral strobe began a flare that illuminated its entire underside.

"You'll note white belly markings during the strobes," Drummond pointed out. "The Leaguers have put a pair up front and a few more arranged asymmetrically aft. We don't know what they are, yet, but we think they might be part of a new weapons system. Wilf, that separation line at the midspan trailing edge break: what does that look like to you?"

Brim squinted as the display froze in place. "Hard to tell from this distance," he said, voice booming at first in the abrupt silence, "but by the shape, I'll wager it's some kind of outboard control emitter for the steering engine; especially if that's a Drive exhaust area at the trailing edge of the smaller chevron."

"Our feelings exactly," Drummond said, starting the display—and the sound—again. "Our on-site observer thought so, too. And for the record, *he* estimated its altitude at about eight thousand irals, with a speed of maybe four hundred fifty to five hundred c'lenyts per metacycle. Probably not ground-shaking information by itself, but you'll note the lack of a shock wave anywhere. That means that the Gorn-Hoff designers are finally starting to pay attention to planetary performance. In an atmosphere."

Abruptly, the desert dissolved into a classic starscape somewhere in deep, silent space. "Now," the still-invisible Drummond said in a much lowered voice, "we'll show you what the ship looks like out in its real element. We took these shots ourselves, from one of our newest benders: I.F.S. *Apparition*, the first ship we've built that can transmit *all* spectra through her hull, even N-rays." He laughed. "Don't get your hopes up for her, gentlemen. Even though she's really quite imperceptible to every detector we know about, *Apparition*'s only marginally better in performance than the rest of the benders: theirs *and* ours. Her extra transmission capability takes its usual toll in power. So a lot of the shots were made while she was simply dodging out of the way."

As Brim watched, fascinated, the angular Gorn-Hoff appeared again, this time at the left side of the display, moving slowly across the starscape at a much-increased LightSpeed number.

"This sequence was taken during one of the earliest flights," Drummond explained. "The crew appeared to be getting her ready for some sort of trials. You'll notice Brim's 'control emitter' is partially deflected downward, and four auxiliary cooling panels mounted over what we think are the Drive chambers have deployed."

Moments later two Gantheisser 380 chase ships appeared at the edge of the display, moving much faster than the Gorn-Hoff in the same direction.

"Those two are going in for a 'rolling pickup,'" Drummond commented as the new cruiser began to gain speed with her control surfaces moving slowly to a fair position. After a few moments only the outboard steering emitters displayed any detectable movement while both chase ships moved into place on her flanks.

The Gorn-Hoff continued to accelerate straight ahead and quickly outpaced the much slower Imperial spy ship. She seemed to maintain this constant acceleration for several cycles, trailing a strangely wavering green wake that was wider, but not so bright, as ones from the single-crystal Gantheisser chase ships. She had gained several c'lenyts when she started a shallow-banked turn to starboard: the first noticeable attitude change since the start of its run. This continued until she reversed direction completely, rolling level on a collision course with the bender

—which rapidly moved out of the big ship's flight path as it passed close to starboard.

Throughout this maneuver, the lead Gantheisser stayed some 250 irals away from the cruiser's starboard tip, closing briefly to a distance of perhaps half the span of the main chevron during the flight.

The second Gantheisser maintained a much wider spacing throughout the trials, moving from one side to the other in maneuvers that Brim felt were clearly made to attain optimum holography angles.

For the next few cycles, the Leaguers conducted standard stability, control, and handling maneuvers. Brim recognized pitch and yaw doublets, bank-to-roll performance checks, level turns, and a final "wind-up turn" before the Gorn-Hoff resumed its high-speed cruise—away from the clearly hard-driven bender.

"She looks good to a number of our analysts," Drummond observed. "She's 'nimble,' in their words. Especially her roll rate, which appears excellent for such a big starship. They also characterize her as 'well damped—very good directionally.' "

Brim silently agreed. He'd caught only a single overshoot in response to a yaw doublet. Clearly, she would be an excellent disruptor platform.

The Leaguers were now making quarter banks and moving at a relatively high rate of attack when they turned once again into the path of the bender, flashed past, and headed off toward a small squadron of support ships that materialized off toward galactic center. To Brim, she looked rock solid—easy to control.

"You mentioned disruptors a while back," Calhoun said. "I have na seen onythin' that luiks like ordnance to me. What *do* we know about her weapons systems?"

"Very little," Drummond admitted. "Detailed analysis on these holograms has turned up mounting rings for seven large turrets, probably twin-mounts like *Starfury*'s. But that's the only hard information we have." He nodded, as if making a decision. "My own guess says they'll carry the new 375-mmi disruptors they've licensed from Theobold Interspace in Lixor."

"Good old Lixor," Calhoun growled. "Wee wonder they're always neutral. They build such a bankroll sellin' to both sides that they still show a hefty profit after payin' off the eventual victors."

"Whatever else people say about the credit-grabbing zu-keeds," Drummond said with a laugh, "they make damned fine disruptors."

Brim nodded. "From what I've read, those new Theobolds are *superfocused*. First production models of a whole new technology. And fourteen ought to land a *lot* of energy at the target."

"Right on both counts, Brim," Drummond agreed. "They are superfocused and a salvo *ought* to land a tremendous load of energy. But that's precisely where we think we've caught them in a very serious mistake."

"Mistake?" Brim asked.

"Aye," Calhoun assured him. "Sounds like they've made quite a ship from where I sit."

"True enough," Drummond said. "They have—except for one small detail. You'll note how thin the cross section is."

Calhoun shrugged. "Small target at a lot of angles—plus tremendous thrust diffusion. And everybody knows what *that* does for maneuverability. What's wrong with that?"

"*Starfury*'s firepower came as a terrible blow to the Gorn-Hoff designers," Drummond said. "They'd designed their new ship with ultra-high performance foremost in their minds—Theobolds had already taken care of their artillery issues. They didn't have a reflecting Drive, however, so they had to achieve their performance in other ways, including that new hull shape. But that very low-profile shape deprived 'em of the two extra plasma generators we put in *Starfury* just to power the disruptors. And the new Theobolds take a *lot* of energy."

Brim felt his eyes widen. "You mean . . . ?"

"Precisely, my good Helmsman," Drummond said with a smile. "While *Starfury* can fire a full twelve-disruptor salvo—at full power—every twenty clicks, we've calculated that the P.1065 here can MAX-fire no more than six of its fourteen Theobolds simultaneously, and even that will drastically alter the ship's velocity—above or below LightSpeed." The display dissolved again, this time to reveal the General standing at the podium beneath a strong spotlight. He pursed his lips, thought for a moment, then shook his head. "Of course," he added, "they *could* fire all fourteen of 'em at some low-energy setting, but . . ." He shrugged. "It's all theoretical right now, of course. But despite the energy problems they've run into: those Leaguers have come up with something very good again. And if I know anything about their xaxtdamned starships, it will probably *also* be very dangerous."

Brim had little trouble supporting Drummond's prediction. Over the years, he had been through enough battles with the Leaguers—and their machines—to underestimate neither. . . .

Shortly after dawn, Brim and Calhoun inaugurated briefing operations on stolid, old Admiral Carlisle A. H. Gumberton, Chief of Fleet Operations. With him were Admiral Frank B. Farleigh, a flighted being from A'zurn who had worked his way from the ranks to the post of Commander in Chief, Home Fleet; Admiral Bruce Meedars, a graduate of the Dytasburg Academy and Director of Fleet HyperDrive Propulsion since Brim could remember; Rear Admiral John F. Varn, newly appointed Commandant of the Helmsman's Academy; and the scholarly Vice Admiral Daniel L. Cowper, Chief of Imperial Operations for Bender Technology. All were old-line, battle-hardened warriors whose true feelings concerning CIGAs and their ilk were well beyond question.

Calhoun led off with a detailed description of The Plan, immediately after which he became embroiled by what can only be described as a three-way grilling by Admirals Gumberton, Meedars, and Cowper that lasted nearly two metacycles. The staff officers were all highly cautious, neither damning nor adopting the ideas as presented; people at that level of responsibility had to be extremely careful. Gumberton, for example, concerned himself with the issue of resources: Fleet strength. "The CIGAs have made these hard times, Cal," he asserted. "Ship numbers are way below critical levels. The whole Empire—at least the part that gives a damn—is counting on those units. What would we do if war suddenly broke out and we suddenly had to destroy some of those new Leaguer space forts . . . ?"

Calhoun fielded that question along with nearly a hundred

others before the day was over. It was apparent from the beginning that selling Calhoun's idea was going to be no easy thing. Yet, doubtlessly, it *was* possible. If the Flag Officers were hesitant, they were also interested: at least willing to consider Calhoun's proposition on its face value. Moreover, during the next weeks, they promised to send their subordinates to be briefed, also. And *those officers*, the advisers, would become the advocates who would actually sell the project.

When Brim's turn came to speak, he barely encountered resistance at all. His subject matter had to do with black-and-white topics such as engineering and performance depictions of *Starfury* and the ships that would follow her from the stocks. The men he faced were all starsailors whose very blood flowed with a love of starships and the vast open reaches of the starry Universe. They were all ears, and clearly liked what they heard.

As usual, Brim's stay in Avalon was nearly all work—often all day and all night. And during his all-too-few moments of free time, he was frequently so tired that he could only stagger to a chair for a few moments of catnapping. Clearly, it was not an idyllic time in his life; there simply was too much work for that. But it kept him from thinking how lonely he had become. It seemed to be a matter of course.

Only a single worrisome incident marred those hectic weeks at the Admiralty Annex—aside from almost-incessant CIGA demonstrations against one thing or another all over the city. Anti-CIGA security at the old building was nearly airtight, as it should have been, considering that it was quietly managed by Sodeskayans. But even Bears were tried to their limits by the nearly impossible restrictions that had to be placed on their activities in the name of secrecy. For example, the old complex was, after all, Admiralty property. Ostensibly, therefore, it was open to Blue Capes of every persuasion—including CIGAs. The Bears (and their colleagues) had outright responsibility to recognize Congress members and direct them to "safe" areas where they could be properly evaluated. But they could expect no help from other security organizations—nor did they particularly want it.

Visitors who arrived at the old complex by mistake, or out of genuine curiosity, were dealt with pleasantly and sent on their way. Others, clearly there to discover what it was that attracted so many senior officers to an out-of-the-way building complex, were offered "verifiable" false information by apparently pro-CIGA guards. However, those who were not satisfied with these measures were dealt with swiftly, meeting with disastrous traffic accidents or fast-acting viral illnesses before they could report to their masters. Fortunately, only a few CIGAs required such extreme treatment: too few to raise flags of alarm among the traitors.

The Sodeskayan guards did their work so quietly that the building's inhabitants were normally unaware of their activities. One morning nearly two weeks into the Avalonian new year, however, while Calhoun was busy presenting to Flotilla Commanders of the 108th Attack Squadron, Brim noticed an attractive Lieutenant enter the room behind a steward carrying steaming decanters of fresh cvceese'. The elder Carescrian himself was so deeply engrossed with a huge holographic representation of Fluvanna that he clearly failed to notice the woman, even when her eyes began to dart everywhere.

Brim watched the woman carefully. Something about her didn't check. A look in her eye? A bearing that belied her rank of Lieutenant? Perhaps it was the way her hands nervously twiddled with her collar buttons? Whatever it was, something began to set all his personal danger flags. He decided to take no chances and started out of his chair to investigate, but before he was halfway across the floor, Barbousse arrived at the woman's side, bowing courteously and requesting her identification disk.

With no provocation whatsoever, she began to shout at the big rating. "How *dare* you question an officer?" she shrieked, stopping Calhoun in midsentence and turning every head in the room while she moved quickly toward the exit.

Brim stopped in his tracks, then swung off toward the door, reaching it before her hand could activate the latch. "*I* question you," he said firmly. "Will you please produce your ID for the Chief, Lieutenant?"

The woman's eyes narrowed as she nervously played with the

two gold buttons on either side of her collar. "What right have you to ask for my identification?" she demanded, her eyes betraying a moment of fear as a huge Bear entered the room from a sliding panel in the rear wall. "Can't you see I'm a Blue Cape like the rest of you?" she shrieked. "Is it a crime to be lost in an old government building like this?"

The Bear bowed politely, then stepped directly in front of the woman, his great bulk blocking her view of the room while he rolled his head backward to peer nearsightedly through a pair of huge eyeglasses. "I doubt it, madame," he rumbled in a gentle, cultivated bass voice. "Although I am not a member of the Imperial Fleet, as such, I am certain that it is never a crime to become lost. Especially in such a confusing edifice as the old Admiralty building here. Otherwise, I should have become incarcerated weeks ago."

"See?" she demanded, looking from Brim to Barbousse. "You heard him. Now, let me out of here. I have important business—"

"One slight problem, madame," the Bear interrupted, placing a six-fingered hand on the woman's sleeve as she attempted to move to one side of him.

"And what is *that*?" she demanded, staring angrily at the Sodeskayan.

"Your collar buttons, madame," he replied uncomfortably, as if somehow dismayed by his own words. "They are ingeniously concealed cameras—but then, you know that." He sighed. "What a shame," he added, "that you succeeded in some small part of your mission. The buttons were already transmitting when my machines detected their radiation—and of course squelched them. Let us hope that the purloined information you managed to send was at least limited. Mr. Barbousse," he said, turning to the big rating, "would you open the door for my Imperial colleagues? They will need to process this charming young woman."

Instantly, the woman's hand opened to reveal a tiny vial that she raised almost to her mouth.

The Bear's reaction belied his massive size. He grabbed the woman's wrists before her hands were halfway toward her lips.

"It would be a great disgrace," he said "were such a beautiful human as yourself to take her own life." Then his eyes hardened, and curled lips revealed his fangs. "Especially," he added, "before my Imperial colleagues can wring some useful information from your traitorous personage."

Moments later three able-looking Blue Capes gagged the woman and muscled her from the room. "My deepest apologies, sirs," the Bear said, bowing deeply at the door. "It is always most difficult maintaining security in a free domain." Grimly he tripped the latch. "May the Universe grant us all that my job never, *ever* grows easier. . . ." Then he stepped into the hall and gently closed the door behind him.

As Calhoun completed his part of the briefing, Brim could only stare at the floor and worry. Even though the Sodeskayan had managed to limit how much information the woman could transmit, there was no telling just how much she *had* managed to get out—nor what it would ultimately mean to the Leaguer analysts who would receive the covert information.

Midway through their third week of briefings, Barbousse chauffeured Brim and Calhoun to an out-of-the-way Imperial Marine installation where they could meet Drummond with no question about security *whatsoever*.

"Your briefings have gone well, gentlemen," the General said, leaning back in a tall chair with his hands around a thick mug of cvceese'. "Everyone's got real concerns about Fluvanna and our dependence on her crystal seeds, so your ideas have been most welcome."

Calhoun pursed his lips. "I could usually tell when I ha' them in the palm o' my hand," he said, "soon as the questions started." He nodded at Brim. "And o' course every Blue Cape worth his salt wanted to hear aboot *Starfury*, so my countryman here couldn't miss. They *loved* ev'ry word he spoke. But there's ane question I ne'er did get an answer for, Brother Drummond. Is *anybody* willin' to help me *staff* these new ships?"

Drummond smiled soberly and shook his head. "Pretty sparse crowd banging on my door to do that," he admitted. "We're not the only ones who see a war coming, you know. And everyone wants to keep his own organization staffed so he can fight it." He furrowed his brow and pulled himself to the table again. "Unfortunately, that's not your only problem, Cal," he continued.

"What else?" Calhoun demanded, his brow wrinkling in concern.

Drummond's face took on a rare look of annoyance, almost frustration. "It's another 'people problem,' " he replied, "and one that I'm half ashamed to mention. You see, a number of otherwise-loyal officers refuse to support the plan at all, even though they believe in it. Their fear is that influential, high-ranking CIGA brass within the Admiralty may get wind of the operation, and if it fails, they'll root out the ones who cooperated and ruin their careers."

"I thought of that myself," Calhoun said, taking a deep breath. "I simply did na want to b'lieve it." He frowned and chewed his lower lip. "If that's the kind of slime we have to rely on these days, we might as well join Amherst's xaxtdamned CIGAs. At least they have some sort of common goal."

Drummond smiled bleakly and nodded understandingly. "I know how you feel, Cal," he said. "I hate dealing weakness like that, myself. But until we encounter a sentient that doesn't have emotions, we're going to have to endure cupidity of one form or another. The one recompense is that the Leaguers put up with the same things—and their thralls, the CIGAs, have to be prime examples of that sort of weakness. Imagine what it's like to deal with utterly contemptible pukes like Puvis Amherst."

Calhoun abruptly chuckled. "Aye," he said, winking at Brim with a look of comic satisfaction. "I can na imagine much worse punishment myself." Then he returned his attention to Drummond. "Neither does it do much to change the situation, either," he continued at length. "There are a lot of normally loyal officers in the Fleet who simply don't support the plan. And that's bad, because Prince Onrad's one requirement was that we generate some solid support among—"

Abruptly Barbousse opened the outer door and stepped inside. "His Highness, Vice Admiral Onrad," he announced as calmly as if the appearance of a Crown Prince were an everyday occurrence. Barbousse *was* unflappable.

Onrad strode into the room only a heartbeat after all three officers jumped to attention. He wore an open Fleet Cloak over the standard Flag Officer's service dress: peaked cap with a double row of embroidered oak leaves, blue reefer jacket, and matching trousers with black boots. Four and a half stripes were embroidered on his cuffs. He wore no decorations save his Battle of Atalanta Service ribbon. "Seats, gentlemen," he said briskly, throwing his cloak onto a desk across the room and taking an office chair beside Calhoun. "Well, Drummond," he demanded, "how have our two Carescrian friends faired with the Admiralty staff?"

Drummond pursed his lips. "*They've* done brilliantly, Your Highness" he said after a moment's thought. "I've heard reports of only a few disagreements, and those are from known malcontents." Then he frowned. "I think if there has been any ill-fairing, it's been with our Admiralty itself. Everybody gives us lip service, but nobody is willing to provide crews."

Onrad nodded and slouched easily in the straight-backed office chair. He was one of those catlike persons who could look comfortable in a thousand-odd positions yet lose none of his dignity for it. "Yes," he said. "I suppose I'd expected that. I don't believe I would want to give up staff were I in their positions, either." He turned his gaze at Brim. "Wilf," he demanded, "how do you feel about temporarily resigning your commission in the Fleet to get this job done? Would you go along with something like that?"

Caught off guard by Onrad's forthright question, Brim needed a moment to sort out his thoughts. Finally he looked the Prince directly in his eye. "Your Highness," he said calmly, "after doing a lot of thinking about how things seem to be going for the Empire right now, I'd take my chances and follow Commodore Calhoun into the Fluvannian Fleet. But I'd *only* do that because I believe that unless we act quickly we are liable to lose our Empire itself, and then my commission won't be worth much anyway."

"Well then," Onrad said with a smile. "That pretty much settles things, as far as I can see. . . . ."

Brim interrupted by raising his index finger. "You didn't let me finish, Your Highness," he said.

Onrad raised an eyebrow, clearly unused to such interruptions. "All right, Brim," he said. "Continue."

"Thank you, Your Highness," Brim said. Over the years, he'd learned that the headstrong Prince actually counted on such interruptions, even though he had never learned to like them. "If I hadn't given a lot of thought to the state of our Empire," he started, "if I hadn't read a lot of exceedingly classified intelligence about what is really going on within the League, then probably I would turn the Commodore's offer down flat."

Onrad's eyebrows joined over the bridge of his nose in a mighty scowl. "And just what do you mean by that?"

"Well," Brim started, "imagine for a moment that you were not Crown Prince of an Empire but rather some career member of the Fleet—officer or rating, it doesn't matter." He poured himself a mug of cvceese' while he put the proper words together. "It's not all that easy to get a career berth in our Fleet," he continued. "Officers have to successfully complete a formidable education—then demonstrate its results in a battery of daunting tests. And ratings must fulfill all sorts of difficult skill and intelligence requirements." He took a deep breath and peered into the Prince's eyes. "If you don't have proper connections—and most of us Blue Capes don't—then entering the Fleet takes a long time, and sometimes a bit of luck, too."

Onrad nodded in agreement. "I understand all you've told me, Brim," he said. "But I've already said that they'd leave the Fleet only temporarily. I fail to see any problem there."

Brim continued unperturbed. "The problem, Your Highness," he said, "is that nowhere have I heard a *guarantee* that an officer's commission would be waiting or that a rating would regain his berth when this Fluvanna operation terminates."

"What?" Onrad growled. "Haven't I already said it?"

"Begging Your Highness's pardon," Brim retorted, "but *I* know what it's like to be legislated out of the Fleet. And believe me, so do a lot of other people. Nearly everyone on today's active-duty roster has seen how easy it is to find one's self on the outside, including the CIGAs who are going to consider this to be the most beneficial purge of the organization possible— lots of the best old-time fighters gone in one easy sweep. Were I a CIGA, I'd do my utmost to make sure none of them ever got a chance to serve again. Much as we all dislike the fact, Puvis Amherst heads up a *very* powerful, Empire-wide organization—enough to make me awfully leery about putting my commission in any kind of jeopardy."

Onrad frowned in sudden understanding. "Yes," he said, stroking his beard thoughtfully. "I see what you mean now. It's going to take some sort of *tangible* guarantee, isn't it?"

"To my way of thinking it is," Brim replied. "Oh, there will be a number of us who will go along without one, but I suspect we won't be enough to staff eleven Starfury-class ships."

"For what it's worth, I think he's right, Your Highness," Drummond seconded.

"What sort of guarantee would they want?" Onrad demanded.

Calhoun smiled. "Like in a game of cre'el, Your Highness," he said. "Something that beats a CIGA resource."

"Like what?" Onrad persisted.

"These days, only Emperors beat CIGAs," Drummond said, "begging the Prince's pardon, of course."

Suddenly Onrad closed his eyes and nodded. "*Now* I understand," he said. "They'd want something 'in writing,' to coin an ancient phrase."

"That's the way I see it, Your Highness," Brim said, relaxing in his chair. He'd done his part; the rest was now up to Onrad.

The Prince leaned an elbow on Drummond's desk and stroked his short beard again, deep in his own thoughts. After a long pause, he nodded to Brim. "It's reasonable," he said. "The damn CIGAs are going to lose their power shortly after we find ourselves in a war with the League again. But until they are shown up for the wrong-headed idiots they are, we'll need that guarantee. And I'll provide it—through my father, the Emperor, of course. Some sort of immutable warranty that people can

carry with them.'' He nodded his head. Count on it, gentlemen.''
Then he looked up and smiled. ''Do we have *that* out of the
way, now?''

''Next topic, Your Highness,'' Calhoun said with a lopsided
grin.

''How about you, Brim?'' Onrad demanded.

''I'm ready, Your Highness.''

''Drummond?''

The General's nod was all Onrad needed. ''All right, then,''
he chuckled to Calhoun. ''To continue with the original purpose
of my visit, it appears that you and Brim have sold the Fluvanna
concept. I can find almost no active opposition among the people
who count. In fact, there even seems to be a groundswell building
for its implementation, although as you have eloquently pointed
out no one is clamoring to staff the ships.''

Calhoun began to speak, but Onrad pointed a finger at him.

''You're going to tell me about the idiots in the Fleet who
fear the CIGAs and won't back you because they think you might
fail. Right?''

''Aye, Your Highness,'' Calhoun said with a grin. ''I figured
you had a right to know everything, e'en if some of it was na
good.''

''I always try to understand the downside issues first,'' Onrad
said. ''Often, that's the quickest way to see the bright side.''

''Xaxtdamned cowards don't bother Your Highness?'' Calhoun demanded hotly.

''Oh, they bother me, I suppose,'' Onrad replied. ''But people
like that are usually just weak, not disloyal. I pretty well know
who they are, now—largely through your fortuitous efforts the
last few weeks. Not so much threats as *empty spaces* that need
to be filled.'' He nodded thoughtfully. ''We'll simply never
assign them a position of responsibility again. That way, they
can still be useful to us without putting anyone in danger during
times of stress.''

''In that case,'' Calhoun said with a nod, ''it's probably time
to involve the Fluvannians, too. We've made a lot of assumptions
aboot their willingness to be part of this wee scam.''

"They'll come through for us," Drummond assured him. "I've known the Nabob since he was a child and I had just joined His Majesty's Foreign Service." He frowned. "A singular sort of person. But you know that, Your Highness. You've met him."

Onrad nodded. "Mustafa's 'singular,' all right," he said. "But only in how he reflects a society very much unlike ours. And of course, he's an *absolute* ruler. Feels he's Nabob by divine pronouncement—from the Universe itself. He doesn't have to put up with a legislature at all. He calls all the shots he wants to call; delegates the rest."

"Luckily, he's delegated considerable power to a real friend of the Empire," Drummond observed.

"Yes," Onrad agreed. "Old Beyazh, the Ambassador—one of the great rue' of our times, from what I hear."

"At least he'll listen," Drummond said. "Might have to find him a good-looking blonde for a while, but he'll come around."

Calhoun grinned conspiratorially. "I'll tell you how to gat on old Beyazh's guid side, in a hurry"—he chuckled—"aside from providin' him some guid-lookin' woman. He's an auld starsailor. Years ago, he commanded ane o' those antiques that make up their 'Fleet.' I'll wager he'd swap his eye teeth for a ride in a ship like *Starfury*."

"Hmm," Onrad said with raised eyebrows as he turned to peer at Brim. "How *is* our 'pocket battlecruiser' these days?"

Brim felt his cheeks burn. "I've only got secondhand news, Your Highness," he admitted, "but Lieutenant Tissaurd reports that *Starfury*'s fit-out is almost complete—with all trials modifications finished last week."

"Would you like to get back to your ship?" Onrad asked.

Brim peered at Calhoun. "Would I, Commodore?" he asked histrionically.

"You'd think I'd dragged him from his own first-born child, Your Highness," Calhoun guffawed. Then he turned to Brim. "All right, my fellow Carescrian," he said, "I suppose it's time I let you go back and take over your ship. You've certainly done me proud here in Avalon."

"And I suspect we'll be needing *Starfury* soon for a bit of bribery after brother Calhoun here works his magic on Ambassador Beyazh,'' Onrad observed with a chuckle. "All very legal, of course."

"But of course, Your Highness," Brim said with as serious a mien as he could muster.

"Think you could come up with some quick transportation back to Bromwich for Commander Brim?" Onrad asked Drummond.

The latter looked up from his workstation. "Thought that might be coming, Your Highness," he said, winking at Brim. "S.S. *Empress of Brockton* embarks at midday tomorrow. Suppose you could be aboard?"

Brim smiled. "I could leave tonight," he said.

"Good," Drummond said. "In that case, I won't have to switch your tickets."

Brim frowned. "I don't understand," he said.

"Well," Drummond explained, "I thought you might be a little bored in the evenings, so I ticketed both you and your friend Barbousse on the S.S. *Arkadia*. She lifts in just five metacycles. . . ."

A week later, with Barbousse thoroughly in command of *Starfury*'s seventy-five nonrated starsailors, Brim had a chance to meet with Tissaurd in the newly carpeted wardroom, bringing himself up-to-date concerning the ship's fitting out. Like most wardrooms on major Imperial warships, *Starfury*'s was divided into two richly wood-paneled compartments: a dining room and a lounge separated by a serving pantry with counter access to both. The dining area contained a U-shaped table hand-hewn from dark rennel oak, twenty-five matching chairs, and a number of wooden sideboards for serving. In the lounge, a score of leather armchairs and divans generally faced the ship's crest: a crimson shield outlined in gold containing stylized bolts of yellow lightning discharging from a blazing orange star. Above this, the ship's motto, "Go Boldly!" appeared in old-fashioned symbolic characters. On an adjoining bulkhead hung the same large portrait of Emperor Greyffin IV that Brim had encountered in his first ship at the beginning of his career. Below this was an array of workstations; Brim and Tissaurd sat at the leftmost display/interface, and from Tissaurd's exquisitely detailed records, the Carescrian could see that nearly a full complement of stores had already been stowed, and that nearly all Admiralty inspections had been passed with high grades. He looked at the woman beside him who had so ably shouldered his duties and shook his head in wonder. "You've done well, Number One," he said.

"Better than you expected, Skipper?" she asked, clearly daring him to admit he'd worried that she could handle the job without him.

Brim laughed in spite of himself. "Yeah," he admitted, looking around the comfortable room, "I suppose that's true." Was it because she'd caught him being himself, or was it because she was so damned cute—or a combination of both.

"It's all right," she said with a mysterious little smile. "I just wanted to make certain I could read you."

"Read me?" Brim asked.

"I read people," Tissaurd stated calmly. "I've been doing it for years."

"I don't understand," Brim said.

Tissaurd gently patted his shoulder. "You don't have to," she said. "I'll take care of it for both of us."

Owen Morris, *Starfury*'s COMM Officer, strode into the wardroom before their conversation could continue. He handed Brim a sealed plastic envelope—the kind that usually contained ship's departure orders. "Hot from the crypto-KA'PPA, Skipper," he announced. "Untouched by human hands."

The envelope was marked SECRET; all sortie orders were sent as classified documents in peacetime; classification rose precipitously during wartime. Both Tissaurd and Morris were cleared for top secret and better, so Brim opened the envelope immediately.

    ASD86DASFLKJH8QT3-05   GROUP   35291   31/
    52010
    [SECRET]
    FM: ADMIRALTY COMFLEETOPS, AP34T

TO: W. A. BRIM, COMMANDER, I.F. @K 5054
INFO: DRUMMOND @AG-9200J

<AW09N7019925VPQ3994T8Q23558714988>

DEPARTURE ORDERS

1. YOU WILL PREPARE FOR DEPARTURE BROM-
WICH SOON AS PRACTICABLE. IMMEDIATELY
NOTIFY AP34T ESTIMATED DATE/TIME OF
LIFT-OFF.

2. SET DIRECT COURSE FOR MAGOR CITY,
ORDU, DOMINION OF FLUVANNA. PREPARA-
TIONS YOUR ARRIVAL ARE.CURRENTLY UN-
DER WAY.

3. YOU WILL BOARD SPECIAL DIPLOMATIC
PASSENGER AT GALACTIC COORDINATES
ZC*931/460:19.

[END SECRET]

ASD86DASFLKJH8QT3-05

Brim showed the brief message first to Morris, then to Tissaurd. "How soon can we lift ship, Number One?" he asked.

The tiny officer frowned for a moment. "Move over, Skipper," she said. "I'll need to check a few items at the workstation."

Brim slid aside, then stood to watch over her shoulder.

"The ship herself is ready," Tissaurd said absently, calling
floods of multicolored data cascading over the workstation's
display, merging it with other streams, then blending elements
into synthesized journals. "We're missing a second spare-parts
kit for the K-P Drives and a few supplies the Admiralty considers
critical—like gortam sealant."

"Gortam sealant?" Brim exclaimed. "Ridiculous. I use gortam sealant around the ion-chamber window on my gravcycle. That stuff's been around for a millennium.''

Tissaurd smiled over her shoulder. "I know," she said with a shrug. "But that didn't stop K-P from using it in their newest reflecting Drives. And we have to stock it—with some other out-of-the way stuff that has me pretty well stymied. I've got a couple of search parties out combing the city. But if we can't find it in Bromwich, then we'll probably have to lift ship without it.''

Brim stepped back from behind the workstation chair. "You'd lift ship without a full complement of Admiralty stores?" he asked in feigned horror.

"Maybe not the Drive spares," Tissaurd said calmly, "but I'd damned well hate to hang up a whole starship over a case of gortam sealant.''

"You mean that, don't you?" Brim asked with a frown, looking the tiny officer directly in the eye.

"You bet," Tissaurd answered. "Would you have it any other way, Skipper?"

"Not on your life, Number One," he replied, putting a hand on her shoulder.

"That's a relief," Tissaurd laughed. She looked up at Morris. "Owen, my friend," she said, "you could have been witness to the destruction of a budding career just now."

"I wasn't terribly worried," the COMM Officer said with a grin.

"Either was she"—Brim chuckled—"I think she can read my mind.''

"You'd be surprised what I can read," Tissaurd bantered.

"Hmm," Brim said theatrically, "do you suppose you can read the whereabouts of a spare-parts kit?"

Tissaurd closed her eyes and pinched the bridge of her nose. "Yee-e-e-s-s," she said, "it is coming to me." Suddenly she was busy with the workstation again. "Ah *yes*!" she exclaimed. "The answer magically springs to life in the crystal before me. Behold!''

" 'This evening, Darkness:45,' " Brim quoted from the workstation display. "Truly conjured magic."

"What can I say?" Tissaud said modestly, examining the perfect manicure of her right hand. "Madame Tissaud foretells all, especially with the workstation before her."

"I wouldn't have believed any of this if it hadn't gone on before m' very eyes," Morris said in feigned amazement.

"Either would I," Brim said, glancing out a Hyperscreen port where a large, old-fashioned skimmer had just pulled up to the brow entrance at the side of *Starfury*'s gravity pool. On its side, large letters proclaimed:

INTERSTELLAR SEALANTS

SERVING BROMWICH SHIPWRIGHTS SINCE 51005

Moments later, he watched the huge figure of Utrillo Barbousse returning through the brow with a large carton balanced on his broad right shoulder. GORTAM SEALANT was stamped prominently along the side. "How does tomorrow morning sound for lifting ship?" he asked.

Tissaurd thought for a moment. "Morning:2:00?" she offered presently.

"Sounds good to me," Brim said. "Morris," he said with a nod, "send that as an estimated time of departure to AP34T, the Admiralty. Got that?"

"Aye, Skipper," Morris acknowledged. "ETD of Morning:2:00 to Admiralty AP34T. I'll get out the word."

Starfury departed precisely on time the next morning—with all required stores in place.

Less than five Standard Days later, Dawn:3:10 found the new cruiser charging through the blackness of space a few hundred c'lenyts aft of perhaps the most distinguished Imperial battleship of all times, I.F.S. *Queen Elidean*, name ship of the five massive battleships that first mounted 406-mmi disruptors and, on completion thirty years previously, were considered to be the finest, most powerful warships in existence. Now fresh from a two-year refit, the grand old starship looked even more splendid than ever, with a multifaceted, box-type superstructure that housed everything that her old-fashioned stacked bridges had carried: navigating room, communications center, and conning tower topped by a powerful HyperLight rangefinder on the top. Even the KA'PPA tower was reduced in height and repositioned aft, yet there was no mistaking the huge, superfiring casemates with their monstrous disruptors that had blasted Kabul Anak's superbattleship *Rengas* to tangled wreckage in the great battle for Atalanta. Despite his many years in space, Brim had yet to see a starship that approached her beauty in simple perfection of line and layout. At the time she was launched, she quickly gained a reputation as the best-looking warship of her day, with none able to match the perfect balance of her design. He had loved the old ship the moment he laid eyes on her.

And no matter how often their paths crossed afterward, he never failed to be awestruck by her colossal dimensions. Steadying himself, he began the ticklish business of conning *Starfury* to the old battleship's starboard boarding aperture. He'd sent Tissaurd to the extreme port side of the bridge with bearing scanners as soon as he had solid visual sighting of the old battleship—and, of course, KA'PPAed a proper Imperial salute. For the last few cycles now, he'd checked the *Queen*'s course and speed with his own eyes, steering a few degrees from the signaled course and a bit faster.

Some Helmsmen he knew considered close-in approaches to a target ship as exhibitions of prowess at the helm, often bragging that such maneuvering facilitated the rigging of optical moorings and "pipes," as midspace connecting brows were called. During his early career on Carescrian ore barges, that kind of precarious maneuvering was part of his workaday existence, so it represented nothing special to him. However, over the years, he'd proven to himself that it seldom had any beneficial effect on the time required for docking evolutions. And in the Fleet it was foolish to get unnecessarily close to any other ship, since the only *serious* mistake one could make was getting so close as to cause a collision. If the years had taught Wilf Brim anything, it was pragmatism when it came to driving starships.

As demanded by protocol, *Starfury*, in her role of junior ship, would moor to the *Queen*'s pipe, and to that end, he presently watched hatches sliding open in the battleship's flanks to uncover an array of fender projectors centered on the boarding aperture. "Ready, Number One?" he asked.

"Ready on the starboard wing," Tissaurd reported. Save for the velvet thunder of the Drive from below, her voice was the only sound in *Starfury*'s bridge—the other occupants were either completely immersed by their duties or themselves enthralled by the very drama of the moment.

"*STARFURY* CLEARED TO APPROACH *QUEEN ELIDEAN*, STARBOARD EMBARKING APERTURE," Brim's KA'PPA display announced directly. "LOCAL GRAVITY INFLUENCES NEUTRAL." Simultaneously, *Queen Elidean*'s director lamps began to flash a pattern amidships.

"All hands to stations for deep-space mooring," he directed on the blower. "All hands to stations for deep-space mooring. Muster honor party to the main boarding chamber on the double." Then, turning to the KA'PPA system, he dispatched his own signal, "*STARFURY* ACKNOWLEDGES STARBOARD EMBARKING APERTURE." Now, it was time for the business of helmsmanship. Carefully increasing speed, he began by bringing *Starfury*'s head a little more to port with deft control inputs that gently increased the *Queen*'s relative bearing in reverse proportion to her distance ahead, checking every few moments with Tissaurd, who had glued her eye to the bearing scanners. When the old battleship was about a thousand irals ahead, Tissaurd reported a bearing of three points from course; by the time they narrowed the distance to approximately five hundred irals, the bearing had doubled. And while he flew, Brim also made his own checks, glancing aft to compare *Starfury*'s flowing cobalt Drive plume with *Queen Elidean*'s broad wake of emerald-green. Long ago he'd developed his own rule of thumb to cover such maneuvers: he was usually well positioned during an approach whenever he maintained some fifteen irals of space between the two wakes.

Brim's instruments showed *Starfury* to be traveling at some five times the battleship's cruising velocity when he arrived off a point approximately three hundred irals astern of her aperture. Judging now by instinct alone, he gradually reduced power and allowed momentum, or "surge," to cover the remaining irals to the boarding aperture, while natural HyperLight retro-induction (toward Sheldon's Great Constant at LightSpeed) bled off velocity proportional to the cube root of *Starfury*'s net mass. By the time she was abreast the battleship's aperture, the pipe had already started to deploy in a flashing welter of director beams.

"Stand by to receive pipe alongside to port," he piped. "Stand by to receive pipe alongside to port!"

Moments later he gradually reversed two of the ship's Drive units; until both starships were running about fifty irals apart, matched perfectly in course and speed, while the pipe connected noisily to *Starfury*'s main accommodation port. He'd done it again. . . .

Taking stock of his control settings, he slaved his helm to the battleship's, relinquished the con to an exhausted (but grinning) Nadia Tissaurd, and set out at a run toward the main deck to welcome the Fluvannian dignitary.

CHAPTER 4

Showing the Flag

Puffing after his sprint from the bridge, Brim arrived at the main boarding chamber only clicks before the Fluvannian Ambassador. *Starfury*'s little marching band had already begun braying out the intolerable agglomeration of groans, squeaks, and wheezing noises that, in aggregate, composed the perfectly awe-inspiring Fluvannian national anthem, "Our Dulcet Star Rises Shrill O'er the Fo'zelii." Calhoun and Drummond both had sent the Carescrian introductory literature about Fluvanna and Fluvannians. But none of it was adequate preparation for the individual who appeared as the great boarding hatch popped inward, then slid aside on its massive guides.

Beyazh the Ambassador was erect, fierce, and patriarchal in every feature. Were it not for his stately progress across *Starfury*'s main boarding lobby, he might have been mistaken for some heroic statue come to life from Courtland Plaza in Avalon. Wearing very full and baggy black cotton bloomers, a high-necked white shirt under a short black silken jacket, and a crimson fez around which was tied a white turban, the man looked like every Fluvannian travel poster Brim had ever seen—even to soft, black leather boots turned up at the toes. He had great, dense eyebrows; glowering, deep-set eyes that spoke of ten thousand days peering into the blackness of Hyperspace; and a gigantic ebony mustache whose stilettolike ends were twisted nearly vertical. He was followed out of the airlock by a confused gaggle of bobbing travel cases in every color of the spectrum.

After what seemed to be a lifetime, *Starfury*'s hard-pressed volunteer musicians (most from Disruptor sections, with exception of two clearly tone-deaf cooks) ceased their dreadful labors, and the boarding chamber fell silent except for muted thunder from the Drive. The Fluvannian bowed deeply from the waist, then straightened and touched first his forehead and next his lips in a sweeping gesture that ended with his right hand turned palm upward toward Brim—an intergalactic gesture of goodwill. "Fluvannian diplomatic party requests permission to board I.F.S. *Starfury*," he announced solemnly, rising to a dignified position of attention and this time saluting in a more contemporary style.

Impressed, Brim returned the salute briskly. "Permission granted, Your Excellency," he said, "with my personal welcome."

"Stand by to cast off the pipe," Tissaurd's voice ordered over the blower. "Stand by to cast off the pipe." Moments later the massive hatch glided silently back in position and sealed itself with a quiet hiss.

Brim dismissed the ship's band while Beyazh strode across the chamber offering his hand in a modern handshake—and abdicating the job of transferring his luggage to a crew of bemused ratings.

"If I remember anything about my days as a starsailor," the big man said, "you are anxious to oversee our disengagement from the *Queen*, Captain Brim."

Heavy repulsion motors whirred inside the aperture—above them on the bridge, Tissaurd was already retracting the huge lug bolts that held *Queen Elidean*'s pipe in place. "You remember well, Your Excellency," Brim remarked. "Would you grant me the honor of your company on the bridge?"

"As our Sodeskayan friends might say, Captain," the Fluvannian replied with a smile, " 'Coarse winds and bitter snow deter no crag wolves.' Is that not so?"

Brim swallowed. "Absolutely, Your Excellency," he replied with hardly a pause. "This way please." Fluvanna promised to be an *unusual* place indeed.

Brim and Beyazh found jump seats on the bridge just in time to watch *Queen Elidean*'s golden pipe disappear into its aperture. Moments later the battleship's director beams winked out. "Deep-space mooring operations are completed," Tissaurd piped throughout the ship. "All hands carry out normal and routine work in accordance with previous instructions."

Beyazh contemplated Tissaurd with ill-concealed interest. "Your First Lieutenant?" he asked.

"She is, Your Excellency," Brim replied.

The Ambassador's eyebrows rose momentarily. "Truly alluring," he remarked, raising an eyebrow, "tiny, yet so perfect—and no youngster, either. Captain," he said. "I must meet this gorgeous woman at the first opportunity."

Momentarily taken aback, Brim opened his mouth, but the Ambassador continued with a sigh.

"Ah, Captain," he said, "calm yourself. I shall not force myself on your most seductive First Lieutenant. I have more breeding than that. But if she is conducive to—shall we say—the inconsequential attentions of a middle-aged man with a salt-and-pepper beard, well. . . ." He shrugged casually, but his eyes warned that he meant business.

Brim forced aside a grin. He didn't blame the Ambassador one iota; he almost told the man so, but at the last moment decided that he ought to be as professional as possible with this high-level diplomat, at least until he got to know him. "Lieutenant Tissaurd's personal life is of no concern aboard ship, Mr. Ambassador," he said stiffly, "except in that it affects her performance as an officer." Suddenly he felt as stuffy as his words.

"Excellent," Beyazh commented absently as he peered at Tissaurd through narrowed eyes. "I should enjoy a tour of the ship, Captain. Do you suppose you could arrange to free this magnificent woman from her duties?"

"Er . . . now?" Brim asked.

"But of course," Beyazh answered with a look bordering on disdain. "Only a fool would dawdle when presented with such an opportunity. Come, Captain. I applaud your professional disregard of this seductive woman's obvious charm. But I have no such impediment, and only a limited time to act." He raised his bushy eyebrows. "Shall we be about it, then?"

"I shall relieve her myself," Brim said, leading Beyazh forward to the two Helmsmans' stations. Now *here* was a man of action, clearly attracted to beautiful women. And Tissaurd *was* a beautiful woman.

"I am eternally in your debt," the bearded man said in a tone that strongly augured otherwise. Clearly, he was also used to getting his own way most of the time.

When they reached the forward end of the bridge, it was almost as if Tissaurd had been expecting them, for she turned in her seat the instant Brim touched her shoulder. Her smile was enough to light the whole bridge. "Why, Captain Brim," she said, "who *is* this utterly handsome man you've brought onto the bridge with you?"

Beyazh didn't wait for an introduction. Sweeping past Brim, he grasped Tissaurd's perfectly manicured fingers and kissed them gravely. "Lieutenant Tissaurd," he murmured, looking into her eyes from a deep bow, "I am known as Beyazh, a humble Fluvannian politician—and I am deeply honored to be in thy presence."

Brim swore he could hear Tissaurd purr like a Halacian Rothcat.

"I am honored by *thy* presence," she said quietly—almost *privately*. Her eyes were completely alert, yet her face had a languid aspect that could only be described—at the moment—as carnal. "How may I make this passage more meaningful to thee?" she asked, a little too assertively for Brim's likes.

"Ah, Lieutenant," Beyazh sighed, "I have so little time to discover the delights of this ship. Perhaps I can persuade you to be my tutor. By all that is holy, and perhaps a little that is unholy, as well," he added with a wink, "I vow to inwardly digest thy every word as if it were an ort of the purest gold."

"I should be honored to be thy guide in all the passages and chambers of this ship," Tissaurd said, gleefully settling into her role. "Just so soon as my watch at the helm is finished."

"My passion for this ship is such that I may not be able to tarry that long," Beyazh moaned. He looked beseechingly at Brim. "Captain," he said. "You *did* promise to relieve Lieutenant Tissaurd of her present duties, did you not?"

Brim took a deep breath. "I did," he admitted, now struggling to smother the smile that threatened to inundate his face.

"In that case, I beseech you to do your duty," the Fluvannian said, his eyes again fastened on Brim's as if the request were actually an order.

"Number One," Brim said, feeling ridiculously as if he were about to relate something that the good-looking officer already knew, "I promised Ambassador Beyazh that I would stand the last metacycles of your watch myself."

"Oh, Captain," Tissaurd said in an excited voice, "how thoughtful! And of course, *Starfury* is already running under autohelm."

Brim smiled in spite of himself as Tissaurd led Beyazh into the aft companionway. She could be so awfully appealing. And whatever else *he* might turn out to be, it seemed clear that the Fluvannian Ambassador was a man of action who also recognized a well-turned ankle when he saw one. All in all, *Starfury*'s first trip to Fluvanna promised to be a lively one—at the very least.

FLUVANNA

Kingdom of Fluvanna

Nabob: Mustafa IX Eyren, The Magnificent

Planets: 916; **Inhabited:** 8

Andronicus, Calleri'l, Dragases, Ordu, Voso Gannit, Voso Gola, Voso Tuvalu, and Wogoria

Population: (est. 52009) 47,250,000 (average annual growth: 2.2%)

Capital: Magor, Ordu

Monetary Unit: Fluvannian Credit

Language: Fluvannian

Economic Summary: Gross Dominion Product: Ç166 billion; Per-capita Income: Ç1,460; Habitable Land used for agriculture: 43%; Principal Products: cotton, mu'occo tobacco, cereals, sugar beets, nuts; Labor Force in Industry: 16%; Major Products: celecoid quartz kernels, textiles, processed foods, hullmetal; Natural Resources: celecoid quartz kernels, chromate, copper; Exports: celecoid quartz kernels, cotton, mu'occo tobacco, fruits, nuts, processed livestock; Major Trading Partners: The Empire and associated states, esp. Sodeskaya.

GENERAL

Most modern travelers visit Fluvanna to observe its rich heritage of archaeological sites and historical monuments. Numerous cultures have flourished there over a span of millennia, at least ten abandoning unique artifacts before the dawn of recorded history. Magor, the capital city, is located on Ordu, largest of eight planets supporting permanent population centers. With an enormous variety of topography and scenery ranging from semitropical vacation planets with white sand beaches and rivieras of colorful flora (Ordu, Andronicus, and Dragases), dense rain forests and vcee' plantations (Wogoria and Calleri'l), to rugged landscapes of the Voso Triad, gateways of the domain's celecoid quartz kernel growing areas, linchpins of Fluvannian economic life.

As many writers on Fluvanna have remarked, this is a domain that stands astride two mutually repelling elements: an overwhelming historical heritage and the inexorable march of progress. With one foot in the past and the other in the present, the population is gripped in a cultural schizophrenia that often seems confusing to outsiders, but which is always a source of considerable interest.

Contemporary Fluvanna may at first strike the visitors as a somber and troubled domain, having suffered in recent years from severe economic and political problems. But this has not in the least diminished the genuine warmth and friendliness of the Fluvannians themselves, whose hospitality to visitors is proverbial. One should be prepared to encounter the Fluvannian greeting wherever he goes on these friendly planets: *"Zin ilegs'oh!"* (Welcome!), responding with *"Kud lubs'oh!"* (We are pleased to be here!).

> *New Consort Guidebook*
> *for*
> *Fluvanna*

Brim piloted *Starfury* to lightward over downtown Magor while Beyazh provided a running travelogue from his observer's seat directly behind Tissaurd in the CoHelmsman's position.

"Magnificent!" the diplomat enthused, waxing poetic as he peered out over the starship's nose. "A golden island surrounded by a garland of waters, if you will." He pointed through the Hyperscreens. "That garland is the Hiemial, an incomparably beautiful waterway that flows from Lake Gonfall—which we overflew only moments ago—into the Gulf of Varn, that large body of water you can see ahead of us. Its two branches separate the ancient, insular part of the city from its more modern boroughs and suburbs on either side. I myself live just beyond the left branch, near the great domed structure atop that first range of hills.''

"The harbor section is on the far bank of that branch, I take it," Brim commented.

"Correct, Captain," Beyazh said. "The 'Levantine Quarter,' as it is known. A military base forms its boundary upriver, farthest from the Gulf. You can see a number of our capital ships are in port today."

Brim nodded musingly. Even from this altitude he could see that the warships were clearly from bygone epochs. Calhoun's advisement of their years, however, had done little to prepare him for how really ancient they were. The fleet yard looked more like a colossal museum than a military base. Two were clearly of the ancient *Charles Martel* design with ventral armament in the "lozenge" arrangement favored by starship designers of more than five hundred Standard Years past: twin-mount center-pivot turrets mounted fore and aft and two more on either beam sponsored out over the tumblehome. Others shipped two squat KA'PPA masts with flying decks running between them. Altogether, an odd collection of antiquated warships from all over the galaxy.

"Opposite the Levantine," Beyazh continued after a deep breath, "across that large bridge midway along the island—is the most impressive basilica ever constructed by the Gradgroat-Norchelites."

"With exception of the great monastery of Atalanta, perhaps," Brim interrupted dryly, trimming the ship's head a little beyond the published landing vector to adjust for a strong cross-wind.

"Ah yes," Beyazh said, interrupting his discourse, "I have admired the Atalantan campaign ribbon you wear. You were there at the Battle of Atalanta to see the monastery go, weren't you?"

"No," Brim answered. "I was out in space aboard Regula Collingswood's *Defiant*," Brim replied. "But I followed the action by KA'PPA after Nik Ursis deciphered the Norchelite maxim."

" 'In destruction is resurrection; the path of power leads through truth,' " Beyazh quoted while his hand unconsciously began to massage the back of Tissaurd's neck. "What a surprise *that* turned out to be!"

Brim nodded, glancing across at the man just in time to see Tissaurd smile a little, then slap the caressing hand without taking her eyes off the readouts before her.

"Imperial K5054," a Fluvannian controller warned from the COMM panel. "Traffic lightward bound: League cruiser L1037, twelve irals at red-orange."

Brim glanced out the starboard Hyperscreens as a big Gorn-Hoff GH-210 cruiser materialized out of the distance in a tight bank, curving around onto a parallel path into the landing zone. "Thank you, ma'am," he acknowledged, "I have him."

The Leaguer ship was as angular as *Starfury* was contoured, and had clearly just come directly from outer space because her complex conformation of deck houses and great frowning bridge were still glowing from the heat of entry. She also appeared larger, by perhaps ten percent, although her heterogeneous nature made this nearly impossible to estimate by sight. The bristling armament she carried, however, was anything but equivocal: fifteen 321-mmi disruptors were a powerful battery by anyone's reckoning, even though any one of them was smaller than *Starfury*'s twelve battleship-size 406s. Brim watched cautiously as the big ship bore down on him at what seemed like reckless speed—sailing in peacetime rig and war paint, as the saying went.

"Coming this way awfully fast, isn't he?" Beyazh commented in a needling tone of voice. "Do you suppose you ought to give way to him?"

Brim continued steadily on course. "He's probably coming a bit faster than necessary," he said calmly, "but I doubt if he's outside the control envelope for that type of Gorn-Hoff. I'm keeping an eye on him."

Silence descended on the bridge as the crew watched thirty-some thousand milstons of hullmetal bearing down on them like a meteor. Only at the last possible moment did the Leaguers swing onto a new heading, impinging on *Starfury*'s airspace by nearly half a c'lenyt before settling down on a parallel track.

"Sloppy helmsmanship," Tissaurd commented after a few moments, but even her voice had a slight edge to it.

"Do you think perhaps they wanted us to move over?" Brim asked with a grin.

"I was about to suggest something like that," Beyazh said, but there was clear approval in his eyes.

"Imperial K5054: you are four c'lenyts from the marker," announced the controller. "Secure the localizer above two thousand five hundred irals. You are cleared for instrument landing, two seven left approach."

"Cleared for instrument landing two seven left approach Imperial K5054," Brim acknowledged. Checking his altitude, he gently heeled the cruiser into a shallow bank—away from the Leaguer ship at the same time it banked in the other direction, obviously getting its own simultaneous landing clearance. "I think we'll keep an eye out for that one," Brim said, starting down toward a ruby beacon that had just begun to flash from the distant surface of the Gulf. On the nav panel before him, two units of different hues quickly merged into a third.

"Localizer and glideslope captured," Tissaurd advised.

"Imperial K5054, contact Levantine Tower one two six five five," the Controller directed.

"Good day from Imperial K5054, and thanks for the help," Brim responded.

Moments later Tissaurd was on the blower: "All hands to landing stations. All hands to landing stations." From aft, a siren howled, accompanied by the sound of running feet. Odd bumps and rumbles throughout the bridge spoke of cvceese' mugs and personal gear being stowed in all sorts of unapproved nooks and crannies.

"COMM frequency redirected," Tissaurd announced.

Brim confirmed her on the panel. "Thanks, Number One," he replied. "Imperial K5054 checking in at two thousand on final for two seven left approach."

"Imperial K5054: Tower Levantine clears for two seven left

landing approach; wind zero nine zero at fifteen, gusts to forty-five.''

The genius of *Starfury*'s designer Mark Valerian always shone like a star during landings. The ship was steady as a rock, in nearly any kind of weather—and today's could only be classed as perfect. The spoilers deployed automatically at fifteen hundred irals without the slightest rumble or pitch change. At the helm, one could feel a slight sinking sensation when the speed brakes deployed, but unless you were actually at the controls, it was nearly impossible to notice.

Brim glanced over at Beyazh, who was staring at the back of Tissaurd's head as if the two were alone on the bridge. Grinning, he concentrated on landing the starship. There was a lot of residual thrust from the six big Admiralty A876 gravity generators, so he normally flew right at reference velocity during descents (instead of adding a little speed for windage, as was the practice), unless of course there *were* heavy gusts or the possibility of sheer. But if there was too much speed, Valerian's new design wouldn't come to hover at standard elevation; she would simply float on and on and on.

With the ruby landing vector beacon steady in the Hyperscreens, he ignored his urge to flare and kept coming down with the gravs at IDLE until her gravity gradient kissed the whitecaps and launched great cascades of spray soaring past the side Hyperscreens. These diminished to a broad rolling wake as they bled off energy and Brim blipped the gravity brakes, sending successions of great spray clouds forward that deluged the Hyperscreens as the big ship thundered to a smooth halt with her pontoons hovering precisely twenty-five irals above the three contoured ''feet'' she pushed in the surface of the bay. Through the overhead Hyperscreens, Brim could see an Imperial flag soaring to the apex of the high KA'PPA tower, followed by a brilliant white ensign emblazoned by *Starfury*'s crest. Clearly, Barbousse was back on the job!

''My congratulations,'' Beyazh said in an awed voice. ''A most *perfect* landing.''

''All in a day's work for this Helmsman,'' Tissaurd remarked with her sunny grin. ''Isn't it, Skipper?''

"Thanks, Number One," Brim said half in embarrassment, but her compliment made him proud as a schoolboy.

Suddenly the voice of Surface Control demanded his attention. "Imperial K5054, intersect one seven right without delay; control buoy six five after you cross, then cleared to Levantine G-pool four sixty-seven. Follow pilot boat ninety-one at boreal river entrance."

"Imperial K5054 crossing one seven right for pilot boat ninety-one," Brim acknowledged, taking up a direct course for an antiquated little watercraft that appeared at the mouth of the river. Abruptly, however, the Gorn-Hoff reappeared from starboard with all flags flying. She was on a collision course with *Starfury*—and moving much too fast to be in a harbor.

"Our Leaguer friends again," Beyazh commented with the same taunting look on his face. "It seems as if this time they really mean to cut you off." He spoke as if he were waiting to see what Brim would do about it. "There is always a long wait for pilot boats this time of day in Magor," he added pointedly.

"I see," Brim growled, deliberating only a few clicks before deciding on a course of action—one that matched *Starfury*'s motto, "Go Boldly!" It was clear that the Leaguers had no conception of *Starfury*'s post-landing capabilities; it was also high time someone put a stop to their foolish antics before they did something dangerous. "I'll have military energy to gravs two, three, four, and six, Strana'," he ordered. "Number One: sound the collision alarm to starboard."

"Military to gravs two, three, four, and six," the Bear acknowledged from a display on his console. Her voice was all but drowned out by of sirens sounding through the ship.

"Stand by for collision, starboard side, frame seven fifty-five," Tissaurd announced on the blower. "Stand by for collision, starboard side. All hands close airtight doors forward of frame seven fifty-five."

The cruiser was closing very rapidly now and throwing a huge wake that rose high enough to hide the aft portion of her hull. Without a doubt, the Leaguers intended that *Starfury* would slacken speed or give way, thus relinquishing the pilot boat. The Imperials would then be forced to wait at the entrance to the

Levantine—in clear view of the whole harbor as well as the Fluvannian Fleet—until such time as the next pilot became available.

"If you speed up, you will maintain your right-of-way," Beyazh urged, his voice more of a challenge than a comment. "He'll eventually have to give way." Then he chuckled. "Of course, if he does get ahead of you, you will then be an overtaking vessel—and *he* will perpetually have the right-of-way."

Brim nodded wordlessly, judging distance between the two ships and giving *Starfury*'s crew time to reach their collision stations, just in case.

"Will you really permit him to accomplish this indignity?" Beyazh demanded in a bantering voice. "The pilot boat is assigned to you after all."

For Brim, it was almost as if he were back in Carescria as a youth flying the incredibly dangerous ore barges of the region and racing to be first at the weighing stations. He had quickly discovered that a fractional load delivered *first* at the receiving station was worth a lot more than a full load delivered later. So he'd learned to come back with the holds only partially full on those early runs—it gave him critical reserve maneuverability, acceleration, and—most important—braking energy he needed to win the post-landing "races" that helped bring him to the attention of the Imperial Helmsman's Academy so many years ago. He smiled as he watched the Gorn-Hoff. Whoever was running that ship had never spent much time in Carescria. She was unquestionably moving at her maximum surface speed with no reserve whatsoever.

Abruptly, Brim moved both damper rays forward until they passed from amethyst through to greenish yellow. A sudden growl rose to a crescendo from the pontoons and *Starfury* drove forward in a tremendous burst of speed, throwing prodigious cascades of green water and spray backward into the harbor. Easily drawing ahead of the lumbering Leaguer ship, she first smashed it broadside with a tremendous wave that had begun to curl off below her bows, then drowned it from stem to stern in the tremendous backward deluge from her oversize gravs. Moments later Brim hauled back on the power and applied his gravity brakes, watching in the stern viewers as the Leaguer emerged from the cloud of spray, skewed almost sideways. A great wash shot sideways from her steering engines, but the ship was too far out of control for that. She spun end around three complete revolutions, snapping her KA'PPA tower in a great burst of sparks, and came to a stop canting heavily to starboard with her bow ignominiously dragging the surface.

"Dispatch a signal to the Leaguers," he ordered in a matter-of-fact voice.

"Ready, Captain," a startled COMM rating answered from a display.

"Can we be of assistance?" Brim dictated.

After a moment of silence, the rating cocked his head to one side. "That's all, Captain?" he asked.

Brim smiled. "It'll do for now."

The signal went unanswered.

At the entrance to the canal, Brim looked down over *Starfury*'s nose at the little pilot boat in admiration. A real *floating* boat. He couldn't help wondering what it must be like to look up from a wildly tossing wooden deck to see thirty thousand milstons of starship suspended twenty-five irals above three great, thrashing imprints in the water little more than a hundred irals distant. The noise alone would be dumbfounding. Yet there they were, two men in the yellow slickers common to seafarers everywhere: one was at the controls, the other signaling with flags using the most basic expressions known in the galaxy. Probably, Brim considered, with only a few basic commands to communicate, it *was* a lot more pragmatic to rely on flags than try to match the thousands of known COMM protocols.

As he carefully followed the little boat into Magor's vast system of canals, he got his first close-up look at the city proper. Fleets of ferries, both floating and levitating, darted to and fro among lumbering starfreighters, some larger than *Starfury*. And dodging catlike through all of the disarray, veritable squadrons of fragile-looking sky-caiques took off and landed at all angles with open decks burdened by cargo bound for riotously colored, tented bazaars that topped the age-blackened stone walls of the canal. To port—past at least half a dozen ranks of gravity pools occupied by merchant ships of every size and description—rose the low hill on which the crowded old city was built. Most common among the structures visible through the whitish mist that Beyazh described as "sea haze" were dome-capped buildings of all sizes and heights, many topped by long, elaborately decorated spikes. The lofty cupolas were overlaid in a profusion of materials, ranging from burnished gold and silver to clay tiles—some of the latter magnificently decorated. Interspersed among the domes were slim towers, many reaching hundreds of irals above the other structures. Here and there between stolid-looking stone walls, trees pushed themselves into the light, dwarfed and stunted by years of struggling with the city for essential room to grow. Whiffets of smoke streamed from chimneys as well as the interstices between domes that must have been streets. In a way, its ancient vigor reminded him of the famed starport of Atalanta, half a galaxy away. But where Atalanta—in appearance—was clearly an outpost of Greyffin IV's Empire, Magor looked *foreign* to Brim in every respect.

Within the metacycle, *Starfury* was moored on a gravity pool whose outer perimeter was constructed of stones so badly weather-blackened they reminded Brim of Gimmas Haefdon. Below, a score of thundering repulsion/levitation units dated from at least three centuries in the past. After a moment of consideration, he leaned over the console and directed Tissaurd to order additional levitation energy from *Starfury*'s own gravity units—just in case the ancient units failed. However, he was nearly five cycles too late. Tissaurd had been bothered by the same thing and had already issued the orders on her own. For a moment their eyes met and she smiled, providing Brim with a *most* bothersome feeling of . . . well . . . *deficiency*. As if something important were missing from his life—something like Tissaurd herself. Taking a deep breath, he attempted to dismiss the strange mood, but perversely, it refused to withdraw.

"You look pensive, Skipper," Tissaurd said with an enigmatic sort of presentiment on her face. "Is everything all right?"

Brim looked her in the eye, almost embarrassed by his

thoughts, which were at that moment decidedly unprofessional. "Fine," he declared absently. "Just a little tired. You'll be in charge while I pay the Empire's respects at the palace," he said, the words stiff and ceremonious in his own ears.

"Give my regards to His Nibs, the Magnificent," she said with a little laugh. "I'll try to keep things in one piece here until you return."

Brim made a deep theatrical bow in parody of Beyazh, then strode off aft toward the companionway with a deep frown set on his brow. No time to worry about his own feelings. He had a lot of important things to take care of right now.

Changed into parade dress with a Captain's ceremonial pyrosaber at his left side, Brim stepped off the end of an antique-looking brow into warm, late-afternoon sunlight. He was as ready as Barbousse could make him for his audience with Mustafa IX Eyren, Nabob of Fluvanna. Beneath a stiff, peaked military cap, he wore a Fleet Blue tunic whose narrow lapels were embellished by the single diamond insignia of an Imperial Commander. It was further decorated by a full-dress silver belt, gold buttons, and a gold aiguillette draped over his right shoulder. His white jodhpurs were adorned by two broad blue stripes that ran from his hips into the tops of his riding boots. Hampered by devilish white gloves (that he normally found impossible to draw on without losing his temper at least three times) he felt—as he always did in parade dress—like a doorman for some great, overstuffed hotel. He much preferred the simpler Fleet Cloak that, as ceremony would have it, now draped over his left shoulder like a great, empty sack.

Out in the parking area two gleaming limousine skimmers hovered just off the age-crazed pavement. One, a sleek limousine of contemporary design and manufacture, displayed the Imperial crest of Greyffin IV. Two figures waited beside this elegant vehicle, a green-clad chauffeur and a lanky individual dressed in the dark gray livery of the Imperial Foreign Service. The other conveyance, a great, top-hampered phaeton of astonishing antiquity—as well as unequivocally perfect maintenance—flew a large Fluvannian national flag from its angular starboard bow.

Crimson-uniformed footmen stood rigidly at attention on either side of its open passenger door as if waiting for the Nabob himself. Grinning to himself, Brim wondered who looked the more ridiculous, the footmen or himself.

At that moment Beyazh stepped from the brow, accompanied by Tissaurd. "Welcome to my little Universe, Captain Brim," he rumbled. "I see that your embassy has acted with its accustomed efficiency, so I shall not offer a lift to the palace. Besides," he added under his breath with a wink at Tissaurd, "I am certain they will want to brief you on the latest concerning the bloody idiot Pasha Radiman Korfuzzier."

"Who?" Brim asked.

"Hmm," Beyazh mused. "If you don't already know, perhaps it would be better that you find out from your own people."

"I don't understand," Brim protested with a frown.

"You will, Commander," Beyazh said. Winking at Tissaurd, he started off for the antique limousine, followed by two of *Starfury*'s ratings and the unruly shuffle of traveling cases that accompanied him on his arrival at *Starfury*'s boarding chamber. "I shall join you later, Brim, during your audience with Mustafa Eyren," he called over his shoulder.

Tissaurd turned to reenter the brow. "I don't know anything about it, Skipper," she said. "Honest."

Brim chuckled. "I believe you, Number One," he replied as she started up the moving stairs.

Moments later the Foreign Service man was at his side. A tall, slim man with narrow face, balding head, and intelligent, piercing eyes, he had the serious anonymous demeanor of a lifetime government executive. "Commander Brim," he said, extending his hand—and a holobadge with his picture. "The name's Saltash, George Saltash. Welcome to 'Hospitable Magor,' as the tourist brochures put it." His face broke into a lopsided grin. "We watched your landing out on the bay," he said. "Glad to see Nergol Triannic's bloody minions get what they deserved."

"It appears as if Leaguers try to play rough around here," Brim observed, relieved at once that the man didn't *sound* like a CIGA. "They certainly wouldn't get away with that sort of bilge at any of the other major space ports," he added as they walked across the pavement toward the Imperial limousine. "And through the whole thing, our friend Beyazh was doing everything he could to make me take a more aggressive role. Interesting sort of chap."

"Interesting chap, indeed," Saltash observed, watching the ancient Fluvannian skimmer lurch out of the parking lot. "Seems to know everything we know, at just about the same time we learn it."

"Hmm," Brim pondered momentarily. "He mentioned a Pasha Radiman Korfuzzier. Called him a bloody idiot, or something."

Saltash chuckled grimly. "Well, there you are," he said. "I'm here *personally* to tell you about that same bloody idiot—which he certainly is." He nodded to the chauffeur and climbed in, motioning Brim to follow. "And the reason I'm here is because the information about Korfuzzier is so sensitive they didn't want to beam it to your ship outside intelligence channels. So much for encryption."

Brim followed the man through the opening, gripping the clumsy pyrosaber so he wouldn't trip himself. "Pretty serious stuff, eh?" he asked as the heavy door closed silently behind him.

Saltash nodded emphatically. "The League's trying to jump in here with both feet," he said, tapping on the window that separated the passenger compartment from the driver. "To the palace, Reynolds."

"Aye, Mr. Saltash," the chauffeur replied. Effortlessly, the heavy skimmer lifted and accelerated through a narrow alleyway between mountainous stacks of packing boxes, scattering furry little animals right and left as it gained momentum. After about a thousand irals, this opened onto a somewhat wider thoroughfare that ran between a canyon of squalid—clearly ancient—goods houses, some crumbling from their very antiquity, others relatively new.

"Somehow, I am far from surprised to hear about the Leaguers," Brim chuckled. "I can't imagine they *wouldn't* want to wield a lot of influence here, considering that nearly one hundred percent of our Drive crystals now come from this dominion."

"Indeed," Saltash agreed, almost offhandedly. "But there is a good deal more to it than that. You see, Triannic's friends have decided to annex the *whole* dominion, and are even now in the midst of their final plans. . . ." As he spoke, the chauffeur veered smoothly left into a cross street, then headed out across a wide bridge whose side lanes were clogged by a riotous confusion of tents in which merchants seemed to be offering every sort of merchandise recognized in the known Universe.

The bridge, at least, was one Brim recognized from the air, and he was able to get his bearings as the limousine weaved and dodged through the clamorous traffic. Once back over land, the crowded avenue veered to starboard and continued directly for the center of a colossal, dome-topped building.

While the chauffeur fought his way along the teeming thoroughfare, Saltash provided Brim with information received only that morning, courtesy of the same Sodeskayan Intelligence services that had time and time again proven to be nearly infallible. According to the Bears, Pasha Radiman Korfuzzier, an unintelligent and rather hotheaded brother of the Fluvannian Grand Potentate, had been carrying on an affair with a beautiful woman who, unknown to him, was a clandestine agent of the League. By clever manipulation, she had made Korfuzzier insanely jealous of the League's own Ambassador—who, himself, was ignorant of the plot. The agent had been given permission from Tarrott to "sacrifice" the Ambassador by having him publicly murdered by her royal lover—thus precipitating a carefully orchestrated campaign of denunciation against the Fluvannian government that would culminate in a "provoked" League invasion and takeover.

Further, the Sodeskayans intimated that, as planned, the incident would take place spontaneously, making it extremely difficult to predict—and thereby prevent. Because of this, the Imperial Foreign Service had quietly assigned 'round-the-clock, plainclothes guards to both Korfuzzier and the Ambassador whenever either departed his quarters. Presently, all possible preparations had been accomplished; now, the Imperials could only wait for the actual deed to transpire. . . .

Saltash's Imperial limousine was admitted to the palace grounds scant cycles after the diplomat finished his briefing. "We'll talk more of this later," he said. "Inside the grounds, here, we can't be certain of our security, even in a protected limousine. The Leaguers have made some impressive inroads."

Brim's eyebrows rose. "They've wired the palace grounds?" he asked in amazement.

"We think so," Saltash replied. "The Fluvannian state security organization is riddled with Leaguers." Then he sat back in the seat and indicated the vast palace gardens that surrounded them. "Might as well enjoy the scenery," he said. "It's quite well known throughout the galaxy, and not everyone gets to see it in person."

Brim looked around him; Saltash certainly had a point. And although the spacious courtyard could never compare to the huge campus in which the Gradgroat-Norchelite monastery had once rested, it was altogether impressive in its own—"foreign"— way. Outlined by a wall that Brim remembered from the air as being roughly octagonal in shape, the Royal Compound was dotted by colossal shade trees in reds, oranges, and greens, accented by lofty fountains; domed, pergolalike structures with intricately carved surfaces and massive balustrades; huge stone urns in myriad graceful shapes; and a network of glistening walkways arranged in wild, geometric patterns. Heroic statues had been erected where walkways intersected, and vivid banners thundered in the breeze from lofty flagpoles. The limousine drew to a halt at the end of a queue of similar vehicles that extended into a stately portico of crimson stone. At least thirty footmen, dressed in matching crimson, stood in attendance. "What's the significance of all the red?" Brim asked as the big car inched its way forward.

"The celebration of Zaborew," Saltash answered. "It's a quasi-religious holiday period of some sort, though I doubt if anyone understands the whole significance anymore. Most of the feast days have something to do with a series of victories against some deadly force from outside the galaxy. But the exact nature of that force is never really described, at least in the feasts I've been privileged to attend." He grinned as they finally glided under the portico. "Lots of excellent food and magnificent, homegrown Logish Meem, so I've never found much reason to complain about their slipshod historical reckoning."

The Carescrian grinned as a red-clad footman stepped up to open the door. "A man after my own heart," he said. "Where good food and Logish Meem are concerned, wise men ask as few questions as possible. I learned that from friends in Sodeskaya." Then he stepped onto the pavement, adjusted his sword, and followed Saltash through the most ornate set of doors he had seen since the Grand Koundourities Hotel in Atalanta. Both were horridly overdone.

Brim was immediately relieved to find that an "audience" with Nabob Mustafa was not something that people did by themselves. To the right of a semicircular area curtained off by huge, red velvet draperies, at least thirty others were lined up, preening themselves and talking to one or more coadjutors. The throne room itself was a lofty structure, shaped as if it were the interior of an incredibly large and ornate bedouin tent whose walls and roof were lined by giant carpets. Clearly, the Nabob's roots were nomadic—but well before the dawn of recorded history. "Anything I ought to know about this?" he asked.

Saltash shook his head. "Old Mustafa holds these audiences every other day, year in and year out. And from what I understand, most of them are serious—requiring some sort of judgment that immediately becomes law. You'll make a nice change of pace for him."

"Good," Brim laughed. "I'll take very little of his time, then. . . ."

"Don't count on it," Beyazh laughed, joining the two Imperials in the midst of their conversation. "What you'll do is answer questions until he runs out of them. And he'll have a few, believe me. I've just spoken to him. He's excited that you're here—with *Starfury*, of course. . . ." The Minister's next words were completely overpowered by a great braying of trumpets that terminated in respectful silence as the curtains parted to reveal the high throne of Fluvanna: A small, straight-backed chair made of what appeared to be solid gold. It was dramatically lighted by a single beam of ghostly luminescence.

Standing beside the throne, Mustafa IX Eyren, The Magnificent, was a small, stout man with a dark, round face; at least three double chins; small, perceptive eyes peering from behind a pair of enormous spectacles; and truly prodigious mustaches that ended in waxed spikes extending considerably outboard of his ears. He was dressed in baggy scarlet silk knee britches; brilliantly polished riding boots with pointed, turned-up toes; a high-necked tunic of white brocade embroidered in gold; and a crimson fez with a long, blue tassel denoting his royal status. When he clapped his hands twice in rapid succession, a large contingent of musicians began yerking out the national anthem and everyone in the room dropped to their knees—everyone except Brim and Saltash. Imperials bowed to no one, especially Imperials in Imperial uniforms. The traditional prohibition had been in effect since time immemorial, and was seldom taken to heart by dominions whose customs required outward signs of obeisance.

When the room had become silent, a voice from the rear snapped off half a dozen Fluvannian words, and a group of men made their way to a small, ornate carpet placed directly before the throne. There, they once more dropped to their knees until sharp commands from the Nabob himself brought them to their feet. Mustafa now relaxed and sat on his throne, bidding the petitioners to begin with a casual wave of the hand.

"You won't have long to wait," Beyazh whispered under his breath. "Nabob Mustafa instructed me to inform you that he will hear two of the shortest cases first, in deference to his own countrymen. You will be called third."

Brim nodded. "I appreciate that," he said.

"Mustafa appreciates *Starfury*," Beyazh chuckled darkly. "He isn't too anxious for a League takeover, either. . . ."

As Beyazh predicted, the first audience lasted no more than fifteen cycles; the second lasted scarcely half that long. Abruptly someone pronounced a rapid-fire string of mostly unintelligible sounds that contained the words "Wilf Brim" and "*Starfury*," whereupon Saltash tapped the Carescrian on his arm. "We're up, Commander," he chuckled, starting across the floor toward the throne. "Let's see if the two of us together can put together a single interview—and don't forget, Nabobs *always* speak first."

The two men stopped a few irals from the throne and came to attention while Brim saluted. Mustafa eyed them with interest, a small smile on his pudgy face. He twisted one side of his mustache, frowned, nodded, then smiled again and cordially pronounced a string of noises that sounded to Brim like a choleric Xythun warbling turtle.

"His Magnificence extends his personal welcome as well as those of his people," Saltash translated.

Brim thought a moment. "Please convey to His Magnificence that I am deeply honored by his greeting, as is the company of my starship."

Saltash grunted and warbled back, then fell expectantly silent.

Mustafa looked amused and nodded. Again he pronounced a string of grunts and warbles, this time with a very serious look on his face.

"His Magnificence has learned that *Starfury* is perhaps the greatest warship in the known Universe," the diplomat said. "He wonders if you agree."

Brim grinned and looked the Nabob directly in his eye. "Tell Mustafa that he can bet his kingdom on that ship and the crew that flies her," he said proudly. "As well as the Starfuries that will follow her from the building yards."

Saltash had just begun his warbling translation when Mustafa held an imperious hand in the air for silence. The little man looked Brim directly in the eye. "Because I very well *may* bet my kingdom on *Starfury*," he began in perfect, but Rhodorian-tinged, Avalonian, "I wish to hear in your own words what there is about this ship that makes you so certain of her fighting powers."

"Your Magnificence," Saltash interrupted in stunned astonishment, "I had no idea. . . ."

Mustafa frowned over his eyeglasses. "Neither do most of

your long-winded Foreign Office colleagues, Saltash,'' he chuckled. ''Prince Onrad assures me you can be trusted.''

Saltash's eyebrows raised appreciatively. ''I am honored, Your Magnificence.''

Mustafa nodded, then focused on Brim. ''With that finished, we can now return to my original question, Commander—concerning what it is about this odd-shaped warship that makes you so certain of her fighting qualities.''

Brim started to reply, but Mustafa raised his hand again. ''Not yet, my Carescrian friend,'' he said. ''I have all of the facts concerning *Starfury* that Sherrington can supply, plus official data from your CIGA-riddled Admiralty.'' He grinned. ''I even have a significant body of classified information that my friend Baxter Calhoun has forwarded during the past few Standard Months. So I already know a great deal about the ship and her unique qualities. The information I require from you is your 'feel,' your very personal instinct of how these unique qualities of Starfury-class starships have *combined*, now that you have had a chance to get to know her. Is she, Commander, a true 'fighting ship,' or merely an object of considerable beauty?'' He smiled. ''Like a lovely woman of little intelligence.''

Brim considered for a long moment before he attempted a reply. Clearly, this Nabob was no mere figurehead. At some point in his life, he must have commanded starships—conceivably a number of them. Somehow, it made the job easier. ''First off, Your Magnificence,'' he began at length, ''*Starfury* is truly a Helmsman's starship. In every meaning of the word. . . .'' He described the feeling he had at her controls, the rock steady feel of her helm, the easy power from the reflecting Drives, the speed, the pure joy of being at the controls of a faultless ship. He described the perfect integration of man and machine that permitted a crew to concentrate on *operating* the ship—not the ship herself. He told about the improved cooling system installed at Gimmas Haefdon, described the incredible destructive power of her disruptor batteries. And all through his dialogue, Mustafa *listened*—not as surfeited royalty listens with boredom in his eyes, but with almost childlike intensity—and not a single interruption.

When at last Brim fell silent, the little Nabob smiled. "That good, eh?" he asked.

"That good, Your Magnificence," Brim assured him.

The Nabob considered for a moment, then nodded to Saltash. "Leave us for a moment, my Imperial friend," he ordered.

With a nod, Saltash stepped off the carpet.

"All right, Brim," the Nabob said. "For that kind of a discourse, you deserve to know that you have erased the last doubts from my mind. I shall permit our mutual friend Drummond to stew for a few days more, but it seems pointless that you should be deprived of the knowledge. You have convinced me—as all the literature in the galaxy could not—that I should accept Prince Onrad's offer. Before one of my weeks has passed, the concordat will be made." He smiled. *"Zin ilegs' oh!"* he said.

"Kud lubs' oh!" Brim replied, returning the Nabob's smile. With that, he saluted, stepped backward from the carpet, and the audience was at an end.

CHAPTER 5

The Volunteer

By the time Brim returned to *Starfury*, the ship was abuzz with news that the whole crew was invited to Mustafa's palace as part of the Feast of Zaborew. During Brim's audience, royal messengers had delivered separate invitations: one for the wardroom, one for the enlisted mess. Officers were summoned to a "Grand Banquet" followed by a formal cotillion; a carnival with a great festal board would be set up on the palace grounds for the lower decks.

"And it's not just for our crew," Tissaurd declared with an excited smile from across a wardroom table, "they've sent invitations to every government ship in the harbor, including the Leaguers."

"Folks take feasts seriously around here," Brim observed, sipping his cvceese' with a grin. "When is this grand soiree?"

"Tomorrow evening," Tissaurd replied, a wistful look momentarily passing her eyes. "I've arranged the watch so I can be there."

"Great, Number One," Brim replied. "Perhaps I can even get you to take my arm on the way." The last seemed to slip out on its own, surprising Brim as much as it seemed to affect Tissaurd.

The petite officer smiled with a sidelong glance that made it clear she had not expected his words. "I'd have loved that, Skipper," she said with a disconcerted little frown, "but I'm afraid I'm already spoken for. Beyazh drove over with the first messengers, and . . . well. . . ."

Brim felt his cheeks flush as a surge of disappointment swept him fore and aft. "Just my luck," he said with what he hoped was an easygoing smile. "The locals always have the first word."

"I'll save you a dance, Skipper," Tissaurd said encouragingly.

"Then the evening won't be a total loss," he said, now feeling more embarrassment than anything else—he *had*, after all, put a junior officer on the spot, "But a word of warning to you," he added, "I'm a dreadful hoofer."

"I'll look forward to having you prove that, Skipper," Tissaurd chuckled.

"Wear your heaviest boots, then," Brim quipped, hurrying off for the Drive chambers to inspect a plasma-tube repair. Afterward, however, try as he might, he had very little luck shedding a feeling of disappointment that naggled him throughout a restless night. . . .

As luck would have it, Brim, Beyazh, and Tissaurd all arrived simultaneously at the main hatch the next evening. Lieutenant Herbig Günter, who had volunteered for Duty Officer during the fête on religious grounds, gave a low wolf whistle as the latter passed his station. "If I'd known you were going to look like that, Nadia," he said, "I mightn't have followed the church rules so closely and asked you myself."

"Too late, Günter," Tissaurd bantered, "I'm spoken for tonight. Ambassador Beyazh has taken on the job of escort for this sortie." She looked positively stunning in her black formal uniform. Edged with embroidered braid, her frock coat was cut away in the front over a low, square-cut bodice trimmed with lace that revealed large areas of ample breasts. Knee-length in back, the coat had two slits reaching to the waistline with a huge gold military button at the top of each slit. Narrow lapels faced with golden embroidery, shoulder boards bearing the three stars of a Lieutenant, and an impressive row of service ribbons completed the embellishments. Beneath the coat, she wore slender black silk breeches buttoned at the sides that extended over her knees and ended in narrow golden bands. Sheer black hose covered her shapely calves, and she wore high-heeled slippers that only just revealed her toes.

"Er, lucky you, Ambassador," Herbig said, his face coloring slightly as he opened the ship's register so that they could sign out.

Standing behind them, Brim felt his own cheeks flush. "Good evening, Ambassador. Er, taking in the dance?" he asked, feeling asinine as the words left his mouth.

Tissaurd finished signing and looked up with a distracted aspect while Beyazh turned and extended his hand to the Carescrian.

"Ah, good evening, Captain Brim," the diplomat said. "Yes, we certainly are taking in the ball. All day I have looked forward to escorting the loveliest woman at the palace. Even the Nabob will be envious tonight." He laughed. "All Magor will envy me."

Brim signed out and followed them uncomfortably through the throng of officers moving along the forward brow. Below, the parking area was filled with huge omnibuses of very recent manufacture. Clearly, Fluvannian tastes ran to modern when it came to public transportation. Directly off the stairs, however, one of the Nabob's huge phaeton skimmers idled quietly at the curb: another great top-hampered vehicle of tremendous elegance and considerable antiquity. As Beyazh's boot touched the pavement, footmen came to attention on either side of the entrance hatch.

"Ride with us to the palace, Commander Brim," the diplomat offered grandly. "Mustafa the Magnificent has sent this lordly antique to carry only me and my lovely escort to the palace. We have ample room, as you can see. Will you do us the honor?"

Brim glanced at Tissaurd and attempted another gallant smile—that probably failed. "I thank you," he said with a little bow, "but I think it would be better for me to ride with the others. If you will excuse me?"

"I understand," Beyazh said. "I shall look forward to your presence at the ball, where I am certain, Nadia has saved you at least one dance."

Moments later Brim watched him gently hand her into a passenger compartment that almost defied description. High, arched windows of beveled crystal surmounted a luxurious gray velvet couch that appeared to run the entire circumference of the room except for the entrance—and there were pillows everywhere! Then the footman closed the door and the big machine glided from the parking lot like the wraith of a great ship.

Brim's own bus ride to the palace was much too rapid, even at the slow speed the huge bus could make through the crowded streets. Directly he was delivered to the ornate side entrance he had seen on his first visit. Inside, at the end of a long corridor, strains of gentle music vied with the murmur of conversation and the ringing assonance of crystal glassware. He checked his hat and queued up at a short line of officers waiting to enter the hall, fidgeting impatiently; he always felt remotely uncomfortable when he was announced. At last, he heard a paige proclaim, "Commander Wilf Brim, I.F., Captain of I.F.S. *Starfury*." Lively music battled the loud conversation and clinking of glasses as he stepped onto the broad staircase amid a smattering of polite applause. The warm air was thick with perfumes and spiced smoke from mu'occo and camarge cigarettes. Below, the room was packed with brightly colored gowns, half-bared bosoms, military uniforms of every hue and cast, and a farrago of people: Bears, flighted beings, and a host of other sentients.

No sooner had the Carescrian reached the bottom than Saltash bounced from the crowd, a goblet of meem in his hand. "Wilf—it's about time," he said, steering through the crowd toward a gilded alcove in the shape of a great seashell. The people inside were clearly influential, just because they were there. But they somehow *looked* influential, too. "A lot of important people have been waiting to met you," the diplomat said. "Mustafa's pretty well kept you to himself since you arrived."

As they passed, a tall Imperial Captain with a CIGA ribbon on his Fleet Cloak turned his head and glared. "War lover," he hissed angrily.

Brim passed the man without a glance. "I didn't know there were any of them here," he said.

"The zukeeds are everywhere," Saltash answered, shouldering his way between two gesticulating League officers who were, to all outward appearances, bickering over some arcane point of military courtesy, "including some of the people you are about to meet."

As they climbed two steps that set the seashell off from the rest of the room, a goblet appeared in Brim's hand, delicately placed there by a bright yellow-clad servant hovering nearby with a tray of replenishments. Moments later, the Carescrian found himself surrounded by a crush of curious faces. He shook hands with people whose names he forgot the moment they were pronounced and fielded a host of questions revealing a distinct sense of apprehension at the League's general posture toward their "precious Dominion." During a moment of relative quiet, he reflected on the real root of their fears: actual concern for their homeland or merely a hazard to the privileges they enjoyed under the present regime. Clearly, they would be the farthest from the battle lines when the fighting began. The wealthiest always seemed to find some plausible excuse.

At that moment, Beyazh swept through the crowd with Tissaurd in tow calling, "Time to dine! Time to dine!" The latter offered Brim her arm as she passed. "Grab on, Skipper," she called, "with this crowd of locusts, the good stuff can't last long."

Brim hooked on and was towed at high speed from the seashell (nearly tripping down the steps), through the rollicking crowd, and into a lavishly furnished banquet room whose tapestried walls and gilded sideboys might have graced an Avalonian palace. Mustafa truly honored his nomadic roots, but he also took a back seat to no one when it came to rococo sophistication and splendor. The three had just reached one of the long, sparkling tables piled high with food when they pulled up short at a flurry of activity near the huge pointed archway that formed one end of the room. Presently, Nabob Mustafa IX Eyren (The Magnificent) strode into the hall with a tall and exquisitely formed woman dressed from head to foot in light green robes of diaphanous material.

She had an almond-shaped face framed by satiny black, shoulder-length hair, a long patrician nose, full lips, and enormous green eyes that fairly sparkled with cool intelligence.

Such a woman could *only* be Raddisma, the Nabob's favorite Consort, but no HoloPicture Brim had seen came even close to doing justice to her beauty. He found himself straightaway fascinated by the woman's natural grace as the couple swept through the crowd like fast cruisers at a Fleet review. The moment they took their seats at center table, the guests eagerly sat in a great scraping of chairs and rustle of gowns.

Brim had little time to contemplate the Consort's exotic beauty, for the moment Beyazh had seated Tissaurd, she grabbed his sleeve and pulled him into the chair next to her. "You'll not get off that easily this evening, Skipper," she pronounced with mock severity. "I'm determined to have my dance with you." As a footman passed, she held up her goblet for a refill of Logish Meem, then turned to toast something with Beyazh—who was already in deep conversation with a portly Galite'er from the League. When she returned her gaze to him, Brim noticed color in her cheeks, as if she had emptied more than one goblet prior to the banquet. If anything, it made her look even lovelier than normal, and Brim was feeling the two he had already downed himself. As the corps of servants in bright yellow uniforms began to serve their first course, he found himself at considerable pains to avoid staring at her décolleté. Again and again.

The feast itself would have slaked the appetites of a battle squadron during Brim's blockading days. There were whole courses of fish prepared in every conceivable manner. He recognized the lavender scales of a delicate Feloo trout; he'd eaten a whole meal of them in Sodeskaya during his Mitchell Trophy days. Most of the others were disguised by rich sauces. Next came twelve kinds of game fowl from Ordu's own dense Boreal forests, each prepared with a different kind of spiced dressing. Afterward there were lavishly decorated courses of sweetmeats; vegetables, cold as well as hot; and uncounted trays of condiments and cheeses. And through it all, footmen constantly hovered over the table refilling goblets with Logish Meem of the finest vintages. Toward the end of the sweetmeats, he noticed with slight disapproval that Tissaurd had continued to drain her goblet a number of times—but, then, so had he. In fact, he was experiencing increased difficulty in his campaign to avoid staring at the ample expanse of breasts revealed by the deep cut of her formal uniform.

Abruptly, Beyazh excused himself to escort a Lutzian Army General to Mustafa's table, and Tissaurd lost no time capturing Brim's eyes with hers. "Skipper," she charged in a confidential voice, "you have been staring at my breasts all evening." She ran her tongue over her lips for a moment, then winked. "Tell me, do you like what you see?"

Brim felt his face flush. "You've clearly caught me, Number One," he admitted with an embarrassed grin. "And, yes, I like what I see very much. The only word that really comes to mind is 'magnificent.' "

He was saved from further embarrassment by Ogmar Vossell, the Prime Minister, who abruptly gathered his ample potbelly within a voluminous set of robes and stood with a full goblet of meem raised to the room. "And now," he bellowed in a deep bass voice that easily carried above the hubbub, "before the ladies retire, I hereby present the royal toast!"

Chairs scraped and glasses spilled (to the accompaniment of shrieks and anguished groans) while the tipsy guests clamored unsteadily to their feet. Considerable time elapsed before the room quieted sufficiently for the ceremony to proceed.

"To his Fluvannian Majesty, Nabob Mustafa IX Eyren, The Magnificent!" Vossell shouted at length, weaving slightly from side to side.

"His Fluvannian Majesty, Nabob Mustafa IX Eyren, The Magnificent!" the guests bellowed in return. "Long may he rule! Long may he live!" Shortly after their cheering subsided into ambient hubbub, Beyazh returned to his seat and, nodding politely to Brim, proceeded to monopolize Tissaurd until all rose and the women began their traditional migration into the ball-room.

"I think I may be embarrassed in the morning for what I said, Skipper," she whispered as she stopped beside his chair.

"I don't know why," Brim answered quietly. "I *was* staring, you know."

"I sort of hoped you might be, Skipper," she said, squeezing his forearm for a moment. "After all, I *did* have them out for you to admire tonight, even if it's Beyazh who plays with them later on." Then, with a rush of color in her cheeks, she joined the throng of women exiting the dining hall. "Don't forget my dance," she called over her shoulder, and was lost almost instantly in a crush of much taller women.

Brim marveled to himself. On a starship's bridge, Tissaurd was clearly one of the best, most talented First Lieutenants in the Fleet. But she was also a damnably good-looking, sexy woman when she wanted to be. And ethically distant as they might be to each other while serving on the same bridge, he felt quite honored that she had thought enough of him to reveal the flesh-and-blood woman he knew lived beneath her professional veneer.

Cigarettes and pipes of all manner, form, and content were quickly passed among the guests by a whole platoon of yellow-clad footmen. Brim refused them all; smoking never had been one of his vices. He did, however, accept a huge snifter of delightful (and elsewhere ridiculously expensive) Fluvannian spring brandy that he managed to nurse while he listened to the talk around him. It was mostly political, as foreign to him as the bridge of a starship would be to most of them. He tried to concentrate on the trivial questions of influential people with whom Saltash constantly confronted him, but somehow Tissaurd's voice kept interrupting with, "After all, I *did* have them out for you to admire tonight." It was awfully good to know that she was human.

Mercifully, Nabob Mustafa relinquished his hold on the male attendees earlier than usual and forthwith gave his royal permission for the ball to begin. . . .

Brim was a terrible social dancer. He'd received scant training in the art, and what little education he'd been forced to endure at the Helmsman's Academy he'd wasted out of pure embarrassment. He could throw the trickiest starships around with the best in the galaxy. He had utter confidence in his ability to make safe landfall in ships that others would have abandoned as derelicts or crashed. He even reckoned himself a reasonably competent lover; certainly he'd endured no open complaints in the last few years. But put him on a dance floor with responsibility for leading a woman in time to music (about which he understood *nothing*!) and he immediately turned into a fumbling, staggering nitwit whose hands went embarrassingly cold anytime he even *thought* about the arcane business. As was his habit at such affairs, he stayed well away from the actual dance floor, usually at the bar, carrying on conversations with whom he could and keeping a watchful eye for women who were not familiar with his particular brand of abominable footwork.

He was doing just that, in one of Mustafa's intimate, darkly paneled palace bars when, without warning, Tissaurd poked her head inside and pointed a gloved finger as if it were a blaster. "I-T-'S T-I-M-E," she mouthed theatrically.

Brim felt his heart thump in panic while his hands instantly drained of warmth. His mind whirled with the million-odd excuses he had catalogued over the years. None seemed to fit.

Grinning at his obvious discomfort, Tissaurd motioned with her head toward the ballroom. "N-O-W!" the gamin officer mouthed, thrusting her breasts ever so slightly toward him while maintaining an aspect of virginal innocence.

At that Brim gave up in a rush of meem-induced self-indulgence. If he could dance with anyone, it would certainly be Tissaurd! After all, weren't they the finest flight-bridge team in the known Universe and beyond? Downing the last dregs of his meem, he swept around the end of the bar, gathered her in his arm, and led the way toward the ballroom as if he actually knew what he was doing.

Unfortunately, once deployed on the dance floor with the tiny officer in his arms, he *still* could only shuffle, more or less with what he supposed people referred to as "the beat."

Surprisingly, Tissaurd didn't seem to mind; she even appeared to enjoy herself as she impudently pressed her breasts into his chest. And wonder of wonders, he even found himself enjoying the experience, especially the sensation of holding his tiny comrade close in his arms. Somehow, he had failed to notice before, but her short hair was scented with the most erotic perfume imaginable!

He had just begun to relax and enjoy himself when, most abruptly, there was no more music. He felt his face flush, wondering how long he had continued his silly shuffling without it. Other couples were already changing partners or heading off the dance floor completely. He looked down at Tissaud to find her eyes closed and her head resting on his chest as if she hadn't noticed, either. She was still moving to his own ungainly rhythm. Taking a deep breath, he awkwardly whispered, "I think it's over, Nadia."

"I know, Wilf," she replied languidly, with her eyes still closed. "I've decided to ignore it. We'll both be back aboard *Starfury* all too soon as it is. I'll have to be 'Number One' again instead of Nadia, and you'll be the Skipper who can't even think of cuddling me like you're doing right now. So I've simply willed time to stop. One can do anything she pleases when she's drunk."

"Nadia . . ." Brim started to say, but a hand grasped his shoulder firmly.

"Sorry, Commander," a tall diplomat declared with a smile, "but this is my dance with the Lieutenant, I believe."

Instantly, Tissaud came awake. "Legate Zumwalter," she exclaimed, winking surreptitiously at Brim as she slipped from his arms. "Why, I was just looking for you!"

Brim bowed. "It has been a pleasure, Lieutenant," he said.

"It has *indeed* been a pleasure, Commander," she replied, capturing his eyes in hers and holding them for a moment, "one I shall not soon forget."

"Nor I," Brim answered, then bowing to the diplomat, he turned and made his way to the sidelines.

Soon afterward, he returned to the ship and a *very* lonely night.

In the days following the ball, Saltash returned Brim to the palace often for presentations to influential Fluvannians both in the government and civilian sectors. One morning, after hectic presentations to flag-grade officers of the Fluvannian Home Fleet, they were strolling back to the embassy skimmer through the great hall of the palace when Brim spied a hulking figure who somehow looked familiar. With a great hooked nose and a shaggy red beard, the man was dressed in flowing white robes topped by a brilliant blue fez and looked a great deal like the images of Pasha Korfuzzier that Brim had seen. He was moving stealthily from pillar to pillar in a most suspicious manner. "That's the Pasha, isn't it?" Brim asked.

"Sweet merciful Universe," Saltash swore under his breath, "it is." He stopped in his tracks with a worried look on his face, scanning the room. "And *there*'s Ambassador Zacristy," he gasped a moment later, "directly across from us." Even as he spoke, Korfuzzier drew two snub-nosed blasters from his robes and raised them in the general direction of the Leaguer diplomat. But before he could so much as aim, tiny sirens began to shriek throughout the crowd, and at least ten Imperial agents appeared from nowhere, resolutely trying to wrestle him to the pavement.

Korfuzzier was a huge man, however, and not easily overpowered. Roaring with maniacal fury, he sent hapless agents flying in every direction, then aimed the powerful weapons at two of his assailants, burning them completely in half before he turned to search out his original quarry. By this time, however, Zacristy was nowhere to be seen, so in frustrated rage, Korfuzzier began to randomly spray the crowd.

At the first shots, Brim blindly threw himself over a nearby woman, pressing her close to the cold marble floor as great bolts of lethal energy crackled close overhead. Moments later he roared in pain as a wild shot burned across his back. Grinding his teeth, he struggled to remain motionless and avoid a second burst while the hard-working Imperial agents again subdued Korfuzzier. This time, however, they disarmed him as well. Gradually the screaming subsided, and the hall fell into a shocked silence. "Are you all right?" Brim whispered to the woman, instantly feeling foolish because she couldn't possibly understand his language.

"I shall be quite all right as soon as you let me up," she returned laughingly—in perfect Avalonian.

Before he could comply, however, the shocked Brim found himself harshly dragged to his feet and pinioned between two enormous eunuchs dressed in the black-and-gold checked robes of the Harem staff who shouted at him angrily in what must have been Vulgate Fluvannian. In the distance, he could see Saltash haplessly trying to push his way through the noisy crowd.

"How dare you defile Raddisma, the Nabob's most cherished Consort, pagan?" a third eunuch demanded in Avalonian. This one was at least a quarter again as large as his partners. "Speak," he growled shrilly, "before we *make* you speak!"

Brim helplessly glanced at the woman he had tried to protect—indeed, it *was* Raddisma, favorite Consort of the Nabob. And today, he noticed—in spite of the circumstances—she had managed to be even more beautiful than he remembered from the banquet.

When the woman commanded something imperiously in Fluvannian, at least a dozen servants gathered to help her to her feet. At the same time, the three eunuchs released Brim with chastened looks on their faces.

"A fine way to reward you, Commander," Raddisma laughed in a dusky, feminine voice while she straightened her hair. "You very probably saved my life," she added with an appraising look.

Brim had no sooner opened his mouth to answer when he, the eunuchs, and the Consort were surrounded by a solid wall of scarlet-uniformed soldiers who opened a narrow passage in their ranks to admit Nabob Mustafa himself. "Raddisma," the little man puffed, clearly out of breath, then continued with an unintelligible string of Fluvannian.

The tall woman bowed and answered with a long soliloquy, also in Fluvannian, nodding often toward Brim.

"Commander Brim," the Nabob said at length in Avalonian, turning for the first time from his Consort. "Forgive me," he said. "My mind was clearly elsewhere." He placed a ring-bedecked hand on Brim's forearm. "Raddisma tells me that you saved her life by shielding her with your own body. Are you hurt?"

Brim smiled. "Only my Fleet Cloak, Your Magnificence," he said. "The rest of me seems to be in fine fettle."

The Nabob smiled grimly. "This bravery of yours will not go unremembered, Commander," he said with a serious mien. "I find I am *considerably* in your debt this trip."

"Not at all, Your Magnificence," Brim replied. "I was honored to serve."

Abruptly the little Nabob saluted in a contemporary manner. "Nevertheless," he said, "you will find that I do not forget those whom I owe."

Startled, Brim returned the salute, but before he could utter a word, the wall of troops opened once more, then followed the Nabob across the floor in the direction from which he had come, leaving Brim once more with Raddisma and her eunuchs.

Mustafa's Consort still had that appraising look in her eyes. "You are Commander Brim?" she asked. "Captain of the *Starfury*?" she asked.

"At your service, ma'am," Brim replied.

"I think you *did* save my life, Commander," Raddisma declared with a mysterious smile on her full lips. "There can be no question about it. Someday, I shall see to it that you are appropriately rewarded, in a personal manner, of course."

Brim bowed gallantly. "Your safety is my greatest reward, ma'am," he said, but when their eyes met, he thought she might just have something *specific* on her mind. "I shall look forward to our next meeting," he added with a great deal of truth.

"As will I," she answered regally. "*As will I.* . . ." Bowing slightly, she swept by his arm, passed him a secret little wink, and disappeared into the crowd that had again begun to move freely through the colossal hall.

Moments later, Saltash arrived at his side. "When I saw who you tackled," the envoy said, "I reckoned the best thing was to let you work things out for yourself."

Brim nodded phlegmatically. "Mighty decent of you, neighbor," he quipped. "I enjoyed the eunuchs especially. Big zukeeds, those."

"Well"—Saltash shrugged—"except for them, it couldn't

have been all *that* uncomfortable. I mean, Raddisma isn't the worst person to end up on a floor with, now, is she?''

"I can't remember," Brim grumped. "I was so thraggling scared, I didn't notice a thing until the eunuchs got me, that is. And just look what happened to my Fleet Cape." He turned his back.

"Ouch," Saltash swore. "That *will* be difficult to fix."

"I'm going to bill the Fleet," Brim chuckled darkly. "It's a line-of-duty reimbursable if I ever saw one and they're xaxtdamn lucky they don't have to repair *me*, too."

"In all seriousness," Saltash said, "we couldn't have wished for anything better to happen."

"We *what*?"

"Well," Saltash answered, "both the Pasha and his favorite bedmate are unquestionably in your debt—and by proxy, so is Fluvanna. That lady calls a lot of the shots around here."

"I get the distinct impression she didn't call *those* shots," Brim quipped.

"Very funny," Saltash chuckled. "Nevertheless, I think you'll find that your discomfiture was all for a good cause."

Brim grinned. "I'll try to remember that the next time some dimbulb tries to broil my back with a blaster. Voot's greasy beard!''

During the next week, in his capacity as Commander of a visiting warship, Brim attended more State receptions than he cared to remember. He also put on weight from all the rich food, in spite of his three- and four-c'lenyt morning exercise runs (the normally sedentary Fluvannians thought him quite mad, and often shouted their opinions as he puffed along the dawn-shadowed streets).

One evening, he and Saltash were at a refreshment center after completing the reception line for still another midweek ball when the diplomat nodded toward the main entrance. "I say!" he exclaimed with obvious interest. "Now *there*'s one I haven't seen before. Simply exquisite!"

Chuckling, Brim turned his head for a glimpse; Saltash seldom missed a well-turned ankle. Suddenly his heart stopped and he almost dropped his goblet. "Sweet *suffering* Universe," he gasped under his breath.

"What was that?" Saltash asked, his face taking on a look of consternation. "Wilf, old boy," he said, "you've gone absolutely pale. Are you all right?"

At that moment, a paige's voice called out from the ballroom, "Grand Duke Rogan LaKarn, Absolute Ruler of The Torond, and Grand Duchess Margot Effer'wyck-LaKarn, Princess of the Effer'wyck Dominions."

Brim could only stand dumbfounded, his whole being absorbed by the moment. Once, a thousand years before, Margot Effer'wyck-LaKarn had been his one true love, and he, hers. They met nearly fourteen years previously at a wardroom party aboard old I.F.S. *Truculent* at the beginning of Brim's military career.

"Intriguing," Saltash mused, peering at Brim with considerable interest. "If I remember correctly, she was forced into a political marriage with LaKarn by Emperor Greyffin IV himself. Usually we keep track of friendships with important people. We should have had notification of one like that."

Brim could only shake his head—all references to his relationship with Margot Effer'wyck had been quashed years ago on direct orders from the palace. While Saltash continued to talk, he watched Margot enter the reception line and turn her face for a moment toward the refreshment area, instantly locking gazes with him. She seemed to falter for a moment, recovered, then continued into the line with a startled expression on her face. As always, her strawberry-blond hair was piled in fashionable disarray, framing a perfect oval face, languid eyes, generous lips, and a brow that frowned when she smiled—as it did while she charmed the Nabob within an inch of his life. She wore a glamorous gown in her favorite shade of apricot that set off her ample figure in a most voluptuous way. A small, snug string of elegant Zenniér pearls shone fashionably at her neck.

Behind the Princess stood Rogan LaKarn, her husband. His body was still hideously twisted after a run-in with Brim years previously. He was dressed in an elegant formal outfit that hid some of the damage, but not all. He turned momentarily with a quizzical frown on his countenance, then met Brim's eyes with a flash of abhorrence.

Brim returned his look with a stony implacability until the once-handsome Baron turned to meet the Nabob himself.

"Doesn't look as if *that* one much likes you," Saltash remarked. "I take it the two of you have squared off before?"

"It's a long story," Brim growled pointedly; then he let the subject drop.

Wisely, so did Saltash. . . .

Brim found himself busy almost the entire evening, meeting what seemed like half of the Fluvannian population. He and Margot Effer'wyck locked glances a number of times, but one of them always seemed to be busy when the other was momentarily free. At last, however, Zacristy, the League Ambassador, disappeared with LaKarn and a scowling Mustafa IX Eyren through one of the Nabob's secret exits. Immediately, the ball settled into what was clearly a second phase; this one more of relaxed socializing than the spirited political mixing after the reception line. Brim was all too glad to accompany Saltash to the bar for another goblet of Logish Meem.

"Hmm," the diplomat mused, "a private audience, no less. Well, I don't suppose I ought to be surprised. After all, LaKarn is more or less the equivalent of a king back in The Torond, even if he is only a figurehead for the Leaguers."

Brim was about to comment when he felt a hand gently touch his arm. Turning slowly, he felt his heart catch once more. "Margot," he whispered, peering into her liquid blue eyes and hoping his voice wouldn't betray the emotion he felt. Clearly, she had aged. She had lines on her face that he couldn't remember. And at close range, he could see that her figure was considerably more ample than when she specialized in perilous covert missions to League planets. Too, her eyes now showed a muzziness that hadn't been there before the TimeWeed. But for all that, to him she was at least as beautiful as she ever had been, perhaps even more so in her maturity. "Baroness La-Karn," he said calmly as he could, "m-may I present The Honorable George Saltash of His Imperial Majesty's Foreign

Service? Sir Saltash, Her Serene Majesty, Princess Margot Effer'wyck of the Effer'wyck Dominions and Grand Baroness of The Torond.''

"I am honored, madame," Saltash mumbled, bowing deeply from the waist to kiss her gloved hand.

"As am I, Sir Saltash," she said, narrowing her eyes coolly. "You are well known by my husband's diplomatic services."

"Yes," Saltash said, "I suppose I am." He met her gaze with a steely look that told Brim they may never have met, but clearly each had encountered the other's power at one time or another. The diplomat bowed again, this time with a formal click of his heels. "Princess," he said formally, "Commander Brim: I am summoned for a moment to our limousine."

"By all means, Sir Saltash," Margot purred, extending her hand for another kiss.

For a long time following the diplomat's departure, Brim and Margot stood silently, staring into each other's eyes. Then, as if they had been together only metacycles before, she took his hands in hers. "Hello, Wilf Brim," she said in her dusky, perfectly modulated voice. "It's been a long time."

"A century, at least," Brim stammered. "H-how have you been, Margot? I mean. . . ."

"Are you asking about the TimeWeed, Wilf?" she asked, her eyes peering all the way to his soul.

Brim nodded silently.

"Nothing has changed, Wilf," she said with almost no emotion. "For addicts, death is the only release. The Weed now keeps me alive."

"You appear to have it a lot more under control than before," Brim observed, recalling more than one time when she had seemed to be almost totally under its influence, like a drunk.

"I won't need more until morning," she replied. "Increased tolerance permits larger doses—they're cumulative, in case you hadn't heard. It provides me with longer stretches of being human than I had before." She lifted a goblet of Logish Meem from a passing servant's tray and looked thoughtfully into it before taking a sip. "Life is still treating you well?" she asked at some length.

Brim took a deep breath. "Years ago when we met," he said, "I would never have believed how generous Lady Fortune has been to me lately." Then he paused, reminded sharply of the loneliness he had experienced after dancing with Tissaurd, and suddenly it seemed to be time for conversation on *any* other subject. "How is your son Rogan?" he asked.

"Growing into a young man," she replied, "nearly six. Can you believe it?"

Brim smiled. "I remember when he was born," he said, staring off into the past. "It was the day of the first post-war Mitchell Trophy race."

"You remember well," Margot said with a little smile. "Then I am not completely gone from your life, am I?"

Surprised, Brim peered into her eyes and frowned. "Gone?" he asked, then stared at the floor while he attempted to comprehend her words. "Margot," he continued at length. "There is no way you will *ever* be gone from my life—at least from my past. Many of my most fond memories center around you."

"But your future?" she pressed quietly. "What of your future, Wilf? Am I any part of your dreams?"

"Should you be?" he asked. "You have not touched me for years."

She frowned. "How could I have touched you? Half a galaxy has separated us until today."

"One touches," Brim said gently, "and then one *touches*." He gently placed his hand on her arm. "Margot," he continued, "addicts touch only their addictions, and you are clearly not addicted to me."

She closed her eyes for a moment. "Perhaps it seems that way, Wilf," she said, barely whispering, "but . . ."

At that moment, a tall Leaguer dressed in a Controller's severe black service uniform, peaked cap, and knee-length riding boots forced his way so close beside her that she nearly lost her balance. His gold shoulder straps bore two large diamond-shaped devices, indicating that he was a Galite'er, the equivalent of a Rear Admiral in the Imperial Fleet. "Is this person bothering you, Princess?" he asked with grandiose disdain.

"N-no, Galite'er Hoffman," she replied, "he is an old friend."

"A friend?" Hoffman said, narrowing his eyes and turning his head to peer disdainfully at Brim. "How can that be? He is nothing but an Imperial."

Brim smiled and calmly looked up into the Leaguer's face. The blue cast of his skin and total lack of body hair identified him as a Varoldian from the Ta'am Region. "How badly is it you want trouble, mister?" the Carescrian asked in a quiet voice. "With the kind of manners you've shown me so far, I can be *very* creative."

"Wilf, no!" Margot gasped in a frightened whisper. She took the Leaguer's arm. "Come, Galite'er Hoffman," she said. "I am ready to return to the ship."

"An intelligent decision," Hoffman said, examining his spotless blue fingernails. "Your Imperial friend here is deeply in your debt. I should have enjoyed breaking him in half."

Brim gripped the back of a nearby chair, stayed from mayhem only by the look of panic in Margot's eyes. "Until we meet again, Princess," he said, bowing deeply from the waist.

Without acknowledging him in any way, she followed Hoffman into the colorful throng. Brim watched her reappear shortly afterward at the main entrance, where three more Varoldians conducted her into a black limousine waiting under the portico.

"What in the Universe was *that* all about?" Saltash demanded, pushing his way to Brim's side with a look of concern on his face.

"I wish I knew," Brim answered, the shock of hearing Margot's voice just beginning to sink in.

"Well, what did you say to him?" Saltash asked.

"Who?" Brim answered distantly.

"Wilf—the *Galite'er*."

Brim chuckled. "Oh, the Galite'er? Don't pay any attention to him; he's only a guard."

"But why did he take the Princess away? What were the two of you talking about?"

"We had really only begun to talk," Brim replied with a

frown. "Odd, that. In retrospect, it almost seems as if the bloody Leaguer had been waiting for something to happen."

"And that's all?"

"I'm afraid that's it, friend," Brim said, draining his goblet. "Damned strange evening, though. I haven't seen Margot for years, yet there she was, talking to me as if . . . well . . . as if we'd been apart only days. And then . . ." He stopped in the middle of his sentence as Rogan LaKarn hobbled painfully into the refreshment center. Once handsome, the man's face had become as twisted with hate and anger as his body. It would still be years until his spinal nerve trunks had regenerated to a point that they could be rebuilt by a healing machine.

"Ah, Brim," the Baron muttered, ignoring Saltash's presence completely, "I am told that my so-called wife is no better at staying away from you today than she was years ago." He laughed. "Well, you'll want to think twice before jumping into bed with her now that she's on TimeWeed. Let me guarantee that she needs it after a dose of love—physically *must* have it. And, as I am certain you are aware, the smoke she exhales will kill you, especially in the doses she now requires."

Brim looked grimly at the man's twisted body. "LaKarn," he growled, "if it would save that woman from the filth of TimeWeed, I'd break your spine again. Gladly. But since there is nothing I can do about Margot, I am simply going to leave." Turning to Saltash, he clapped the diplomat on his shoulder. "You can talk to him if you wish, my friend, but I am heading back to *Starfury*."

"Ah yes, *Starfury*," LaKarn crowed as if he had heard nothing Brim uttered. "Then you will be most interested in the arrival tomorrow afternoon of an old acquaintance of yours." He laughed bitterly. "I am certain that you will be on hand to welcome Kirsh Valentin when he arrives in a preproduction model of the League's new Gorn-Hoff P. 1065. I understand that you and that shameless space pirate Baxter Calhoun have spent considerable time assessing covert recordings of the prototype."

Brim stiffened as yet another shock from the past collided with his mind. Kirsh Valentin. Handsome, intelligent, accomplished, and in too many ways as talented as himself, Valentin had been the Carescrian's arch enemy since the Leaguer egregiously tortured him as a helpless prisoner aboard a Leaguer patrol ship. Afterward, their paths continued to cross, in both war and the ensuing peace. And each time they did, Brim managed to frustrate Valentin's evil aspirations until the Leaguer's original disdain turned to cold and bitter hate. "I cannot imagine the meaning of your words concerning Baxter Calhoun," Brim lied calmly, "or recordings of some new Gorn-Hoff."

LaKarn's eyes filled with cold hate. "But you do remember Kirsh Valentin, don't you, Imperial gangster?"

Brim nodded, ignoring the insult from a man who could no longer defend himself. "How could I forget a man who has almost killed me three times?" he asked with a dour smile. Valentin had been responsible for at least three—and perhaps more—attempts at Brim's life in the fifteen Standard Years that had elapsed since their first encounter.

"Perhaps next time will prove the charm," LaKarn countered with a smile. "Or the time after that."

"I wouldn't hold my breath," Brim countered evenly. "Kirsh isn't really very good at it, you know."

"Practice makes perfect, Brim," LaKarn growled, then abruptly turned to Saltash. "My respects, Councillor," he said, awkwardly clicking his heels. Without a backward glance, he hobbled back into the crush of revelers.

During the ride home in Saltash's sleek limousine, Brim began to prepare himself for another "peacetime" encounter with his old enemy. He had neither seen nor spoken to the man since the Mitchell Trophy races, where he had been involved in an unsuccessful plot that would have blown Brim and his Sherrington M-6B into subatomic components. But even as he stepped onto *Starfury*'s entry chamber, he found that Tissaurd had the ship at lift-off stations with orders to loose for space immediately, destination: Avalon. . . .

Starfury raised Avalon in record time, mooring in the military complex near Grand Imperial Terminal on the sixth day out from Magor. Had anyone at the Admiralty been interested in those sorts of things, the crossing could have gone into the record books. But setting records in *Starfury* was almost too easy. And actually recording the event in an "official" manner required a lot of advance planning that simply wasn't possible with an active military ship.

Brim switched the propulsion controls to Strana' Zaftrak and got to his feet, idly watching a big government limousine draw to a halt at the foot of the brow in a cloud of powdery snow. Its sleek lines were somehow out of place among the angular dockyard vehicles parked nearby. Curious, he leaned his elbows on the coaming behind his recliner and watched while a liveried chauffeur hurried to open the passenger compartment door for a familiar-looking woman in mufti . . . *Regula Collingswood*— his skipper from I.F.S. *Truculent.*

"Take over, Tissaurd!" he barked. "Farnsworth. Call down to the Duty Officer on the double! Order him to watch for Captain Regula Collingswood at the main port; then tell Chief Barbousse to show her to the wardroom—he'll recognize her!"

"Aye, Captain," the two officers replied in unison, switching on their intercoms with raised eyebrows that seemed to have replicated themselves everywhere on the bridge.

Brim felt his face burn as he sprinted for the companionway. How soon people forgot. In her days of active service, Collingswood had been one of the finest skippers in the Imperial Fleet. At his cabin, he rinsed his face and struggled into a clean uniform, then dashed into the corridor, dodged along three crowded companionways, and arrived at the wardroom just as Barbousse served the elegant ex-officer a sparkling goblet of Logish Meem. "Captain Collingswood!" he huffed before she could take the first sip. "What a *great* surprise!"

Collingswood was a statuesque woman who never, even for a moment, let the power of her high station interfere with the basic femininity that shaped virtually everything about her personality. She was statuesque, tall, and ageless with a long patrician nose, piercing hazel eyes, and soft, graying chestnut hair that she wore in natural curls. Dressed in a beige business suit with huge, puffed shoulders, and fronted by great cascades of lace, she appeared to be completely ageless—which, Brim considered, she probably was. Shortly after Nergol Triannic foisted the disastrous Treaty of Garak on the war-weary Empire, she had resigned her commission and married Admiral Erat Plutron, her whispered long-time lover, who—as a recently elected member of the Imperial Parliament—had become a major opponent of the CIGAs. Now, for some reason, she was here in Avalon to meet I.F.S. *Starfury*. She smiled as she indicated a second chair Barbousse had drawn to the table. "Wilf Brim," she demanded, "when are you going to remember that my name is Regula—not Captain?"

Brim bowed, took her hand, and kissed it. "Right now—I think," he said, slipping into the chair just as Barbousse quietly placed a goblet of Logish Meem before him. "Thanks, Chief," he said, touching the big rating's arm. "Sometimes, only very special friends will do."

Barbousse gave a little wink and smiled. "Special friends are most honored to offer their assistance, Captain—er—*Captains*." Then he vanished into the Steward's room like a specter.

"I thought you were still at Bemus Manor," Brim said. "And here you are in a government limousine, no less. What's happening?"

Collingswood smiled. "Well," she explained, "ever since Erat was elected to Parliament, I seem to have become more and more involved with the Admiralty, at least the non-CIGA people there. And since starfleets require organizers as well as disruptors, Harry Drummond asked me to become his Operations Director." She laughed. "I even get a salary."

Brim rolled his eyes. "What are you going to do with *all* that wealth?" he asked jestingly.

"Donate it to the Fleet Relief Drive, of course," she said with a little smile. Then she chuckled. "As willing as I was to trade in my Blue Cape for a comfortable business suit, I never *could* get that far away from the Fleet. It's been a part of me too long."

Brim savored the ancient Logish Meem that Barbousse had ordered from the ship's well-stocked meem vaults. "Somehow, I didn't think you'd last," he admitted, "especially after you got involved with the Imperial Starflight Society." Then he frowned. "But . . ."

Collingswood grinned. "But why am I here?" she interrupted.

"Well," he answered, "with nothing but a two-and-a-half-stripe Commander for her Captain, *Starfury* isn't often met by Directors in big government limousine skimmers."

Collingswood nodded. "Probably that is true sometimes, Wilf," she said. "But today, *you* are expected at the Imperial palace in a little more than a cycle so you can personally assist Commodore Calhoun and General Drummond when they brief Greyffin IV on the Fluvanna Plan. They scheduled the whole thing around *Starfury*'s return, and you know what a hectic schedule Greyffin IV keeps every day." She smiled. "So at least for this exercise, you're a very important person, Wilf Brim."

"It's not difficult to be important when you command the only starship in the game," Brim chuckled. "I suspect I'll be a lot less in demand when deliveries start on the production Starfuries."

Collingswood sat back to sip her Logish Meem with an enigmatic smile on her face. "We'll see about that, Captain Brim," she said. "We'll see. . . ."

"Saltash tells me that you've taken Magor by storm," Drummond chuckled, clapping Brim on the back as they sat in one of the palace's elegant waiting rooms.

"Tough on clothes, tho'," Calhoun interjected. "I signed the order for your replacement uniform yesterday." He chuckled. "Brim, you act like a lightnin' rod when it comes to trouble."

The younger Carescrian laughed. "If it weren't for the honor of the thing, Commodore," he quipped, "I'd just as soon someone else had the title."

"Aye," Drummond said. "I can understand that, all right."

"At any rate," Calhoun declared, "Mustafa is ane hundred percent in support o' the plan. An' a lot o' that decision had to do wi' his impression o' you. He's already ordered his embassy here on Avalon to sign the papers just so soon as we draft them up."

"Now," Drummond interjected with a nod of his head, "all we have to do is to make certain our own Emperor's behind the plan."

"An'," Calhoun said, nodding toward the door of the elaborate waiting room, "I believe that we gat to begin that process immediately."

Brim turned to confront an Imperial paige, dressed in a traditional high-collared blue uniform with four gold frogs down the front of the tunic. He carried a gilded AnGrail reed at least six irals tall.

"This way, gentlemen," the paige said, bowing from the waist. Straightening, he pointed his AnGrail at the rear of the room and part of the wall simply vanished. Beyond was a huge oval chamber whose elegant walls were entirely lined by lofty beveled mirrors inscribed with intricate scrollwork. Colorful renderings of legendary flighted beings and baroque starships decorated the ceiling above a trompe l'oeil arbor "supported" on ornate columns separating the mirrors. At one end of the room was a huge rococo table beneath a canopy of deep blue velvet, and beside the table stood the slim form of Emperor Greyffin IV, Grand Galactic Emperor, Prince of the Reggio Star Cluster, and Rightful Protector of the Heavens.

A spare man of medium build—neither young nor old—Greyffin still looked surprisingly like the portraits that hung in every Fleet starship large enough to have a wardroom. He was dressed in a magnificently tailored Fleet uniform adorned by the insignia of a full Admiral. His hair, a little grayer than Brim remembered, was still short, parted on the left, and combed straight back from his narrow face. He had close-set gray eyes on either side of a prominent, squarish sort of nose and a diminutive, pointed beard. As the three officers approached his table, he returned their salutes with that particular bearing of total impenetrability that seems to define people who are both very wealthy and very powerful.

Offering his hand first to Baxter Calhoun, then to General Drummond, he turned at last to Brim and smiled warmly. "Good afternoon, Commander," he said, extending his hand. "It has been quite some time since I've been referred to as 'His Nibs,' to my face."

Brim felt his cheeks flush. He'd done that inadvertently the night Greyffin awarded him the Imperial Comet. Then, as now, the Emperor seemed to value the little slip as a rather good joke. "Your Majesty," he said, solemnly shaking the Emperor's hand, "I have been extremely careful ever since to look *before* I speak."

"A pity," Greyffin chuckled under his breath. "You're probably spoiling everyone's fun." Then nodding to Calhoun, he took his place in a huge, high-backed chair behind the table. "Baxter," he said, "Onrad's privately described your plan to save Fluvanna in spite of the CIGAs." He raised his eyebrows. "About time to let me in on the details, eh?"

"Aye, Your Majesty," Calhoun replied, immediately swinging into what must have been his ten-thousandth presentation. Brim and Drummond stepped clear of the projectors and took seats at the side of the room, doing their best to appear as if fresh information were reaching their ears, too. Mercifully, the elder Carescrian had prepared a capsulated version for the Emperor, so he spoke for little more than a half metacycle. But during that short time, he covered every important factor. And just as he finished, Prince Onrad strode into the room to stand by Greyffin's side.

"Well, Father," he asked with a grave look, "what do you think?"

The Emperor nodded thoughtfully, joining the tips of his fingers and thumbs. "Wonderful," he pronounced at length. "Just the right treatment. Completely beyond the CIGAs. Bloody wonderful. In fact, Baxter," he said, angling his head toward Calhoun, "during the past week, I have mulled over some ideas about your staffing problem."

"I'm all ears, Your Majesty," Calhoun declared. "We need ev'ry bit o' help we can gat wi' that particular problem."

The Emperor took a deep breath and frowned. "It seems that the bloody CIGAs have forced some of our finest officers and starsailors from the Fleet in the last few years," he mused grimly. "Commander Brim knows," he added with a wink. "Now assuming that some of them have the forbearance and patriotism he exhibited, what would happen if I personally extended them an offer to rejoin the Fleet at their old grades plus one promotion? Shouldn't at least a few of them come through for us?"

"Counting *Starfury* herself, we'll need to find volunteers for *eleven* ships," Onrad warned.

The Emperor shook his head. "Commander Brim already has a crew," he said. "If what I hear is correct, he will lose only a few when he announces that *Starfury*'s been leased. So you will only need enough for ten." He looked around the room while passing his fingers among the beams from a tiny panel of lights near his right hand. "Here, let me read an offer I've had drafted." He frowned as he peered onto his tabletop where a display lit his face from beneath. "First," he began, "by Imperial Edict, all candidates, officers, and enlisted alike will be offered special one-year reserve commissions and enlistments in the Imperial Fleet at their previous grade plus one. To obtain these, however, they will be required to 'disappear,' serving in the Fluvannian Fleet as mercenaries in what will be known as the Imperial Volunteer Group, or IVG for short."

"What happens after the year is over?" Onrad asked.

"Afterward," Greyffin continued, glancing up from the table, "if I decide not to extend the term of service, I shall personally guarantee each volunteer a permanent place in the Imperial Fleet—working at his or her IVG specialty and rank." He looked at Brim and smiled. "I shall extend the same sort of offer to certain persons who already have positions in the Fleet, including *Starfury*'s entire crew. It will, of course, require them to resign their commissions. But each will have my personal guarantee that they may return." Turning to Calhoun, he raised eyebrows. "How does that sound, Baxter?"

Calhoun grinned. "I think your personal guarantee wull do it nicely, Your Majesty," he said. "That's all I would ever need."

"Good," Greyffin said. "Harry? Wilf? Is there anything you want to change?"

"Nothing, Your Majesty," Calhoun said.

Brim shook his head, bemused at hearing the Emperor use his first name. "Nothing, Your Majesty," he seconded.

"In that case," Greyffin declared, applying thumb and forefinger to a minute signing window on the tabletop, "it is now a proclamation. Onrad, call in the Fluvannian Ambassador and we shall begin 'recruiting' immediately."

In less than a cycle, they were joined by a tall, slender woman in fashionable Avalonian dress. She had straight black hair that reached her shoulders and bangs cut straight across her high forehead. Her calm, almond-shaped eyes complemented a long, narrow nose and wickedly thin lips. She wore a restrained business suit, all in black, with a white ruffled blouse and a skirt so long it revealed only high-heeled slippers and a hint of slim ankle. "Your Majesty," she said, bowing almost double.

"Madame Orenzii," Greyffin said, nodding from his chair. "These men are the vanguard of the warship crews who will soon fortify your fleet. May I present General Harry Drummond, Commodore Baxter Calhoun, and Commander Wilf Brim."

Orenzii bowed to Onrad, then looked from one officer to the other until her eyes stopped at Brim. "You are captain of the *Starfury*, are you not?" she asked with no trace of an accent.

"I am, Madame Orenzii," Brim answered.

The woman laughed. "Raddisma made me promise that I should not leave the castle without thanking you once more for saving her life," she said.

Brim felt his cheeks burn again. "I think Consort Raddisma gives me credit for a great deal more than I accomplished," he replied.

Orenzii bowed with only a wink for comment, then turned to face the Emperor. "Your Majesty," she said, "I have been empowered by Nabob Mustafa IX Eyren, The Magnificent, to begin recruiting as soon as qualified space crews can be located."

At that, Calhoun stepped to the Emperor's table and bowed. "I should count it an honor to become the first volunteer," he declared proudly.

"Your Majesty," Orenzii asked, turning to the Emperor, "is your office perhaps available for this historic occasion?"

Greyffin smiled, peering down at the work surface of his table. "I detect the fine hand of my son here," he commented with a chuckle. "The necessary documents have already appeared on this display—including my own. Even the signing window is activated, no doubt for the Commodore's fingerprints, eh?"

"Well," Onrad admitted, "I *did* make a few preparations for this meeting. Nothing elaborate, of course, but . . ."

The Emperor shook his head. "Hmm," he muttered wryly, "since everything appears to be in good order, I suppose we proceed. Commodore," he said, rising from his chair, "come sit here. You may as well be comfortable while you sign away a year of your life."

Calhoun took his place at the table, carefully reading the displayed contracts. "All right," he said at some length, "I'll sign." Twice, he placed his thumb and forefinger on the signing windows with a flourish. Then, Orenzii signed for her government.

"Congratulations!" she said, shaking Calhoun's hand with great gusto. "You are now a Commodore in the Royal Fluvannian Fleet."

"It is a great approbation, madame," Calhoun said gallantly as he stepped back from the table and fixed his eyes pointedly on Brim.

His were not the only eyes peering in that direction. "Well, Commander," the Emperor said, "shall I assume you also intend to volunteer?"

"Poor Brim," Onrad observed with a broad smile. "He only won back his commission two years ago."

Greyffin chuckled gently. "Don't think of this as losing your commission again, Commander. The next year ought to be much like an assignment to a very special covert mission. That should be nothing new to you."

"Aye, Your Majesty," Brim agreed, settling into the Emperor's chair. Before him, shimmering on the surface of the table, were three lettered documents. On his left was a Form 889A, VOLUNTARY TERMINATION OF FLEET SERVICE, everyone joked about the forms, but in the eyes of idealists like Brim, they were suicide notes. Next to it was a one-year commission for service in the Fluvannian Fleet at the rank of Commander. On its right, the Emperor's guarantee was dynamically changing contents as writers elsewhere in the palace attempted to hammer out a legal document at a dead run. Brim waited until the characters had stabilized, then read the new parts, and eventually signed all three documents.

"Good of you to sign," Onrad remarked. "I noticed Father's

pledge going through at least three drafts while you tried to read it.''

Brim chuckled in spite of the solemnity of the occasion. ''I managed to read one complete draft, Your Highness,'' he said. ''I'm no space lawyer, but it seems all right to me.''

''The Fleet takes another hit,'' Onrad said facetiously. ''Scratch one Commodore and a Commander.''

''Yes,'' the Emperor agreed dourly. ''And the absurd part of it is that we aren't even CIGAs.'' He shook his head sadly. ''A terrible darkness is settling over the galaxy, even as we meet here. What a terrible shame that we may contend with it only in secret and by guile for fear of inciting the enemy. . . .''

The next evening, Brim dined alone in a quiet bistro just off Courtland Plaza where he and Margot used to rendezvous during the early years of her marriage to Rogan LaKarn. It was a place known for stiff white linen, discreet service, excellent food, and what the Carescrian had grown to know, and respect, as ''good music.'' He came here often when he was in Avalon, after the press of the dinner crowd, to dine quietly and reflect on his day's activities, which today centered around Nergol Triannic's Treaty of Garak. The document had served its creator well during the spurious ''peace'' it had enabled. But it was quite clear that both the treaty and its peace had outworn their usefulness to the League of Dark Stars—and both would soon be shattered by their creator.

He stared blindly off into the dark, smoky room as he sipped a goblet of Logish Meem and mused about the year ahead. There would be a war; that was almost a given. What concerned him even more than the war was its ultimate outcome, because win or lose, it would also end the familiar, centuries-old civilization that Greyffin IV's Empire had enjoyed in relatively affluent comfort. He frowned a little as a tall figure stopped beside his table and, when it didn't go away, glanced up—in sudden disgust.

There, glowering like the threat of a bad cold, was the choleric visage of Puvis Amherst, chief of the CIGAs. With a Fleet Cloak draped across the right shoulder of his impeccable dress uniform, the man still cut an impressive figure—in spite of a most conspicuous absence of battle ribbons on his chest. ''Well, Carescrian,'' he said with a curled lip, ''you have clearly continued your warlike activities in spite of my *personal* warning to you last year in the Admiralty. What do you have to say for yourself?''

Brim fought down a strong urge to punch the overweening clown in his nose, then relaxed with a smile of contempt. ''Your warning wasn't frightening enough, Amherst,'' he said. ''I assume that you have noticed I am still very much alive.''

''Antagonism toward our friends in the League will *yet* cost your worthless life, Brim,'' Amherst spat back with venom. His eyes narrowed. ''And you *will* address me by my title of Commodore, as regulations require, *Commander* Brim. I have warned you about that often.''

''Not often enough, zukeed,'' Brim said quietly. ''As I said last year, the best title you'll get from me is 'traitor,' at least so long as you remain the local CIGA boss.''

Amherst glared at Brim for a moment, clutching the lapels of his tunic. ''Grand Imperial CIGA Dominator,'' he snarled, his face now crimson with rage.

''Traitor,'' Brim corrected with an assured smile.

''Arrogant Carescrian zukeed,'' Amherst gasped, as if he were short of breath. ''You have no more respect for the uniform of your dominion than does that perfectly awful countryman of yours, Baxter Calhoun.''

''It's not the uniform we discredit, Amherst,'' Brim amended with a grin, ''just the wearer. Nothing stupid about Carescrians.''

Only a reddening face betrayed the effect of Brim's retort. ''So you will become a Fluvannian thrall with your reprehensible mentor, will you?'' Amherst growled. Then he laughed arrogantly. ''Nothing that you or your warmongering associates carry out escapes my purview.''

Brim shrugged with equanimity and kept his silence.

''Warmonger,'' the CIGA snapped after long moments of silence. ''You will *yet* bring disaster down on our heads, in spite of our labors to preserve the peace.''

Brim shook his head. ''That's where you're wrong, Amherst,'' he said, locking glances with his old shipmate. ''We talked about that a year ago in your office. I don't want war any more than you do—or any of your CIGAs. In fact, I work toward peace every bit as desperately as anyone else, yourself included. The difference is that I want an *honorable* peace: one that preserves our Imperial heritage with all the very mortal faults that make it habitable. And that can only be done with *strength*, like a powerful fleet. You and your CIGAs would preserve the peace by capitulation. But in that way, we become slaves to Nergol Triannic's League of Dark Stars, under the yoke of his Time-Weed-soaked Controllers. And no matter how imperfect our old Empire has become over the years, it is a thousandfold better than *anything* like that.''

''You would still sacrifice men and women to the insatiable maw of war,'' Amherst demanded, ''when you have seen firsthand—as well as I have—how horrible that is?''

''Now *that* defines a principal difference between you and me,'' Brim replied steadily. ''Battle was shattering to you. I saw that in person while we shipped together aboard old *Truculent*. It was so frightening that your father used his influence to remove you from all further combat assignments.'' He narrowed his eyes. ''The rest of us, on the other hand, went on fighting—and do so today—because the loss of our freedom frightens us a lot worse than the loss of our lives! Without freedom, life doesn't have much value for most of us. Believe me, Amherst, I've seen that on every planet we've had to liberate from your good friends, the Leaguers.''

Amherst's eyes narrowed in dark anger. ''Are you,'' he asked with a quivering voice, ''suggesting that I am a coward?''

''No accusation at all, Amherst,'' Brim stated calmly. ''It's a statement of fact. You *are* a coward, pure and simple. And so are the rest of your craven CIGAs.''

Amherst went completely rigid, his hands trembling as he drew his fingers into fists. ''I shall make you pay dearly for that, Brim,'' he spat through colorless lips stretched over clenched teeth.

''We'll see, Amherst,'' Brim replied calmly. ''But you'd better keep an eye on your own back, or you'll eventually lose the chance. If the League wins, the first Imperials they'll use for target practice are you CIGAs. They always get rid of unstable elements first. Makes places easier to rule." He laughed grimly as he held the man's gaze with his own. "And if the League *doesn't* win after it restarts the war," he added, "then likely as not, you'll gasp out your life swinging at the end of a rope, because lynch mobs don't wait for legal justice."

A momentary shadow of fear clouded Amherst's proud visage, but he recovered swiftly and again grasped his lapels in a pose of high dudgeon. "Were you in uniform, Brim, I should have you thrown in Avalon's darkest prison for that sort of presumptive insolence."

"But you can't," Brim replied with a smile. "In the first place, you don't have a witness. And besides, zukeed, you implied it yourself: I am now an officer in the Fluvannian Fleet. Throwing me in prison would cause an international incident."

"Low-life Carescrian slime," Amherst swore under his breath. "Then I was right!" His face became a mask of ghastly anger. "You will know my power someday, mark those words well." With that, he whirled around and stormed away from the table—directly into a busboy laden with a large tray of dirty dishes. The clattering avalanche of disintegrating plates and silverware focused every eye on the CIGA leader.

In the shocked silence that followed, Brim whispered over his shoulder, "Psst! Commodore. . . ."

Momentarily stunned with embarrassment, Amherst turned. "What now, Brim?" he demanded.

"Watch your step, old man," Brim warned him with a straight face.

The enraged CIGA nearly lost his footing on the pile of shattered crockery, then retreated among the tables toward the door. As he exited, he was trailed by a beautiful blond man wearing the uniform of an ensign.

Brim took a deep breath as conversation resumed in the dining room, then shook his head in frustration. It was people like that who had doomed the comfortable civilization he lived in. With the Admiralty riddled by powerful CIGAs like him and the Fleet reduced to a shadow of its former self, the next war was going to be a lot more destructive than most Imperials could imagine. He'd just missed seeing the League's new Gorn-Hoff killer-cruiser in Fluvanna, but it promised to be a *most* destructive ship. It would have to be, if only to survive fights with Starfuries. He sipped his meem thoughtfully. Before the coming war was over, even Avalon itself would feel the power of ships like that just as the poor souls in the outskirts of the Empire—like Carescria—did at the beginning of the last war. People had no idea what was in store for them. As the Emperor had so aptly put it, a terrible darkness was settling rapidly over the whole galaxy, and everyone—without exception—would in one way or another be most devastatingly affected by it.

Only days later, Calhoun departed abruptly—and in mufti—for little Beta Jago, a small but wealthy dominion that had been high on Nergol Triannic's "want list" since before the previous war. Only great sacrifices on the part of the Imperial Fleet had saved the little star system then, and now the League clearly intended to finish the job they had started so many years previously.

When Brim saw him off from the Sodeskayan section of the Grand Imperial Terminal, he had real feelings of concern, not only for Calhoun who was knowingly putting himself at risk, but also for himself. Without question, if anything happened to the elder Carescrian, he would be forced to take on much more of the IVG's administrative and political tasks. And he did not feel he was ready to perform *either* of the duties, especially the political ones.

Precisely one week later, civilized dominions throughout the galaxy received their first electrifying shock of what many recognized to be the beginning of the next war: Nergol Triannic's League attacked and overran the tiny dominion of Beta Jago, capturing all five populated planets in little more than three Standard Days. Almost immediately, news of atrocities began to leak from behind the little dominion's sealed borders. Brutal Controllers were quick to extract a frightful toll of the citizens, phlegmatically murdering thousands of the weak and elderly, as well as notable enemies, merely to satisfy the basic expedient of reducing occupation costs. Significantly many of the staunchest Leaguer proponents among the native Beta Jago populace were among the first to die. As the Bears always predicted, traitors were considered to be among the most inconsistent elements in a civilization. And inconsistency was a most notably difficult attribute to govern.

Messages from Calhoun, of course, ceased immediately. But by that time, Brim had no more time to squander on worries. He was caught up with preparations for transferring *Starfury*— and as many of her crew as possible—to a new base of operations in Fluvanna. Clearly, that strategic little dominion would be next on Triannic's list of conquests.

CHAPTER 6

Fluvanna

"Almost time, Cap'm," Barbousse warned.

Grimly, Brim checked his timepiece; it was. "Thanks, Chief," he said, straightening his Fleet Cloak. It was a job he found *most* difficult—notwithstanding years of practice. "Let's get it over with," he grunted.

Barbousse nodded and stepped out onto the stage, paused dramatically for a moment, then shouted, "THE CAP'M!"

Directly, *Starfury*'s ninety-one officers and ratings jumped to their feet in a confusion of scrapes and coughs that belied any capacity whatsoever for running a starship.

When the room became still, Brim strode to the lectern, peering apprehensively out into the auditorium Drummond had reserved for him in the Admiralty Annex. He was going to considerably upset these people before much more of the morning had passed. "Seats," he ordered crisply.

After another round of shuffling and scraping, a semblance of quiet returned to the room.

"I have a strange announcement this afternoon," Brim continued abruptly, "as well as what may be the strangest proposition you've been offered this side of Voot's tangled beard."

Frowns of curiosity appeared everywhere.

"First," he continued briskly, "it is my bizarre duty to inform you that I.F.S. *Starfury* has been leased to the Fluvannian government for a period of at least a year. She will depart Avalon as soon as she can be prepared.''

A momentary stillness fell like a chill over the room, followed by an angry stir of bewildered dismay.

"*Starfury*?" someone asked. "Leased?"

"To *Fluvanna*. . .?"

"Somebody sure sold us out to the CIGAs this time."

"'Oo 'av the bloody Wogs got to crew her, anyhow? She's no thraggling antique like the rest of their so-called Fleet!''

Brim held up his hand. "Before you say anything more," he enjoined, "let me offer that proposition I mentioned."

Grudgingly, order returned to the room.

"How many of you would like to sign up for the Fluvannian Fleet," he asked, "with no change in rank?"

This time, the room stayed silent for a few shocked moments. "Captain Brim," one of the Drive Room officers called out by and by, "have you joined the CIGAs, or something?"

"Yeah!" another joined in hotly. "Why in the Universe would any of *us* want to join the Fluvannian Fleet?"

"Well," Brim replied easily, "one reason might be to continue serving in *Starfury*. As Petty Officer Kenzie pointed out, someone's got to run her, and right now, *we're* the only ones in the known Universe with any practical experience."

"When you use the word 'we,' Captain Brim," one of Barbousse's assistants demanded warily, "does that include *you*, too?"

"You bet it does, Singleton," Brim replied. "I signed up more than a week ago, with Commodore Calhoun. They're fitting our new Fluvannian uniforms as I speak." Smiling, he held up his hand once more for silence—he definitely had their attention now. "Here's the whole story," he continued and launched into an abbreviated version of Calhoun's standard presentation—to which he added a description of Greyffin IV's guarantee. By the time he finished, the room had become very still indeed. "The deck is again open for questions," he offered, "this time, I'm accepting serious ones."

After a long time, a single hand went up. "What about the

ones of us who might be killed in the line of duty?'' a Gunnery Officer asked.

"Good for the estate, if nothing else,'' Brim answered grimly. "Death and disability benefits are separately paid by *each* government, giving you a one hundred percent increase, because both Services pay Admiralty scale."

"How about maintenance for the ship, Captain?'' another asked.

"That,'' Brim answered truthfully, "will be a real challenge. You've seen Magor yourselves, and we're to be based at a place called Varnholm, nearly a thousand c'lenyts nearer the boreal pole—where facilities are described by the Fluvannians themselves as . . . he consulted his notes . . . 'somewhat deteriorated.' I've only seen HoloPictures, but I tend to agree with the descriptions."

"You're right, Captain,'' the officer agreed. "It sounds like a real challenge to me."

"Commander Brim,'' an expensively uniformed newcomer asked, "how long do we have to consider this, er, offer?''

"Until morning,'' Brim said. "We embark for Fluvanna as soon as the ship is prepared to lift."

"And if we decide we've had enough of that backwater, what then, Captain?''

"You get an instant transfer somewhere else in the Fleet,'' Brim replied. "That's why I've got to know your decision almost immediately. Replacements are difficult to find, and we're in a hurry."

"I'm ready now!'' somebody shouted from the audience.

"Yeah, me, too,'' another seconded. "Where do we sign up?''

Half surprised by the response, Brim pointed to a work table that Barbousse and a Fluvannian representative had just plugged into a secure data outlet near the door. "You sign up with Mr. Barbousse at the table back there,'' he said. "He'll also help you transfer out, if you're of a mind to do that. . . .''

Directly following the meeting, fifteen officers and seventy ratings had signed themselves into the Fluvannian Fleet, leaving one officer and five ordinary starsailors to be replaced the next day.

The following morning, however, pudgy Sublieutenant Vasil Huugo of the Communications Section, a native Avalonian, reported back aboard after consulting with his family during an all-night session. His signature completed wardroom staffing with no changes in personnel. But by midday, Barbousse appeared on the bridge with bad news. "It looks like none of the five refusing spacemen have shown a change of heart, Cap'm," he reported with a frown.

"Hmm," Brim muttered, looking up from a test sequence a Logics Mate was running on his power console. "Any of 'em going to be hard to replace?"

"Not if you know where to look, Cap'm," the big rating answered with a wink.

Within a metacycle, a sleek military van pulled up at the foot of the brow to disgorge five of the toughest-looking Petty Officers the Carescrian believed he had *ever* encountered: scars, eye patches, artificial limbs; collectively, they had them all. As the group stumped through the ship's hatch, each made a peculiar little bow to Barbousse, who stood quietly to one side with his arms folded, nodding in return. Brim wanted to know *nothing* about their backgrounds. Barbousse had picked them, and he was certain they would turn out to be the most reliable—and able—hands on the ship.

In a few days, all forms and contracts were duly signed while ninety-two sets of Fluvannian uniforms changed hands. Brim and his crew of "mercenaries" set course for Magor on 31/52011 aboard a completely reprovisioned R.F.S. *Starfury*, newest, most modern warship in the Fluvannian Fleet. They made landfall at Varnholm little more than six days later (after another "unofficial" record run), where they discovered to their dismay that conditions were far worse than the Fluvannians had led them to believe.

The age-blackened stone ruin of Varnholm Hall was *very* desolate, standing some distance from the scruffy village it once ruled on a barren, rocky slope that overlooked storm-tossed Penard Bay. Below, spoiling what little strand existed between the slope and the deep waters of the bay, lay two long rows of ancient stone gravity pools, remnant of a mining operation that had petered out more than a century in the past. Many of those on the seaward side had tumbled walls, victims of the storms frequenting that particularly depressing corner of the planet. As promised, however, four of the timeworn structures reported themselves to be operational when *Starfury* descended out of the overcast, and two of *them* appeared to be large enough for a cruiser.

Viewed from the air, the hall itself—or rather what remained of it—was a melancholy relic, tediously rectangular with crumbling stumps of towers at each corner and a half-ruined gate house on its landward end. A huge, central dome had rolled completely off the main foundations and lay to one side like some great shattered piece of crockery. Thick stone curtain walls between the tower stumps were reasonably complete, but any battlements on them had all but disappeared over the years.

"Not very promising," Brim commented bleakly as Tissaurd banked *Starfury* into a climbing turn and headed out to sea for a landing. He glanced back at the receding shoreline. "Especially the xaxtdamned gravity pools." In little more than one Standard Month, they would have to coax a minimum of fifteen into operation: eleven Starfuries and four ancient ED-4 freighters that Calhoun had managed to secure at the last moment. And that would allow no guests or—worse—spares when the century-old repulsion generators broke down, as they inevitably would, no matter how methodically they might be maintained.

Within cycles of their landfall, Tissaurd had taxied to the largest gravity pool, nudging *Starfury*'s prow just over the seaward rim before she braked to a halt. "Looks all right to me, Skipper," she said, peering over the nose through the Hyperscreens. "What do you think?"

Brim rubbed his chin. Below, six huge, extraordinarily old-looking repulsion generators were somehow filling the great pit with a reassuring amber glow. On top of the far wall, a number of villagers had gathered in small groups and were variously waving, jumping up and down, and holding their ears against the deafening rumble that would be coming from both the gravity pool and *Starfury* herself. Clearly, the semi-abandoned star anchorage relied on local residents when it was time to deploy the pool's optical mooring devices. "I guess I don't have any gems of wisdom for you, Number One," he admitted at length. "Maybe you ought to play it safe like you did in Magor and keep a little lift on the ship herself—just in case."

Tissaurd nodded agreement. "Strana'," she said, "how about maintaining about five percent hover on her for a while?"

"Five percent hover is now minimum," Zaftrak responded presently.

Tissaurd nodded and turned her attention to a small monitor between the Helmsmans' consoles. It displayed the visage of a bearded man with a large nose—and an even larger mustache —who wore typical Fluvannian apparel, including one of the ubiquitous crimson fezes. "Mr. Bogwa'zzi," she pronounced carefully, "I shall appreciate your assistance now."

The man nodded. "Switching I am the machine now to power," he said in Avalonian with a great toothy grin, clearly proud of this linguistic achievement. On the far wall of the gravity pool, a ruby light blazed out from what appeared to be a globe mounted on a tripod. The figure of a man beside it waved—at the same time Bogwa'zzi's head bobbed in the monitor. "Can you scrutinize this beam?" he asked.

"I, er, scrutinize the beam, Mr. Bogwa'zzi," Tissaurd acknowledged with a grin. "You may now activate its side lobes."

As Brim watched from his station on the port side of *Starfury*'s bridge, the beam began to separate into vertical lines. He knew that it would remain steady for Tissaurd in her more central console, but for Powderham, the Navigator seated behind the starboard Hyperscreens, it would now be broken into horizontal lines.

"Side lobes, ah, how do you say . . . ?"

"Activated," Tissaurd prompted.

"Ah yes, *activated*," the Fluvannian reported a moment later.

"Thank you, Mr. Bogwa'zzi," Tissaurd replied, nodding to herself as if she had just completed some internal checklist. "All docking cupolas: stand by your mooring beams," she ordered over the blower. When each had acknowledged, she began to nudge the ship forward with deft thrusts of her fingers over the power console, then applied full gravity brakes almost immediately.

Starfury came to a stop nearly halfway over the pool with her stern still extending out over the roiling strand, kicking up a hail of rocks from the shallow bottom.

Abruptly Tissaurd rose and stood with hands on hips, surveying the situation for nearly half a cycle, before appearing to reach some decision. "Send the bow beam over," she commanded. Instantly a powerful shaft of greenish-yellow light shimmered out from *Starfury*'s bow and contacted a great optical bollard centered in the inland wall of the pool. "Send over the forward bow springs, too," she ordered after a further moment of study, "port and starboard." Instantly the forward springs crackled to matching bollards on the side walls.

Brim nodded in approval. Tissaurd was playing it safe. *Starfury* could winch herself onto the old gravity pool. With the primitive docking devices available, it was an intelligent course to follow. Even at their lowest power settings, the ship's gravity generators were clearly too powerful for this kind of maneuvering without high-precision tracking devices these ancient pools clearly lacked.

"Take the bow and forward springs to the warping head and heave 'round," Tissaurd continued in terms that considerably predated star flight itself. The first three mooring beams flashed brilliantly as they took the strain and began to draw the big ship forward onto the pool. A moment later the diminutive officer ordered both aft bow springs sent over and followed these with the two sets of quarter springs as the optical cleats came in range of their particular bollards on the pool walls. Only when *Starfury*'s stern approached the seaward wall did she give the order to avast heaving on the three beams forward. The cruiser now had sufficient headway to coast the rest of the way into the pool on her own.

At last, with the stern just inboard of the wall, Tissaurd projected the stern beam to the seaward wall and immediately called for a "check," holding heavy tension on the blazing shaft of light, but letting it slip as necessary to prevent it from overloading the projector circuits and possibly blowing a fuse. Moments later,

Starfury snubbed to a gentle halt—amid a round of applause on the bridge. The ship was almost perfectly centered over the six generators beneath her hull. ''Double up all beams,'' the grinning Tissaurd ordered as she secured her helm and joined hands above her head in a little sign of victory.

Brim smiled to himself as a rust-mottled brow squeaked and squealed out from the ancient control shack. Tissaurd richly deserved the applause. She had done a magnificent job.

During the next week, Brim's worst concerns proved far too conservative. Had the base been only ''somewhat deteriorated,'' as advertised, things might have been reasonably manageable. Unfortunately, ''nonexistent'' did a better job of describing many of the critical services necessary for sustaining a fleet of up-to-date starships like *Starfury*.

He had been reasonably prepared, for example, to deal with the remote area's dearth of up-to-date medical facilities, and had made certain that *Starfury*'s sickbay was crowded with medical supplies. In addition, the first ED-4 was already on its lumbering way with much of its cargo hold dedicated to healing machines and life-support systems. But he still had to find somewhere to house the whole medical complex. Good as they might be, starship sickbays could offer temporary care at best. Unfortunately, he had few choices outside the ruined castle itself.

At least housing and administrative spaces posed no problem to operations. Nor did sustenance for the crews. Ships that could operate for extended periods in deep space simply provided these amenities as part and parcel of their essential operations. Repair and maintenance facilities were, however, *totally* lacking, and those constituted another matter completely. He'd dispatched his other three ED-4s to Bromwich for spare parts the day he'd lifted *Starfury* for Fluvanna. But maintenance *parts* were not the same as maintenance *facilities*, and both would be necessary if there were any chance at all of keeping the IVG ships spaceworthy—especially under combat conditions.

He'd first attempted to find help in Fluvanna itself. However, shortly after the Leaguers found out about *Starfury*'s affiliation with the Fluvannian Fleet, all attempts to procure heavy equipment from local sources fell on deaf ears. Beyazh had used his considerable influence to change the situation, but Nergol Triannic's minions had a powerful presence in Magor, and they were now exerting every scrap of influence they could muster to insure failure of the new "Imperial base" so close to the capital they coveted.

Likewise, procurement efforts from home produced little in the way of results—except that these refusals were at least sent with sympathy. Even Drummond's best efforts had been stopped cold by the enraged Puvis Amherst and his CIGAs, whose anti-Fleet efforts had been further galvanized when the Emperor's IVG offer became public. Some of their demonstrations had even become violent, including one in Courtland Plaza on the Admiralty stairs that left seven Fleet officers and fifteen riot police injured—along with fifty-nine hospitalized CIGAs.

Brim had just returned from a hike to the ruined manor and was sitting disconsolately in the wardroom nursing a short meem when Tissaurd slid into a chair beside him and signaled the Steward for a goblet of her own. "You don't look happy, Skipper," she said with a serious mien. "And you haven't since we got here. Want to talk?"

Brim grimaced. "I guess I'm not very good at hiding my feelings, am I?" he said.

"Not from somebody who's gotten to know you as well as I have," she chuckled. "And that doesn't even count my little verbal indiscretion at the Mustafa's party a while back."

"I wish it were as easy as admiring your décolleté, Number One," he replied with a grin. "Unfortunately, this problem has to do with heavy maintenance equipment."

"I kind of thought that might be it," she said, lifting her goblet from the Steward's tray. "Especially since the manor's old meem cellars will serve nicely as our base hospital. So what's the problem? Barbousse's work crews have already repaired five gravity pools. And except for *Starfury* herself, you'll be starting off with brand-new starships and all the spares you can use for a while."

"What's the *problem*?" Brim demanded in a harried voice. "Tissaurd: an easier question might be what *isn't* a problem.

Gravity pools are only the beginning of starship maintenance—especially in combat situations. What we need are machine shops, gantry cranes big enough to change Drive crystals, gravity pads." He thought for a moment. "You know," he said presently, "the kind of heavy equipment *Refit Enterprise* provided at Gimmas Haefdon. They couldn't have changed our space radiators without that kind of support."

Tissaurd shrugged and sipped her meem. "Sorry, Skipper," she said gently. "I guess I knew all that. I simply wasn't ready to start tackling those problems yet. They're too far in the future."

"Problems are never too far in the future," Brim said didactically.

"They are if there's nothing you can do about them," Tissaurd countered firmly. "I've found that when I've reached a brick wall about a problem that's still off in the future, it's a good idea to simply step back and wait for something to change. It usually does, and then I can go at the problem again using a different set of parameters—with perhaps a better chance of doing something about it."

Brim nodded. "Tell me about brick walls," he grumbled. "I've done everything I could think of today and achieved no perceptible results at all."

"Oh, you may have gotten more results than you imagine," Tissaurd said with a little nod. "Maybe you started that *very* something that will eventually make everything work out the way you want. Of course, you may *not* have, either. The only thing you know for certain right now is that *nothing* is for certain. And that's good, because if nothing changes, then you're still at your brick wall. Right?"

"Right," Brim admitted sheepishly. After that, they sat in silence for a long while with nothing to say.

"Good meem," she said at last, staring into her goblet.

"Yeah," Brim replied.

"Too bad we're shipmates," Tissaurd said quietly, draining the last of her meem.

"Why do you say that, Number One?" Brim asked.

"Because," the petite officer answered, setting her goblet on the table and getting to her feet, "with your problems, you need a woman to take you to bed for a spell—and it can't be me."

Brim looked up and shook his head. "I think you're right, Nadia," he said wryly. "Twice."

"I'm sorriest about the second part," she said as she started for the hatch.

"So am I," Brim called after her; then she was gone.

After the landfall of their first ancient ED-4 transport and its cargo of medical equipment, Commander Penelope Hesternal, *Starfury*'s Medical Officer, immediately established an excellent field hospital in the deep, cool cellars of the ruined hall—staffing it with a bevy of handsome male nurses she recruited during a diplomatic run to Magor. Only days later, the other ED-4s arrived from Bromwich with spare parts literally cramming their holds. Within metacycles, Barbousse and three crews of starsailors (augmented by hefty teams of locals) commenced 'round-the-clock efforts to reactivate the site's ancient gravity pools. And for those not otherwise occupied, either Brim or Tissaurd took *Starfury* aloft twice a day for gunnery drills and "swapping" classes during which everyone got a chance to suffer someone else's duty station. It allowed little time to become bored with the desolate surroundings or grouse about the primitive conditions—or focus on any of the hundred and one troubles that can result from a combination of monotony and the close proximity of shipboard life.

Almost before they knew it, a morning arrived when the first pair of Starfury MK-1s were due: R.F.S. *Starsovereign* and R.F.S *Starglory*. Brim and Ambassador Beyazh had just emerged from an inspection tour of the new hospital, and were standing alongside the crumbling stone walls of Varnholm Hall where the Ambassador's launch hovered, ready for takeoff.

"Captain," the Ambassador prompted, cocking his head to one side and staring out to sea, "did you hear that?"

Brim nodded. "Sounds like Admiralty-type gravity generators to me," he said, looking out over crested, gray-green rollers marching endlessly against the ancient gravity pools at the foot of the piebald slope. "It's either our first two Starfuries or the very grandfather of all thunderstorms, Mr. Ambassador," he replied. *Starfury* herself hovered quietly below on one of the inboard pools, testing her moorings in the gusty—and perpetual—wind.

"So the adventure resumes," Beyazh said grimly, glancing up at Varnholm's perpetual overcast as if he could see the ships from where he stood.

Brim nodded. "And the wounds and the deaths," he added.

The Ambassador pursed his lips as the thunder swiftly rose in volume. "Why is it we always end up shooting at each other when we have disagreements?" he growled. "If there really is a Universe who cares and loves, like the Gradygroats teach, then how can war be *permitted* to happen?"

Brim had no response to the man's words—in any case, they were all but drowned out by the velvet thunder of two Starfury-class starships descending majestically out of the overcast little more than a c'lenyt offshore. The big ships paralleled the coast for a time, keeping close formation and tearing the cloud base into long tubes of furiously swirling tatters. Abruptly *Starfury*'s KA'PPA beacon began to strobe from the pool site, and in perfect concert, the MK-1s heeled fifty degrees to starboard and swung out to sea, their massive shapes hazed by wild vortices of gravitons pouring from their pontoons before they disappeared in Varnholm's perpetual sea mist.

Less than a cycle afterward, a siren wailed and the renewed section of gravity pools came alive with groups of people gathering here and there to don protective garments, start repulsion generators, move large wheeled cylinders about, and make last-moment adjustments to a multitude of tripod-mounted globes that glowed with every color of the spectrum. The prodigious figure of Barbousse could be seen at the end of an instrument jetty, his Fleet Cloak streaming in the wind as he activated one of Varnholm's ancient magnetic beacons with an enormous metal crank. Brim watched the operations with emotional fascination —almost pride. Imperial Blue Capes possessed a certain mystique: a whole set of skills and mettle that were never totally understood by landsmen. No matter what was required of them, they carried out their duties with an air of confidence and imperturbability that came as much from constant testing as it did from millenniums-old tradition. And it made them practically infallible.

Far out to sea, the thundering generators abruptly changed pitch, then continued in a much reduced note. "Sounds as if they're down," Beyazh observed, "and you'd better be on your way to greet them, Mr. Base Commander."

Brim laughed. "Not me," he protested. "I've got my hands full just trying to keep *Starfury* out of trouble."

The Ambassador frowned. "Captain," he said in a very serious voice, "whether or not you like it—or even feel particularly *ready* for it—you are right now in command of this so-called base. It was set up on *your* orders by people from the starship *you* command. In other words, it's *yours*. At least until Commodore Calhoun finds his way back from Beta Jagow."

Brim bit his lip. "I suppose you're right, aren't you," he said.

"Never question a Diplomatic Officer," Beyazh chuckled. "Greatest bunch of know-it-alls in the galaxy. Sometimes, we're even right—as I am now."

"I guess I hadn't been thinking about much else except how to get the base in shape," Brim replied. "And if I *had* thought of taking charge," he added with a chuckle, "I might have quit work on the spot."

"Too late for that now," Beyazh said didactically, sending a perfectly horrid parody of the Fleet salute Brim's way. "You'd better get yourself down there so you can greet the newcomers when they arrive. Someone *has* to be in charge, my friend."

Brim returned the salute and started down the hill. "See you again, Mr. Ambassador," he said.

"Safely—in Avalon, one hopes," Beyazh called after him. "Once you take out that space fort the Leaguers are building."

Brim laughed in spite of himself. Clearly, few secrets escaped the purview of His Excellency. In the next moments, two shadows, darker than the mist, loomed perhaps one and a half c'lenyts out to sea. These rapidly defined themselves into R.F.S. *Starsovereign* and R.F.S *Starglory* with their distinctive tri-hulls and great batteries of disruptors. The two starships were keeping close station abreast as they drove toward shore, majestic and powerful, the sea creaming away from triple footprints while shimmering KA'PPA rings spread deliberately from tall masts that remained serenely steady against the gray sky. Within cycles, *Starsovereign* had lined up on the number 23 gravity pool, and presently the big ship was secured. Moments later the noise of her generators died in a haze of stray gravitons that drifted away in the afternoon grayness in a big, shimmering cloud. *Starglory* moored on pool number 19 shortly afterward —just as Brim arrived at the brow.

"You'll be goin' aboard, Captain Brim?" the brow operator, a leading Torpedoman, called over the noise of the repulsion generators while he guided a newly painted gangway toward the ship's main hatch.

Brim considered for a moment, peering up at the bustle in *Starsovereign*'s bridge, then he shook his head. "I don't think so, Garrivacchio," he said. "But when you have the connections secure, make to the Captain . . . ah . . . 'Thanks in advance for . . . the bottle of Logish Meem you will bring with you to my cabin aboard *Starfury* at Evening:0:30.' Got that?"

" 'Thanks in advance for the bottle of Logish Meem you will bring with you to my cabin aboard *Starfury* at' . . . um . . . 'Evening:0:30,' Captain," Garrivacchio repeated with a grin.

"You've got it," Brim said. "And pass that same message on to the Captain of R.F.S. *Starglory* immediately you secure the brow."

"Ave, Captain," the Torpedoman assured him with a quick salute. "I'll have the same message delivered within five cycles."

At precisely thirty cycles past the Evening watch, Barbousse answered a polite tapping on the door to Brim's stateroom.

"Come in, gentlemen," Brim said, extending his hand to the first officer over the coaming, "Wilf Brim, here."

"Fortune McKenzie, of *Starglory*," the other said with a grin, offering his hand while he turned over a bottle of obviously Logish Meem to Barbousse. He was a short man, stocky and powerfully built, who clearly had not an ounce of fat on his body. His foursquare face was framed by a close-cut beard and short gray hair. He had a small, rather common nose, a thin mouth, and the mortally precise eyes of a savant marksman. Brim recognized the man immediately. Long ago, *Starglory*'s Master had served with Commander Englyde Zantir, the famous leader of Destroyer Flotilla 91, as an Imperial Marine. Indeed, there was nothing phony about the man's prowess as a military Helmsman, either. Two great scars ran from his forehead to his chin, souvenirs of a thousand-odd hand-to-hand skirmishes with the League—and he had applied the same fighting skills to piloting an E-Class destroyer in the Battle of Atalanta: keen eyes, swift reactions, and a dashing spirit. "I think the gentleman behind me will need little introduction to you," McKenzie added, grinning.

Brim looked up just in time to see a tall, blond Commander in an impeccable uniform step over the coaming. He had blue eyes that sparkled with good-natured humor, a grand promontory for a nose, and the droll, confident smile reserved for the very rich. "I say," the man muttered with a fictitious look of confusion, "have you chaps any idea which way Avalon might be. I'm from *Starsovereign*, and our navigator got frightfully confused about a day ago. . . ."

"Toby Moulding!" Brim exclaimed. "What in the crazy name of Voot are *you* doing here?"

Moulding grinned and handed Barbousse a magnum of Logish Meem so ancient that the bottle was actually made of *glass*. "I suppose I shall be doing the same as you and Commander McKenzie," he said, grasping Brim's hand. "It's my understanding that the poor benighted Fluvannians have hired us to fly these bloody buses around, frightening Leaguers, and such. That's how I'm to earn my modest living, at any rate."

"I suppose you two have more time in Starfuries than anyone else in the Universe," McKenzie said with a grin. "If I weren't so hardheaded, I think I'd be intimidated."

"Let *him* intimidate you," Moulding replied, pointing to Brim, "not me. Aside from the metacycles I've spent training in *Starsovereign*, all I've done is chase the man around in some of Mark Valerian's racers."

"Well, that's chasing I never got a chance to do," McKenzie replied.

"Before this is over," Brim predicted, "we'll all probably have more chasing than we want."

"Amen," the ex-gunner agreed, taking a goblet of Logish Meem Barbousse served discreetly from a magnificent silver tray that Brim couldn't remember seeing before.

"And speaking of 'tired,' old chap," Moulding interjected, "you must be damned tired yourself after getting this base set up." He sipped his meem and looked appraisingly into the goblet. "Excellent," he said at length, "like the job you've done around here. Calhoun's lucky they had you to put in charge."

Brim was about to comment about *that* when Beyazh's words echoed in his ear: *Someone* has *to be in charge, my friend.* The man was right. "Only till the Commodore shows up," he hedged.

"*That* could be a while," McKenzie commented. "Last I heard of Baxter, he was somewhere in Beta Jagow when the League attacked."

"True," Brim said with a grimace, "but I'm far from giving up on him yet."

"If I know Calhoun," Moulding interjected, "he's not only safe in Beta Jagow, he's also doing something that will eventually cause the bloody Leaguers a *lot* of trouble. Mark my words."

"I hope you're right," Brim said, peering into his meem for a moment. "I *certainly* hope you're right."

By the time the evening was over, the three officers managed to resurrect at least an aeon of war history, while putting away a *lot* of Logish Meem.

Early next morning, Brim balanced himself—and one mighty hangover—atop *Starfury*'s bridge, a dizzying seventy irals from the surface of the gravity pool while Barbousse supervised a sealant repair to Hyperscreen panel 81D. As their little party of maintenance ratings eased the heavy crystal plate back in place, his ears picked up the thunder of approaching gravity generators. Big ones. And they were *definitely* not the Galaxy 10-320-B1Cs that powered ancient ED-4s below Light Speed velocities. Looking up into the overcast, he frowned. "If those are League ships, we could be in *big* trouble," he grumbled to Barbousse. "Wonder why Tissaurd hasn't sounded some sort of warning."

Barbousse nodded. "I can't say as I know, Cap'm," he replied, "but I'd really find that hard to believe that Lieutenant Tissaurd is prone to makin' mistakes like that."

Brim nodded, but the noise continued to vex him, especially since the mysterious starship continued to circle, hidden in the dense overcast. Finally Tissaurd herself popped through the hatch. "Oh, there you are, Skipper," she called. "That's a ship from the Sodeskayan national space line, AkroKahn, up there with a cargo of spare parts. And your friend Nik Ursis is on board, demanding Chief Barbousse's personal guarantee of a bottle of good Logish Meem before they'll land."

Brim and Barbousse looked at each other for a moment. "Thank the Universe the crews got those extra pools going yesterday," the latter whispered, casting his eyes skyward.

Brim looked down at Tissaurd for a moment. "Seems to me you said a few words about starting something that could bring down a wall, didn't you?"

The tiny officer grinned. "Watch out for flying bricks," she said. Then, spontaneously, both broke out laughing.

"What do you think, Chief," Brim said to Barbousse after a few moments, "are you going to let 'em land?"

"I think I'd better, Cap'm," the big rating said with a look of mock concern. "Strikes me they might just stay up there till we do." Then he winked. "Besides, I've stashed away a few cases of Grompers, vintage '81, that I know Polkovnik Ursis especially relishes."

"Why am I not surprised?" Brim laughed. "Then we'll deliver a case in person! Number One," he ordered, "message Ursis that the Chief capitulates unconditionally, and"—he thought for a moment—"yes, as soon as they moor, he will lead a party to their brow and surrender the meem."

"I'll have that relayed to the Bears," Tissaurd chuckled with an overdone salute and disappeared into the hatch.

"Call Moulding and McKenzie, too," Brim called after her with a grin. "They ought to share in the capitulation, after all."

"An' we'll finish here in plenty of time for all that, Cap'm," Barbousse promised, casting a baleful eye at the three maintenance hands, "won't we, gentlemen?"

"Aye, Chief!" the trio said in unison, bending to their work with renewed fervor. No one ever questioned Barbousse's ability to get action out of work parties.

Indeed, the work detail completed their task in record time. Brim finished his inspection long before the giant, bluff-bowed AkroKahn freighter thundered in from the swirling mists, stark white except for the line's distinctive red hull stripe and wreathed six-pointed stars on either side of the bridge, aft of the Hyperscreens.

Sacha Muromets was one of the Sodeskayan Morzik-class freighters: big, good-looking starships of twenty thousand milstons, intended for the general carrying trade, but each had accommodations for passengers as well. Out of the corner of his eye, the Carescrian saw a beacon begin to flash on one of the newly refurbished gravity pools and the starship's taxiing speed dropped off as the Helmsman brought her head around. Then, as she came abeam of the beacon, she swung hard to port with the gray waters thumping and foaming under her hull until she drove onto the pool like a ship half her size, putting mooring beams across in a most spacemanlike manner. The Imperial ground crews had her secured in a matter of cycles.

"Nice," Barbousse said quietly. "I'll wager it's a Bear at the helm."

"Nice indeed," Brim chuckled, leading the way back through the hatch and into the starship, "but I wouldn't touch your wager with a ten-iral pole. . . ." The occasional Bears who chose to fly starships were always superb pilots. Cursed with relatively poor eyesight in comparison to other spacefaring races, most Sodeskayans preferred to employ their vast intellectual energies by engineering vessels for others to operate.

Trailed by a dusty-looking case of rare old Logish Meem, the little party arrived at the gravity pool only moments before Ursis stepped from the brow, resplendent in full Sodeskayan military regalia: high black boots, an olive-green greatcoat, and a billed service cap, all trimmed in crimson. Bright crimson epaulettes with the three gold stars of a Sodeskayan Polkovnik embellished his broad shoulders.

Brim saluted. "I thought you'd be at Dytasburg," he shouted over the din of six thundering repulsion generators. "It can't even be time for midterms yet, is it?"

"Academy is in good hands, Wyilf Ansor," Ursis replied, returning the salute with a sober look. "Dr. Borodov has come out of retirement to act as Dean until I return. My place is here at present; Sodeskayan intelligence organizations believe Great War will shortly resume." Then his brown eyes softened as he extended his hand. "Is good to be working with you again, my furless friend."

Brim gripped the huge Bear's delicate, six-fingered hand. "I'm awfully glad to see you for a number of reasons, Nik," he said, looking his old friend in the eyes. "And I've brought a number of people whom I know feel the same way."

Ursis looked up and grinned as the others saluted in unison. "Ah *yes*," he boomed, returning the salute with a huge, toothy grin, "Chief Barbousse and his surrender party! Come!" he ordered, sweeping the little group into the brow with his arm. "At top of stairs, Steward will lead you to place where we sacrifice some prisoners!"

Cycles later, in the *Muromets*'s comfortable main dining saloon, he greeted Moulding and Tissaurd, then introduced himself to McKenzie before shaking Barbousse's hand. "Chief," he said, placing a fraternal arm around the big rating's shoulders, "is been long time. Where did you manage to disappear after war? You did even better job than friend Brim here."

Barbousse blushed for a moment, then grinned. "Other people have asked me that, too, Polkovnik Ursis," he said with a mock-serious look, "but I can't seem to remember. Must be one of those memory lapses they talk about."

"I understand," the Bear replied, matching Barbousse's look of concern. Then he winked. "I think Calhoun himself must have had lapse when he put three of us on another operation together, eh?"

"You've heard from Calhoun?" Brim interrupted.

"But of course, Wyilf Ansor," Ursis replied. "Message came through secure network—from covert field operative, of course. He said you needed maintenance apparatus. So I brought some of what you need—a whole ship full, vould you believe? And more is on way."

Brim shook his head in amazement. Somehow, it all made some sort of sense. Bear sense, anyway. "When did you hear from him?" he asked.

Ursis shrugged. "Perhaps two Standard Weeks ago," he replied with a frown. "The Commodore isn't in touch with you?"

"I don't suppose he could be, now that I think about it," Brim said. "Beta Jago's an occupied dominion now, and most of our Imperial intelligence organizations are riddled with CI-GAs."

"He got in touch with us instead," Ursis said, lighting up one of the Sodeskayan's dreaded Zempa pipes. "Is same thing; we Sodeskayans are Imperials, too, in own way. So you got your supplies *and* me—although tomorrow I must temporarily return with *Muromets* to Sodeskayan before my own induction into Fluvannian Fleet." Then he smiled broadly. "But," he added, "according to friend Harry Drummond, combination of you, Chief Barbousse, and myself comprises perhaps greatest threat to League in existence. Is that not so?"

"If nothing else," Brim said, trying unsuccessfully to ignore the Zempa smoke that—at least to humans—smelled a lot like burning yaggloz wool, "we are certainly a great threat to much of the Universe's Logish Meem."

"Aha!" the Bear said, grinning now so his fang gems gleamed. "Until war actually *does* resume, we should certainly attempt to make good on such threats. Speaking of which. . . ."

"Speaking of which . . ." Brim continued, "you said something about Grompers, vintage '81, didn't you, Chief?"

"Absolutely, Cap'm," Barbousse replied with a twinkle in his eyes, indicating the dusty meem case that hovered just inside the room.

"Grompers '81?" the Bear said, holding an index finger in

the air. "Ah, but I *knew* there must be good reason I travel nearly halfway across galaxy to end up in remote parts of Fluvanna. Chief, you will do honors . . . ?"

Just before a slightly woozy Brim turned in that evening, he heard a light tapping at his door. Barbousse was in the hall with a sealed envelope. "Personal message for you, Cap'm," he said quietly. "I thought I'd seal the hardcopy and deliver it personally on the way to m' cabin."

Brim nodded. "Which is all the way at the other end of the hull," he observed with a frown.

"Beggin' the Cap'm's pardon," Barbousse said, handing over a sealed blue plastic envelope, "but . . . well, it *was* a personal message, an' all."

Brim squeezed the man's forearm. "You take damned good care of me, Utrillo Barbousse," he said.

Barbousse grinned. "Don't want anythin' to happen to you, Cap'm," he said. "It'd be too easy goin' back to the Governor's privateer—an' then I'd probably get myself killed."

"What makes you think it'll be any different with me?" Brim asked. "We went through some pretty hairy times during the last war."

"Well, Cap'm," Barbousse replied emphatically, "there's no way I can refute *that*, now. But if I *do* have to get myself killed, at least with you I'll go in service to the Empire. An' that's mortally important to me." He shrugged. "Besides," he added, "we *have* had some excitin' times together, haven't we, sir? Like when we captured that bender with the little spin-grav launch from I.F.S. *Intractable*."

"It's rarely been boring," Brim chuckled, recalling that they had nearly been vaporized a number of times during that desperate action.

"Good night, Cap'm," Barbousse said, interrupting Brim's reverie. "You'll want to be woken early so you and Polkovnik Ursis can work on settin' up that covert supply line to Commissioner Gallsworthy at the Atalanta Fleet Base. *Sacha Muromets* is scheduled to lift before midday."

"Thanks, Chief," Brim said, starting to shut the door.

"Oh, an', Cap'm . . ." Barbousse added.

"Yes, Chief?"

"Probably, you won't want to wait until morning to read the message I brought," the big rating said with a quick salute. Then he hurried off down the hall.

Brim settled wearily into an expensive ophet-leather recliner. It was one of the few luxuries he afforded himself in *Starfury*'s commodious Captain's cabin. He peered at the envelope. No clue there: Barbousse had sealed the message into a standard unclassified hardcopy container. Frowning, he ripped off the side of the envelope, puffed it open, and extracted a single sheet of common message plastic used to record unclassified KA'PPA messages. It was from an old acquaintance, and its short message made his heart feel as if it would burst from his chest.

QQOW-97RTRV762349HUSE GROUP KJ64L 132/52010

FROM: H. AMBRIDGE, RUDOLPHO, THE TOROND

TO: LCDR. W. A. BRIM, R.F.F.
CAPTAIN, R.F.S. *STARFURY*
VARNHOLM HALL, ORDU, FLUVANNA.

COMMANDER BRIM:

HER SERENE MAJESTY, GRAND DUCHESS MARGOT EFFER'WYCK-LAKARN BIDS ME INFORM YOU OF HER PLANNED MORNING ARRIVAL IN MAGOR 136/5210 ABOARD T.S.S. *KATUKA* FOR THE STATE CELEBRATION OF NABOB EYREN'S FIFTIETH BIRTH ANNIVERSARY. THE DUCHESS WILL REPRESENT THE TOROND IN LIEU OF GRAND DUKE ROGAN WHOSE SCHEDULE PRECLUDES HIS ATTENDANCE. SHE SENDS THESE WORDS FOR YOU:

O' THAT 'TWERE POSSIBLE
AFTER LONG GRIEF AND PAIN
TO FIND THE ARMS OF MY TRUE LOVE
ROUND ME ONCE AGAIN!
LARITIEES   /31887

THIS MESSAGE ALSO CONTAINS MY OWN
WARMEST REGARDS FROM OVER THE YEARS,
COMMANDER.

SINCERELY,
HOGGET AMBRIDGE,
CHAUFFEUR TO PRINCESS MARGOT

QQOW-97RTRV762349HUSE

It was almost as if the message had been sent by the Margot of old—the woman he had known and loved before her disastrous addiction to the Leaguers' TimeWeed. Even the old poetry was there—a deep bond they had shared only moments after they met. In seven days he would see her again—an invitation to the Nabob's huge soiree had already been delivered to all the officers of the IVG. Would she turn out to be real, or was this another perversity dreamed up by the Leaguers? Seven days!
Starfury's Captain passed an exceedingly unsettled night. . . .

Even with Brim's normal overload of work, the next seven days passed like seven years—*Standard* Years. Three of his ED-4s arrived with overloads of critical materiel, and close on their heels was another Starfury: I.F.S. *Starspite*, captained by a long-time friend of Brim's from Atalanta, Commander Stefan MacAlda. And still another pair of Starfuries was due early the following week. Events like these seemed only remotely significant, at least on a personal level. Did miracles really occur? Could Margot someday actually conquer her deadly addiction? At one point, he actually calculated the metacycles (Standard as well as local) remaining before he would have a chance to see for himself. And the daydreaming affected his work. Not a lot, but enough that at least one of his crew recognized that his mind was often elsewhere—and she had no problem bringing it to his attention.

"Voot's beard, Skipper," Tissaurd demanded the morning before Margot's arrival, "where in xaxt are you these days?" She'd found him alone on the bridge, staring out to sea at a time when he *should* have been making quarters inspections. "All of a sudden, you're not Wilf Brim anymore," she protested in frustration, "except when you're at the controls. And even *then* you fly like some sort of an analog. What gives? Your insufferable friend Barbousse knows, but I can't get a thing out of him."

Brim reached inside his tunic and silently handed her his message from Ambridge.

Frowning, Tissaurd seated herself at the right-hand helm and unfolded the sheet of plastic, staring at the text as if she were trying to insert herself *inside* the words. "I guess I'm not surprised," she said at length. "Word got around that you two met at one of Mustafa's parties a while back."

Brim nodded. "The last I'd seen her was a couple of years ago, and she'd been in *bad* shape. I guess I just"—he shrugged—"wrote her off at the time. It was terrible."

Tissaurd narrowed her eyes as she rose from her seat and quietly took a place behind him. "Isn't she the Leaguer Baroness who got herself addicted to TimeWeed?"

"She's not exactly a Leaguer," Brim protested.

"Sorry, Skipper," Tissaurd replied, "but The Torond's close enough for me."

"I know," Brim conceded without turning around "I guess I just don't see her that way. You had to know her before she married that zukeed LaKarn. She was a different person then— and she seemed like her old self at the ball."

"She seemed like she'd thrown the habit, then?" Tissaurd asked, gently kneading the back of his neck.

"No," Brim replied. "She talked about having a greater tolerance for it, or something. But she *looked* . . . well . . . normal, for lack of a better word. And she acted rationally, too. You know, almost as if everything were all right, again."

"That's pretty unusual from what I hear about TimeWeed."

Brim closed his eyes. "Who knows?" he responded at length. "I certainly have no idea."

"Sounds to me as if you hadn't *really* written her off, Skipper."

"That's not entirely right, Number One," Brim corrected. "I *had* written her off; I just hadn't stopped caring. And until I got the note, I didn't realize how much I still cared."

Tissaurd rested her hand gently on his shoulder. "It's not that easy to shut off an old love, is it, Skipper?" she said.

Brim turned in his seat and shook his head. "Sounds as if you know from experience, Number One," he said.

"Yeah," Tissaurd answered, her eyes focused somewhere else in both space and moment, "I do."

"I'm sorry," Brim ruminated, "I didn't know."

"I never told you about him, Skipper," she said. "And neither of us is famous like you and your princess, so you'd never have heard. But he was beautiful."

"I'm still sorry," Brim said, touching her hand. "Do you still think of him a lot?"

She nodded. "Too much," she said. "It gets in the way at the damndest times." Then she looked him in the eye. "Luckily," she said, placing both hands on his shoulders, "I am not captain of this ship, so it isn't much noticed. And when it is, well, I'm simply having an off day. But you, Captain Brim, aren't *allowed* to have off days."

Brim winced. "It shows that much?" he asked, feeling his cheeks burn.

"Probably not *that* much," she assured him with a little smile. "But those of us who know and love you *do* notice. And, of course, *Starfury* doesn't run as well—nor does this confounded base you've managed to carve out of nowhere." She scowled. "By Voot's beard, if that LaKarn woman *were* a Leaguer, this would be one clever way of undermining the Empire's attempt to establish a base here."

It was now Brim's turn to scowl. "You didn't know her during the war, Number One," he said hotly. "Margot may have become a lot of things I don't approve of, but she's *not* a traitor. I know that in my heart."

Tissaurd looked him in the eye. "I'd be the last one to question your judgment, Skipper," she returned, "but the heart seems like a poor place to look for danger, if you ask me."

"Nobody's asking, Number One," Brim said pointedly.

"I understand," Tissaurd replied quickly. "Still, I'm looking forward to meeting this woman. You will introduce me, won't you?" she asked. "I've always wanted to meet a Princess."

Brim reined in his temper. "Yeah," he conceded, "I'll introduce you." Then he shrugged. "And I'll make xaxtdamned sure that I quit going around like a love-struck teenager," he added, "at least in public." He grimaced. "I'm sorry if I've acted like a fool, Number One."

"Like a human," Tissaurd corrected. "Like a *man*." With that, she headed for the aft companionway, leaving him alone with his thoughts in *Starfury*'s quiet, empty bridge.

On Mustafa's birth anniversary the next day, Brim and nearly half of the wardroom mess embarked for Magor aboard one of *Starfury*'s fast launches, flying in finger-four formation with launches from the other three ships. Moulding flew wingman for Brim, and McKenzie led *Starconstant*'s Carrie Hogan to form the second pair. Back at Varnholm Hall, the remaining IVG crew members had been placed on increased alert status, just in case. Too many unidentified "civilian" ships were now passing overhead each day to warrant any complaisance at all so far as Brim was concerned. The new base was nowhere near any of the planet's established commercial airways.

On final over Magor's harbor, Brim had little difficulty locating T.S.S. *Katuka*, The Torond-manufactured Dampier DA 79-II that would have borne Margot to the celebration. Unquestionably the most important warships manufactured so far by The Torond, these new Dampiers had quickly established themselves as tough competitors during the short battle for Beta Jago. Angular in design (the only way to produce in quantity with skills and tools available in The Torond), these deltoid ships were powered by three P.XI RC.40 Drive crystals and a brace of primitive, but reliable, Schleicher ASK 13 gravity generators. The one parked below on a gravity pool appeared to carry six 280-mmi disruptors in triple-mount turrets mounted at the two aft topside vertices of its hull; from intelligence briefings, Brim knew these were matched by three additional triple-mounts in similar belly mountings at all three hull vertices. The ships had been highly successful against the outmoded starships of Beta Jago, but Brim guessed they would quickly meet their match in new generations of fighting machines like *Starfury*.

The ex-Imperials had no sooner landed and secured their launches to mobile gravity pads in Magor's Levantine District than they were ushered into three magnificent omnibus skimmers that set off for the palace immediately. As base commander by default, Brim found himself seated in the front of the first omnibus with a Fluvannian General who clearly had been detailed to escort them by virtue of his ability to speak Avalonian. The man made it very evident he felt the job was largely beneath his station, especially since his highest ranking charge was two grades short of his own. "How do you find working for the Fluvannian Fleet, Commander?" he drawled without introducing himself, clearly uninterested in Brim's answer, whatever it might be.

"It's working out, General," Brim said noncommittally. "We've made a lot of progress with the base."

"Ah, yes, Varnholm Hall," the General said, peering approvingly at his perfectly manicured fingernails. "A bit out of the way, I suppose, but a fine location for you mercenaries."

Brim frowned. "I see," he said, stifling a smile. *Mercenaries*, were they? He'd been called a lot of names over the years, but never a "mercenary." In a perverse sort of way, he almost felt honored by the sobriquet. . . .

After clearing the reception line, Brim and Tissaurd quickly located another of Mustafa's glorious little palace bars. This one's walls were covered in odd-shaped mirrors framed by elaborate baroque scrollwork and embellished in gold. The ceiling was formed in the shape of a giant seashell, glowing 'round about its scalloped periphery with muted light. And, of course, it had a good view of the Grand Entry Hall. Brim had been most adamant about that.

"You haven't taken your eyes off the doorway since we arrived, Skipper," Tissaurd commented, sipping a Logish Meem. She wore her dress uniform even lower on her breasts than it had been at the last ball. "How come you aren't ogling my cleavage tonight?" she asked salaciously, shifting her torso to reveal a hint of dark, studded aureole in the folds of lace. "Mustafa certainly seemed to enjoy what he saw."

Brim grinned as he felt his cheeks burn. "Oh, I haven't missed those, Number One," he assured her, peering quite deliberately now.

Deftly, she checked the bartender—who was noisily occupied with an ice machine at the other end of the room—then momentarily slipped the top of her dress far enough to reveal a small distended nipple, stunningly brown against her creamy skin and the folds of Imperial lace. "Do you think your friend Moulding might be interested in this as much as you seem to be?" she asked.

"I have no doubt you'll get his attention," Brim answered, experiencing a very compelling sensation in his own loins. Tiny as she was, the woman had magnificent breasts. He marveled at how she managed to conceal them as well as she did.

"Good," she replied, nodding her head thoughtfully. "Because I intend to seduce that man tonight, just as soon as I meet this Princess who's got her claws in *you* years after she ought to." Abruptly she frowned and focused her eyes into the hall beyond. "And I'll bet that's *her* out there right now," she said, nimbly moving the top of her dress higher again.

Brim peered into the hall for the millionth time. This time, however, there she was, being helped out of her evening coat by five severe-looking women outfitted in bright green dress uniforms from The Torond. He felt his heart soar. She was dressed in a high-necked silken apricot dress with spike-heeled slippers that made her statuesque legs look even longer than they were. And as always, her strawberry-blond hair was arranged in carefully styled disarray. "Margot," he whispered more to himself than to anyone else.

Beside him, Tissaurd squeezed her chin in thought for a moment. "Well," she commented cattily, "they clearly eat well at Baron LaKarn's court, don't they?"

Brim smiled. In truth, the ample Princess had become even more so with the passing years. "Yeah," he had to agree, "she's put on a few stoneweights, Number One." Even so, she was still almost perfectly proportioned, and—at least to Brim—perhaps the most voluptuous woman in the Universe. Once, he'd known each secret alcove and recess of her body as well as he knew his own.

Afterward, they sat in silence, watching the Princess make her way through the long reception line. When—at last—Mustafa finished his ogling (clearly, his tastes were similar to Brim's), Tissaurd looked up and nodded. "All right, Skipper," she said, sliding gracefully from the bar stool, "let's get this inspection over with. I've had an itch—in a very personal location—to ravish your aristocratic friend Moulding since the day he arrived."

Brim frowned as he stepped to the floor. "Well, don't feel this is some sort of task you have to accomplish," he said, slightly chafed by her attitude.

"Oh, but I do," she assured him, then she looked him directly in the eye and winked. "I'm simply doing what I can to make sure you stay in one piece for a while, Skipper. Sooner or later, one of us will be transferred; then it'll be *your* turn to be seduced. I'm looking forward to that."

Brim laughed. "Don't hold your breath, Number One," he said with a grin. "You're the best First Lieutenant I can imagine. I'm not about to let you go for a *long* time."

"I can wait, Skipper," the gamin officer said as they made their way across the floor. "I'm being, shall we say, 'serviced,' on a pretty regular basis now that the other ships are beginning to arrive. But I keep wondering how long you can hold out, because I don't have the impression anybody's taking care of you." She peered through the crowd at Margot. "Hmm," she said appraisingly. "Perhaps. . . ." Taking his arm, she stopped him and looked up into his face. "Wilf Brim," she said with a very serious expression on her face, "if you can talk that one into a bed tonight, do it. I'll personally guarantee transportation back to *Starfury* after, say"—she thought for a moment—"I ought to have your friend pretty well worn out by midday. So call me after that. All right?"

Brim shook his head gloomily. "I doubt if I'll have to bother you, Nadia. This will be the first time we've been together for a lot of years."

"Good," Tissaurd laughed. "She'll be all the more appreciative once she's on her back. And for xaxt sake, remember to take your time!" Then she smiled. "Now get yourself over there and say hello so you can introduce me."

Margot met his eyes only moments later, and almost instantly, the one-time lovers were hand in hand, as if they had been apart no more than a few short days. "Wilf," she whispered breathlessly, "thank the Universe. I was so afraid you might not come."

"But you sent a message," Brim said. "How could I ignore something like that from you?"

Margot dropped her eyes to the floor. "It took more than a year for me to discover why you'd broken Rogan's back," she said. "I must have seemed like some sort of animal, lying there naked on the floor while he offered you my body if you'd join the League."

"You were too far gone with TimeWeed to know anything about it," Brim replied, trying desperately to force the abominable scene from his mind. "And what I did to your husband afterward," he added through pain-clenched teeth, "was the product of . . . well . . . simple insanity, I suppose. I hardly remember doing it." He drew her closer. "You seem to be different now," he added after a long silence.

"I am," she answered with a sad little nod, "but only to the extent that I described the last time we met." She shook her head. "Don't let it fool you, Wilf," she warned. "When I need it, I *need* it. Withdrawal symptoms are disastrous—and they occur almost immediately following the first cravings. . . ."

Suddenly, Tissaurd appeared beside them. "Skipper," she interrupted with a guileless smile, "I can't wait forever for an introduction."

Frowning, Margot turned to glance at the tiny officer's intrusion, then abruptly went rigid, as if something had momentarily startled her. "Hello," she said warily, brushing an offending lock of blond hair back in place.

"Margot—er . . . Princess Effer'wyck LaKarn," Brim stammered, "may I present Nadia Tissaurd, First Lieutenant of His Magnificence's starship R.F.S. *Starfury*?"

"Oh, yes, it is R.F.S., isn't it?" Margot remarked, her eyes narrowing as if she were suddenly facing some sort of menace. "Well, it pleases me to meet you, Nadia," she replied, extending her gloved hand to be kissed in the Grand Manner. "I'd heard you were all Fluvannians now," she said.

"Not Fluvannians, mercenaries," Tissaurd corrected, looking up at Margot with a little smile. She took the proffered hand and shook it politely, then for a few moments, she seemed to freeze time while she peered deeply into the Princess's eyes.

Suddenly Margot blanched as if she had been physically penetrated. "W-what have you done in my head?" she demanded, her eyes widening with something that looked a lot like fear.

Tissaurd slowly relaxed like a small viper uncoiling. "*Done*, Princess?" she asked with a malign little smile that Brim had never encountered before. "I don't understand." Abruptly she stepped back and resumed her original artless pose—except for her eyes. They had taken on a look of implacable anger.

Margot impulsively brought her fingertips to her lips. "Well . . ." she stammered, clearly at a loss of words.

"No matter," Tissaurd continued, raising a hand in gentle approbation. "Your Highness," she said, "it has truly been an honor to make your acquaintance, and I look forward to the next time we meet." Then, turning to Brim: "Captain, I shall await your summons early tomorrow afternoon." Before either could utter a word of reply, her tiny form had disappeared in the ever-growing crowd of revelers.

The two stood in relative silence for long moments before

Margot recovered sufficiently to speak. "*That* woman is your First Lieutenant?" she demanded.

Brim nodded. "She's the best, so far as I'm concerned."

"But, do you trust her—really?"

"Often with my life," Brim replied.

"That may someday turn out to be a foolish decision, Wilf Brim," she warned quietly.

"I noticed a few sparks fly when you two got within firing range," Brim joked in a lame attempt to defuse the ticklish situation.

"Sparks flew on *both* sides," Margot said, appearing to quickly recoup her aplomb. "An interesting one, that Tissaurd," she mused. "She might be good at what she does around a starship, but were I you, I'd never take my eyes off her."

Brim grimaced. "I . . . ah . . . will try to . . . keep that in mind, Margot," he equivocated.

"Well, no matter, Wilf," Margot said after a few more moments of silence. "I certainly have no business criticizing your crew in the first place. It's just that I should certainly hate to have anything untoward happen to you," she added, placing an arm around his waist. "Especially now that we will finally have some access to each other after all the years of separation."

Brim felt her breast pressing his arm and took a deep breath. "Margot," he sighed, "what will that access do to us? Haven't we been through enough pain over each other?"

"Pain, like gratification, is a part of life, my once and future lover," she whispered, guiding him toward the door. "I think Mustafa decreed romantic dancing in a number of his ballrooms. Let's see what threads of pleasure we can pick up after all the years we've been apart."

Immediately, Brim felt the old fear of dancing suddenly rise in his chest. Then he recalled the delight he'd felt while Tissaurd matched his artless shuffle. She'd even seemed to enjoy it! He shrugged—why not? "I'd love to, Margot," he said while his hands begin to warm all by themselves. Less than a metacycle later, they decided to share the night.

CHAPTER 7

Command

Brim awoke in a lavish suite belonging to one of Magor's larger downtown hotels. Early dawn softly illuminated the room from behind an ornate shade and Margot's golden curls tickled his ear as she slept peacefully in the crook of his arm. Only a slight odor of TimeWeed permeated the air; she had taken care of her addiction in an adjoining bedroom.

Gently easing her head to the pillow, he sat up and regarded her luxuriant form beneath the stained silken bed linen. In many ways, she was even more beautiful than she had been years in the past. Heavier, of course, but somehow all the more desirable for it. And she'd made love as ingeniously and strenuously as ever. Universe, had she! He found himself quite tender following her spectacularly uninhibited ministrations. She indeed had made it a night to remember, almost as though she were trying to atone for the missing years.

Yet in the light dawn, he realized that something had been subtly absent during their lovemaking. Oh, his lust had been as well slaked, no doubt about that. And unless the Princess-cum-Baroness had lately become a talented actress in her own right, so had hers. Nevertheless, *something* had been missing. He couldn't quite focus in on its exact nature; but instinctively he understood it was quite central to the passion they once shared.

And without it, he found a strange void in his soul that in the past would have been fulfilled during their lovemaking.

What *was* it?

Lack of sleep benumbed his concentration as he struggled to somehow characterize the emptiness. Was it even real, or had he dreamed of a reunion with Margot for so many years that nothing could live up to his expectations? And for that matter, why was Tissaurd so skeptical about the whole thing? Suddenly nothing made sense anymore, and the comfortable fulfillment he had anticipated only metacycles before was quickly turning to bewildered misgivings.

As he fretted, Margot opened her eyes and smiled languidly, pushing the sheet down past her knees. "Good morning, my lover," she whispered while a hint of last evening's perfume caressed Brim's nostrils from the warmth of her lush body. " 'The night is past and all its sweets are gone!' " she recited in a whisper. " 'Sweet voice, sweet lips, strong hand, and stalwart breast. . . .' Oh, Wilf, so few moments of this heaven remain with us. Can you fill me with your manfulness once more before I must return to another existence?"

Brim peered at her lush beauty. "If only that return weren't necessary," he said.

" 'If only,' " Margot sighed with a faraway look. "The most melancholy words in the Universe, perhaps." She took a deep breath and closed her eyes. "I smoked my last pinch of The Weed just after we made love the last time—I waited until you were asleep. And within"—she peered at her miniature timepiece glowing from a bedside table—"within three metacycles I must return to the ship and beg for more or suffer the tortures of the specially damned. It's better than a chain, Wilf. They don't need guards. They *know* I'll be back." She stretched out her arms to him. "Hurry, my love," she urged, "make me forget that I no longer control this body of mine."

While tears stung his eyes, Brim knelt between her drawn-up legs and gently lifted her head. "Margot, darling," he whispered as he willed himself ready, "you're the one who knows about this . . . disease. Isn't there *any* cure?"

"Death," Margot whispered, almost as if she loved the word

itself. "It has become my only hope." Biting her lip, she drew him on top of her "Yes . . ." she sighed urgently, while he plunged himself into a tiny Universe of swollen, wet flesh. "*Yes*," she groaned through clenched teeth. Her voice caught momentarily, then she closed her eyes and clasped him fiercely. "Fill me *now*!"

Short metacycles afterward, Brim brooded in the right seat of a small launch with Tissaurd at the controls beside him. Since lift-off at the Levantine, only muted thunder from the spin-grav had broken the silence in the cockpit. At last, the tiny officer turned in her seat. "Skipper," she said, "you're mighty quiet for someone whom I suspect has spent the night making love. A lack of sleep perhaps or something else?"

Brim angled his head. "I haven't heard much from you, either, Number One," he retorted, unable to break his bleak mood.

"A *healthy* lack of sleep in my case," Tissaurd replied, glancing quickly at the NAV panels. "Your friend Moulding seduces very easily." Then she frowned. "You will notice, however, my dear Skipper, that *I* have a rather satisfied smirk on my face—which *you* do not. Did I make a bad assumption about how you spent the night?"

"No, Number One," Brim said, staring blindly through the windshield as they bounced through a turbulent area of clouds. "The Princess and I seduced each other early and often." He made a bitter little chuckle. "I'm even pleasantly tender from it all."

"But . . ." Tissaurd probed.

"But?"

"You sounded as if 'but' was the next word you were going to say."

Brim snorted. "Yeah," he admitted bleakly. "It was. Only I decided not to."

"You mean you don't want to talk about it," Tissaurd prompted.

"No," Brim answered after a time. "I suppose I wouldn't mind talking about it if I could only define what that particular 'it' is."

"I don't understand," Tissaurd said with a frown.

Brim nodded. "That's just it, Number One," he replied. "Neither do I. But after all that lovemaking, there was something *missing*." He turned to face her as she flew. "And that 'something'—whatever it was—must be terribly important, because I've come away with this awful feeling of emptiness."

Tissaurd checked the autohelm and relaxed in her seat, turning her head only after long moments of what appeared to be concentration. "Interesting," she said, "the difference between last night and the previous time you two met at one of Mustafa's parties. It was my understanding that on her first visit, she was escorted by a bunch of Leaguers. Is that right?"

Brim nodded. "That's right," he affirmed, glad for the change of topic. "Mean thragglers, too. Four Varoldians."

"Universe," Tissaurd muttered. "They *are* mean. Sure sounds as if the zukeeds wanted to keep the Princess away from people."

"Seemed that way at the time," Brim agreed. "But they'd certainly gotten that nonsense out of their systems this *trip*. You saw it: she got there with only five retainers in tow—all from The Torond."

"Yeah," Tissaurd said, narrowing her eyes. "It doesn't make sense, somehow."

"Nothing seems to make much sense these days," Brim said, wrinkling his nose.

Tissaurd adjusted the autohelm and started a gentle descent toward the tattered gray cloud base. "Maybe that's true," she said after a long silence. Then she turned to look him full in the face. "But maybe, Wilf Brim," she said, "just *maybe* it makes all the sense in the Universe." Moments later she had picked up Varnholm's new localizer beacon, and there was little time for idle talk.

Precisely one week later, *Sacha Muromets* arrived again, completely unannounced as on her first arrival. Aboard were another load of scarce parts; Nik Ursis, now a Fluvannian Captain; and Commodore Baxter Calhoun, the latter casually dressed in his white IVG uniform as if he had merely been away on an overnight trip to Magor.

"Commodore!" Brim whooped in surprise at the foot of the brow. "You've had a number of us worried, the last month or so."

"Rumors o' my demise are often vastly overrated," Calhoun drawled modestly, returning Brim's salute. Hands on his hips, he sauntered to an inland wall of the gravity pool with the two officers in his wake. "Nik tells me you've done guid, thorough work here," he said, peering up and down the berthing area where eleven Starfury cruisers now floated in a seemingly random pattern optimized to reduce the effect of an attack from space. "I'd have a hard time refutin' him from whar I stand." He smiled. "Good job, young Brim. O' course," he added with a wink, "I should hae expected nothin' less—especially wi' Barbousse and the comely Lieutenant Tissaurd to do most of the really difficult work."

"I hardly needed to lift a finger," Brim said sardonically.

"Oh, I'm certain o' that, laddie," Calhoun chuckled, clapping the younger Carescrian on his shoulder. "But nonetheless, it's guid progress you've made in my absence. I'm right proud o' you."

"I'll be more than glad to turn everything back over to you now—except Starfury," Brim said.

"Oh, you will, will you?" Calhoun said. "What makes you think I'll be able to gat it all done? Outside o' brother Ursis here, hae you seen any Fluvannian staff officers come off the brow?"

Brim frowned. "Not a one, Commodore," he admitted.

"What does that lead you to believe, young Brim?" Calhoun asked, winking slyly at the Bear.

"Somehow," Brim said, "I have the oddest feeling that you have it in mind to delegate some authority."

"Nothing odd aboot that," Calhoun said. "I plan to parcel the management o' this place among a number of you—at the general crew members' meeting that you wull call for Evening:3:00 in Sacha's hold. All right?"

"Sounds good to me," Brim said, "I think."

"Whar's your sense of adventure, m'boy?" Calhoun asked.

"Commodore," Brim said, "when you get a look like that in your eye, it's usually time to go underground."

"Trust me," Calhoun said.

"Should I do that, Nik?" Brim inquired of the Bear.

Ursis rolled his eyes to the heavens. "Probably not," he said, "but since both of us work for him now, I see little choice in matter."

"Evening:3:00, Commodore," Brim repeated. "I'll have them here." Then, saluting once more, he started back along the top of the gravity pool. As usual, he had a lot of work to do and only a limited time in which to do it.

By Evening:2:40, with still ten cycles to go, *Sacha Muromets*'s cavernous main hold was filled with nearly eleven hundred IVG mercenaries. Only a few duty officers remained with their various warships. Everyone had heard about the legendary Baxter Calhoun; few, however, had ever as much as seen his face.

A speaking platform of packing crates had been jury-rigged against a forward bulkhead; the IVGs sat on the floor or stood three and five deep around the periphery. At precisely Evening:2:48, Barbousse climbed to the rostrum, paused for the crowd to notice him, then shouted "THE COMMODORE!" in his loudest voice.

It took a few moments before that many people could scramble to their feet and come to attention, but at precisely Evening:3:00, Commodore Baxter Calhoun, R.F.S., mounted to the boards in utter silence, his footfalls and the ship's distant generators were the only sounds that could be detected in the giant chamber. He stood for a long moment, handsome and ageless as he had been when Brim first encountered him aboard I.F.S. *Defiant* at the beginning of that ship's tragically short career. Then he seemed to relax and his face twisted into what passed for a grin of approval. "Seats," he said. He hardly had to raise his voice.

Moments later, when quiet had again returned to the room, Calhoun placed his hands on his hips and began, legs akimbo, as if he were braced on the deck of some ancient surface vessel. "Fellow Imperials," he held forth in a strong, confident voice, "we are aboot to embark on a desperate an' dangerous mission.

'Tis o' wee importance whose uniform we wear: blue capes or white, the enemy wull be the same—and but little changed from the last cycle o' war we lived through. Leaguers are capable, brave, an' utterly merciless. I've seen them up close as well as their ships. Both are excellent—and *dangerous*." He let the words soak in for a moment before he continued. "In a lot o' places these days, they are already considered to be invincible. *But*," he said with great emphasis, "*they can be beaten!* I hae seen it done with gr'at regularity by ill-equipped forces o' much smaller size. An' I am here to show you how it is done. . . ."

For the next solid metacycle, he delivered a top-level glimpse of the Leaguers and the tactics they used. "To beat them," he urged, "learn how privateers fight their battles. They are *always* outnumbered by squadrons of defenders, but they seldom find themselves deprived of the quarry they seek." He described how privateers battle in pairs, using ultra-fast ships to drive through hostile formations, shooting quickly and accurately with heavy armament, then breaking away before massed superior firepower can be brought to bear against them—often without scoring clean kills. In his view, serious damage spread widely among the ships of an enemy squadron could win more battles than actual kills. He claimed he'd seen the principle proven time and time again as the outnumbered ships of Beta Jago slashed squadrons from The Torond to ribbons. "And the poor Beta-Jagans war usin' surplus ships from the last conflict," he asserted. "Your Starfuries were literally *made* for this kind o' fighting—the right ships at absolutely the right time. . . ."

At the end of his discourse, the assembled IVGs broke into wild applause that lasted until the grinning Calhoun was forced to hold up his hands and demand silence. When the chamber had again quieted sufficiently that he could make himself heard, he called Brim and McKenzie to the platform. "Startin' today," he continued in a clear voice, "I hae decided to group your ships into twa squadrons; we'll call 'em the Reds and the Blues for the moment. Brim here will command the Reds, our offensive element, with eight ships; McKenzie's Blues will patrol near Ordu as a base defense with the remaining three reserve ships. . . ."

Immediately after the meeting, Brim asked Moulding if he would lead the second attack quad. "Probably signing you up for suicide," he said, only half in jest. "But then, you already did that when you came aboard the IVG in the first place."

The aristocratic Moulding smiled grimly. "You and I made a bloody good team against the League during the Mitchell Trophy races," he said. "It would be a damn shame to deprive Nergol Triannic the benefit of our services over something so inconsequential as death."

They started their campaign early the next morning. . . .

Within three weeks, nine Starfuries had been damaged in training accidents and thirty IVGs had gone back home because of the utterly primitive existence at Varnholm. Calhoun doggedly drove Brim and McKenzie to instruct their charges in tactics and put them through wartime maneuvers in the new starships—that continued to suffer damage by crews unfamiliar with the powerful craft under conditions of maximum performance. One waggish Commander painted five Fluvannian flags over the main hatch of his Starfury; he'd caused an accident that laid up five other ships for a week, thus qualifying himself and his crew as Leaguer aces. Even the practiced Moulding, accustomed to quick, near-vertical landings in Sherrington racers, nearly wiped out one evening after a tiring mock battle because the infinitely heavier Starfuries were designed for long, gentle approaches. He then poured on too much power when he lifted the porpoising starship off for another attempt at landfall and nearly blew up a whole row of generators. Gradually, however, the accidents subsided, and the hard-working IVGs began to hammer their squadrons into tough, capable fighting units.

Unfortunately, the training had cost Calhoun many of the spares Brim so carefully hoarded. And none of the ships had yet seen actual combat of any kind. . . .

During the next six weeks, relations between Fluvanna and the League rapidly deteriorated, the latter taking issue with nearly every element of foreign policy introduced by Mustafa's Foreign Ministry. Almost on a daily basis, OverGalite'er Hanna Notrom's Ministry for Public Consensus filled all possible news channels with her demands for "justice" on one trumped-up pretense or another.

Then, on 273/52010, R.F.S. *Rurik*, an ancient Fluvannian armored cruiser, disappeared without a trace in close proximity to a League-Torond battle exercise. When Fluvannian Search and Rescue squadrons converged on the last reported position of the old vessel, they were brusquely warned off with tremendous disruptor fire from strange new warships in the conformation of double chevrons. And the powerful barrages were clearly not fired in warning; they were *ranging shots*.

After a few weeks, the old ship was written off and added to the long catalog of vessels that had simply vanished into the great maw of the Universe. But R.F.S. *Rurik*—and her crew— were not easily forgotten, either in Fluvanna or the Imperial Admiralty. And whispered accusations surfaced from one end of the galaxy to the other.

The situation was headed rapidly from bad to worse when Brim abruptly received another message from Ambridge, Margot's chauffeur. The Princess would again visit Magor during the next Standard Week, this time on what the old servant termed a "last-moment peacekeeping mission." Of course, she hoped that Brim would be available for an evening rendezvous; she would contact him when she arrived.

Tissaurd was distinctly negative when the subject came up during an early morning with Brim in *Starfury*'s wardroom. "And I'm not alone in this, Skipper," the tiny officer declared, shaking her finger at him. "The Chief's upset, too. I asked him."

Brim frowned. "The Chief?" he demanded. "What does Barbousse know about all this?" He paused. "And how did *you* find out about it before I told you?"

"Skipper," Tissaurd said, "you know as well as I do. When a personal message comes into the COMM room, the whole ship knows what it says, especially when the Skipper's on the address. It's called a 'grapevine.' "

"A 'grapevine'?" Brim demanded. "What the xaxt is a grapevine?"

"Real grapevines are something like a logus bush, I think,"

Tissaurd answered with a frown. "Spreading plants of some sort that grow on one of the little Rhodorian planets. But you get the meaning. Look how the word spread when you got the unclassified message about old R.F.S. *Rurik*."

"WUN-der-ful," Brim grumped. "Isn't there any privacy at all?"

Tissaurd smiled. "Not through the unclassified message room, there isn't."

Brim was about to open his mouth when Tissaurd put her hand on his arm. "And I'm not finished, *Mister* Wilf Brim," she continued. "We'll clear up the thraggling COMM center some other time. Right now—when there's nobody else in the wardroom—I want to talk about that Princess of yours, because, frankly, I don't think she has your best interests at heart. And that's putting it mildly."

"What're you trying to tell me?" Brim demanded.

"Is that question coming from *Captain* Brim or my friend and associate Wilf?" she demanded.

"Wilf," Brim grumped.

"In that case," Tissaurd said, looking him directly in the eye, "it is my studied opinion that your Margot Effer'wyck—or whoever is in control of *that* particular Margot Effer'wyck—is out to make serious trouble for you."

"Trouble? Margot?"

"That's the way I read things the one time I spoke to her," Tissaurd answered. "Possibly *serious* trouble. I think a liaison with her right now might prove to be dangerous."

"Oh, come on, Nadia," Brim snapped with a sudden feeling of harassment. "I know I said something was missing in our lovemaking a while back. But surely *that* doesn't qualify as danger, does it?"

"There is no way I can prove anything, Wilf," Tissaurd said. "But since the Chief thinks there's something wrong, too, maybe you ought to talk to him before you simply dismiss this out of hand."

By this time, Brim had heard enough. With a faltering grip on his temper he rose to his feet and scowled down at the tiny officer. "Nadia," he growled, "I understand and *appreciate* your concern for my well-being. I also appreciate the Chief's. But xaxtdamnit, I will *not* tolerate you two prying any further into my personal life, no matter what your good intentions are. Do you understand?''

"Your call, Wilf," Tissaurd said with an easygoing shrug. "You won't hear any more from me. Sorry I got you upset."

Brim turned toward the door. "I am *not* upset," he grumped as he started for the bridge. But he was. And for the next two days, avoided all but the most official contact with either Tissaurd or his old friend Barbousse. . . .

As Ambridge promised in his message, Margot contacted Brim shortly after her arrival in Magor aboard another of The Torond's powerful Dampier D.A. 79-II cruisers. "Tonight," she pledged breathlessly, "I have informed my retainers that I shall dine at the Palmerston—alone. Can you join me?"

"Of course," Brim answered. Somehow, it made sense. The Palmerston Club, located at the edge of Magor's diplomatic sector, was a purlieu of those who longed for the distant elegance of cities in more sophisticated homelands. To Brim, it always invoked thoughts of the quiet, elegant clubs in Avalon's urbane Courtland district. "It will be perfect . . ." he said.

It was.

He caught an early-afternoon shuttle to Magor and arrived at nearly the same instant as she. They surrendered their rented skimmers to white-gloved valets in happy silence before walking arm in arm under a long canopy toward the elaborately carved stone doorway of the Palmerston. Inside, a *very* formal major-domo dressed in ruffled shirt, cutaway coat with long tails, satin knickers and stockings, and slippers—all in white—recognized them by name and bowed elaborately. "Ah, Captain Brim, Baroness LaKarn," he rhapsodized, "you honor our humble establishment."

"Thank you, Westley," Brim said. "It is always a pleasure to visit the Palmerston." With Margot on his arm, he followed the man along a thickly carpeted passageway lined with huge portraits of antique landscapes. This led into a candle-lit chamber filled with the most compelling odors of food, perfumes, and smoke—both from a great fireplace and spiced cigarettes of a dozen exotic persuasions. The ceiling was low for its expanse, and supported by huge wooden beams that gave the impression of antiquity. Sinuous music from a string orchestra blended with the faint clatter of tableware and hushed conversations in a dozen languages as they made their way among tables occupied by all manner of patrons: human, Bearish, flighted, reptilian—even a threesome of the pellucid Spirit races from outside the Home Galaxy who had only recently deigned to trade with their more substantially propagated neighbors. Brim's table, not far from the glowing fireplace, was perfectly located for discreet privacy.

"I love this place, Wilf," Margot whispered as the steward decanted a fine old vintage of Logish Meem.

"I do too," Brim agreed softly. The warm, dimly lighted room was comfortable in a very intimate manner that he couldn't quite put his finger on.

"What does it remind you of?" she asked suddenly.

Brim frowned. "Well," he began, sipping the superb old meem, "it *does* look a lot like those places off Courtland Plaza in Avalon, I suppose."

Margot smiled and nodded. "It's *designed* to look like one of those. But what else does it remind you of?"

Brim peered around the room. He'd dined here on a number of occasions, and indeed, there *had* been something familiar about it. But he'd seen so many similar establishments over the years . . . then it struck him. "The Mermaid Tavern on Gimmas Haefdon!" he exclaimed. "Of course."

"Isn't it wonderful?" Margot said dreamily. "It brings back so many good memories. Remember the first time we met there?" Her eyes focused somewhere in a different time and space. "You'd swallowed one of those locator transponders, and just as you were going to ask me upstairs, the Base called you up for duty."

"I never was certain," Brim said with a rueful smile. "*Would* you have gone upstairs with me?"

Margot smiled mysteriously. "That's my secret," she said. "But I will confess I was giving it some *thorough* preconsideration at the time—just in case you might ask."

Brim sighed theatrically. "Life is a lot too short to miss chances like that."

"Over the years, we've more than made up for that one opportunity, wouldn't you say?" Margot asked with a suggestive little smile.

"Even once or twice at the Mermaid Tavern, if memory serves," Brim answered easily. "Yet I'm not sure we ever did make up for that particular night—or *could*. Some opportunities are so fundamentally unique they pretty much exist in their own Universe. Think about it," he said, looking Margot directly in the eye. "That was during the one special time in our lives when we weren't yet certain how the other would react. A time of . . . exploration, I suppose—special excitement." Instinctively, he took her hand. "By the time we *did* eventually fall in bed together, we were good friends, and I think both of us knew it was only a matter of time until it happened. Remember? You had most of your dress off just inside your suite at the Embassy. And we were rutting for all we were worth only a few cycles later."

"Yes," Margot whispered, her cheeks coloring. "I'd built up to it in my mind the whole evening." She smiled. "I couldn't wait to feel you inside me. I'd been drenching my scanties since our first dance."

"Even though I stepped all over your feet?" Brim asked.

"I wasn't really concentrating much on my feet at the time, Commander Brim," she laughed. "Or anybody I danced with, that night either—except you." She smiled. "But if I remember correctly, lover, you were exceedingly ready yourself that evening."

Brim nodded, his cheeks burning. "I'll admit that I'm beginning to feel that way right now," he said, experiencing a characteristic fullness in his loins. "If we keep talking like this, I'm not going to be interested at all in supper. At least until we . . . ah."

Margot smiled, considerable tinges of pink appearing high in her cheeks. "We shall, my lover," she said, raising her goblet. "But first, shall we fuel the fires of our passion?"

"Seems like a more sane idea to me," Brim admitted, raising

his own goblet to hers. "That way, we won't have to interrupt anything later. Besides," he said with a smile, "the Palmerston Club *is* a wonderful place to dine."

"I chose it for a number of reasons," she said, staring with half-closed eyes as she sipped her meem. "The atmosphere and food go without saying—but the *location*: that serves our *other* needs as well."

Brim frowned. "They have rooms here?" he asked, instinctively staring toward the ceiling.

"Well," Margot giggled, "not quite upstairs, my impatient lover, but only a short distance away—through a little park— is a lovely country inn, converted from an ancient grist mill; the old millrace is even intact beside it. Part of the Palmerston, of course." She licked her lips sensually. "Since an evening begun in a place like this can only appropriately end in a bed . . ."

". . . It seems natural that they provide the beds," Brim finished with a grin.

"But of course," Margot assured him. "Anything else would be a downright waste. That is why, Commander Brim, I reserved a suite there for us when I called for the table."

Even with *that* resolved, Brim found himself hurrying through an excellent supper. Some instincts were much stronger than others. . . .

Brim felt just the slightest bit tipsy as he and Margot crossed the street arm in arm and entered the little park across from the Palmerston. Ahead in the dim glow of ancient street lamps, a picturesque inn beckoned from the far end of the path. "Tell me about your scanties tonight," he whispered in her ear, savoring the perfume of her hair.

"You'll have firsthand information shortly," she giggled, squeezing his waist. "How about yours?"

"Probably that's the reason they keep it so dark in there," he replied as a breeze cooled his face, "otherwise a number of us would have been embarrassed." They were approaching a copse of young trees and bushes planted around the periphery of what appeared to be a sizable boulder. Ahead, he could hear the millrace. He listened for a moment, relishing the sound. Then above the rushing water came a momentary scraping ahead in the dark copse. He tensed, hairs bristling on the back of his neck. "Did you hear that?" he whispered.

Margot put her hand to her throat and took her arm from around his back. "N-no, Wilf," she replied in a voice suddenly tight with fear. "I heard nothing."

The sound came again. This time, there was no mistaking his imagination. Brim stopped in his tracks. "Something's wrong, Margot," he whispered instinctively, pushing her into a clump of bushes. "Stay here and don't move," he ordered, then drew his service blaster. At the same moment two dark figures burst silently at him from the left. Whirling while he fired a long, high-energy burst, he saw them jackknife in a froth of blood as the powerful weapon literally cut both in half.

An instant later he sensed scuffling in an archway behind him. Going to the ground again, he glimpsed three figures racing his way, each firing *silenced* blast pikes from the hip. As he rolled behind a bush, a blinding thunderbolt shredded his hiding place in a blizzard of branches and leaves. Reflexively, he snapped to a firing position and let off another long volley of shots, but these went wild as the trio scattered and dove for the flagstones.

At that moment the energy pack in his blaster bleeped empty.

"Voot, you miserable zukeed!" he swore under his breath, but it was his own fault. In spite of regulations, he habitually neglected his side arms. After all, it was peacetime, wasn't it? Before his assailants could properly aim, he desperately sprinted for the boulder and dove behind its mass through an eerily silent fusillade of wild shots, blinding flashes of light, and stinging stone chips. Struggling desperately to catch his breath, he snapped out the old energy pack and snapped in a new one, forcing himself to take a long, deep breath before tensing his legs in a shallow crouch. A split click later, he came out from behind the boulder firing for all he was worth, but again the men had disappeared.

Or had they?

Spontaneously flinging himself to the ground again, he only just dodged a whole welter of silent discharges that rent the air precisely where he had been standing. Firing blindly, he jumped behind the boulder again, trembling like a leaf. In the instant he'd had to take stock of the situation, there appeared to be at least ten people running toward him from the center of the park, shooting silently as they came.

Brim pursed his lips and frowned. Surprise and audacity had saved him before—and they were his only hope now. That, and saving his one remaining energy pack. With no time to worry about Margot, he thumbed the blaster to its lowest conservation setting—any hit would disable at this distance—and started making his way carefully toward the other side of the boulder. Abruptly he froze in his tracks: someone was running toward him from *that* direction—and making a terrible racket as he trampled cocksuredly through the weeds. Clearly, whoever it was didn't consider Wilf Brim to be much of a combatant. . . .

The first thing to appear around the side of the boulder was the barrel of a blast pike, extended almost an iral by the ribbed barrel of a silencer. Brim grabbed it and nearly screamed in pain; his fingers instantly froze to the supercooled metal, but he hung on grimly for all he was worth. From that point, things were quick and silent. He jerked the silencer fiercely and pulled with all his might. Clearly surprised by the onslaught, his assailant stumbled and nearly lost his footing, but recovered quickly and tried to bring the big weapon to bear anyway. With the detached calm of a long-time warrior, Brim stepped in close to block the swing, gripped his assailant by both biceps, and brought up his knee hard. With a look of utter agony, the man dropped his pike and sucked in breath for a howl of pain. But before a sound could escape his lips, Brim stiff-armed, crooked his hand into a right angle, then drove it under the man's jawbone like a pile driver. A stab of pain flashed along his arm and shoulder as he heard neck bones crack—his assailant went down like a sack.

Retrieving the blast pike, Brim ran a quick self-test while he peered at the body, already rank with the odor of feces. Masked. Powerfully built. Dressed in black with no obvious means of identification. A professional, he considered with a shudder— probably one of the Leaguer Agnords; they'd made an attempt on his life the previous year. Only Lady Fortune—and a large dose of Leaguer arrogance—had so far saved him from their second try.

The pike sounded quietly as its self-test ended—three-quarters charged. It would do a lot more damage than his blaster. As he replaced the latter in its holster, he heard skimmers brake to a halt out in the park. Turning, he quietly retraced his steps while doors slammed and a sudden fusillade of heavy weapons flashed and snorted to a quick crescendo that quickly evolved into quieter sounds of running feet and muffled grunts of pain. He had just rounded the boulder again when he froze—this time in horror, his heart thumping wildly in his chest.

Now *he* had been mortally careless—and was about to pay dearly for his own foolish imprudence. . . .

On a patio not ten irals distant, the figure of a man was illuminated from the side by the lights of two van skimmers. He was pointing a blaster directly at Brim's face, but for some reason had not yet fired. As the Carescrian trembled in terrified fascination, the man slowly lowered his powerful weapon, almost as if he had changed his mind.

Still staring at Brim from a masked face, he slowly leaned forward and crumpled onto his knees, the blaster clattering heavily to the flagstones. After moments that passed like years, he noisily struggled for breath, then leaned forward again, this time going to his hands. Slowly—in utter silence—he bowed his head, no longer showing any interest in Brim at all. There came a sound of wet gagging, and finally the man's arms gave out. He slumped forward on his face and lay quite still, as if he had gone to sleep. A throwing knife protruded from between his shoulder blades, just to the right of center, buried nearly to its hilt. At least twenty irals beyond, the huge silhouette of Utrillo Barbousse stood motionless against the lamplight, arms folded, legs akimbo.

Out in the park, guarded by two of Barbousse's tough replacement Chiefs and Nadia Tissaurd, six more bodies sprawled on the grass in awkward attitudes of violent death. Miraculously, the furious little skirmish had taken place without disturbing anyone in the Palmerston, no more than four or five hundred irals distant. Brim found himself trembling as he looked at the bodies, mouths agape as if they were gasping for air. One of them could have easily been *him*! Then—abruptly—he blundered to his senses. "Great thraggling Universe!" he exclaimed. "Where's Margot?"

"Yes," Tissaud said, peering around the park as she holstered her blaster, "where *is* that LaKarn woman?"

Brim sprinted for the bushes where he had pushed her, but she was gone, only an indentation in the grass remained to prove that anyone had been there at all. "Have you seen her, Chief?" he demanded.

"No, Cap'm," Barbousse said. "When we arrived in the vans, all we could see was the crowd of Agnords—and a lot of quiet blastin'."

"Sweet mother of Voot," Brim swore, suddenly terrified for her life, "we've got to find her."

"You *bet* we've got to find her," Tissaud growled again, her eyes hard with anger. Putting her fingertips to the bridge of her nose, she closed her eyes, and began to turn slowly this way and that. She continued in silence until, after some moments, she stopped abruptly. "There," she said, pointing her arm unequivocally toward a small maintenance building beside the far bridge approach wall. She took two steps forward. "Bring her to me," she said as if her eyes were open, "from the shed!"

Immediately, the two Chiefs set off at a trot, covering the distance in a matter of clicks. Together, they dove into the little building and emerged moments later, supporting a figure between them that could only be Margot LaKarn. She was stumbling along between them as if she were drunk.

Stunned—as much by Tissaud's feat as by the sight of Margot in the hands of the Chiefs—Brim could only shake his head. "How did you manage *that*, Number One?" he whispered.

"I . . . ah . . . just happened to see her move in the doorway," the tiny officer said, clearly at pains to avoid his eyes.

"Gorksroar," Brim said quietly. "Your eyes were closed."

"Begging the Captain's pardon," she said, "but that's my explanation. Take it or leave it—sir; this is a bad time for a disagreement."

Brim frowned, then nodded. "For now, Number One," he said, "I'll take it." He had to.

While they waited for Margot and her captors to arrive, three more of Barbousse's Chiefs reappeared from the trees nearby. Two were half carrying a clearly wounded assassin; the third was dragging still another corpse by its feet. Without a word, Brim and Barbousse took charge of the wounded man, holding him erect by throwing his arms over their shoulders. "What do you think, Cap'm?" the big rating asked as he peeled the man's mask from his face. "Looks like an Agnord to me."

"That's the only thing I could think of," Brim said, struggling to steady his voice.

The man groaned when Barbousse lifted his chin to the light, and a thick bubble of blood oozed from the corner of his mouth. "I'll make sure," Barbousse said, then quietly mumbled a few unintelligible phrases into a blood-smeared ear.

These seemed to momentarily revive the prisoner, who croaked out a weak reply before his head fell limply to his chest again.

"Definitely an Agnord, Cap'm," Barbousse said in a matter-of-fact voice. "I ran into plenty of them during my tours on the Governor's ship. I slipped him the 'First Precept'—in his own language."

"The 'First Precept'?"

" 'Death before capture,' " Barbousse explained. "Assassination's sort of a religion with them. The worst humiliation they know is being taken prisoner. The ones I've run into so far really would rather die."

"So what did he say?" Brim demanded as the three Chiefs began to dump bodies off the bridge and into the millrace.

"He begged me to kill him," Barbousse said matter-of-factly.

"Maybe he's trying to protect secret information," Tissaurd said, keeping a weather eye on the hesitant approach of Margot and her captors.

Barbousse shook his head. "I rather doubt if he has much information to protect, Lieutenant," he said deferentially. "From what I've been able to learn, Agnords mostly take other people's orders and carry them out."

"Then, y-you'd actually . . . kill him?" she asked with a look of horror.

"Aye, ma'am," Barbousse said calmly, "unless you or the Commander has objections. We'll have to do *something* with him, no matter what we decide about anything else. The Leaguers won't admit they've seen him before. And it'll be dicey getting him back to Varnholm the way he is right now. Somebody'll sure want to know how he got hurt—right before they demand the ID he doesn't have."

"Why can't we just leave him here?" Brim asked as the two Chiefs brought Margot to an unsteady halt directly in front of Tissaurd.

"Well," Barbousse answered with perfect logic, "if we leave him here and he *does* die, then there's another body that should have been thrown off the bridge. With the millrace spreadin' 'em around the neighborhood a bit, there'll be less cause for a big investigation. . . ."

". . . And if he *doesn't* die," Brim finished with a nod, "then he can cause a pile of trouble for us with assault charges. Even if we *could* manage to explain the whole thing away, just getting involved would be bad for the IVG. They take stuff like this seriously here in Fluvanna."

"That's the way I see the situation, Cap'm," Barbousse seconded. "And since this Leaguer gentleman really *does* want to cash in, I can't see any reason to ignore his wishes."

Brim was suddenly aware of Margot, who seemed to be avoiding everyone's eyes—including his own. Her hair was disheveled and she fairly reeked of TimeWeed. No wonder she'd looked the way she did. Forcing back a rising gorge, he nodded to Barbousse. "Kill him," he said.

"Aye, Cap'm," Barbousse replied, knuckling his forehead. Gently lifting the wounded Agnord in his arms, he headed for the stand of young trees nearby.

Brim turned as Tissaurd began to speak. "What were you doing in that building, LaKarn?" she demanded. "You didn't lift a finger to help the Captain. Why?"

"I—I did everything I could," Margot said in a dull voice, still avoiding Brim's eyes. "But I wasn't armed," she slurred, weaving back and forth on her feet. "I . . . er . . . ran for the inn to call for the police."

"Interesting," Tissaud said. "I wonder where those police are. You'd think even Fluvannians would have shown up by now."

"I c-couldn't get anyone to answer the door," Margot answered. "I t-tried. . . ."

From the corner of his eye, Brim watched Barbousse emerge on the far side of the trees, striding briskly toward the bridge with a limp form slung over his shoulder.

"Nobody answered the door?" Tissaud exclaimed in open disbelief. "That's Gorksroar, pure and simple! Palmerston managers are at that desk all night, *every* night. I ought to know; I get laid there now and then myself!" She shook her head for a moment, then dismissed the Baroness with an angry wave of her hand. "Let her go," she said to the Chiefs. "That was all I needed to hear."

The two immediately released their prisoner, who staggered a few steps, then lost her balance and collapsed in a heap on the grass.

"WUN-der-ful," Tissaud growled while Brim hurried to help Margot to her feet. "Skipper, how in Voot's name can you do that when this blond zukeed just set you up for a pack of Agnords?"

"We can't just leave her here," Brim replied, nearly overcome with anguish.

"The Cap'm's right, Lieutenant," Barbousse put in, cleaning his knife with a dark-colored handkerchief. "I think we probably *had* better get the Princess back to her ship; otherwise . . ." He raised his hands in supplication.

"I know," Tissaud pouted, "another 'inter-domain incident.' Right?"

"Aye, Lieutenant," Barbousse said quietly.

While Brim helplessly supported the flaccid wreck of a woman he had once loved, he saw bright headlight beams swing into the park and race toward him. At the last moment, their source —an arrogant Majestat-Baron limousine skimmer—slewed sideways and came to a halt no more than twenty irals from where he stood, its powerful generators purring at idle. Four tall Controllers from the League catapulted out of the passenger compartment and strode imperiously toward Brim and Margot, completely ignoring the array of powerful blasters aimed at their heads.

"Baroness," one of them said as if she were alone in the park, "where have you been, my dear? We were *worried*."

Margot absently touched a lock of her hair and turned slowly to face the four sinister figures before her. "I h-have . . . been out to supper," she slurred, reaching toward him like a small child.

"We shall return you to your ship immediately, Your Highness," the Controller said, taking an outstretched arm.

"Get your xaxtdamned hands off her," Brim growled, but Barbousse appeared wraithlike at his side to gently place a restraining hand on his forearm.

"It's better this way, Cap'm" the big rating said in a low voice. "She'll need her TimeWeed soon enough."

Brim ground his teeth while bitter tears filled his eyes. Barbousse was right. It was the *only* way.

Now completely supported by the big Controller, Margot turned toward him one last time, and he felt he could almost touch her mind. Almost. . . . With an unfathomable expression in her eyes, she stumbled into the limousine; a moment later she was gone once more from his life in a cool breeze of gravitons and receding tail lamps.

Followed by Tissaurd in one of the IVG vans, Brim returned his rented skimmer, then climbed in beside his diminutive First Lieutenant while she drove back to the launch that had carried her and the Chiefs from Varnholm. The woman was clearly angry: too much for any relevant conversation. All she would say concerning the fracas that night—and for a long time to come—was, "That LaKarn woman is no longer your friend, Wilf Brim. Mark my words. She is out to have you *killed*."

During the three weeks following Brim's "incident" at Palmerston Park, relations between the League of Dark Stars and Fluvanna deteriorated at an even speedier rate than before, with accusations and counteraccusations spicing each new edition of the media. Strangely enough—at least to Brim—the Leaguers themselves continued to breathe life into the disappearance of R.F.S. *Rurik*. Insisting that the old armored cruiser was being hidden somewhere by Fluvanna's own Admiralty, they continued a succession of accusations that she was actually a spy ship. Further, they alleged that she had been used routinely for covert operations against the League and her allies, especially The Torond. The aspersions made no sense, but then, politics of any ilk made little sense to Brim.

One morning just before dawn, he was on his way back to *Starfury* from a chilly, predawn jog along the strand when Ursis met him at gravity pool one, where S.S. *Maksim Litvinov*, one of the big AkroKahn cargo liners, had moored the night before. The Sodeskayan had a look of deep concern on his face as he waved Brim to a halt.

"Morning, Nik," Brim panted, grabbing the Bear's huge biceps in friendship. "You look mighty concerned for such an early juncture."

Ursis nodded and placed a six-fingered hand over Brim's. "Deeply sorry to interrupt exercise, Wilf Ansor," he called over the roar of nearby repulsion generators, "but Commodore Calhoun asked that you be notified immediately."

Brim frowned, noting the uninterrupted succession of ghostly rings spreading from the ship's tall KA'PPA tower—something was definitely up. "Notified about what?" he asked. "Sounds bad."

"Perhaps 'inevitable' is better word than 'bad,' " the Bear said, "but 'appalling' also applies—'disastrous,' as well. In short, my furless friend, war has restarted or"—he checked the huge, old-fashioned timepiece he kept in a special pocket—"*will* have started in about two metacycles." He shook his head. "Sodeskayan intelligence organizations are best in Universe, yet not infallible. Were they perfect, we should have information you are about to learn at least two Standard Days in past. As things stand, we know what is about to happen, but we have no time to prevent it without revealing our sources." Glancing up for a moment at the big ship's lofty bridge, he bowed and indicated the brow. "Commodore Calhoun requests your sweaty presence in the Communications Room," he said, "immediately."

Brim nodded, suddenly aware of the cold, gray morning around him—it seemed appropriate—then he stepped into the brow. Moments later he and Ursis were striding along a passageway deep within the hull of the great vessel. "Kind of laid out like a warship with the COMM room down here between the Drive bays," Brim commented with a smile.

"A warship?" Ursis gasped, his eyebrows raised in mock surprise. "But how could that be? We Sodeskayans are *always* peaceful."

"Except when you're angry," Brim said.

"Is true," Ursis admitted with a grin, then held up a tutorial finger. " 'Lightning and snug caves seldom bleach fur of young crag wolves,' as they say."

"As they say . . ." Brim averred, his eyes raised to the heavens.

"I knew you'd understand," the Bear said, fastidiously examining his claws.

When they arrived at *Litvinov*'s COMM room, Brim was ushered directly into the ultra-secret transmission chamber. Calhoun sat at one of the big KA'PPA consoles, busily operating the complex mechanism himself from an old-fashioned keyboard. Beside him in chairs hastily drawn up to form a temporary conference room, Moulding and McKenzie sipped steaming hot cvceese'. Motioning Brim to a third chair drawn up beside the console, the Commodore completed his KA'PPA conversation —if interactive transmission of ancient symbolic characters could be considered "conversation"—then he turned and scowled. "For your information, Brim," he said angrily, "'tis but a few metacycles afore Nergol Triannic begins war on Fluvanna." He shook his head. "And there is nothin' any o' us can do aboot it."

"I don't understand," Brim said.

"You wull in a moment," Calhoun growled. "An' shortly

after that, you'll need to hae your ships out in space. I've already ordered Tissaurd to ready your Red squadron for immediate lift-off."

"I still don't know what . . ." Brim started, but Calhoun cut him off with a wave of the hand.

"Neither do these two gentlemen with me," the Commodore said. "I've been waiting for you, laddie." He sat back in the console's recliner for a moment, studying a screen full of characters from the KA'PPA, then swiveled to face the three Captains. "When you've got mair time, gentlemen, you'll be able to read the whole thing, just as it unfolded on the KA'PPA," he said. "But for the nonce, you'll have to do with my personal synopsis. Otherwise, you might miss the first event. An' I don't think any of you wull want to do that." With that, he launched into such an account of double-dealing and treachery that Brim found himself absolutely staggered.

CHAPTER 8

Prelude to Chaos

"Turns out," Calhoun began, "that auld R.F.S. *Rurik* ne'er was lost, at least so far as the bloody League was concerned. They captured her the day she was reported missing—and she's in their hands right noo."

"Why?" Brim asked in astonishment. "What in the name of Voot would they want with that antique?"

"And how did they manage to snatch her before she at least got off a couple of messages?" Moulding interjected.

Calhoun laughed. "Young Brim, we'll get to the question aboot *why* they did it in a moment. Your friend's *how* is a lot easier." He turned to Moulding. "They blew away the auld ship's KA'PPA mast with their first salvo, then before she could slow enough for a normal transmission, they blanketed her with a bubble of free electrons. *Rurik* never had a chance."

"They got her KA'PPA with the first salvo?" Brim gasped. "But they must have fired at fantastic range; otherwise, the Fluvannian crew would have done a lot of broadcasting when they saw the Leaguer cruiser bearing down on them."

Calhoun nodded his head. "All too true, laddie," he said. "'Twas definitely a lang-range shot. Nergol Triannic hae fine gunners in his fleet; we've known that since the last war. But there's still anither part o' the story," he added. "Through Mustafa, we've learned that Leaguers weren't prevaricatin' aboot one thing, at least. *Rurik* actually was on a spy mission. That's another reason her captain waited too long afore she called for help.'' For a moment, his gray eyes focused on another time and another place. ''A fine woman, she was,'' he growled quietly. ''The zukeeds will pay in blood for the likes o' her. A *lot* o' blood.''

''I suppose she was spying on that new Leaguer space fort on the Zonga'ar asteroid shoal,'' McKenzie said.

''That's what Nik Ursis tells me, but there's a lot more to it than that. So I'll let him tell you about the rest in person—it's his Intelligence service that's supplied most of the information.''

Everyone turned toward the huge Sodeskayan who was sharing a workstation with a smaller female Bear whom Brim guessed was *very* attractive. She was small, reddish in color, and had a most compelling sparkle in her eyes. She also had large, furry ears, a mark of exceptional beauty among Sodeskayans he had met so far.

''*Rurik* was indeed spying,'' Ursis declared while he slowly rose to his feet, ''on that new space fort at Zonga'ar the Leaguers have constructed just outside the fifty light-year demarcation between Fluvanna's occupied planets and intragalactic space. It seems clear now that they're building it as a base for their campaign against Fluvanna—and that will make it one of our principal targets. The squadron that took *Rurik* embarked from that base, so it is already serving limited use. Eventually, we shall have to take it out.'' He pursed his lips. ''Indications are that they've initially housed three squadrons of Dampier cruisers from The Torond there. You'll be fighting those ships first.''

''Somehow, I'm not surprised,'' Moulding said. ''Leaguers have a history of letting other people fight their wars for them. At least in the beginning.''

''I guess it all leads back to my first question, then,'' Brim persisted. ''Why did they bother to capture the old spy ship anyway? If they had good enough fire control to blow off a KA'PPA mast at long range, why didn't they simply put a salvo right through the hull? I can't imagine an ancient armored cruiser being much use to a squadron of new Dampiers.''

The Bear nodded. "That is where the *real* treachery comes in," he growled, glancing up at a time display mounted over the KA'PPA console. "In little more than two metacycles, a Leaguer crew of Agnords flying old *Rurik* will attack and destroy the S.S. *Lombog*, a small passenger liner run by the League's own Central Bureau of Transport. The little vessel is traveling with every stateroom booked. She lifted three days ago from Tarrott, bound for Voso Gola, the Fluvannian vacation planet. Triannic's Pan-Dominion Tour Service offered special low prices to government employees on furlough."

"Sweet thraggling Universe," Moulding whispered in horror. "Now it makes sense. Triannic will use the attack on S.S. *Lombog* to . . ." He couldn't finish his sentence.

"Nergol Triannic will use the attack as an excuse to declare war on Fluvanna," Ursis said, taking control of the conversation again, "for as everyone knows, starships are considered sovereign territory just as if they were part of a planet somewhere. So when it seems that S.S. *Lombog* is destroyed on direct orders of Mustafa himself, it will be just as if he had ordered an attack on one of the Leaguer planets."

"And *Rurik* will be crewed by Agnords," McKenzie groaned, still wide-eyed with horror.

"Only at first, my friend," Ursis replied. "Those bloody Leaguers are a lot more unscrupulous than that. At their orders, the Agnords murdered everyone aboard *Rurik* soon after she was boarded, then towed her back to their new space fort and preserved the bodies. As soon as they patched up *Rurik* enough to fly—evidently, that was late yesterday—they lifted off and are now ready for their 'attack' on *Lombog*. When that's done, they'll put those same corpses back in *Rurik* at the exact stations where they were killed. Then they'll exit the old cruiser in a launch while a couple of The Torond's new Dampiers burn *it*, in turn—leaving just enough debris for positive identification."

"After that," Brim interjected, "Hanna Notrom's Ministry for Public Consensus will shriek that a 'hideous crime' has been perpetrated by Fluvanna, and shortly thereafter, Nergol Triannic will declare war in the name of *defense*."

"You've got it, laddie," Calhoun broke in. "That is *precisely* how they wull prevent Prince Onrad from quickly invoking our Mutual Assistance Treaty wi' Fluvanna. The crime wull be so heinous—literally hundreds of innocent civilians burned to death aboard the harmless *Lombog*—that the CIGAs wull have little trouble tying the Admiralty in political knots, at least long enough for the Leaguers and their allies to make a guid start on things here in Fluvanna.''

''Eventually the CIGAs have to lose that fight,'' Brim interjected. ''They won't be able to hold back the treaty forever.''

''Aye,'' Calhoun agreed grimly, ''but such a day wull come only after lang parliamentary debates. That, o' course, is why we are here.'' He glanced up at the time display again. ''Well,'' he said grimly, ''if the Leaguers are punctual as they are normally, the attack on *Lombog* wull begin precisely two cycles from now, give or take a few clicks for gravity corrections out there.'' He nodded toward the door. ''It's high time the three o' you get your Starfuries out in space; no telling what kind of timetable they're on. The first Dampier attacks could come quickly.'' He nodded. ''You'll be able to follow this travesty as it unfolds thro' the news media. Today, I'll ride with Brim; Nik wull keep us posted by KA'PPA as the Sodeskayans come up with new information. Oh and, McKenzie, you and Brim wull trade one starship each mission we fly. That way, nobody will be left behind without a bit of combat experience. Any questions?''

''Only one, Commodore,'' Moulding said. ''How will we find out when Fluvanna has declared war back? I assume we oughtn't to go around blowing up Toronder warships until all the paperwork's done.''

Calhoun made a cold smile. ''Your assumption's dead wrong, my friend,'' he said dourly. ''After the first media announcements, feel free to blast any Toronders you see, as well as any ship that belongs to their bosses, the Leaguers. Certain enemy vessels wull be off limits during the next week or so, like the anes that carry their diplomatic staff back home. But I'll specifically identify those for you. From noo through the end o' the war, consider them all fair game—and shoot before you find yourself bein' shot at. Got that?''

"Got it," Brim said, getting up from his chair. He turned to Moulding. "Toby, I'll see you out on the bay at . . . let's make it Dawn:2:50."

"Dawn:2:50," Moulding confirmed. He grinned. "Don't be surprised if I'm there a little early. I think I started getting myself ready for this a long time ago. . . ."

Less than two metacycles later, at precisely Morning:1:17, Brim lifted R.F.S. *Starfury* from Penard Bay under a heavy overcast with Stefan MacAlda's R.F.S. *Starspite* tucked close to starboard and half a length astern. Moments later they thundered over Varnholm Hall. Below, Brim glimpsed a small crowd waving from the keep, then abruptly the outside Universe was swallowed by a gray blanket of cloud. On the other side of the Hyperscreens, only a radiance in the whiteness marked the planet's star, Ephail, but a good Helmsman could judge the angle of climb by that alone.

At about twelve thousand irals they came out into clear air, and Brim, almost blinded by the brilliant whiteness on all sides, glimpsed deep blue sky above him. Soon, they were climbing steadily through a crystalline-clear atmosphere. Below, the receding planet speedily became a plain of white cotton where nothing stirred. As far as the eye could see—for hundreds, soon thousands of square c'lenyts—stretched soft cloud-continents with occasional crevasses between them like wide rivers. Brim never tired of the spectacle; it was part and parcel of the milieu called space flight.

As *Starfury* climbed out toward space, Ephail kept the whole bridge wrapped in brilliant gold light. Brim held it in the same position on his right, flying with the exhilaration that landsmen could only imagine, occasionally turning his head to insure that MacAlda was still keeping R.F.S. *Starspite* in position to starboard. Off to port, the second pair of Starfuries, R.F.S. *Starvengeance* and R.F.S. *Starconstant*, were climbing at the same speed as MacAlda and himself, all four ships at different relative altitudes. Looking back along their shimmering flight path, he watched Moulding in R.F.S. *Starsovereign* lead the second four-ship quad out of the clouds. Then the brightness outside began to fail with the atmosphere, and they started into the utter darkness of space.

Just after they thundered past the ninety-five-thousand-c'lenyt flight level—still well below LightSpeed—he heard Calhoun's globular display beep for the arrival of an urgent, TOP SECRET transmission. Moments later, his did, too. He passed his hand over a blinking enabler on the console beside him. Instantly, Ursis's furry visage filled the globe.

"The war has begun," the Bear announced grimly. "*Lombog* transmitted a series of urgent calls for assistance only moments before she was actually attacked. Clearly, *Rurik*'s captors learned her old disruptors quickly and thoroughly. They worked ever so slowly, nibbling away at the liner's hull until only the control and COMM chambers were intact. It gave the poor crew a maximum time to scream for help—and KA'PPA word of the 'attack' all over the Universe."

Immediately after the Bear signed off, Calhoun's visage filled the display, eyes narrowed with a look of determination. "As Ursis put things, it's started noo," he growled. "Make nae mistake. Probably we'll see no action for the next few days, but you'll want to keep someone mannin' the search gear at 'Action Stations' from now on."

As Calhoun predicted, within a metacycle, Hanna Notrom's Ministry for Public Consensus began to KA'PPA streams of invective to every news bureau in the Universe. These transmissions were accepted by *Starfury*'s KA'PPA-COMM at the same instant they were received everywhere else in the Universe. By this manner, Brim and the crew of *Starfury* followed the carefully orchestrated scenario as it rapidly unfolded.

Using the *Lombog*'s broadcast pleas for assistance as "proof" of Fluvannian transgression, the League's military Chiefs immediately ordered "full mobilization of forces." All this by KA'PPA-COMM before "normal" messages could be transported by mail aboard starships that could outspeed radio waves. Clearly, the event had been planned well in advance and thoroughly rehearsed throughout the League and its network of allies.

Early the next Standard Day, Triannic's huge Ministry of

Diplomacy produced a long list of impossible demands the Fluvannians must immediately satisfy.

In Avalon, it was clear that Puvis Amherst and his minions had been well prepared for their part of the action. Hastily organized but superbly coordinated CIGA demonstrations occurred simultaneously at the palace and the Admiralty, only metacycles following the first KA'PPAed announcement of the declaration. These neatly strangled all initial demands for invocation of the mutual defense pact with Fluvanna. And when voices of reason refused to be silenced, powerful CIGAs in the General Parliament—who doubtlessly had been well rehearsed for such an event—smothered the whole matter in an absolute morass of governmental debate.

Among the IVG, the days following delivery of Triannic's demands to Fluvanna were an unending test of everyone's patience. It was clear that an attack would follow shortly after any declaration of war, and the strain of patrolling became a double-edged sword: day after day, the routine never changed from watch to watch, yet the anxiety of waiting for the unexpected was almost unbearable. Moreover, each time Calhoun urged Mustafa to let the IVG go after the Leaguers' space fort with a "surgical" strike in anticipation of attacks on the Fluvannian homeland, the Nabob deferred, maintaining that "We shall let history record that Leaguers delivered the first blow."

"What if it's the Leaguers who write the history?" Calhoun asked time and time again.

"Then so be it," the Nabob replied, folding his arms in a symbol of finality. And thus it was that when the declaration of war finally came—just ninety-seven Standard Days following *Rurik*'s initial disappearance—Brim was leading Quad One on a roving orbital patrol, some two thousand c'lenyts out from Ordu and nowhere near the fort. Moulding led the second quad, keeping to the opposite hemisphere. Close in, McKenzie's three ships hovered in synchronous orbit, approximately seventy-five c'lenyts above Magor itself. Between them, at about one thousand c'lenyts distance, six quads of Mustafa's pristine antiques cruised in a roughly spherical pattern. Calhoun, who had ordered the defensive pattern on a tip from the Sodeskayans, today was riding aboard McKenzie's *Starglory*. All the ships were traveling well below LightSpeed; if an attack against the planet were imminent—as the elder Carescrian strongly suspected—the enemy would have to slow considerably to fire their disruptors at a "stationary" target.

Just prior to the Dawn watch, Brim was finishing breakfast in the wardroom and going through a stack of routine KA'PPA dispatches when the deck vibrated slightly under his boots. Simultaneously, the whine from *Starfury*'s power primaries raised in pitch—followed at once by a substantial boost in the thunder from Zaftrak's big Admiralty generators out in the pontoons. Moments later sirens whooped throughout the ship.

"General quarters! General quarters—all hands man your action stations! General quarters! General quarters—all hands man your action stations!" Brim's calm was shattered as he raced for the bridge. Boots thumped on the deck as running figures scampered to their posts, groping for antiradiation gear and battlesuit helmets, making sure at least two air cartridges were secured loosely around their waists.

"Special duty starsailors to your stations! Secure all airtight doors! Down all deadlights!"

"I'll take the con, Number One," he said to Tissaurd, sliding breathlessly into the left-hand helm.

"You're welcome to it *today*, Skipper," Tissaurd said with a grin—as if it were just another exercise.

It passed Brim's mind that the tiny woman enjoyed perhaps the strongest character on the ship. She was positively unflappable. He checked his helmet and air cartridges, then tightened his seat gravity to MAXIMUM and ran a quick systems check. Behind him, the whole bridge hummed with similar checkouts: power, propulsion, fire control, damage control, communications, sensing systems, medical. Outside on the pontoons, he watched A and B turrets swing and elevate their twin 406-mmi disruptors as firing crews ran final systems checks. Overhead, the business ends of two more 406s, these belonging to E turret, traversed past the dorsal Hyperscreens. He knew that three other emplacements performed similar oblations out of sight beneath the pontoons and hull. In the distance, nearly out of range, a few suspicious lights were now moving improperly against the great canopy of stars.

Abruptly, one of the gun layers broke the relative silence of the bridge. "Look out, chaps. Here they come." His voice was strangely calm, as if he had been giving that same sort of warning for years. At one time, he had, of course, during the *last* war. As Emperor Greyffin IV once so succinctly pointed out, experience *counted*. Moments later, a proximity alarm sounded.

Brim banked *Starfury* in a slight left turn and looked up to confront at least twenty-five starships coming at them, slowed below LightSpeed for a ground attack. Even though he couldn't identify them, they were uniquely from The Torond. The untidy formation and nervously juddering graviton plumes were unmistakable. As the disruptors swung up to meet them, his thoughts momentarily touched on his unresolved feelings for Margot Effer'wyck. Then, before he could concentrate, an old Helmsman's Academy instructor's voice echoed ancient Fleet doggerel: "Beware the ships wot bear out of a glare, me boy."

Brim closed his mind to all of it. This was his very purpose for being. Nothing else mattered. "All killing systems energize," he ordered over the blower.

As his muscles keyed to the oncoming challenge, he pictured Chief Baranev and his Sodeskayan Propulsion Engineers out in the pontoons with their gravity generators, sealed in a brightly lit hell of noise and hair-raising energy. He switched his COMM to the work chambers. "You people in the pontoons," he ordered grimly, "take to your lifeglobes if I give the word. No heroics; got that?" He didn't wait for an answer. He'd seem too many people burn in streams of escaping energy from radiation fires. It was a slow, painful death.

Everybody would be at his action station now . . . waiting. There were no passengers aboard warships; even people like cooks and disbursing clerks would be down with the damage-control parties. He thought about Penelope Hesternal back at the base hospital. She'd be getting ready for the first casualties of the war. On the far side of Tissaurd's station, the Navigator was correcting a HoloChart in his oversize globular display. The firing crews in the next stations aft were busily tracking possible targets in their arcane language of pure mathematics. Beside him, Tissaurd followed his every move, ready to take over instantly should he be disabled.

"Warn the generator rooms, Strana'," he said into a display, "I'll want maximum thrust when I give the word."

The Bear nodded silently and turned to her own displays.

Suddenly Brim's introspection vanished. He altered course toward the squadron of graviton plumes and called out, "All gravity generators, full power." He was ready to fight.

A moment later Zaftrak's furry visage appeared in a COMM display, her mouth open to speak.

Brim spoke up before she could utter a word. "I know what the Chief and his Drive crews are saying down there, Strana'," he said, "but I want everything they've got—*now*!" Baranev —hefty, even for a Sodeskayan—was the best Drive crew supervisor in the business, but sometimes he loved his equipment a little *too* much.

Zaftrak's face disappeared from the display and moments later the whine from all ten K-P K23971 plasma generators simultaneously rose in pitch while rolling thunder from the big Admiralty A876s shook the very deck; stars began to cascade past the Hyperscreens in an insane flood. *Starfury* was made for tearing along like this, above and below LightSpeed. She was in her element now.

Ahead, the squadron of graviton plumes fanned out and veered to meet them.

"Break port!" Brim commanded to the other starships in his quad. "Climbing!"

At nearly the same instant, Brim's power indicators reached their rated maximum three thousand standard thrust units. Outside, the oncoming ships had defined themselves into Dampier D.A. 79-IIs, driving in toward Magor. He made for the first group, and all space seemed to explode as the big 406s discharged. An instant later the leading Dampier lit up with explosions—but the focus was 'way short. Three or four shimmering energy puffs nonetheless appeared in the Dampier's wake. Even near misses from a brace of 406s could be deadly.

Two more Dampiers made a tight turn, bringing themselves

head-on. Energy beams from their 280-mmi disruptors formed long, glittering tentacles snaking remorselessly toward *Starfury*, at the last moment curling down just under her hull. In the next instant, all space became a swimming kaleidoscope of The Torond's black triangle insignias. At half the speed of light, Brim sensed rather than saw the presence of starships circling 'round until suddenly his eyes fixed on one of them.

"There's one!" he shouted.

Immediately half the battery swung aft. "We see him, Captain," a deep voice called tensely from a display.

Brim didn't even acknowledge. The big Dampier was still circling, its black triangles edged with yellow, Hyperscreens glittering in Ephail's bright starlight as she banked back and forth, settling on an opponent.

"Tracking. . . ."

"Out of range and closing. . . ."

Suddenly the Dampier appeared to spot them.

"Good proximity alarms," Tissaurd commented dryly.

The enemy ship fell off to starboard in a tight turn. Two shimmering streamers of gravitons appeared at her extremities from the steering engines. Without warning, she climbed vertically at tremendous speed, then violently flipped over on her back, disruptors firing spasmodically as their director systems tumbled. Brim flinched. In a moment of frenzy, her Helmsman had overcontrolled and outrun the steering engines. Now the big ship continued in the same direction, flat, on momentum alone. Such a mistake was easy to make with the new breeds of powerful ships that had begun to appear subsequent to the final Mitchell Trophy races. This mistake, however, would *also* be fatal. *Starfury* was narrowing the distance quickly.

Brim listened to one of the Director crews behind his helm. "Range nine thirty-one Green and closing. . . ."

He watched the long-nosed Dampier grow in the Hyperscreens. She was so close now he could see the blue radiation flames close in where her graviton plumes began. She was almost factory new. The electron waste gates abaft her crystal chambers were hardly stained. Too late, her turrets were beginning to swing!

"Bearing one one nine. . . ."

"Steady. . . ."

Brim held *Starfury* on course as if she were on rails.

"Fire!"

The graceful Sherrington cruiser shuddered as if she had encountered some great cosmic wall, while eight huge disruptors tore at the warp and woof of space itself. Simultaneously, the Dampier's sharp, clear image ahead shook and began to disintegrate. Her bridge Hyperscreens burst into glittering fragments and the two forward turrets spun into the slipstream like toys. The hits advanced aft toward her inactive Hyperspeed Drive section in a series of disastrous explosions and sparks that glittered along her hull until a spurt of radiation fire and debris erupted just aft of her main deckhouse. In the wink of an eye, a blackish-red cloud of raw energy mingled with the burning collapsium particles.

Brim pushed over on the controls and veered out of the way. As *Starfury* flicked off, he had a last vision of the big Dampier exploding in a cloud of energy and light. Then he was past, Calhoun's voice thundering in his mind: *Slash and fire, lad. No toe-to-toe!*

The whole episode had lasted no more than a few clicks.

To the right, Brim watched another *Starfury* break off and head behind a Dampier. He caught a glimpse of its markings: K5058. Moulding. Swerving to cover him, the Carescrian avoided several determined attacks by going into a tight spiral —but *Starfury* was traveling too fast to follow. Ahead, *Starsovereign* began to fire, her disruptors disgorging long trails of glittering energy.

Of a sudden, proximity alarms went off all over the bridge, while a series of terrific explosions blasted *Starfury* sideways. A near miss from somewhere! The starboard turrets swung violently, loosing huge bolts of energy that shook the speeding cruiser even farther off course. Brim fought the controls as a great shadow momentarily blanketed the overhead Hyperscreens. A Dampier's enormous, heat-streaked belly flashed only a few irals above the bridge. He had missed *Starfury* and was going after Moulding.

"Watch out, Skipper," Tissaurd exclaimed, "that zukeed's taken a real dislike to Toby!"

Instinctively, Brim hauled back on the power, listening to the disruptor trainers and watching the forward tubes elevate, then immediately open fire. The mighty fusillade of raw energy belched forth by six 406s at point-blank range hammered into the Dampier precisely where the forward dorsal turret pierced her armored hull—with devastating results. Shaken in its course, the big starship skidded violently to the left as its whole bow from the bridge forward folded up in a shower of sparks and hullmetal fragments that smashed her aft Drive shields and whizzed past *Starfury* in a hail of debris.

The Carescrian had hardly recovered from his surprise when *Starfury* was attacked by six other Dampiers. The whole Universe seemed to go wild again in an insane turmoil of monstrous explosions and lurid flashes of light, while the gun crews defended the ship as if they were possessed. Brim felt sweat pouring off his face. He had to keep turning constantly, with the Dampiers dogging his every move.

Then one of the Dampiers took a moment too long recovering from its attack. Four of *Starfury*'s big disruptors fired immediately with murderous effect. A cluster of tremendous explosions blasted its main deckhouse just beneath the bridge, and the cruiser faltered as if it had smashed into a large asteroid. Brim never looked back. *Slash and fire. Slash and fire. . . .*

Then, abruptly, the Dampiers showed signs of flagging and soon thereafter turned on their heels. Brim and the other Starfuries gave chase for a moment to start them on their way, then all turned and headed for Varnholm Hall—just as the first of the "regular" Fluvannian Fleet units reached the battle area. Brim left them with orders to continue their patrol, another thousand c'lenyts out. They'd at least make a good early warning group.

On the way home from the rout, they passed at least three squadrons of elderly Fluvannian warships clawing their way into space. "A day late and a credit short, if y' ask me, Skipper," Tissaurd commented.

Brim laughed grimly and took a deep breath. His adrenaline was only now coming under control. "I suppose that's true,

Number One," he said. "But how would you feel about flying out to meet a squadron of Dampiers in one of those antiques?"

The tiny officer thought for a moment and gave her own grim little snort. "You're right," she said angrily. "Were I aboard one of those pitiful antiques, I think I might be a day late myself, now that you mention it—because clearly that poor excuse for a fleet is a *lot* of credits short." She scowled bitterly. "Mustafa has undoubtedly saved himself, and his treasury, a lot of wealth over the years by buying up everybody else's cast-off warships. But guess who's making up the difference now that he's got a war on his hands. . . ."

During the next Standard Month, Calhoun's superbly equipped and trained IVG—"assisting powerful units of the Fluvannian Home Fleet," as the media reported almost daily—handily repulsed a score of raids from the Leaguer space fort, with disastrous results for the Toronder starfleets and "acceptable" damage to the leased Starfuries.

The IVG's advantage was the Starfuries' superior speed combined with awesome firepower and generous armor. These enabled them to swoop into enemy formations, produce devastating harm in a matter of moments, then speed away before their quarry could effectively react. According to the Sodeskayans, the unorthodox tactics actually rattled Toronder crews, who were trained for more conventional warfare. Despite the ample firepower of their Dampiers, the big ships were no match for Starfuries, and they were usually easy victims for the aggressive IVG crews. But every one of the ex-Imperials knew that sooner or later, the League would tire of its thralls' overlong effort to subdue Fluvanna; then there would be Gorn-Hoffs to deal with as well.

And indeed, the change began less than a week later, manifesting itself in revised enemy tactics called "doubling," whereby escorting squadrons of Dampiers were escorted by a squadron of the League's powerful new Gorn-Hoff 262A-1As, first production version of the P.1065. These stood off maddeningly from the battles until it was certain that the Dampiers had fought themselves into a corner (as they usually did). Then the Leaguers would jump into the fray, effectively tripling odds against the IVG. To no one's particular surprise, the new Gorn-Hoff 262s were *superb* warships; in many ways the equal of Mark Valerian's Starfuries—in some, superior.

Happily, during the months imposed between Calhoun's initial briefings on the Leaguers' new, chevron-contoured prototype and Brim's first personal encounters with production versions, Sodeskayan intelligence sources were able to provide considerable data on the new Leaguer ships. So their startling performance came as no surprise. It was a fortunate thing, too. For unbeknown to the ex-Imperials, the squadrons of "easy" Dampier opponents had been making them moderately lax. And even with ample forewarning, they still turned out to be a nasty surprise on the day they first showed up.

Brim had *Starfury* in the middle of a frenzied melee well below LightSpeed. With his quad outnumbered three-to-one by Dampiers, the Carescrian had been flying for all he was worth, twisting and turning, trying to set up shots for his disruptor crews while nursing the generators, scanning the instruments, and watching for the few scrappy Toronder skippers who yet remained among their savaged squadrons. Just as the enemy crews appeared to be getting ready to pack it in for another day, his eyes caught a second group of ships cruising high off the port bows. *These*, however, were making curious, oscillating Drive wakes—like ones he recalled from the endless Gorn-Hoff P.1065 briefings he'd been forced to sit through in Avalon. "Everyone on his toes," he broadcast to the bridge crews, "we've got some special company, Purple Apex."

Tissaurd needed only a glance through the forward Hyperscreens. "Bloody Gorn-Hoffs," she swore under her breath. "The new 262s! We've *got* to take out that xaxtdamned fort somehow."

Brim nodded grimly. "If we ever have a moment when we're not fighting for our lives." Abruptly, the Drive wakes flickered out and the enemy starships slowed to Hypospeed. He switched on the COMM and set it for GENERAL. "Special threat alert, all firing crews!" he announced throughout the ship. "Hands prepare for unknown enemy warships. Special threat alert, all firing crews. Hands prepare for unknown enemy warships!"

A moment later the Dampiers literally evaporated in breakneck retreat and the Leaguer warships surged forward to replace them. Brim no sooner disengaged from the last fleeing Toronder than he was immersed in a fight where suddenly life and death hung in the balance. He pulled *Starfury* into a half loop, passing so close to a pair of the big Gorn-Hoffs that for a moment he could see through their bridge Hyperscreens—but the three ships passed so closely to each other that none could bring its disruptors to bear. The Gorn-Hoffs followed in their own half loop, but by this time, Brim had cranked *Starfury* into a tight turn and the IVG disruptor crews were able to get off two good volleys from eight 406s that sparkled along the left-hand Leaguer's starboard "wing" and blasted one of its 375-mmi turrets out into space like a top.

A hail of return fire smashed the Sherrington cruiser aside like a cork in a millrace, blanking the Hyperscreens momentarily and pulsing the cabin gravity so that Brim's restraints constricted painfully around his body.

The Carescrian tightened his turn, *Starfury*'s rugged spaceframe groaning in protest as the steering engines struggled to bring the speeding ship onto a new course. But they had him cold, sitting on *his* tail as if they were under tow. As he angrily ground his teeth, he realized that they had probably been watching him for several cycles and planning the whole thing.

From their position, he guessed they would expect him to tuck *Starfury*'s nose under and try to run for it. Instead, he twisted upward and *toward* them in a corkscrew. He'd guessed right! As he thundered at them, it was *they* who had had to turn.

But the zukeeds had been ready for *that*, too! Two more Gorn-Hoffs suddenly appeared directly in his path; clearly they'd been waiting on the chance that he might do the unexpected.

Brim was a brave starsailor—and survivor of more than his share of battles against "impossible" odds—but those battles had also made him smart. Clearly, anytime one ship was up against four that were flown by crews of *that* caliber, the prudent thing to do was to execute a well-known maneuver known as "getting the xaxt out of there." As an old Carescrian proverb put things: *It's no disgrace to run if you are scared.*

He was!

Accelerating to the upper limits of *Starfury*'s Hypospeed envelope, he zigzagged and skidded like a madman in an attempt to break for home. But the four Gorn-Hoffs hung on like Drive cement, two high and two low—just out of lethal range. . . .

Why didn't they fire?

Spasms of anxiety danced up and down Brim's spine like ice. He glanced at Tissaurd who was sitting bolt upright in her seat, her forehead beaded with sweat.

"Aren't the zukeeds going to fire?" she growled through clenched teeth. "We could thraggling die of old age!"

Starfury had become easy meat, sandwiched between two pairs of expert crews. Her main armament was divided among four attackers, and the percentage certainty of destroying one of the Leaguer ships with a salvo of only three disruptors was a little less than fifty percent. Sooner or later, somebody would make a mistake, which at least one of the Leaguers would spot instantly. After that. . . .

And then it came to him. "A mistake!" he half shouted. "*Now* I remember!"

"Mistake?" Tissaurd asked, glancing his way for a moment. "What do you remember? *Whose?*"

Brim grunted, hauling the big starship around in a tight curve with the four Leaguers still hot on his tail. "Gorn-Hoff's design team made the mistake," he growled, checking the rearview display on his panel. "They didn't build enough power into those new ships of theirs to fly at top speed and simultaneously fire all fourteen of those new superfocused Theobold disruptors at maximum power."

Tissaurd met his eye. "Voot's beard!" she exclaimed. "That's true. I remember it from somebody's briefing—yours, probably."

Brim nodded. "Like right now," he said, "those four ships on our tail can probably muster no more than eight of their Theobold 375s apiece. I figure that gives each of them something like a forty-five percent certainty of destroying us, per salvo: about the same chance we have of getting one of them with three of our 406s. But since that certainty percentage isn't additive among the four ships, those twenty-four big Theobolds behind us *still* share only a single ship's forty-five percent chance of stopping us." He laughed grimly as he steered into yet another extreme maneuver. "It's a standoff, so long as I can keep them from catching up. At this speed, if they fire, they'll also deprive their generators of energy, cutting into their ability to maneuver." He chuckled. "Of course, they could fire a bigger salvo at lower power—and change the percentages significantly. But with a proportional decrease in range, they'd come closer to our 406s. And then they might not get off any shots—*ever*."

At that moment, one of the low Gorn-Hoffs became vulnerable as it attempted to follow Brim's wild maneuvering and blocked his partner's field of fire. But for only an instant.

That was all it took.

Straightaway, Brim pushed over, drew back on the power, and as *Starfury*'s nose came down, the disruptor crews fired a terrific salvo ahead of the errant Leaguer. Perhaps the enemy Helmsman didn't even *see* the thick bolt of energy sizzling past in front of him, but at any rate, he flew right into it, with devastating effect. The concentrated firepower of six 406-mmi disruptors tore her entire bow away, along with the bridge, then rippled along the hull until it blasted her Drive section open like an overripe fruit. Rescue globes popped into the doomed ship's wake as the few surviving crew ejected. Then clicks later, the big Gorn-Hoff exploded in a blinding flash, bombarding its partner with a hail of hullmetal shards and whirling debris.

When the Hyperscreens cleared, *Starfury*'s twelve main disruptors were now tracking four apiece among the remaining Gorn-Hoffs, and his kill probability had now risen to fifty-eight percent. Moreover, the surviving low Leaguer had clearly been damaged by its exploding partner. Huge areas along its starboard "wing" had been shattered and raked with debris.

Had Brim been either of the two high Leaguers above him in such a situation, he would have attacked at that very moment, counting on surprise for extra protection. They didn't, hesitating for one fateful moment while *he* decided to attack. In the wink of an eye, he pulled back on the nose and judiciously applied full power, coming over at them in a complete renversment with *Starfury*'s steering engines howling in protest.

The Leaguers were caught with their battlesuits at half mast. Before *Starfury*'s disruptor crews could set up for another salvo, they turned and fled, accelerating toward LightSpeed on maximum output. Brim supposed that the sight of their exploding colleague might have taken much of the fight out of them.

It didn't take any fight out of Brim. He lit off after all three of them—annoyed with them and downright angry at himself.

Starfury was faster, especially so after they passed into Hyperspeeds. And the damaged Gorn-Hoff immediately began to fall behind, clearly experiencing Drive trouble. Remorselessly, Brim continued to close in until, at about five thousand c'lenyts distance, the laggard began stunting. It didn't do any good. *Starfury* easily stuck with him, just out of range, until Ulfilas Meesha's disruptor crews fired a burst directly into Gorn-Hoff's stern that blasted through her Drive tubes and directly into the power chambers.

There were no rescue globes before or after that explosion. The ship and everything associated with it passed directly to subatomic particles in a single hellish detonation.

Afterward, Brim sullenly headed for home to report that he had blundered into a trap and had come out of it with two victories. *Starfury* now had nineteen confirmed kills, but—to himself—he felt that the two Gorn-Hoffs should have counted at least double. And now the IVG would have to take out the fort *whatever* the costs might be. It had become a simple matter of survival. He resolved to take it up with Calhoun as soon as he made landfall. Then, as he readied the ship for reentry, a globular display on Brim's COMM unit winked into life with a three-chime priority signal.

"Incoming Precedence-One message for you, Captain," a KA'PPA rating announced, "from Polkovnik Ursis back at Varnholm."

"A KA'PPA message?" Brim demanded. "We're below LightSpeed."

"It's a KA'PPA, Captain," the rating said.

"Very well," Brim said with a frown. "Put it on the display."
He glanced at Tissaurd. "What could be so important that he
needs to tell us before we land—and by KA'PPA?"

The tiny officer shrugged. "Beats me, Skipper," she said,
leaning across her left-hand console to watch the old-fashioned
characters appear on Brim's KA'PPA screen.

BNO-987HO97BFD GROUP Z98V09 13/52011
[UNCLASSIFIED]

FROM: N. Y. URSIS, CAPTAIN, R.F.F. @ VARN-
HOLM HALL, ORDU

TO: B. O. CALHOUN, COMMODORE, R.F.F.
COMMANDER, VARNHOLM HALL
IVG DETACHMENT
@ R.F.S. *STARGLORY*

COPIES:
W. A. BRIM, CMDR, R.F.F. @ R.F.S. *STARFURY*
F. L. MCKENZIE, CMDR, R.F.F. @ R.F.S. *STAR-*
GLORY
T. D. MOULDING, CMDR, R.F.F. @ R.F.S. *STAR-*
SOVEREIGN

<EAS0923YOIAVSK70W45OIUH>

IS OFFICIAL NOTIFICATION I.F.S. *QUEEN ELI-*
DEAN ARRIVED VARNHOLM HALL PRECISELY
FIFTEEN CYCLES PAST. LOCAL ABSENCE
LARGE GRAVITY POOLS REQUIRES RETURN
TO PARKING ORBIT APPROXIMATELY 150
C'LENYTS ALTITUDE. NO OVERT ACTION TO-
WARD VARNHOLM BASE IMPLIED, HOSTILE
OR OTHERWISE. QUEEN CARRIES [NOTE
RANK] VICE ADMIRAL PUVIS AMHERST DE-
MANDING IMMEDIATE MEETING UPON YOUR

RETURN TO BASE. LEAGUE PASSENGERS POS-
SIBLE.

WITH MOST CHEERFUL REGARDS
N. Y. URSIS, CAPTAIN, IVG

[END UNCLASSIFIED]
BN0-987HO97BFD GROUP Z98V09 13/52011

"Sweet thraggling Universe," Brim swore softly. "Puvis
Amherst—scum of the Empire and a Vice Admiral to boot."
He shook his head angrily and scowled at Tissaurd. "The CIGAs
are sure up to something, sneaking a battleship to Varnholm—
and I'll bet none of *our* people knew about it. We'd have been
warned, otherwise. No wonder Nik KA'PPAed—and in the
clear."

"Yeah," Tissaurd agreed with a nod, "everybody in the Universe who wants to pick up that message will read it."

Brim glowered as he scanned his instrument panels. "The
Commodore's got trouble now," he growled. "Amherst might
be a scoundrel, but he's quick as a whipsnake—and a thousand
times more dangerous."

"I sort of got that idea," Tissaurd said, backing away from
his obvious rage.

"That's what I like about you, Number One," Brim chuckled,
focusing through the forward Hyperscreens as an altitude warning
began to flash on his nav panel. "You catch on fast." He
switched on his COMM and contacted the Varnholm traffic controller. "Fleet K5054 descending through two hundred
c'lenyts," he said.

"Fleet K5054: fly heading two thirty-five," the base replied.
"Orbital traffic, fifty c'lenyts ahead of you: Imperial battleship."

"Two thirty-five heading; orbital traffic in fifty," Brim acknowledged. He glanced at Tissaurd. "Universe," he said, "the
Queen herself. Amherst brought heavy support with him."

"Yeah," Tissaurd responded, squinting through the Hyperscreens. "I think I have her in sight."

"Fleet K5054," the controller broke in, "not to exceed forty-five hundred on the run-in; there's quite a bit of returning traffic right now; you'll probably have an eight- or nine-c'lenyt final it looks like.''

Brim activated *Starfury*'s powerful retarders and the ship began to slow. "OK, forty-five hundred on the speed, Fleet K5054," he replied, then peered ahead into the distance to a colossal, wedge-shaped form that was growing by the moment in the Hyperscreens as they approached. "Yeah," he said, "I see her. We'll pass within c'lenyts."

Tissaurd peered ahead as if she were mesmerized. "Sweet thraggling Universe, but she's beautiful, Skipper," she whispered aloud.

Brim nodded. The grand old ship had always been a symbol of everything worthwhile about the Empire she represented. "We'll have the salute, Number One," he said,

"Aye, Skipper," Tissaurd replied, touching a portion of her COMM console.

Overhead, KA'PPA rings shimmered out from *Starfury*'s KA'PPA mast in the age-old Imperial salute; Brim had no need to check his console for the message, "MAY STARS LIGHT ALL THY PATHS," nor the answer that shimmered forth from the battleship's lofty transmitter, "AND THY PATHS, STAR TRAVELERS." As *Starfury* swept past no more than five or six c'lenyts from that majestic panorama of casemated turrets and wide-shouldered hull, the old warship looked powerful simply idling in orbit. He felt hairs tingle on the back of his neck. *Queen Elidean* and her four consorts were from another age—one that was dying even as the present war began. The future belonged to newer, smaller, more powerful breeds like Starfuries, and all too soon great ships like the *Queen* would fade into Universal darkness.

With the battleship receding in the distance, Brim's COMM panel came alive again: "Fleet K5054, check in with Varnholm Approach one one nine point four."

"One one nine point four, Fleet K5054," Brim acknowledged. Then he put the *Queen* from his mind. He had a starship to land, and afterward, it was very probable that he would have to help deal with Puvis Amherst. There was much to prepare. . . .

As Brim swept over Varnholm Hall on final, he spotted a launch on one of the gravity pools that was bigger than anything Starfuries could carry. Clearly, Puvis Amherst had arrived. McKenzie's *Starglory* was nearby, already moored on her own gravity pool, so Calhoun was there as well. Brim took a deep breath to calm himself. He could imagine the conversations that were taking place.

Setting *Starfury* down with a minimum of runout, he hauled the big ship around in great cascades of spray, and taxied back to the pool area at high speed. Well-practiced docking crews quickly had the big cruiser secure on her pool, at which time Ursis arrived at the foot of the brow, shading his eyes and squinting up at the bridge. He beckoned emphatically when Brim waved.

"Take care of her, Number One," the Carescrian ordered, sliding out of his recliner and heading back through the bridge at a trot. He took the companionways two steps at a time and arrived at the entry chamber even while the hatch was sliding aside. Ursis met him on the other side.

"The Commodore wants both of us in his office on the double," the Bear said. "Moulding and McKenzie are there already with Amherst. I saw an additional human emerge from their launch and join them, but I could not tell who it was."

Brim nodded, and the two trotted along the maze of stone catwalks that led to what was once an assay laboratory: leftover from Varnholm's original existence as a mining port. Two IVG guards—*big* Sodeskayan Sergeants, originally from the Special Security Corps—stood watchfully on either side of the door. Dwarfed at their sides were two human guards, wearing Imperial Fleet Cloaks embellished by large CIGA crests, who were casting worried glances at their IVG counterparts. As Brim and Ursis approached, one of the Bears opened the door, then both came to attention and saluted. The Imperials did not . . . until one of the Bears growled something in a low, menacing voice. At that, both humans immediately sprang to attention and saluted as if their lives depended on it. Brim stifled a laugh and returned their salutes. The terrified CIGAs were probably correct!

Inside the cramped "lobby," Barbousse and a third CIGA starsailor stood side by side, each holding a blast pike at the trail-arms position. Barbousse and the CIGA both saluted at the same time—smartly. Either Barbousse already had this one trained, or they'd actually run across a CIGA with some class. Barbousse opened the door and nodded. "Polkovnik Ursis, Cap'm Brim," he announced, "Commodore Calhoun asks that you go right in." Then he looked Brim directly in the eye and rolled his eyes to the ceiling.

Frowning, Brim nodded, and deferring to Ursis's superior rank, strode in first—nearly stumbling in surprise as their entry interrupted Amherst in the middle of a sentence. So *that* was what the big rating silently tried to warn him about! Seated before the glowering Calhoun's makeshift workstation were *four* men, not three: Toby Moulding, Fortune McKenzie, Puvis Amherst, and *Kirsh Valentin*—the latter smiling as if he were specially pleased to see the look of astonishment on Brim's face.

"Well, Brim," Amherst growled through clenched teeth, "it is high time you returned from your bloodthirsty work, *war lover!*"

The Carescrian glanced at Valentin only just in time to see him wipe a look of amusement from his face. Tall, slim, and handsome in his jet-black tunic, shirt, jodhpurs, and glossy riding boots, the cavalier Provost knew full well what Amherst was; Leaguers had no more respect for him or his CIGAs than did most Imperials. "What was that, Amherst?" Brim demanded.

"How many times must you be reminded, low-life Carescrian, that I am to be addressed by my title?" Amherst whined, indignantly jumping from his chair.

"More times than you've got," Brim replied calmly. "I have better respect for your Leaguer friend Valentin, here—at least he's never tried to be anything more than an enemy. The best *you'll* ever hear from me is 'traitor.' "

When Ursis finally lost his battle to stifle a guffaw, Amherst swung on his heel and confronted Calhoun. "*Commodore!*" he screeched, his face turning a livid red, "*do* something about these men of yours!"

Calhoun only shrugged. "I doubt if I can noo, Admiral," he said. "They're all a wee out o' control, you know. Especially Brim."

That was more than either Moulding or McKenzie could suffer. They covered their mouths while their faces turned red as zago-beets.

By now, even Valentin was struggling to maintain his composure. "Admiral Amherst," he suggested uneasily. "Perhaps you should not—as you yourself suggest—lower yourself to intercourse with such despicable tatterdemalions as these . . . *mercenaries*." He pronounced the latter as if it were an especially vile scurrility. "Might it not be more fitting that I—who have not yet reached true flag rank—deal with your inferiors?"

Amherst frowned, considering this. "Yes," he agreed at length, gathering his injured pride into a heroic pose, "I believe that might be appropriate."

"Excellent," Valentin said, rising slowly. He stood for a few moments in silence while Amherst continued to pose, then cleared his throat pointedly.

Amherst started slightly and turned to peer down his nose at the Leaguer.

"If you please, Admiral," Valentin said coldly.

"Oh," Amherst said, almost in surprise. "Ahem . . . yes. . . ." He resumed his seat with great dignity.

"Commodore," Valentin said, turning to face Calhoun, "my Imperial colleague, Admiral Amherst, has brought your venerated battleship *Queen Elidean* to Fluvanna not by request of the League of Dark Stars, but by acclaim from an equally peace-loving segment of your own Empire: the Congress of Intra-Galactic Accord." He paused for a moment to look around the room. "We do not address you here today in your guise of Fluvannians but as the members of Greyffin's Imperial Fleet that you assuredly are. Do you understand?"

Calhoun nodded. "You may continue, Valentin," he said noncommittally.

The Leaguer sneered and turned to Brim. "To think that once

you might have been legitimate, Brim, as an officer in the League Fleet," he said. "Instead, your foolish prejudice has led to this berth working for a low-life pirate—hiding your shame behind the uniform of the corrupt Nabob of Fluvanna."

Brim steepled his fingers together and forced himself to relax. "Time will tell, Valentin," he said, "which of us turns out to be legitimate. But meanwhile, I feel a lot more comfortable right where I am than serving as toady to a contemptible kennel of butchers like the Leaguers I've met so far."

Amherst gasped, and started out of his chair, but Valentin pushed him back without even taking his eyes from Brim—as if the CIGA were nothing more than a bothersome child. The Leaguer's eyes flashed with cold rage. "Those words will someday cost your life, Carescrian," he hissed through clenched teeth.

"I've heard you promise that a number of times, Valentin," Brim replied calmly. "But you'll have to work faster than you've worked so far. Otherwise, I'm liable to die of old age first."

Calhoun interrupted. "Valentin," he growled, "you claim you have some sort of message for all of us. Alright, let's have it. You can let Brim make a fool of you later, when you aren't wasting time for so many other people."

Valentin's eyebrows rose in rage and he opened his mouth to speak, but Calhoun cut him off with a scowl that would shred hullmetal. "An' remember this, you black-suited punk," he growled, "I'll grant that it took a lot of intestinal fortitude for you to show up here alone. You've never been anythin' if you haven't been brave, Kirsh Valentin. But you *are* sittin' here as my guest. It's not the other way around. So say what you have to say an' then get you an' your recreant friend out o'here the fastest way you can. Do you understand, Provost?"

"I understand, Commodore," Valentin said quietly, his whole expression dripping with enmity.

"Then begin, mon," Calhoun prompted.

"First," Valentin said, glancing around the room, "I shall remind you all that no state of war exists between the League and your Empire." Then he turned to Calhoun. "Oh, you were clever in leasing these Starfuries to the Fluvannian government," he said in a low, menacing voice. "We can do nothing about that—nor the fact that we will have to contend with your defense of this wretched dominion. However," he continued with a droll smile, "in the interests of conciliation, our harmony-loving Imperial colleagues have gathered a full battle crew of heroic reconciliators aboard I.F.S. *Queen Elidean*. And—in the interests of peace—these brave men and women from all walks of Imperial life are prepared to give their lives protecting the new space fortifications we have recently completed just off the shoals of Zonga'ar."

Brim felt a chill cut wickedly along his spine while he ground his teeth in rage.

"They *wha'*?" Calhoun demanded angrily.

Valentin smiled cruelly. "I believe you heard me, Commodore," he purred, once more in possession of the upper hand. "A group of highly patriotic CIGAs in the Imperial battleship *Queen Elidean* will take up station orbiting our newest deep-space fortification located in the shoals of Zonga'ar." He peered down his nose at Brim. "I'm certain you know where that is, gentlemen." Then he laughed. "And if you dare to attack it, you will first have to deal with one of the most powerful battleships in the known universe—with her normal complement of escorts." He stopped for a moment to inspect his perfect manicure. "Of course, you will also be attacking your own Empire, and—should any of you survive such a fight—might eventually have to answer to retaliation from other Starfuries. A great irony, gentlemen, is it not?"

Calhoun's face grew red, but aside from that, he evinced no other emotion. "Are you quite finished?" he demanded at length.

Valentin nodded and motioned to Amherst. "Did I cover that well, Admiral?" he asked solicitously.

"With excellence," Amherst said, looking around the room as if he himself had uttered the words. "Do any of you have questions?" he asked.

"Only one," Calhoun said.

"And that is?"

"How soon do you twa think it will take to get your loathsome bodies off this planet?'' he growled. ''Because if it takes you any mair than ten cycles—at the outside—I shall personally blow you away myself. Understand?''

''How dare you, Commodore?'' Amherst demanded hotly.

Calhoun rose from his desk and moved like lightning. In the flash of an eye, he had Amherst's lapels in his fists, and he was shaking the lanky CIGA like a rat in a terrier's mouth. ''*This* is how I dare, you miserable traitor.'' He lifted the terrified CIGA to his feet, spun him toward the door, and propelled him through with a tremendous kick to the posterior. Then drawing himself to his full height, he turned on Valentin. But the Leaguer was already on his way.

''I shall leave without your assistance, Commodore,'' he said. Then he turned to Brim. ''But you, Carescrian—and you, Toby Moulding—you will remember what I have said despite this lickspittle . . . er . . . *colleague* of mine. To attack that fortification, you will have to deal *first* with your own *Queen Elidean*.'' He laughed. ''That ought to send a few N rays to dampen your plans, my perennial Carescrian adversary.''

Brim smiled grimly. ''It does, Valentin,'' he admitted. ''You've done a good job—so far. But this war's only begun.'' He turned to Moulding. ''Do you recall what it was you said to this gentleman just before the Mitchell Trophy race back in Oh-four?''

Moulding smiled. ''You mean there in front of the Leaguer shed, just after you'd driven the skimmer through all those flower gardens?''

''Yeah,'' Brim replied. ''That's it.''

'' 'Races are never won,' '' Moulding quoted didactically, '' 'until the finish line is crossed.' Remember?''

''I remember,'' Valentin said, flashing a smile that fairly dripped with contempt, ''but you must certainly *also* recall that I not only crossed the finish line that day, I won.''

Brim nodded. ''That you did, Valentin,'' he agreed. ''But that was one race among many. And it put the trophy in your possession for only a single year. I am certain you *also* remember who finally retired the Mitchell permanently.''

''You do have a point,'' Valentin said. Then, surprisingly,

he saluted. "Gentlemen," he said, "we shall eventually meet again in space—and there continue our . . . *race* . . . for the lack of a better word." He smiled grimly. "The trophy we retire in that competition will be considerably more consequential than the Mitchell." Then, turning on his heel, he strode through the door. . . .

Amherst's launch was airborne *well* before Calhoun's ten-cycle deadline.

With the coming of the new Leaguer ships, Nergol Triannic's second war took a considerably more dangerous twist. Toronders and their Dampiers had been a minimal threat to IVG Starfuries. Clearly, they had inflicted damage; no one fights a war without inflicting *some* injury. But most of it had been minor, and even though the eleven leased ships were significantly outnumbered, not a single volunteer had been killed.

That ended immediately following Brim's first, admittedly providential, double victory. The Leaguers were natural warriors, superbly trained and equipped. Their very next raid left three Starfuries crippled, one for more than a week because of the IVG's primitive repair facilities. Moreover, during *that* raid, five Dampiers got through to Magor, where they caused the first significant ground damage of the war. Five additional Dampiers that attempted a simultaneous raid against Varnholm Hall were all badly damaged by McKenzie's reserve force before they could fire a single bolt at the gravity pools.

A week later, however, it was *Starfury*'s turn for damage. . . .

Brim was leading both attack quads on a regular defensive patrol roughly five thousand c'lenyts out from Ordu when they came on at least twenty-four Gorn-Hoffs in four groups of six. Immediately, he went in to attack, hitting at least two on their way through the Leaguers' formation. Then he remembered that he had no faithful MacAlda guarding his tail, as *Starspite* had turned back with grav trouble shortly after takeoff. He was about to rejoin for a second attack when Moulding called with the other six Starfuries to give his rough position. Brim said that he was in the same general area. Spotting six shimmering graviton contrails, he immediately climbed toward them. He was little more than five c'lenyts away when—instead of graceful, three-piece Sherrington hulls—he sighted the angular shapes of . . . Dampiers!

Peeling off in a violent maneuver, he raced directly away from the big planet to lower his visibility, then swung rapidly to port and kept *Starfury* turning as tightly as he possibly could. For a few cycles, they all spun around in a crazed globe perhaps five c'lenyts in diameter until Brim threw maximum power to the gravs and tried another maneuver—a steep drive *toward* Ordu. Five of the Toronder Helmsmen stuck grimly behind him, and as he reached fifteen hundred c'lenyts, he could see eruptions of blinding light from *very* near misses. The deck bucked from their energy waves. Suddenly, he heard a faint, rapid, two-beat thud and *Starfury* shuddered while half his energy display turned bright red.

"Direct hit in the starboard power chamber," Chief Baranev reported from the power distribution center, deep within *Starfury*'s hull. The indefatigable old Bear spoke as if he were announcing some sort of sporting event.

"Flood both starboard power chambers with N rays!" Brim ordered, switching one of his view globes to the view below decks. He winced. The Aft chamber had been opened to space like an old-fashioned tin of fish. A huge radiation fire in one of the Krasni-Peych plasma generators was just coming under control as the N rays saturated its collapsium fuel. However, great bolts of runaway energy were still arcing to the chamber walls, bathing the chamber in lurid reddish-yellow light as if it were a scene from the Gradygroats' vision of Hell. And through it all, burly figures of Sodeskayan Bears scurried here and there, dragging portable N-ray mains and struggling with half-melted control systems.

A moment later Brim heard Strana' Zaftrak counting over the intercom.

"Thirteen crag volves . . . fourteen crag volves . . . fifteen crag volves . . ." she counted, as if she hardly dared to take a breath.

Tissaurd glanced across at him. "What's she counting, Skipper?" she demanded.

"Clicks, Number One," Brim replied, his heart in his mouth. "We just took a hit in power chamber eight. If she can count all the way to thirty, the N rays will have damped any radiation fires and we probably won't blow up."

". . . Twenty-one crag volves . . . twenty-two crag volves . . . twenty-three crag volves . . ."

"Power's out to the main disruptors, Skipper!" Ulfilas warned.

"Very well," Brim said between clenched teeth. He careened to port again. The ship now felt heavy and difficult to maneuver, as if a delay had been thrust into her normally supple reactions to his control inputs. And the Dampiers were catching up quickly. Clearly, the only hope was to get the main battery going again—if *Starfury* didn't first blow them all to kingdom come.

". . . Twenty-six crag volves . . . twenty-seven crag volves . . . twenty-eight crag volves . . ."

Brim held his breath. . . .

"Thirty crag volves! VOOF!"

There was an immediate and simultaneous exhalation from all over the bridge. Now, they needed *disruptors*!

And so the battle went on: a few turns and then a flat-out run for it, some more turns and then another bout of straightaway. They lost two of the Dampiers, but the other three hung on tenaciously, sensing that *Starfury* was somehow disabled. As soon as Brim sensed they were about to open fire, he had to start turning again. Occasionally Meesha got in a burst with the secondary armament, but the 127-mmi disruptors were more a gesture than a determined attack.

After what seemed like an age, but was in fact only five or so cycles after the Toronders first spotted *Starfury*, the red lights on Brim's power panel suddenly went out.

"We've got power to the disruptors," Meesha whooped triumphantly.

Brim nearly shouted for joy. They'd made it! He let the Dampiers catch up, and approximately three clicks later, all twelve of *Starfury*'s 406s lashed out at her pursuers. By the fourth salvo, two of the Toronders were reduced to space refuse and the third had limped off with fierce radiation fires blazing in at least three locations along her hull.

Brim glanced back at the burning Dampier with a sense of relief. So far, so good. *Now*, however, he had to set his own damaged starship down as quickly as he could. The overworked plasma generators that remained operable would only run her gravs against the planet's gravity for a short time. Already they were overheating. Working quickly, Omar Powderham, *Starfury*'s navigator, expeditiously located a remote Fluvannian base: R.F.F. Station Calshot on frigid Lake Solent—near Ordu's Boreal pole, and Tissaurd radioed ahead for permission to set up a straight-in approach, direct from space. Not surprisingly, they were immediately granted permission. Now, all he had to do was set thirty-four thousand milstons of hullmetal and assorted, more-or-less sentient crew members down on the surface of the planet gently enough so that nobody got hurt. He ground his teeth. It wasn't going to be as easy as he liked to make things appear. . . .

After what seemed like at least a Standard Year, *Starfury* was finally beneath the confused layers of dirty clouds, descending in a graceful glide despite her flagging gravs. A mottled landscape passed rapidly beneath the ship's nose: snow in every direction Brim looked, lighted in patches by thin, wintery sunlight. Everywhere else were shades of white and gray, broken only by occasional green expanses of dense conifer forest. He checked his readouts for the ten-thousandth time—the power quadrant was edging back into the red. *Starfury*'s lift would last for only a few more cycles now. And although her glide ratio *was* better than a rock—it was only *slightly* so. Hunching his back to stop the knot that was forming in the middle of his shoulders, he frowned. The next few cycles might well challenge his worth as a Helmsman.

Ahead, sunlight glinted momentarily from ice covering a slender lake, foreshortened by the angle of their descent. A ruby landing vector shone steadily from the left-hand shore, directly centered on a boiling strip of water melted in the frozen surface.

"Fleet K5054: Calshot Tower clears for one nine right landing approach; wind zero nine zero at fifteen, gusts to forty-five."

"Fleet K054," Brim replied absently, totally absorbed with landing the stricken cruiser. "One nine right. Thank you, ma'am," he grunted. The wind didn't much matter. One way or another, he was coming in. Period.

He was no more than five c'lenyts from touchdown when Voot's Law struck—as somehow he knew it might. Without warning, the generators stammered . . . thundered on for a moment . . . then abruptly quit altogether as his instruments indicated zero thrust!

The bridge went deadly silent, except for the slipstream howling past the Hyperscreens. At this altitude, there was no escape from the hull; everyone knew his life was entirely in Brim's hands—and whatever deities he might personally accredit.

With the determination and nerve that had brought him through a thousand metacycles of mortal danger, the Carescrian guided the big cruiser toward a dead-stick landing on momentum alone. A tiny shore-side village disappeared beneath the bow as Brim willed *Starfury*'s nose a few degrees high.

Nearly there. . . .

"HANG ON!" Brim gasped into the blower. "We're going in!"

Less than a click too late, he spotted the small hill of ice shards that caught his right pontoon and violently slewed the big machine around to the right. Loose equipment cascaded across the bridge in a cacophony of shattered cvceese' mugs and tumbling equipment. More by instinct than anything else, he kicked hard left rudder just as the cruiser smashed through the ice in a cloud of spray and was thrown in the air again. This time, she swung badly to port, and, rolling dangerously, fell heavily to the melted landing strip with a resounding thud on the left pontoon—but pointed the proper direction. He sensed the tail coming up as the tips of the pontoons plunged into the waves, but miraculously, the starship righted itself and glided to a stop, her overheated plasma generators pinging and crackling throughout the main hull. Moments later he glimpsed what appeared to be a squadron of land tractors racing over the ice toward him. The ship might be touching the water, with all the mischief *that* promised, but she *was* down. And safe. . . .

"Voot's beard," Tissaurd said in a shaky voice, opening her helmet in mock disgust, "you'd think there was a war on, or somethin'!"

CHAPTER 9

Strike Force

Clearly, *Starfury* was not the first ship to have crashlanded on Lake Solent. Calshot Station was much too practiced in rescue/salvage operations for such an event to be any sort of rarity. Even before *Starfury* surged to a halt, eight big traction engines were thundering along each side of the melted landing vector, smartly projecting mooring beams to salvage points in the hull as they traveled. At a prearranged signal, they stopped to tension the beams; moments later *Starfury* was firmly moored at sixteen points, stable, although floating helplessly in the water.

"HoloPhone signal from the Base, Skipper," a communications technician reported from Brim's display panel.

Brim nodded and peered out the forward Hyperscreens toward a tall, uniformed man and a slim woman wearing an ankle-length cape who were standing beside a staff skimmer parked at the edge of the ice. "Very well," he said. "I'll take it here."

Presently, the technician was replaced by an angular face with high hollow cheeks, thinning hair, a long nose, and the sensible, intelligent eyes of a born Engineer. "Commodore Atcherly, here, Commander," the man said. "If you're talking from the bridge, I'm over here by the staff skimmer," he said with a little smile.

Brim glanced up to see one of the distant figures wave its arm. "I see you, Commodore," he said.

"Too bad about the ice hill there off the end of the runway," Atcherly mused. His eyebrows raised for a moment as he peered out past his portable communicator. "You've taken considerable battle damage," he added, returning his eyes to the display. "Offhand, I'd say you did an admirable job landing with no propulsion—nearly made it, you know. Anyone hurt on board?"

Brim ground his teeth. "We've a number of casualties, Commodore," he declared while a portable brow clanked into place two decks below at the main boarding lobby. "And . . . many thanks for the fast assistance," he forced himself to add, as medical teams rushed through the crystal tube toward *Starfury*'s sickbay.

Atcherly nodded, as if nothing out of the ordinary had transpired at all. "Next," he mused, "I suppose we'll have to see how quickly we can get that ship of yours out of the water," He scratched his head and frowned. "She's a big one for the salvage equipment we've got to work with here." Abruptly he looked off to his right, mewing unintelligible words in Fluvannian.

Brim again glanced through the Hyperscreens at the two figures. From the HoloPhone, he could hear the woman's voice in the background—familiar, somehow—although her words were also in Fluvannian.

A moment later Atcherly peered into the display again. "I say, Commander," he muttered with a grin, "is your name *Brim* by any chance? I don't think I've given you much of an opportunity to tell me."

Brim felt his cheeks burn. In all the excitement, he'd never even thought of introducing himself—poor manners indeed. "My name is Brim, Commodore," he said. "Wilf Ansor Brim of Mustafa Eyren's Imperial Volunteer Group."

Atcherly nodded and once again looked to his right, saying something to the unseen woman about "Commander Wilf Ansor Brim" and the "IVG."

Suddenly, Atcherly's visage disappeared from the HoloPhone. It was immediately replaced by a glorious combination of oval face, patrician nose, full lips, and enormous, almond-shaped eyes that could only belong to Raddisma, the Nabob's favorite Consort. She wore a loose, fur-trimmed hood that revealed some of her black, shoulder-length hair. Even in his small panel display, she was beautiful—gorgeous was probably a better word, he decided.

"Well, Commander Brim, we meet again," she said in the dusky voice he remembered so well. Her smile alone was enough to melt most of the Station's ice. "It is . . . regrettable," she said pointedly, "that Mustafa has not accompanied me on this trip. But then, Lady Fortune offtimes chooses strange circumstances and localities for the fulfillment of debts, wouldn't you agree?"

Brim's mind raced. Yes! He clearly recalled her words the day he had shielded her body with his: *Someday I shall see to it that you are appropriately rewarded—in a personal manner, of course.* "Most strange, madame," he agreed cautiously, "but all the more delightful because of them." In the corner of his eye, he could see Tissaurd studiously ignoring the proceedings. She was making a bad job of it.

"Indeed," Raddisma said, her eyes narrowing to a presence that could only be described as carnal. "You were unharmed in the, er, *difficult* landfall I watched."

"Completely unharmed, madame," Brim assured her, "although a number of *Starfury*'s crew sustained casualties in a recent battle that, I fear, I must tend to without further delay." He hesitated for a moment, then decided that even a Principal Consort could only say "no." "Might I have the honor of continuing this conversation later in the day?" he asked, heart in his mouth.

Safely beyond the HoloPhone's field of view, Tissaurd wordlessly grinned and pumped her fist in encouragement.

Raddisma's face colored visibly at his words, and she looked genuinely taken aback for a moment.

Brim felt his face begin to color. He'd blown it this time! He braced himself. . . .

"*Casualties?*" she queried with a distraught look—while completely ignoring his proffered invitation. "Commander, I must beg your indulgence that I could lack the basic compassion to inquire about casualties." She shook her head in obvious mortification. "What can I do to make amends?"

"G-E-T L-A-Y-E-D!" Tissaurd mouthed soundlessly.

Cheeks burning while he stifled a grin that threatened to break forth all over his face, Brim considered for only a moment. "Madame Raddisma," he said, glancing at the procession of covered GravLitters that were gliding through the brow to ambulances that hovered at the edge of the ice—many contained the bandaged figures of Bears. "Perhaps you would do me the honor of accompanying me through the base hospital tomorrow, once *Starfury* has been secured," he said. "I know the IVG casualties there would consider your presence a particular honor."

The woman's face slipped for a moment from its regal mien to one of genuine astonishment. "Me?" she asked with a frown, "tour the base hospital with you?"

"But yes, Madame Raddisma," Brim said, bemused at her evident surprise.

"Why . . . I . . . should be *honored* to accompany you on such a tour, Commander Brim," she said, her eyes momentarily flashing with considerable emotion, "at your convenience. I shall await your call tomorrow with great anticipation." Then, turning to Atcherly, she quickly reverted to her accustomed bearing as the Nabob's Principal Consort. "Commodore Atcherly," she directed, this time in faultless Avalonian, "may I assume that Commander Brim and his officers will be requested to attend the reception in my honor tomorrow evening?"

Tissaurd nodded with exaggerated enthusiasm. "Y-E-A-H!" she mouthed.

"Aye, that you may, madame," Atcherly said, replacing Raddisma in Brim's display. He spoke as if he hadn't noticed that she had switched to Avalonian for her query—but clearly he had. "You'll all attend, Commander?" he asked with a little smile.

Brim grinned in spite of himself, fighting to keep his eyes from Tissaurd. "As many of us will attend as possible, Commodore," he replied, "depending, of course, on *Starfury*'s condition by that time." He laughed grimly to himself. Only a few cycles ago, they had been fighting for their very lives. Here at Lake Solent, without *Starfury*'s battle-damaged presence, it might have seemed as if the war had never started.

"I understand your concern, Commander," Atcherly said, "but I think we shall be able to move *Starfury*, in spite of her size." Then he frowned. "*Repairing* her, however," he added, "may turn out to be an altogether different problem—much as I hate to say it."

Nobody hated those words more than Brim. . . .

Judicious application of Calshot's big snow tractors and a miraculous performance by crews deftly operating all six of the Station's medium-duty gravity barges (at a risky 115 percent levitation factor) finally managed to wrestle the light cruiser onto one of the base's five "large" gravity pools. When they concluded their work, Brim, who had watched the delicate operation all afternoon from the bridge, found himself soaked in sweat. Though he was only a helpless bystander, he had probably traveled ten c'lenyts pacing back and forth across the bridge from Hyperscreen to Hyperscreen. It felt as if he had hefted the cruiser on his own shoulders.

"Commodore Atcherly reports the ship is secure, Commander," Barbousse announced, his normally deep bass voice at least an octave higher with the tension on the bridge.

"Very well," Brim replied. "How much time do you suppose the Bears will need for their damage report?"

"I asked Chief Baranev on my way to the bridge," Barbousse said. "He sent his compliments and asked me to tell you that it's at least as bad as it looked when you were there about a cycle ago, but he'll need at least all day tomorrow and perhaps more for a detailed report."

Tissaurd took Brim's arm. "In that case, Skipper . . ." she started.

"In that case *what*, Number One?" Brim asked suspiciously.

"In that case," she repeated, "it is my studied suggestion

that you *command* every officer who has no immediate duty—including yourself—to stand down till morning when we have a better idea of how bad things really are."

"Good idea," Brim admitted. "Put those orders on the blower, if it's still operational, and I'll run over to headquarters and get us set up for the repair effort."

"*Skipper*," Tissaurd said with her hands on her hips, "you didn't hear what I said. *You* need rest as much as anybody. Doesn't he, Chief?" she asked, turning to Barbousse.

The big rating raised his eyes to the overhead Hyperscreens. "Um . . . beggin' the Cap'm's pardon," he stammered, "but . . . um . . . that sounds like good advice to me. Most of us in the Petty Officers Mess are . . . um . . . headin' for our bunks as soon as we can. It's been a *long* day."

"There, Skipper," the tiny officer declared as Barbousse lumbered off toward the companionway. "And you certainly won't be much help to anybody tomorrow if you can't think straight."

Brim nodded. "Thanks, Number One," he said. "That makes sense. I guess I *could* stand some R and R, couldn't I?"

"More than anybody else I know, right now," she said. "And who knows, maybe after the hospital tour tomorrow, this green-eyed 'Consort' can get your mind off that LaKarn woman."

Brim smiled sadly and took a deep breath. "Somehow," he sighed, "I doubt if that will happen."

"It certainly won't if you don't let it," she stated firmly, "or if you fall asleep while you're trying to . . . Well, you get my point."

"Yeah," Brim chuckled, as if she were making a joke, but somehow he knew she meant every word she said. He retired to his cabin shortly afterward.

When a COMM rating woke him before dawn the next morning with a high-priority message, Brim couldn't even remember crawling into his bunk. Clearly, he had slept like a burned-out star, for he felt unusually refreshed—as he often did after pushing himself nearly to the brink of exhaustion.

He spent most of his day inspecting damage and frantically swapping messages with Varnholm—especially Calhoun—and it was late afternoon before he was finally able to leave word for Raddisma that he would meet her in the lobby of the Station hospital at Afternoon:3:00, early enough that they would have time for both a meaningful tour *and* an appearance later at Atch-erly's reception. Following that, he hurried to his cabin where Barbousse had already laid out a fresh uniform.

In the hospital lobby, Mustafa's Consort was even more al-luring than Brim recalled. She entered wearing her same black woolen cape with the fir-trimmed hood; white, high-heeled, ophet-leather boots; and matching gloves. The Carescrian shook his head in admiration. Even largely covered up she was beau-tiful. No wonder the Nabob—who clearly enjoyed his pick of Fluvanna's courtiers (as well as courtesans)—had chosen her above all others! He smiled while two ladies-in-waiting helped her slip out of her cape. Instead of the flowing robes he antic-ipated, she had dressed in contemporary Imperial style, wearing a silky gold crepe cocktail suit (whose backless jacket opened all the way to her slim waist) and a short, shaped skirt that revealed long, *very* shapely slim legs. "Madame Raddisma," he said, "how good of you to come."

She drew off a glove and presented her hand. "It is my plea-sure, Captain Brim," she said in a dusky, modulated voice, her lips forming a little smile as she nodded to the small coterie of physicians gathered nervously at the entrance to the wards. With her hair pulled back from her face and tied in a loose knot at the back of her head, she was more than just stunning. Huge golden rings dangled from her earlobes and she wore an enor-mous sapphire ring on her left hand. She had that enigmatic brand of natural assurance that goes hand in hand with influence. Brim surmised she would have an intelligence as sharp as anyone he had ever encountered. She'd need it to merely survive the cutthroat machinations that he understood characterized the inner circles of Mustafa's court.

He bowed and kissed the soft, warm tips of her fingers. "If I may be so bold," he said, straightening, "you look magnificent this afternoon."

She smiled, obviously pleased. "You may *always* be so bold,

Captain," she answered. Her gaze was like an inspection: outwardly cool and composed—but *absolutely* complete.

Brim nodded to the physicians, then turned to Raddisma. "Shall we begin, then, madame?" he asked, offering his arm.

Nodding to dismiss her maidservants, she grasped his elbow and they proceeded on to the wards. In the cycles since *Starfury* had landed, three of the most gravely wounded Bears and seven humans had already died; however, healing machines were steadily working their magic on other casualties. Six of the throbbing cylinders had opened, and their occupants were even now in various stages of rousing. Raddisma immediately captivated a Sodeskayan Chief who had been working only a few irals from the point of detonation, yet had been miraculously saved by the chance deflection of a falling control panel. In the machine beside him was a pretty electronics technician whose left arm and leg were being regenerated beneath pulsating layers of healing plastic tissue. Saved by her Imperial battlesuit, she had been blown through three vaporized hullmetal bulkheads and remembered nothing of the disaster—which she laughingly agreed was probably the best thing that could have happened under the circumstances. Two machines farther along was a quartermaster's mate who had been attached to a damage-control unit stationed in the power chamber itself. He had actually missed the main force of the hit, but had been caught in the outer margin of a secondary explosion when one of the big plasma generators blew up. The healing machine was rebuilding the top half of his face—but he considered himself lucky. The other nine members of his crew were dead—vaporized. A number of generator technicians in adjoining chambers had been burned through their battlesuits, but were still ambulatory and undergoing antiradiation treatments. Many of them would be available for duty in the morning. All in all, twenty-four of *Starfury*'s crew had been killed or wounded as a result of the hit.

As always, the hospital tour was a sobering experience for Brim. He had been wounded a number of times himself, both in war and in peace—and seriously enough that he could appreciate what it was like to be on the other end of his visit. But Raddisma completely astounded him. Throughout the grisly tour, she acquitted herself like a veteran, as if she encountered such wounds as an everyday occurrence. Moreover, she was witty when she could be, sympathetic when necessary, and even coquettish with some of the wounded crew members. More than once, Brim stood back and marveled at the woman's aplomb. Doubtlessly, she had experienced nothing to match the horror of these hideously wounded individuals. Yet she made each of them feel special in her eyes—as if she *personally* appreciated the sacrifice they had made for her and her domain. When the tour finally ground to a halt, she showed little more wear than if she had just spent an afternoon entertaining at the royal palace at Magor.

In Brim's view, whatever else Raddisma happened to be, she was *also* a trooper, pure and simple.

"Might I offer a lift to the reception, Captain?" she asked in the lobby while her handmaids placed the cloak around her shoulders. "When Mustafa bids me tour in his place, he invariably includes a small fleet of cars."

"I should be honored to ride with you, Madame Raddisma," he replied, shrugging into his Fleet Cloak. The evening was *still* his to enjoy—he had just finished talking to Chief Baranev, and as predicted, there was still no complete estimate of *Starfury*'s damage—except "bad." At the door, he offered Raddisma his arm and they stepped out into a clear, wintery evening agleam with starlight. As the cold air nipped his cheeks, he felt her grip tighten.

"Do not for a moment think that I have forgotten my pledge to repay you personally, Wilf Brim," she whispered without turning her head. "I never—how do you Imperials say—'renege' on a promise." Then she giggled in her husky voice. "Especially when Lady Fortune practically ordained such an assignation for us tonight."

Brim felt a surge of excitement. Did she mean what he *thought* she meant? He took a deep breath and waved off Barbousse waiting in the staff skimmer. Then he turned to look the beautiful Consort straight in the eye. "An assignation with you, Raddisma, would be the crowning glory of a man's life," he said. "But if something of the sort ever came about, I should certainly hope that it was not granted entirely in a spirit of . . . compensation—especially for a debt that I shall never acknowledge in the first place."

She stopped and raised her eyebrows for a moment. "Why, Captain!" she murmured with a look of astonishment. "You saved my life. Remember?" Then, while a tall, alluring chauffeur with fiery red hair and long, gorgeous legs held the door of her limousine skimmer, she stepped gracefully into the passenger compartment and smiled with an expectant look in her huge, almond-shaped eyes. "Come in here, Wilf Brim," she urged, patting the seat beside her, "I want to make certain you understand about my so-called 'debt.' "

Frowning, Brim stepped inside, and as soon as the door had shut, she took his hand and looked deep into his eyes.

"Do you have any idea what it is to be a Consort?" she asked.

"No," Brim admitted. "I suppose I'd never thought much about it."

She smiled, this time a little sadly. "You are not alone, my handsome Captain," she said. "We Consorts are taken more or less for granted throughout the court—most glamorous and successful of all the courtesans. And I am the *most* successful of all—for I have clawed and scratched my way to the top." For a moment her eyes grew hard. "You must understand that one does not reach my position by being a lady, Captain. I used the word 'courtesans' with great care, because Consorts are first and foremost whores. And one maintains her position by competing with other whores—on whore's terms."

Brim felt his eyebrows rise. Of course, he'd guessed as much. It was just that, in Fluvanna, Consorts were considered as a rather extraordinary class. Like wives, only much more significant, in a political sense. It was simply astounding to hear the *Principal* Consort calling the shots as he imagined they really must be.

"Oh, don't get the wrong idea," she continued. "Each of us who holds the title of Consort is also highly educated. We have to be. I myself have earned three academic degrees." She said this with a proud little nod. "One of them in Avalon itself—at your prestigious Estorial Library near the Imperial palace."

"Impressive," Brim said, "but not at all surprising, not after watching you in conversation with the Drive engineers this afternoon. No wonder you so completely mesmerized them. Your long metacycles of study certainly manifest themselves well."

She smiled sadly. "But after all that brain work, it was still only vigorous application of a far different organ that first installed me in Mustafa's court."

Brim pressed her hand. "You can't blame him for that," he said. "You are a *most* beautiful woman."

"Thank you, Captain," she said. "I know I am. And—strange as it must sound in light of my, er, profession—I still find myself with *very* normal urges in the proper circumstances, and with the proper man."

"Such a man would be very fortunate indeed," Brim said. He meant *every* word.

"That," Raddisma said with a smile, "brings us back to our original conversation, then—about debts."

"It does?" Brim asked.

"It certainly does," she said with a little smile. "Because, while your eyes tell me that you *obviously* crave my body, you also evidence at least some respect for Raddisma the woman. And that respect makes you very special, my friend. It also changes the whole complexion of our relationship."

Brim raised an eyebrow.

"Oh, not that kind of change, silly," she said with a little laugh. "You must certainly realize you are *very* attractive in your own right, Wilf Brim, and that alone was enough to draw me to you in the beginning." She laughed in her husky voice. "While your body covered mine in the palace that day, I found myself becoming . . . intensely *stimulated*. And I decided that very day that we, someday, should share a bed, as soon as the opportunity presented itself. Which, of course, it did today. The kind of 'debt' I spoke about this morning had to do with sex, pure and simple. However," she said with a very serious expression, "my attitude changed radically when you invited me to tour the hospital this afternoon. It turned our relationship into something very much more deeper and meaningful—at least to me. Do you understand?''

Brim frowned. ''I think I may, Raddisma,'' he said, recalling most of the other women in his life. Her intellect made her even more desirable—high intelligence nearly always had that effect on him.

''We seem to have arrived at the Officers Club,'' she said presently, peering out the window. ''I feel most fortunate that Dame Fortune has granted us time for this little conversation before we dilute our intellects with . . . hormones, and the like. It has become somehow very important to me that you understand.''

Brim had no words for the rush of emotion he felt for the beautiful woman who had just bared her soul to him. He scarcely had time to kiss her hand before the door opened and a blast of cold air stung his cheeks. Stepping to the pavement, he took a deep breath and bowed with all the dignity he could muster. ''Madame Raddisma,'' he said, offering his hand, ''please allow me.''

Gently taking his fingers, she stepped gracefully from the limousine and nodded regally. ''Thank you, Captain,'' she said in her public voice. ''I look forward to continuing our conversations later this evening.'' Then she winked. ''In somewhat more private circumstances,'' she added in a whisper. With a surreptitious rise of flawlessly plucked eyebrows, she then swept regally through the door as if she were the Nabob himself.

Brim followed in her perfumed wake with an internal frown. Just whose ''private circumstances'' did she have in mind, he wondered. Then he grinned to himself. Lady Fortune would work something out. She'd already invested too much in this particularly magical evening to miscarry so late in the game.

Commodore Atcherly's reception was a small but quite gracious version of a thousand-odd receptions Brim had attended all over the galaxy. He endured a receiving line consisting of Calshot's senior staff officers and their wives—most of whom were anxious to brag that they had spoken to officers from Mustafa Eyren's now-celebrated IVG. Commodore Atcherly occupied the position of honor with his charming and famous wife, a thought creator known far and wide for her delightful historical treatises on the curious artifacts left behind by Fluvanna's previous civilizations.

Tissaud had clearly stationed herself near the end of the line, and was in deep conversation with a handsome Fluvannian Army officer who sported great bushy mustaches, wide shoulders, and a huge chest. The man was, of course, as good as seduced already. Brim fought back a grin as he passed them on his way to the bar. Suddenly Tissaud reached out and snagged his arm. "Captain Brim," she said, as if she were surprised to see him, "may I present . . . er."

"C-Capitan-Comandor Photius," the Fluvannian stumbled with a deep bow.

Brim shook the man's hand—It was soft and warm, like a woman's. Clearly, Mustafa's Army spent little time on maneuvers. "Pleased to meet you, *Capitan*," he said.

"Well, Skipper," Tissaud demanded before either man could utter another word, "*so how are things going tonight?*"

Brim could only grin. "Tonight, Number One," he said, "things *seem* to be going . . . ah . . . swimmingly—at least so far."

"You don't say?" Tissaud commented, her eyebrows raised. "So you're going to . . . a . . ."

"Would the word 'score' be appropriate to your question?" Brim asked caustically.

"What was that?" Photius asked, struggling in vain to keep abreast of the conversation in Avalonian.

" '*More*,' " Tissaud replied with a serious nod of her head. " 'More.' "

"Oh, I see," the man said. "My Avalonian is far from perfect."

"Lucky for you, soldier," Tissaud mumbled in a grinning underbreath, "that it's not your Avalonian I'm interested in tonight." Then she winked at Brim. " 'Score' is most adequate, Skipper," she said. "And . . . *well*? . . ."

"Looks promising, Number One," Brim replied. "If the lady

can once disengage from all the social climbers who want to rub elbows with a palace favorite.''

"She'll disengage, Skipper. I'd bet on it,'' she said, clapping him on the arm.

Brim winked. "We'll see,'' he equivocated. "You'll be on the bridge in the morning?''

"Probably *late* in the morning, Skipper,'' she said with a sidelong glance at the big Fluvannian at her side.

"We'll carry on somehow, Number One,'' Brim said, manifesting a theatrical look of concern. "I don't think *Starfury* will be ready to fly for quite a while yet.'' Then he nodded to Photius and continued on toward the bar.

During the next metacycle, he bought rounds of Logish Meem for Omar Powderham, Owen Morris, and Ulfilas Meesha, but went easy on the spirits himself. Unless Raddisma were in the midst of a tremendous practical joke—to be inflicted on him— he would need to be in command of *all* his faculties later on that evening.

He stared across the gaily decorated ballroom, watching the tall, alluring Consort in spirited conversation with a half-dozen groups of local spouses who looked as if they were about to swoon from the very proximity of so much glamor. He shook his head in admiration. During a single day, this magnificent woman had shown him three very disparate—very real—personalities: one imperious as Mustafa's Consort; one affably gracious in her role as representative of her nation; and one as a most pragmatic human being, making her way in a tough, uncompromising world. He found they all delighted him, each in its own way.

While he sat at Calshot's cozy Officers Club bar passing time until Raddisma could free herself, Tissaud and Photius strolled by on their way to the door. She winked as they passed; then they were gone. Atcherly and his wife stopped to regale him with some of the more preposterous aspects of maintaining a base in the polar regions of the planet. Their warm humor revealed a most genuine love for the frozen land in which they made their home.

Later, after checking *Starfury*'s condition with Baranev for what seemed to be the eleventh million time—and *still* receiving no final assessment of actual damages—Brim joined a group of Fluvannian space officers as they discussed combat techniques against the new Gorn-Hoffs. In spite of their ancient starships, the audacious Fluvannians had developed effective ways to counter the ultra-modern warships they now faced on a daily basis. They had just begun to question him about uprating some of their existing disruptors when Raddisma abruptly appeared at his side, dressed in her long cape and clearly prepared to depart. Surprised—and not a little concerned about their plans—he introduced her to the group, then took the hand she extended to him.

"Commander Brim," she said, "it has been a long day for me, and my ship departs for Magor in the morning. Therefore, it is with considerable regret that I must leave the reception much earlier than I had planned." She glanced around the little group and smiled apologetically. "I have rarely enjoyed such a warm, gracious reception—anywhere. However," she added, turning to Brim as if she were issuing a command, "I need to allow time for availing myself of your kind offer to tour *Starfury*. The Admiralty would be sorely vexed if I blinked away such an opportunity." She met his eyes and for one instant betrayed the hint of excitement he had seen earlier in the limousine.

Brim grinned to himself. So it was *Starfury* that constituted the "discreet circumstances" she had in mind! Well, Lady Fortune was taking a lot for granted tonight—especially in view of the rule that required everyone to sign an entrance/exit log! "Madame Raddisma," he replied, his mind racing to overtake the new turn of events, "as I promised earlier, I . . . er . . . look forward with great pleasure to *personally* conducting your tour." He turned to the clearly envious officers and bowed soberly. "Gentlemen," he said, "duty calls." Nothing more was necessary. Then, with Raddisma on his arm, he made his way directly to the cloakroom.

"I took the chance that you might volunteer, Captain," she whispered while he struggled into his white Fluvannian Fleet Cloak. "I have already dismissed my handmaidens for the evening and summoned a limousine."

Brim considered *Starfury*'s sign-in/out register—that Raddisma simply could *not* sign—and put it out of his mind. By the time they got to the ship, he planned to think of something. After all, he *was* the captain. He smiled mischievously. "Madame Raddisma," he said with a theatrical frown as they strolled to the parking area under a canopy of cold-looking stars, "since nearly everything aboard is classified, the Captain's cabin may be the *only* part of the ship we can tour. Will such a highly restricted tour disappoint you?"

She paused some distance from a huge limousine and regarded him thoughtfully for a moment, then frowned. "Strangely enough, Captain," she said, her breath condensing into puffs of steam, "I believe it would." She pressed his arm. "I find that when I am with you, life takes on a much more serious aspect —as it did when I visited your wounded crew members in the hospital this afternoon."

"I don't understand," Brim said, suddenly confused. ". . . I thought you wanted to . . ."

Raddisma smiled sadly and peered into his eyes. "Dearest Wilf," she said, "I have been ready—anxious, even—to lie with you since our chance conversation on the Commodore's HoloPhone this morning. And I look forward to making love yet tonight. But this afternoon you made me feel as if I might have some value beyond my existence as a fetching bedmate." She touched his hand with an impassioned look. "I already know that I am beautiful," she said, "and I thank the Universe each day for such a gift. But beauty is only that: a legacy from one's parents. I crave to be *more* than that: to achieve a certain significance on my feet—fully clothed, even. Can you understand, Captain Wilf Brim of Avalon's vaunted Imperial Fleet? Or are you so jaded by your own prestige that you cannot envision the unfulfilled yearnings of others?"

Brim closed his eyes for a moment. "Sorry," he muttered presently. "Believe me, Raddisma, I am no stranger to those same yearnings—or the frustration that goes with them." He took her hand. "You were magnificent raising morale in the hospital this afternoon, and will clearly have the same effect on the exhausted teams laboring in the ruined power chambers.

Sometimes," he admitted, "my brains tend to hang between my legs. Will you tour the damaged areas with me tonight before we . . . ?"

"I want that tour very much, Wilf Brim," the beautiful woman interrupted. "And then, I shall expect you to carry me off to your cabin where we can ravish each other—for the remainder of the night."

"You've got a deal, Raddisma," Brim said. He grinned. "Somehow, I think I would wait a long time for the privilege of ravishing a woman like you."

"Strange," she said with a peculiar look in her eyes, "I feel the same way about being ravished by a man like you."

"Let's go inspect a couple of damaged power chambers," he said, and handed her into the limousine again. Moments later they were on their way.

Now, all he had to do was somehow get her to his cabin without recording Raddisma's name on the xaxtdamned register. It wasn't the sign-in time that worried him; her tour of the power chambers would justify that. The sign-*out* time, however, might prove to be embarrassing in the extreme. Especially if someone decided that Mustafa ought to read it!

As the limousine pulled into the parking area beside *Starfury*'s gravity pool, the cruiser's dark bulk made her seem even more massive than she was. Especially with most of her lights extinguished and only a cluster of battle lanterns tossing uneasily in the breeze near the brow portal. Brim stepped out and helped Raddisma to the pavement as guards on either side of the opening snapped to attention.

"You may return to the ship and retire, Tutti," she directed her red-haired chauffeur. "I shall summon you should I desire to be picked up."

"Aye, Madame Raddisma," the woman said, bowing deeply. She quickly stepped into the driver's compartment and the big limousine whirred into the darkness like some great wraith.

Brim pressed Raddisma's hand as she took his arm. "It won't be very pretty in the wrecked chambers," he said quietly. "But then you've already seen worse in the hospital this afternoon."

"I'm prepared, Captain," she said, her voice calm and steady.

"All right," Brim said, wishing that *he* could say the same. Returning the guards' salute, he led her way into a moving staircase while he furiously attempted to come up with *any* even halfway plausible way to finesse Raddisma on board without signing. As they neared the top, however, his mind remained a very frustrated blank.

Only one alternative was left to him, now: brute force (better known as "Captain's privilege"). Unfortunately, if he resorted to that, eventually *everyone* would know what he and the Princess were up to.

Then, suddenly, it was too late. He took a deep breath, smiled reassuringly at Raddisma, and was just about to storm through the boarding hatch when he spied . . . He couldn't *believe* his eyes! There was Barbousse, manning the sign-in desk as if it were his normal duty station. . . . "Good evening, Chief," he said, calmly as he could.

"Evenin', Cap'm," Barbousse returned with a most routine countenance.

"Um . . . Madame Raddisma," Brim said, "m-may I present Master Chief Petty Officer Utrillo Barbousse, who has saved my life on so many occasions that I have lost count. Chief—Madame Raddisma, Principal Consort to the throne of Mustafa Eyren."

Barbousse rose to his feet and bowed formally. "Madame Raddisma," he said, "I am deeply honored."

"As am I, Chief Barbousse," she said, returning a graceful curtsy. Tall as she was, she still had to look up at the huge man.

Brim's eyes strayed to the sign-in log. How in the name of Voot's filth-dripping beard was he going to bluster past somebody like Barbousse? Talk about bad luck. Universe!

"Um, Cap'm," Barbousse intruded on his discomfort, "I'm 'fraid you an' Madame Raddisma will have to go on board without signin' in this evening." He frowned. "Somehow the whole mechanism went out of commission less than a metacycle ago. I just stationed myself here in case someone unauthorized tries to come on board. Never can be too careful, as you say, sir."

Suddenly Brim understood. He closed his eyes in silent thanks.

"Chief," he said when he had recovered the ability to speak, "I shall probably *never* be able to thank you sufficiently for taking over this duty tonight."

"All part of m'job, Cap'm." Barbousse said, knuckling his forehead as Brim and Raddisma started toward the main corridor of the ship. "I'll be here as long as . . . um . . . I'm needed."

Brim nodded; there was nothing else to say.

"It has been a pleasure meeting you, Chief," Raddisma said, stopping to touch the big rating's arm. "Your name comes up often among the ladies at court," she said with a broad smile.

Barbousse blushed. "Um . . . well . . . those fine ladies always make me feel . . . um . . . pretty wonderful."

Raddisma grinned while her own face colored. "I'm certain they do, Chief," she commented. "And I can see why." Reaching over the desk, she put her hands on his cheeks and gently pulled him down to where she could plant a quick kiss on the tip of his nose. "I think you're pretty wonderful, too." Then she turned to Brim. "Now, Captain," she said, "I am ready to see those damaged power chambers."

Their visit probably cost Brim an aggregate fifty metacycles of work among the damage-control engineers who were totally captivated by Raddisma's natural intelligence and glowing, sympathetic personality. The badly ruptured chambers had been exposed to Lake Solent's damp, cold atmosphere without heat for almost a Standard Day and Raddisma never even had the chance to get out of her great black cloak. Yet wherever she went, she dispensed her own brand of sunny charm that uniquely warmed everything she touched, both physically and spiritually. Sodeskayans nearly always exhibited an appreciation for human women, and the normally rancorous Chief Baranev was no exception. After a few moments conversation with the beautiful Fluvannian, the old Bear would clearly have eaten from her hand.

After a while, Brim found himself daydreaming about their talk in the limousine and wished that she weren't making *quite* so thorough a job of her visit. But he had to admit that nothing he could ever have done himself would have resulted in such a beneficial effect on the tired crews—who still faced working well into the morning. He followed patiently while she listened with great care to each tale of horror and endured a thousand descriptions of damaged systems, from mangled, two-story generators and wave guides to melted electronic circuit assemblies. She must have inspected each linear iral of the jagged tear in *Starfury*'s side, leaning out over the frozen lake literally dozens of times to inspect every major (and minor) detail that someone in the crew deemed important.

Eventually, however, she stopped at Brim's side and smiled at the admiring crowd that had gathered nearby. "My friends," she began in a tired voice, "it has been a long day. Will you please accept my deepest thanks—and Mustafa's appreciation —for the patience you all have shown while you described *Starfury*'s damage to me?" She shook her head and opened her hands. "Only when allowed to witness something like *this* first-hand," she said, "can one begin to comprehend the terrible power of the weapons you face—and understand the prodigious stature of your bravery. Every Fluvannian is deeply in your debt—and I perhaps most of all."

As the ruined chamber echoed with applause and cheering, she took Brim's hand. "Now, my dear Captain," she whispered, "I should rather like to take you up on that offer of a 'highly restricted tour,' as I believe you put it. Do you suppose that might still be arranged?"

Once more, Brim offered his arm. "I can think of nothing more important in the Universe," he said, looking into her great blue eyes.

As they passed through the hatch, Raddisma turned to wave —and caused still another round of applause and cheering.

Outside, Brim looked at her with real approbation. "You were a sensation," he said earnestly. "They loved you."

With power shut off to most of the ship, the only lighting in the log corridor was provided by an occasional hovering battle lantern. She smiled as they walked slowly through the artificial twilight. "Thank you, Wilf," she said in her dusky voice. "I guess I love them, too." Then she winked and pulled his arm around her waist. "And speaking of love," she said, "is there much traffic along this corridor?"

Brim looked around and smiled. "Not at this time of the night," he said, "especially with the power off the way it is."

"Good," she said, stopping in the semidarkness between two of the dim battle lanterns. She turned to face him and slowly began to unfasten her cloak. "I've had a surprise waiting for you since we left the reception," she said as she pulled the garment completely open. "Do you like it?" she asked.

Brim felt himself gasp. Beneath her cloak, the long-legged woman was stark naked. "Raddisma," he mumbled, "you are . . . *magnificent*!" She had small, youthfully upturned breasts with light-colored nipples that pouted from modest, knobby aureoles. Her waist was tiny, with only the merest swelling for a midriff. And as he had guessed, her legs were superb—all the way to her spike-heeled ankle boots! But what absolutely set him on his ear was her crotch. It was completely shaven, featureless except for its great dark cleft that looked all out of proportion without its customary thatch. He simply couldn't take his eyes from it.

"You have never been with a shaved woman before?" she asked, opening her stance provocatively. "It is more or less a trademark with me."

"Never," Brim said bemusedly, running his fingers gently over the smooth flesh. She must have had herself shaved during the reception, for his own chin had already grown more stubble since before their hospital visit.

"Well?" she prompted. "What do you think of my little surprise?"

"U-Universe," Brim stammered, urging her toward the next battle lantern. "Had I guessed what you had in store, I'd never have let you *near* the power chamber."

She laughed, slipping the cloak off completely and handing it to him as she turned her back. "That's why it had to be a surprise, my lover to be," she called over her shoulder while she shook her buttocks. "I don't think you *yet* have any idea how much that little visit meant." Then she winked. "Enough talk," she said with a giggle. "Do you think I can make it all the way to your cabin wearing only my boots, or shall I put my cloak back on? I've enjoyed showing *you* what you want to see, but now I'm getting a little chilly—and more than a little anxious to discover what it is that makes such a protrusion in the front of your trousers.''

Brim grinned as he held the cloak for her to put on. "Much as I hate to cover all that female elegance," he said, "it will be only for a few moments while we cross some of the busier parts of the ship." He laughed ruefully. "And believe me, Raddisma, the sooner I can show you what it is that makes that, er, *protrusion*, the more comfortable I shall be."

She squeezed his arm as they hurried along the corridor. "I'll bet I can show you what to do with that protrusion of yours that is a lot more comfortable than just letting me see it."

"You can?" Brim asked in mock interest. "Really?"

"Trust me," Raddisma laughed.

He did.

And so did she. . . .

Brim awoke the next morning to a gentle tapping on the door to his cabin. "Yes?" he demanded as Raddisma sleepily drew him even closer to her perfumed warmth.

"Cap'm," the deep voice of Barbousse intoned in a stage whisper from the corridor outside. "It'll be light in another metacycle an' a half, sir. I have one of our staff cars waitin' at the brow, and—beggin' both your pardons—but Petty Officer Tutti says that Madame Raddisma ought to be back aboard S.S. *Andenez* before the watch changes."

Brim frowned. "Does that make sense to you?" he asked, looking into great, almond-shaped eyes—that were presently a little out of focus. "Do you know a Petty Officer Tutti?"

Raddisma grimaced and hugged him tighter. "We all have *special* people we can trust," she said sleepily. "Petty Officer Cosa Tutti—that absolutely stunning, red-haired chauffeur you couldn't help oogling—is also my personal Barbousse. I can trust her with anything, and she's quite correct. I need to be aboard *Andenez* before the watch changes."

Brim nodded to out-of-focus eyes and grinned. "I understand, now," he said. Pushing himself up on his elbow, he turned toward the door. "Many thanks, Chief," he called out. "You may tell Ms. Tutti that we will be on our way in . . ." Suddenly Raddisma placed her hand over his mouth.

"At the very most, it can take no more than ten cycles to drive between our two ships," she whispered. "And I for one have not had *nearly* enough of you to last until Lady Fortune once more sees fit for us to share a bed."

Brim felt gentle fingers deftly exploring his crotch, and discovered that his own hand had become curved around a *most* intriguing, moist shape—one that was just now developing the merest beginnings of a rough stubble. "You're right, of course," he said, kissing her gently on the lips. "Chief," he called out, "we'll be ready for that staff car in about a metacycle—or so."

"Aye, Cap'm," Barbousse acknowledged and Brim immediately found his mouth besieged by a great fusillade of wet kisses. Then before he could gain control of the situation, Raddisma silently rolled him onto his back and mounted his loins as if he were some sort of backward horse. Grinning as if she had just discovered something wonderfully new, she arched her back against his drawn-up knees, then threw her naked crotch forward, opening its great crevasse for his inspection with long, graceful fingers. Instantly he felt himself grow ready, and she sank back on him with a huge sigh, enveloping his whole existence in wet, swollen flesh. After that, he found it *most* difficult to keep track of time.

Brim and Barbousse returned Raddisma to her starship with only a few moments to spare, but it was enough. The Consort's alluring chauffeur met their staff car at the foot of the brow. The woman blew Barbousse a long, impassioned kiss—as if she and the Chief had become *extremely* close friends during the evening. Brim nodded with an inward smile as she bundled Raddisma up into the moving staircase and disappeared. "Looks as if you might have enjoyed a little relaxation yourself last evening, Chief," he said.

Barbousse grinned—Brim knew he was blushing. "Aye, Cap'm," he admitted. "Lieutenant Tissaurd got us together by HoloPhone durin' the reception. Warned us we'd better be ready to coordinate things, an' I came straight over here to see her."

He drove quietly for a moment, as if he were savoring his thoughts. "After that," he continued, "we just sort of got . . . well . . . *friendly*. An' after you two were squared away— beggin' the Cap'm's pardon, of course—why, she came over for her own visit to *Starfury*." He laughed quietly. "It was a beautiful evenin', it was," he said, "An' o' course, Ms. Tutti didn't have to waste a lot o' time schmoozin' with the folks in the power chamber. . . ."

Precisely two metacycles later, S.S. *Andenez* embarked Raddisma for home. Brim listened to the thunder of its passage from *Starfury*'s damaged power chamber, and for a moment he lost his ability to concentrate on the distressing details of Chief Baranev's report. A certain portion of his anatomy had become quite tender during the evening; he wondered if hers was, too.

"You look *awfully* relaxed this evening, Skipper," Tissaurd observed over supper in the wardroom.

Brim nodded. "I am," he said, "or, more correctly, I *was*, at any rate."

"I don't understand," the tiny officer said with a frown.

"Well," Brim said with a little smile, "let us say that Chief Baranev destroyed a great deal of last night's 'glow,' shall we say, with his cockeyed afternoon damage report." He shook his head as he sipped a third scalding mug of cvceese'. "I'm sure you know that *Starfury*'s in a bad way."

"I'd heard," Tissaurd said. "Word got around right after the Chief released his report."

Brim nodded. "What hasn't gotten around is Commodore Atcherly's answer to that report."

Tissaurd frowned. "Hmm," she said. "From the look on your face, it wasn't very promising. What did he say?"

"Not a lot," Brim replied, taking a long, thoughtful sip of cvceese'. "Just that it will take a long time for Calshot's maintenance people to make the repairs we need. *Starfury* is simply too big for any of the local facilities. It was all they could do to have her drawn onto their biggest gravity pool. Everything else will have to be done practically by hand."

"I suppose things wouldn't have been much better had we set

her down at Varnholm Hall,'' Tissaurd granted. ''Because we certainly don't have any bigger facilities there.''

Brim nodded. ''That's it, Number One,'' he said. ''And the damned CIGAs are still tying up facilities in all the other ports around Ordu. Calhoun KA'PPAed the situation to Avalon about a metacycle ago.''

''Well, Skipper,'' she said, ''then it's time to remind you of the talk we had on brick walls a while back.''

Brim glowered at the tiny officer. ''I remember,'' he grumped. ''But how in xaxt sake can I just step back and wait for something 'different' to happen? There's a war on!''

''Yeah,'' Tissaurd said with a little smile, ''I'd noticed the war.''

''Well, then?''

''Then, Skipper,'' she said, ''you probably ought to turn in for a few metacycles of sleep tonight, because, war or no war, everything about *Starfury* is stopped *cold*!''

Early the next morning, Calhoun messaged from Varnholm. Brim took it on the bridge, where he was helping run tests on a bank of flight controls.

''I'm aboot to send a launch for you, young Brim,'' Calhoun said. ''You might as well be here helpin' me plan what we're going to do about yon xaxtdamme fort, for there's clearly nothin' much you can do there that Lieutenant Tissaurd can't handle for you.''

Brim could only nod agreement. He hated sitting on his hands. Soon after Calhoun closed the connection, he slid from his seat and started aft to pack an overnight bag when he heard a great rolling thunder overhead, as if a capital ship were making landfall out on Lake Solent. Fighting down a moment's dread, he willed himself calm—had this been a raiding Leaguer, there would have been at least a *little* warning. He glanced up through the Hyperscreens just in time to see a colossal form materialize from the overcast in the still-dim light of dawn—and stopped in his tracks, flabbergasted. Great stowed cranes parked fore and aft like outsize disruptors, monstrous hatches, massive sheer flanks of streaked hullmetal plate, and a low glowering bridge. He'd only seen one Repair and Salvage vessel like that one, ever: Commodore Tor's big *Refit Enterprise*, from Gimmas Haefdon! As the great form hurdled overhead, four familiar shapes descended with her: Starfuries, with whirling condensation contrails streaming from their pontoons. And the Imperial Comet blazed prominently from abaft their bridges. *They* were from home!

While the squadron settled toward the lake—that was even now boiling as landing vectors were cleared in the ice—a COMM rating bustled aft among the control toward him.

"Captain Brim!" he called. "Commodore Calhoun's on the HoloPhone for you again."

"I'll take it here," Brim said, reaching to activate a globular display on a nearby navigator's console. The elder Carescrian's visage appeared almost instantly.

"Well, Brim," he said with a smile. "I understand they made it."

"You mean Commodore Tor and the *Refit Enterprise*?" Brim asked.

"Faith!" Calhoun exclaimed happily. "An' who else were you expectin'?"

Brim grinned. "I wasn't expecting anyone, Commodore," he said. "But I'm sure happy to see Commodore Tor—and the Starfuries. Looks like the Fleet is finally taking some deliveries."

Calhoun nodded. "Those are the nineteenth thru the twenty-second, lad," he said. "An' e'en though they aren't permitted to help us in our efforts, they *are* authorized to defend the *Enterprise* while she puts *Starfury* back to rights."

As Brim watched, the colossal starship set down on the lake with a massive grace all out of proportion to her size. The Starfuries, however, continued on their way and soared effortlessly back into the clouds. "*Enterprise* is down safely, Commodore," he said.

"Good," Calhoun said, "sorry I wasn't able to give you more warnin'. I only found out myself just after I'd talked to you. Brother Drummond played this one mighty close to his vest."

"I'm not surprised, sir," Brim observed, "with the fuss the CIGAs are able to raise at home."

Calhoun nodded. "Weel, m'boy," he said. "You and that crazy Number One o' yours wull want to spend a wee time talkin' wi' Commodore Tor, so I'll temporarily counter my orders havin' you report immediately to Varnholm Hall," he said with a strange little smile. "The Commodore has some information that I'd like you both to hear from him. The man's produced an absolute miracle back at old Gimmas Haefdon."

"A *miracle*?" Commodore?

"You judge it for yourself, young Brim," the Commodore laughed. "An' I shall expect you to report as soon as you and Tissaurd have learned all Tor's willin' to tell you."

"Aye, sir," Brim promised. "I'll be there!" Then he struggled into his Fleet Cloak, turned up the thermostat, and made his way to the main hatch and *Refit Enterprise*.

Later that morning in the wardroom, Tissaurd and Brim met Commodore Tor for a late breakfast. . . .

"How are you today, Nadia?" Tor asked.

"Terrible, Commodore." Tissaurd chuckled with a theatrically demented grin.

"*That's* nice," Tor answered, winking reassuringly at the Steward—whose jaw had suddenly dropped in consternation. "I feel horrible, too."

"Good! Glad to hear it!" Tissaurd exclaimed. "And you, Captain, how are you this snowy morning?"

"Worse than ever, Number One," Brim grumped spuriously. "You, Commodore," he remanded, "have clearly set a bad precedent in *Starfury*'s wardroom."

"Why, Captain Brim," Tor protested, hand on his heart in a gesture of mock innocence, "how can you say that?"

"In Avalonian, mostly," Brim said with a grin. "And you're no better than the Commodore, Number One," he added, pointing an accusatory finger at Tissaurd. Soon afterward, the Steward recovered enough to serve steaming mugs of cvceese' and *Starfury*'s own version of a dish called "battercakes," smothered in a pungent hot syrup—and for the next few cycles, everyone was much too busy for talk.

When conversation eventually resumed—with the third round

of cvceese'—Brim learned that Tor had ordered out maintenance crews from both the Calshot Station and *Enterprise* long before dawn. The huge salvage vessel was now hovering no more than ten irals from *Starfury*'s side, using her own mighty levitating systems instead of a gravity pool. Moreover, huge cranes had already raised the damaged cruiser nearly twelve irals without disturbing anyone aboard. Even as the four officers sipped cvceese' and talked, massive new power chambers rumbled across a temporary bridge between the two hulls, and replacement hullmetal plates were taking shape on glowing collapsium forges deep within the big ship's hold.

"What I don't understand," Brim commented at length, "is how you managed to bring *Enterprise* here in the first place. Especially with an escort of four Starfuries. Since the CIGAs first got wind of the operation, I haven't been able to get help —anywhere."

Tor smiled. "That's probably the reason I'm here, then," he said with a cryptic little smile. "I'm from *nowhere*." He joined the tips of his fingers and appeared to be deep in thought for a few moments. "What I am about to tell you," he said presently, "has been such a carefully guarded secret that even you, Wilf Brim, were kept in the dark about it. They sent you—and you, Lieutenant Tissaurd—off to too many places where you might fall into League hands." He frowned. "With the near-term resumption of hostilities, however," he continued, "the secret of Gimmas Haefdon will be revealed soon enough. So it is time both of you know the whole story."

Tissaurd smiled and nodded her head. "I *thought* something was strange about the 'closed-down' status of that planet every time we flew anywhere near the surface. Those big reactors were always active—everywhere. If the place had *really* been shut down, they would all have been cold."

"You were—and are—correct, Lieutenant," Tor said. "But the power was continuously in use."

"By whom?" Brim asked, frowning.

"Well," Tor said, "by the people who fabricated *Starfury*'s new space radiators, for example."

Brim felt his face flush in embarrassment. "Of course," he said, snapping his fingers. "I thought at the time that you people had pulled off true magic fabricating that in *Enterprise*."

Tor smiled. "*Enterprise*'s crews are good," he said. "But even *they* can't work the kind of miracles something like that would have required." He sat back while the Steward filled his mug with more cvceese', then nodded, as if he had just made up his mind about something. "So far as the CIGAs are concerned," he began at length, "Gimmas Haefdon was closed down more than ten Standard Years ago—except for small-scale maintenance operations and some 'nonessential research.' " His eyes lit up with humor for a moment. "We were careful to make certain that Amherst and his coterie of traitors remained convinced that they made Gimmas into a certifiable *nowhere*. But shortly after its so-called closing, a number of colleagues and myself pulled certain strings to become that 'small-scale maintenance crew' and began turning the base into one of five covert *somewheres* that may yet help to save the Empire from its CIGA cancer."

"What you do there can be *that* critical?" Tissaurd asked.

"Well," Tor replied with a smile, "I'm not authorized to talk about everything, but we certainly build Starfuries at Gimmas. The four new ships that escorted *Enterprise* were built there— they completed their deep-space trials just before we departed for Fluvanna. And," he continued, cleaning his spectacles with a huge white handkerchief, "if you have not already guessed, all four ships are here at the direct orders of Prince Onrad."

"Universe," Tissaurd whispered. "Prince Onrad?"

"He and General Drummond have been keeping close tabs on the situation here in Fluvanna," Tor said. "They waited as long as they could before playing their hand, but with the appearance of the new Gorn-Hoffs, it quickly became clear that Baxter Calhoun would soon need heavy maintenance support. There are five more Enterprise-class salvage and repair ships under construction, but they're far from complete. We were the only game in town, so to speak."

"*Enterprise* is one miraculous game," Brim said appreciatively. "But they certainly did wait until the last possible cycle to send her. If she hadn't already been on your way, *Starfury* would have been out of action for weeks!"

"I know," Tor said sympathetically. "I'm empowered to apologize for both the Prince and General Drummond."

"Doesn't really matter now," Brim allowed pragmatically. "'All's well that ends well,' as *somebody* once observed."

"Actually," Tor said, "it really doesn't end, so to speak."

"I don't understand," Brim said.

"Well," Tor said, "only one of the Starfuries will depart when we've finished here. The other three—along with *Refit Enterprise* will be based at Varnholm Hall. Permanently—or as long as the IVG exists."

"Universe!" Brim exclaimed. "Now *that's* what I call help!" He grinned. "And we can certainly use three more Starfuries, even with rookie crews."

"Hmm," Tor said with a frown. "There, you're in for a bit of a disappointment."

"Why?" Brim demanded.

"It has to do with the Imperial comets they have abaft their bridges," Tor explained with a grimace, "like the ones *Enterprise* wears. They are all ships of the Imperial Fleet—and the Empire isn't just now at war with the League." He peered over his glasses apologetically. "It's only a technicality, of course. But unfortunately. . . ."

"I remember Calhoun telling me about it, now," Brim said, shaking his head in frustration. "So the Starfuries are here to protect *Enterprise*, eh?"

"I'm afraid that's about it—at least until the Emperor can get around the CIGAs in the General Parliament and declare war."

Brim nodded and grinned. "As they put things in Sodeskaya," he said, "it's a lot better than a poke in the eye with a sharp icicle."

Tor nodded sober agreement. "It certainly seems to be that," he observed.

Tissaurd nodded. "And getting back to Gimmas Haefdon for a moment, Commodore," she said, "unless I miss my guess, you're not *just* building Starfuries there, are you? I'll bet you're working on that stripped-down, killer-ship version of *Starfury* people have been whispering about!" She grinned and fixed him with one of her gazes. "I always wondered what somebody like Mark Valerian was doing there just for *Starfury*'s deep-space acceptance trials. He already knew the ship would pass with flying colors."

Tor's face colored and he smiled. "Probably, we ought to discuss killer-ships at a more appropriate time, Lieutenant," he demurred. "But, as I said, we, ah, *do* keep busy out there. . . ." At that moment, a singularly piercing thud sounded from deep within the hull. Tor's eyebrows shot up with real concern. "I think I'm probably needed down there," he said, pushing back his chair, then he stopped and held up his index finger. "Captain Brim," he said, "would it be possible to ask a favor of you and your ship?"

"We are at your service, Commodore," Brim replied.

"Good," the Commodore replied, "Then have your ward-room cook send over the recipe for those, er, 'battercakes' you fed me this morning and I shall be forever in your debt."

"I'll do it debt free, Commodore," Brim promised.

"Good," Tor said, "and I shall expect both of you in *Enterprise*'s wardroom this evening," he said. "Evening and one on the dot."

"We'll be there, Commodore," Brim promised. "Could I bring a few bottles of Logish Meem with me?"

"*Could* you?" Tor asked in astonishment. "But of course, Brim," he said. "You didn't think I'd let you in without them, did you?"

"Well," Brim countered, "under normal circumstances, I'd probably admit that you had me over a barrel, Commodore."

"Well, I do, don't I?" Tor demanded.

"Oh, absolutely, Commodore," Brim answered, "unless you decide that you also want a recipe for the syrup that goes with the battercakes."

Tor looked stunned. "Captain Brim," he groaned in dismay, "do you mean to tell me that the syrup recipe isn't included with the one for the battercakes?"

"No, sir," Brim said. "It's an all-purpose syrup."

"I see," Tor said, frowning as if he were considering some complex engineering problem. "On the other hand," he added, "the cakes themselves *are* delicious. There's no getting around that. So you'd better bring the meem *and* the syrup recipe—just to be sure. You never know how the rest of my day will go." Then, with a grin, he disappeared through the hatch.

Next morning, a gravely hung-over W.A. Brim, Commander, R.F.F., and Captain of the Fluvannian cruiser R.F.F. *Starfury*, unabashedly pulled rank by placing an equally hung-over Nadia Tissaurd, Lt. Commander, R.F.F., in temporary charge of all ship's operations. He then staggered directly to his cabin and slept for nearly a full Standard Day. Privilege, he observed to the outraged Tissaurd, is an insidious endemic—but it is rarely a mortal malady. . . .

CHAPTER 10

Zonga'ar

Starfury was out of action for nearly seven Standard Days. Immediately afterward, however, Brim found himself back in furious—and deadly—combat with what seemed like the total combined fleets of Nergol Triannic *and* Rogan LaKarn. Though Commodore Tor's *Refit Enterprise* kept a significantly larger percentage of Calhoun's little fleet operational, the ever-increasing pace of battle was beginning to make itself felt—and within a month, they lost their first two Starfuries: I.F.S. *Starwarrior* and I.F.S. *Stargallant*. Thereafter, as shrewd Avalonian CIGAs in the General Parliament stretched out Fluvannian Defense Treaty deliberations, IVG conditions inevitably began to deteriorate. And though the ex-Imperials destroyed nearly fifteen Leaguer warships for each Starfury demolished, it didn't take a Drive scientist to understand they couldn't sustain that kind of pace forever—even with Commodore Tor accomplishing feats of maintenance wizardry every metacycle (on the metacycle) or courageous AkroKahn captains running spare parts through the Leaguer blockade in their unarmed civilian transport ships.

Replacements for IVG combat casualties, however, were in *far* shorter supply. Only a trickle of volunteers arrived from Avalon, and many of them had to be smuggled past zealous CIGAs who had infiltrated the Imperial Customs Service. As

Brim's first anniversary in the IVG arrived, he and the other captains found themselves flying with reduced crews as a matter of course while the enemy fleets were clearly growing both in strength and experience. And although they vowed to fight until the last Starfury would no longer lift, that day was clearly on the time horizon, and approaching rapidly.

On the morning after R.F.S. *Starviper* was lost with all hands, Calhoun KA'PPAed an order for Brim and Moulding to report to his office the moment they made landfall. Brim was last in, and arrived from the gravity pool complex at a run. As he hurried through the door, he noticed a tall, grave-looking Bear in earnest conversation with Calhoun, Moulding, Ursis, and Ambassador Beyazh. Wearing a monocle fastened to a delicate gold chain, the Sodeskayan was dressed as a General-Mayor with sky-blue embellishments of the Intelligence Corps. Brim didn't know him, but Ursis and Beyazh clearly did.

"General Probyeda," the Bear said soberly in Avalonian, "is now meeting old friend and shipmate Commander Wilf Ansor Brim, Captain of *Starfury*."

Probyeda turned and extended his hand. "I have heard much that recommends you, Wilf Ansorovich," he said, "both from fryend Nikolai Yanuarievich and Grand Duke Anastas Alexi Borodov."

"General Probyeda," Brim said in surprise. "I am honored to meet you." His words were no empty courtesy. During the last war, Probyeda had distinguished himself in a number of daring covert missions, some of which had never been declassified. And he was also an old friend of the Empire; it was through his offices that the prototype Gorn-Hoff P.1065 had been discovered—and its data released to Drummond.

The Bear smiled and peered through his monocle. "When you and Commander Moulding hear information I bring," he said soberly, "you may revise opinion."

Calhoun placed his hand on the Bear's shoulder board. "General Probyeda isn't makin' small talk, gentlemen," he said, indicating six chairs that had been drawn up around a large globular projector in a corner of the office. "If you'll take seats aboot yon projector, we'll gat this meetin' under way directly."

Moulding grinned at Brim as he slid into an adjoining chair and rolled his eyes to the heavens. "Sounds as if they're planning to make us work for a living," he whispered.

Brim shrugged. "Well," he muttered, "this Fluvannian vacation of ours *could* get to be sort of boring, after a while."

Calhoun got to the point with no preamble whatsoever. "'Tis high time," he began, "that we take on the League's xaxtdamme space fortification immediately; they're beginnin' to hurt us bad. In addition to basin' their Gorn-Hoffs and Dampiers there, the zukeed space weasels have been stockpilin' ground supplies an' troops as well. An' noo it appears their invasion plans for Fluvanna are almost complete, so we hae little choice—*Queen Elidean* or nae." He paused. "We'll be doin' the mission in consort wi' units o' the Fluvannian Fleet, thanks to Ambassador Beyazh, who flew in a month ago from Avalon an' has worked miracles to coordinate things between the two governments."

Beyazh looked at Brim and Moulding. "My take is that the real miracles have been accomplished by these two gentlemen and their colleagues in the Starfuries," he said.

Calhoun pursed his lips. "They may need a few mair miracles afore you're finished dealin' wi' the fort," he continued, "'cause unfortunately the Leaguers hae gone aboot fortifyin' the place beyond all measure." He nodded to Probyeda. "That's wha' the General's here to tell you about, so I'll ask him to start wi' his part o' the briefin'."

Probyeda also wasted no time getting to his point. "Gentlemen," he said, "we Sodeskayans have studied Leaguer fortifications for number of years now, ever since they began building fortified networks. However," he added meaningfully, "they have been unusually careful with this one, going so far as to construct from outside in to preserve secrecy. Because of this, we know relatively little about interior layout, although we have considerable information concerning exterior features and armament." He touched a switch and a three-dimensional image of the Zonga'ar shoal itself materialized above the projector. Small as asteroid collections went, it was named for an enormous old starship, S.S. *Zonga'ar*, that came to ruin against the mass of rocks more than a thousand Standard Years in the past. The longish formation extended no more than eight hundred c'lenyts from tip to tip at the outside and was accumulated—as well as shaped—by the accretion beam of a neighboring space hole. Over the aeons, it had taken the slightly curved shape of a scythe blade, with a roughly triangular cross section that was perhaps ten c'lenyts on a side. The same accretion beam that amassed and shaped it also formed a wide, fast-flowing gravity ribbon that swept past its concave ends like a river. And it was between the accretion beam and the center of the scythe that the Leaguers had built their fortification, positioned near a huge glowing asteroid called Cendar and shielded from the beam itself by the shoal's slightly protruding ends. The same beam, however, also protected the fort from frontal attack. The very act of crossing its treacherous graviton flow made such an assault highly difficult as well as dangerous, even without considering the fort's huge battery of disruptors.

As Probyeda focused his projector on the fort itself, he described great disruptor batteries, armored flanks, and nearly limitless energy supplies—along with rows and rows of parked Dampiers and Gorn-Hoffs, the ones that the IVG had been fighting since the outbreak of war. Before he was finished, the General described one of the most brilliantly conceived fortifications Brim had ever encountered.

"Shaping up to be *some* vacation, eh, Wilf?" Moulding muttered.

"Yeah," Brim agreed under his breath. "You'll be sure to let me know when we start having fun."

Calhoun overheard them and laughed. "I've taken personal steps to bring a little mair firepower to bear for the mission," he said, "but it may arrive a wee late—or not at all. An' disfortunately, we've already put off the raid too lang. They're damme near too strong to deal with right noo." He glanced at Beyazh. "That's where the Ambassador and his Fluvannian Fleet come into the picture. They'll try to draw off the Gorn-Hoffs and Dampiers while we go after the primary target." With that, he and Beyazh launched into a description of a bold and ingenious scheme that left the others in the room nodding with admiration.

Brim was to take command of the eight remaining IVG Starfuries, which he would lead as a unit code-named CLEAVE. His ships would operate in conjunction with units of the Fluvannian Fleet, ostensibly speeding off to intercept a brace of Leaguer supply convoys that were known to be on the way with more ground troops and invasion supplies. At the same time, a second squadron, consisting wholly of ancient Fluvannian warships—Force SMASH—would deploy toward the space fort itself, clearly a suicidal mission against such a target. The key to the operation, however, lay in purposely leaking these plans to the Leaguers—while omitting one small, but significant, detail.

Success depended heavily upon two essential elements: the Leaguers' natural disdain for all but the most up-to-date military equipment and the colossal emptiness of intragalactic space itself. If everything went according to plan, the entire fleet of Dampiers and Gorn-Hoffs would light out after the Starfuries in CLEAVE, ceding the ancient Fluvannian ships of SMASH to the CIGAs in their Imperial battleship—and the powerful disruptors of the fort itself. Less than a cycle into the CLEAVE sortie, however, Brim and his Starfuries would secretly depart from their elderly Fluvannian consorts. Firing off their reflecting Drives, they would sprint through the trackless void on a direct course to the fort, thereby arriving in place of the Fluvannian antiques with weaponry all out of proportion to what the defenders had been led to expect. By the time IVG's ruse was discovered, it would be far too late to send reinforcements.

As the Commodore readily admitted, his strategy wasn't perfect—but it *was* a plan in being. And something had to be done right away if they were to have any chance of averting disaster.

Brim and Moulding conferred for only a moment before they agreed to the mission, and even before the Evening watch was under way, plans were sufficiently complete that Beyazh could leave for Magor to alert the Fluvannian Fleet for a midmorning departure two days hence. He chuckled as Brim accompanied him to his ship. "For years I have searched for some way to make use of the wiring job the bloody Leaguers sneaked into our palace grounds," he said. "It's been most difficult composing small talk so they would think we hadn't discovered the rather amateur job they did."

Brim frowned, unwilling to reveal he'd learned about the wiring job from Saltash on his first day in Fluvanna. "I wasn't aware that the grounds had been wired," he lied.

Beyazh laughed. "In a pig's eye you weren't aware, my good Captain," he said. "But your denial makes you a good soldier in anybody's book—as well as the reason I have more than once been willing to share information with you." He smiled. "And all my patience will be worthwhile tonight—rewarded when I walk in that garden briefing the Nabob with information we actually *want* the Leaguers to hear."

They stopped for a moment at the brow to the fast packet that had brought the Ambassador to Varnholm, and Beyazh turned to grip both of Brim's upper arms. "Captain," he said with a very serious look on his face, "I realize that this mission may well turn out to be one of the most difficult and dangerous of your career."

Brim nodded. "It certainly isn't shaping up to be any kind of a joyride, Mr. Ambassador."

Beyazh looked down at the long, curled tips of his boots. For the first time since Brim had met the man, he seemed to be at a loss for words. "I hope you come back, Wilf Brim," he said finally. "Your bravery makes you a *most* valuable man—not just to Fluvanna or your beloved Empire, but to the whole of Civilization."

"Thank you, sir," Brim replied with emotion. "You honor me." Then he offered his hand. "I shall be back, Mr. Ambassador. You can count on it."

"A number of us will be counting on that, Captain," Beyazh replied, grasping Brim's hand in his. Then he turned and started out across the brow.

As Brim retraced his lonely way along the rows of gravity pools, he reflected on his own words: "I shall be back, Mr. Ambassador. You can count on it." He hoped to the Universe he was right. . . .

* * *

Three Standard Days later, Brim was *there*, scanning the distant asteroid shoal and trying to overlook the excited commotion around him. *Starfury*'s bridge had succumbed to excitement shortly after they slowed through LightSpeed—it wouldn't have been noticeable to everyone; his bridge crew was professional almost to a fault. But he could tell. He was excited himself. And in spite of the detour when they started out with the old ships of Force CLEAVE, they'd made the best of *Starfury*'s astonishing Hyperspeed capability, arriving off the asteroid shoal at about the same time the Leaguers would be expecting to see the real Fluvannians. Now, as they crept toward the still-distant fort at DEAD SLOW, he brought his charts to the global display and studied them for the ten-billionth time. Cendar, the glowing asteroid, was barely visible against the distant curve of the shoal when he called up Ulfilas Meesha on a display. "Ready, Lieutenant?" he asked.

Meesha's spectral gray eyes peered out of the shimmering globe like malevolent wraiths. "Full charges at the turrets, and plasma is running max below, Captain," the Gunnery Officer answered quietly.

"Very well," Brim said, "you may enable the disruptors."

"Aye, Captain," Meesha acknowledged.

Brim listened to the litany that would bring the ship's powerful main armament into life, while outside the turrets unparked and their big tapered firing tubes began to index like athletes limbering themselves before a workout.

"Main battery has completed self-test and is in firing mode, Captain," Meesha reported presently.

Brim nodded, scanning the starry blackness beyond the shoal. Moulding and his four ships were out there somewhere—he hoped. Nudging *Starfury* slightly to starboard, he made a mental note that she was responding well to the low-speed steering-engine update Tor's crew had downloaded via KA'PPA from Gimmas Haefdon two days before. He'd mention it when he got back. If he got back.

In a panel display, he absently watched Chief Kowalski out in A turret patting a massive firing block as if it were alive. Six consoles aft on the bridge, Barbousse stood beside his torpedo station with a foot on the firing console as he helped two novice ratings at a tracking station beside him.

"Wrecked starship off the port bow, Captain," Tissaurd warned.

"Got it," Brim replied; he'd been keeping his eye on it. Even at a distance of two or three c'lenyts, *Zonga'ar*'s colossal wreck was impressive. She'd been opened to space along one whole flank, exposing tiers of huge ruined galleries and melted apparatus that once must have been an interstellar Drive. In other circumstances, the ancient wreck would have been fascinating. At DEAD SLOW, however, the threat from benders in spectral mode was enough to quickly blunt his interest. "Who's running the N-ray detector gear?" he demanded.

"The best, Skipper," Tissaurd replied. "I put Roy Hunt on duty as soon as we slowed through LightSpeed."

Brim nodded. "Hunt's the best," he allowed, scanning the distant shoal again. Ultimately he focused his attention on the target. They'd soon be close enough to spot the massive bulk of *Queen Elidean* in the Leaguer's gravity anchorage. If everything so far had gone according to plan, the grand old ship and her escorts would be practically alone.

Rawlings, an Electro-Optical Systems Officer, appeared in a maintenance display. "Shall I set the Hyperscreens to battle ready?" he asked.

Brim nodded. "Tint 'em down, Matt," he replied. In moments, the Hyperscreens darkened subtly to the shade starsailors knew as "Battle-Tint/331." During actual combat, the 'screens would automatically darken from this tint and return to it as necessary to protect the crew's eyes against the hellish glare of disruptor fire—incoming as well as outgoing.

Abruptly *Starfury* began to skid sideways and "up," in relation to the fort. Brim reset the trim and glanced out to port where he could just pick up the glow of an accretion beam coming off the nearby space hole. Its rush of gravitons was like a crosswind on an old-fashioned aerodynamic vehicle; and he checked his instruments for the proper bearing—this was no time to lose control of the ship.

In a sickbay monitor, he caught Hesternal and her crew energizing banks of healing machines and laying out radiation dressings for the wounds that were certain to come about. For a moment, his mind strayed to Avalon. Did the people back there really appreciate the courageous Imperials he was leading? Could they understand the sacrifices that would soon be made? He snorted grimly. Doubtless there was *appreciation*, for all that—but little comprehension. To *comprehend* what these starsailors would soon endure, one had to be there in *Starfury*'s racing hull, listening to the disruptors fire and feeling the ship lurch when she was hit. One had to *feel* the fear in his own gut—to know that in the next moment, he could be blasted to atomic particles or die screaming in a ruptured battlesuit while his blood boiled in the vacuum of space. One needed to survive that hell of hells called "battle" to really comprehend. And few citizens of Avalon would ever experience *that*. It was why Starfuries and Wilf Brims and Nadia Tissaurds and Utrillo Barbousses and all the other brave starsailors on the mission existed at all: so ordinary folks weren't required to live through such an experience. And because of it, ordinary people would never—*could* never—appreciate, nor even understand, the very special breed of people collectively referred to as "military."

By now, the gravity "crosswind" from the accretion beam had become a problem. The ship was lurching violently in severe graviton turbulence. Brim set his jaw and finessed the controls with all the skill he could bring to bear. Ordinarily, he would have simply used *Starfury*'s tremendous reserves of power to blast her free. However, doing that would also result in a greatly amplified wake from the generators—easily spotted from the base because it would be flowing at almost a right angle to the accretion current. And it certainly wouldn't look like one from a Fluvannian antique.

Brim bit his lip as the turbulence worsened and he struggled to keep on course without increasing speed. No wonder the Leaguers had picked this spot for their space fortification! It was damned near impossible to approach the area unless you came in along the very edge of the asteroid shoal—where they had concentrated extra firepower. The bridge was almost silent as the big starship bucked and pitched through the invisible violence. Beside him, Tissaurd cleared her throat with a look of concern, and he could hear anxious voices behind him. He brushed away a momentary sensation of annoyance. All of them were excellent starsailors, representing aggregate centuries of deep-space experience. As warriors, Voot Himself could not question their bravery. But for half a millennium now, starships had been designed with energy overload capabilities to power out of this sort of situation—and did so as a matter of routine. He ground his teeth and fought the turbulence. There was nothing he could do but endure—and trust that the other three Helmsmen would somehow make it through the storm as well.

As the distance narrowed, Brim could see that the CIGAs in *Queen Elidean* had ominously lighted the great Imperial Comet Crests on either side of her bridge. Pretty evident what *that* meant—they'd been spotted. From the lack of firing, however, it was almost certain that the traitors were uncertain of whom they were facing. "We'll need all the power we can get soon, Strana'," he warned.

The Bear nodded in a display. "I'll tell the Chief," she said.

This brought forth neither questions nor gripes from the pontoons. The deep grumble of Chief Baranev's big plasma generators slowly began to build deep within the hull. That extra power would presently exhaust through waste gates. But when *Starfury* needed it, she wouldn't have to wait.

Then abruptly they cleared the gravity stream. Cheers sounded all over the bridge, even while the colors on Brim's power panel deepened with the increase of ready energy. He glanced outside as the other three ships re-formed in close formation—they'd somehow made it safely through the gravity torrent, too. Now came the hard part. . . .

"They still can't be certain we'll attack at all, with the old *Queen* standing by like that," Brim muttered to Tissaurd as he peered at the distant Leaguer installation, "and surprise is the only edge we'll ever have against those fixed batteries in the space fort. So we'd better be on with this business quickly." He peered at Ulfilas Meesha. His gray eyes looked as if they might bore holes in the status displays before him. "Enable your disruptor triggers, Lieutenant," he said, feeling his breathing grow shallower as the tension mounted. "Now."

"Disruptor triggers are enabled, Captain."

"Check," Brim replied, as always, boggled by the prodigious quantums of energy ready to surge through the mains to the turrets. Outside, the tip of each disruptor began to glow as the mammoth weapons accepted their initial firing charges.

"The *Queen*'s coming up at maximum firing range, Captain," Meesha said in a tense voice.

"Is she tracking us with her firing directors yet?" he asked.

"She is, sir," Meesha replied. "And the fort's main batteries are enabled, too. You can see the fire director beams from here."

Brim nodded. "Very well, Meesha," he said. In Sodeskayan terms, the fat was in the fire now. Next, he punched in Barbousse's torpedo console on a COMM display. "Chief—you going to have trouble putting a spread of torpedoes into the old *Queen* if we have to?" he asked.

"No trouble here, Cap'm," Barbousse replied. "The launcher's already armed with eight 533s, an' they're all energized."

"I mean—blasting an Imperial ship," Brim amended.

Barbousse shook his head. "I appreciate you askin' me, Cap'm," the big rating said. "An' I suppose I love that old ship as much as any Blue Cape. But, Cap'm, when you give an order, it's my duty to carry it out as long as I'm still alive to do it." Then he frowned. "Besides, sir," he said, "it's just like the old girl's been captured anyway—I mean, CIGAs aren't nothin' but Leaguers in Fleet Cloaks."

Brim smiled grimly. "If they fire on us, Chief," he said, "I'll break off *Starfury*'s pass at the fort and we'll make a torpedo run—just like we used to in old *Truculent*. Give 'em whatever it takes. Understand?"

"Understand, Cap'm," the Chief replied with a firm look. No other words were necessary.

Brim turned in his seat for a moment to look back over the bridge. Beside him, Tissaurd was running a last-moment systems check. The firing crews had already begun their litany of target acquisition: "Bearing eight nine; range nine nine one and closing; disruptors steady at two twenty-seven."

Brim nodded to himself. By now, Moulding would either be in position and key his attack on *Starfury*'s—or he was going to miss the whole show. Activating the switch that would soon send an attack signal to his other three Starfuries, he glanced at Tissaurd. "Call it for three cycles, Number One," he ordered and pulled his helmet shut, toggling all five seals in his battlesuit.

The tiny officer nodded grimly, then switched on the blower. "All hands close up battlesuits and stand by for firing run in three cycles," she broadcast as her own battlesuit began to seal.

An almost palpable wave of relief swept the bridge—when the order came to seal battlesuits, things had really started. Brim heard Barbousse talking reassuringly to the novices at the tracking console. "Calmly, lads," he warned, the sound of his voice tinny inside a helmet. "Calmly now. You've important jobs today; you'll do them better if you take a little extra time with the battlesuits. . . ."

A row of consoles nearer, Meesha and his firing crews were making last-moment calibrations, while Strana' Zaftrak filled the bridge with strobing light from her huge power displays. Ahead, through the Hyperscreens, the mammoth Leaguer space fort floated squat and ugly against the undulating backdrop of the asteroid shoal, a malign pustule bristling with KA'PPA antennas and huge disruptors—speckled everywhere by the winking crimson glow of director beams. And directly fronting the grotesque structure hovered *Queen Elidean*. Her CIGA crew had turned the grand old ship's majestic bulk broadside, making it impossible to attack the fort without hitting her first. Additionally, six Imperial attack ships—"escorts"—were moored in a spiral pattern that extended out at least a c'lenyt past the *Queen*. If Amherst's lackeys truly intended to protect the Leaguer fort, then the Imperial ships represented a dangerous gauntlet that would have to be run with each pass at the fort. Unless they were somehow neutralized—or destroyed.

Brim watched a whole new set of director beams wink into life on the knobby surface of the fort. Secondary barbettes, he guessed. His mind's eye conjured rows of black-suited Leaguers at firing consoles, tensely charging their disruptors for close-in combat.

"Open fire *only* at my command," Meesha broadcast to his turret crews.

Brim noticed how quiet the bridge had become now that *Starfury* was committed to the attack.

"Xaxtdamned Leaguers are in for a hard time today," one of the gunnery mates observed aloud. Brim knew the man was especially anxious for the attack to begin; he'd been gravely— and agonizingly—wounded when *Starfury* was brought down. He had a large score to settle.

"Steady, there in C turret . . ." Meesha whispered tensely to one of his displays.

Brim felt the blood lust rise within him. It was always like this in the final moments before battle. He was ready. Clearly, so were the Leaguers and their perfidious CIGA colleagues.

"All hands, stand by for maximum acceleration in ten clicks . . ." Tissaurd announced. "Nine . . ."

Brim studied the fort as he carefully lined up *Starfury* on what the Bears had described as its power center. He poised his hands above the controls. . . .

"Five . . . four . . . three . . ."

Opening the waste gates, Brim fed power to the generators until his damper beams turned a glaring scarlet and begun to pulse just below the DANGER level. The Leaguers would be certain to spot that, but now it wouldn't matter.

"Two . . . one . . . GO!"

At Tissaurd's word, Brim dumped the waste gates and *Starfury* leapt forward like some giant viper after its prey. Through the port Hyperscreens, he could see two other graviton plumes burst into life. To starboard, still another blanked the starscape with its glare. And then they were moving *fast*, accelerating at the ragged edge of the ship's performance envelope in finger-four formation. They skimmed past the first Imperial escort on her port side . . . and beneath the second. Brim could see no visible reaction whatsoever from these clearly surprised crews. But as the little formation sped past the third escort, this time to starboard, the ship's disruptors were unparked and had begun indexing to port. She was much too late to do anything about *this* run, but her crew would be ready for the next.

As they raced above the fourth, no more than two hundred c'lenyts beyond her KA'PPA mast, the CIGAs were tracking and ready to fire. But it quickly became apparent that the Imperial turncoats might be bound by their own set of rules—they failed to shoot. Was it possible, Brim wondered, that they were banned from using their disruptors until a possible adversary actually opened fire on the fort? Almost in mute answer, the fifth and sixth escorts also disappeared in the Starfuries' raging graviton wake without opening fire. Brim almost cheered aloud. He was getting at least one "free" run. After that, he surmised, things would become considerably different!

Then only the old *Queen* stood between them and the fort itself. Compared to her escorts, she looked like a mountain, bristling with the same immense 406-mmi disruptors carried by the Starfuries themselves. And these CIGAs were *ready*. Eight monstrous quad-mount barbettes tracked Brim and his speeding attackers as if their director systems had been locked on for a metacycle. Only once before had Brim looked at the business end of an Imperial disruptor ready to fire—as a prisoner aboard a Leaguer ship. And that time, old I.F.S. *Truculent*'s disruptors were pointing his way in an attempt to save his life. He had the definite impression that none of these CIGAs had his welfare in mind at all.

They skimmed the huge battleship's bow area at tremendous speed. Brim had an impression of a great blurred expanse of Hyperscreens as they coursed past the big ship's bridge. And at last, only the void of space stood between them and the fort.

"Fire!" Meesha shouted over the thundering generators.

All twelve of *Starfury*'s monster 406-mmi disruptors discharged forward in a salvo, juddering the big starship like a giant hammer. Their forward Hyperscreens abruptly dimmed and the Universe itself dissolved for a moment into a great coruscating eruption that seemed to envelop the whole Universe. When the 'screens began to transmit again, it was immediately clear that the other three Starfuries had fired at the same time—and at the same general target. A quartet of tremendous eruptions was in process near the fort's power center that made a good imitation of some volcanic activity Brim had seen a few years back on Tolland-32.

"Good shooting!" he whooped as he pushed up *Starfury*'s nose and skimmed the top of the fort with only a few irals clearance. But the Leaguer's great disruptors were clearly tracking him, so instead of continuing straight on, he hauled *Starfury* straight up in relation to the fort. Return fire began immediately, with a welter of huge explosions that tossed the cruiser around like a leaf in a windstorm. But Brim continued to raise the nose until—as he passed vertical—he started rolling to starboard and went over the top inverted with MacAlda in *Starspite* keeping close formation to port. As he did so, McKenzie and Dowd, his wingman, kept going straight across the track, then crossed over him as he went on his back. Immediately, the firing became sporadic. League gunners were only superb when firing at predictable targets.

Brim and MacAlda kept rolling back in a flat spin on the steering engines alone while McKenzie and Dowd passed over them. Then Brim led back to port with *Starfury*'s nose falling through at the end of the spin, while McKenzie and Dowd turned back to starboard and let their noses fall through underneath him. As the four starships rolled out, they ended up in perfect finger-four formation again, but going in the opposite direction from the way they came in—and by happenstance, directly on course for the six Imperial escorts. The sight of four hard, sleek Starfuries flying at tremendous speed in superb formation—seemingly out of nowhere—must have unnerved the astonished CIGA firing crews, for they began discharging in panic, sending disruptor beams everywhere.

"That's it," Brim broadcast through clenched teeth. "Get the zukeeds. They fired first!" Immediately, each of the four Starfuries picked a particular ship and—with the accuracy born of long, brutal practice—poured a devastating salvo right down into their guts with devastating results. Imperial destroyers were powerful starships in their own rights, but no match whatsoever for cruisers. Especially cruisers armed with battleship-size disruptors. Even near misses were enough to rip open their thin-skinned hulls from stem to stern. Considering the quantums of energy blasted at them, the first four ships perished with surprisingly little radiation fire. They simply came apart at the seams. The surviving two ran for open space without firing a shot.

Brim bit his lip. It wasn't that the little ships had been without teeth. Small as they were in relation to a cruiser, all classes of Imperial destroyers carried the same huge torpedoes as did Starfuries. And they were powerful weapons. Had he gone by the book, after hitting the fort, he would have pulled out straight ahead, then started jinking around to set up for the next run in on the fort. And that would have made the Starfuries targets for six salvos of the powerful weapons. Properly fired, they might have knocked out all four of his ships at the end of their very first run. He shook his head bitterly. CIGAs. . . .

As he swung around to starboard for a second run, he watched the firing crews preparing their big weapons. E turret was always fastest, and as he switched a display to its interior, the crew had already completed their test procedures and the big weapons were ready to fire. Moments later all six turrets reported a status of READY.

Off in the distance, the fort was still battling huge radiation fires where the Starfuries' powerful salvos had landed. And as he watched, Moulding's four Starfuries made their first pass—this time from the direction the fort had originally expected: along the rim of the asteroid shoal. However, now the great batteries were still tracking Brim's four-ship element, which was presently out of range. And before the big disruptors could be retrained on the new threat, forty-eight more 406-mmi disruptors were blasting away at the fort, resulting in a second area of huge radiation fires that quickly spread over nearly a quarter of the fort's irregular surface.

In spite of the obvious damage, Brim wondered how much real harm his ships had actually accomplished with their first passes. Radiation fires occurred when collapsiums were subjected to high-energy impingement—usually by disruptor fire—and began to "un-collapse." The system of reactions gave off tremendous heat and light as a by-product, and thus earned the soubrette "fire." Sustaining such a reaction required significant additional energy, and if other, undamaged collapsiums were available nearby, it could spread rapidly. However, more often than not, such conflagrations were controlled by saturating the runaway reaction with N rays—the very same rays that were used to spot benders in spectral mode. And that is precisely what Brim suspected the Leaguers might be doing at the fort: controlling the radiation fires in an attempt to convince their attackers they had inflicted much more damage than was actually the case. Somehow, he had the feeling that they'd yet to land a telling blow. . . .

Then Moulding's ships cleared the target area, and it was time to line up again. This time, the fort would be triggering off every weapon they could bring to bear, and all eyes were on the *Queen*. Would she open fire, too? Her big turrets were clearly tracking Brim's four Starfuries as they sped toward her. The cruisers' only defense now was to keep jinking: moving up and down, rolling slightly from one side to the other, slipping, skidding— anything to aggravate the enemy's problem of tracking as they aimed their weapons.

But jinking also aggravated the problem of aiming *from* the starships as well. So at some point, the jinking had to stop, replaced by smooth, precision tracking while the IVG's firing crews got ready to do *their* work. That was the payoff, the only reason for being there in the first place. And both the Leaguers and their CIGA lackeys knew it as well as anyone. . . .

It was just as Brim rolled over the top and acquired the fort that old *Queen Elidean*—grand symbol of a proud empire— opened fire on her own kind with a tremendous barrage of raw energy that smashed MacAlda's port pontoon and blasted *Starspite* nearly a thousand irals sideways in a huge eruption of flame and debris. Brim's wingman was out of the fight—and perhaps out of the war.

The Carescrian immediately signaled *Starterror* and *Starspirit* to continue jinking on their run in—and damn the accuracy— then he hauled *Starfury* hard to port. "All right, Chief!" he said angrily into his display, "it's you and me again. Let's get it over with!"

"I'm ready, Cap'm," the big rating said. "Just like in ol' *Truculent*."

Brim smiled grimly as he began to jink violently—all the time lining up for a torpedo run. Barbousse understood. So far as *this* run was concerned, they were the only two on the ship. "Meesha," he growled, "I want you to keep firing those disruptors of ours at the *Queen* as fast as they'll recover. Aim for the bridge if you can. Keep those zukeed CIGAs plastered with plenty of energy. Got that?"

"Got it, Captain," Meesha answered. Moments later *Starfury*'s big disruptors went into rapid-firing mode turning space outside the speeding cruiser into a colossal inferno of light and concussion—and peppering the battleship's thickly armored hide with a barrage of hits that would literally pulverize a lesser ship.

The *Queen* was returning fire in deliberate, deadly salvos. Her CIGA disruptor crews were trying for accuracy; Brim had counted on that—and their deliberation might just save his mission. Up . . . down . . . roll . . . skid . . . slide . . . His jinking had become violent, now. He was literally racing for the great eruptions that marked the battleship's latest salvo, trusting that the fatuous, "peace-loving" CIGA crews would never aim for the same place twice.

The *Queen* . . . proud and beautiful. Brim loved her. Everyone who loved the Fleet loved her!

"Outer doors open," Barbousse reported.

Brim blinked away bitter tears and glanced at his instrument panel where eight indicators had abruptly changed from red to a flickering green. "Outer doors open," he seconded.

At that moment one of Meesha's random salvos hit a section of the *Queen*'s bridge that exploded in a blinding flare of radiation fire, sending wreckage flying in all directions. *That* would hurt the zukeeds who'd stolen her, Brim thought. Maybe they'd quit. "Keep it up, Meesha!" he yelled—just before he was nearly knocked from his recliner by a near miss that pulsed *Starfury*'s gravity system and threw everyone violently against their mechanical restraints. Startled shouts of pain filled the bridge, and Tissaurd turned in her recliner with eyes big as saucers. Reedwich from Damage Control came on immediately, his long, narrow countenance unruffled by the blast. "Clean miss, Captain," he said as calmly as if he were reporting something no more threatening than a burst soil pipe.

"Inner doors open," Barbousse reported through tight lips as the eight flashing lights went to steady green.

Brim glanced at Barbousse in his COMM display; the big rating was hunched over his torpedo console, concentrating for all he was worth, while his face and eyes reflected the patterns of information traversing his displays. "Steady as she goes, Cap'm," he said, without taking his eyes from the displays.

"Steady as she goes," Brim seconded. *Starfury* was now scudding through a hellish cross fire of disruptor fire from both the fort and the battleship, and all he could do was grind his teeth, keep on course—and wait. . . .

"Torpedoes armed . . ." Barbousse announced.

Another near miss blasted *Starfury*'s nose high. Brim fought the controls to another standstill.

"Steady as she goes, Skipper. . . ."

"Steady. . . ."

By now, *Queen Elidean* had grown huge in the Hyperscreens. *Chief*, Brim thought, *are you planning to ram her*?

"Launcher circuits energized," the big rating reported as Brim's second set of eight indicators changed from red to green. "Keep 'er steady, Cap'm. . . ."

The cross fire was so terrible now that Brim had to fight the controls with all his concentration to keep *Starfury* on any semblance of his intended track. The director stabilizing mechanism could make *some* allowances for tracking inconsistencies, but . . .

"Ten," Barbousse announced grimly. "Nine . . . eight . . . seven . . ."

By now, it seemed as if they were riding through a single drawn-out explosion. Only Voot's own luck would bring them through a fire storm like this. *Come on, Barbousse!*

"Four . . . three . . . two . . . one . . . Torpedoes running, Cap'm!"

In the wink of an eye, eight dark spindles—each trailing a coruscating beam of ruby red light—flashed out from beneath *Starfury*'s bridge and headed squarely for the battleship. Instantly Brim threw in full military power, pulled the nose up and rolled out into a violent jink. But he was moments too late. With unbelievable concussion and sound, the whole forward tip of *Starfury*'s starboard pontoon—including A turret—disappeared in a tremendous blast of radiant energy that must have carried away the KA'PPA antenna as well, for the display winked out. Great sparks of molten hullmetal trailed into the starship's wake, while *Starfury* reared up and to the right like a wounded Careandellian riding lizard. Her hull jumped and quivered for a long moment and the generators skipped a beat as Brim fought to bring the skewed ship back under control.

Then, without warning, they were again blasted off course—this time by an even more stupendous explosion. The whole Universe seemed to light up from aft by the birth of some hellacious new star.

"Sweet thraggling Voot!" someone cried aloud. "Look at the *Queen*!"

Suddenly the bridge was alive with startled cries of alarm. And dismay.

"Universe!" Tissaud cried aloud as she stared into an aftview display. "She's *gone*. The *Queen*'s just . . . thraggling . . . *disappeared*!"

Brim had no time for displays *or* the *Queen*, no matter. *Starfury* was hurt herself. He cranked the cruiser to port and then to starboard testing the controls. She was trailing clouds of glittering radiation haze and definitely more sluggish to starboard—but controllable and still very much in the fight.

"A turret's . . . gone," Reedwich reported presently from a station near the damaged area. In the background, Brim could see two battle-suited cooks working desperately at a pile of wreckage that appeared to have pinned a disruptor technician to the deck. The man was screaming weakly over the voice circuits. Two more figures sprawled in awkward positions on the deck nearby—motionless. One lay facedown in a huge puddle of blood that was vacuum boiling to dried solids even as it leaked from a huge gash in the helmet. While he watched, a medical team jogged into view.

"Stand fast!" one of the medics yelled at the cooks. "Don't move that man yet!" He bent over the groaning, half-buried figure and prepared a SuperHypo that would safely penetrate a battlesuit.

"How many casualties?" Brim asked, jinking desperately as he searched for his other two ships among the tremendous blasts pouring from the fort.

"Three dead, six wounded, Captain," he answered. "And, of course, the whole A-turret crew."

"Take care of things the best you can, Reedwich," Brim ordered, his mind already switched over to the problem of joining *Starfury* with her surviving consorts—and then getting back to the business at hand: silencing the fort.

And once again, space came alive with a welter of powerful explosions. The CIGAs might be gone, but the Leaguers were very much alive in their space citadel.

Meesha's gunners fired off a welter of long-range shots at the receding fort as Brim searched for his two consorts. In the midst of a crowded starship bridge, he suddenly felt very much alone. War had a way of doing that, he remembered. With death perched grinning on the back of your recliner, it was xaxtdamned easy to feel alone.

The firing had stopped now that they had outflown the fort's disruptors, and Brim watched *Starterror* and *Starspirit* as they hove into view and rolled into formation on *Starfury*'s starboard flank. Then he gasped as he turned in his seat to glance back toward the fort. Even in dissolution, what remained of the old battleship was magnificent. Barbousse was perhaps the greatest torpedo marksman in the known Universe, and all eight of his powerful missiles had unquestionably found their mark in vulnerable locations. Her once-proud hull was a blazing mass of radiation fire from stem to stern, clear evidence that at least one of the powerful weapons must have burst among the colossal power chambers. A shiver climbed his back like an icy spider. *Queen Elidean* had been destroyed as much by avarice and cowardice as by the torpedoes themselves. He bit his lip. As Ursis was fond of saying, "Life is never necessarily fair—just on-going." In the distance, he watched another swarm of explosions erupt on the face of the fort as Moulding's four cruisers shot past, their disruptors flashing to meet the hail of return fire. And suddenly two great puffs of radiation fire blazed into incandescent life. Brim gasped and bit his lip. In that instant, he knew that two more Starfuries had been destroyed—and judging from the size of the fireballs, there would be no survivors.

"Owen," Brim ordered, "get me a secure channel to Moulding . . . or whoever's in charge now over there."

"Aye, Captain," Morris replied. After a significant stretch of clicks, Moulding's haggard visage filled a display on Brim's console. "Bloody bad out here, Wilf, old chap," he said. "I assume you saw what just happened to *Starswift* and *Starduke*."

"I saw," Brim answered grimly. "Any survivors?"

"Hardly."

"What shape's the fort in after your last run?"

"We've certainly hurt it," Moulding replied. "But it's far from being out of commission—as I assume you can also see."

"Hard to miss that," Brim agreed. "We lost MacAlda a while back, although he *may* make it home."

"What do you think, Wilf?" Moulding growled with his lop-sided grin. "Will the fort buckle under to those radiation fires or will we run out of Starfuries first?"

"It's a toss-up," Brim said. "The only thing for certain is that we *do* still have a chance—so we've got to try." He thought for a moment, then nodded. "Listen, Toby, here's what we're going to do. . . ."

"Captain Brim!" a COMM rating interrupted from a second global display. "There's a message comin' in for you from the fort."

"From the *what*?"

"The fort, Captain. It's a woman, askin' for you . . . um . . . personally. I'm puttin' 'er on channel two—receive only. She says it can't wait, an' I believe 'er." Instantly the rating was replaced by the image of . . .

"Margot!" Brim exclaimed.

"Margot?" Moulding demanded incredulously from his display. "What in the name of Voot's greasy beard does Margot have to do with any of *this*?"

"Hold off a moment, Toby," Brim ordered, staring at the second display in disbelief. Behind Margot, in what appeared to be a small conference chamber, was her lifelong guardian and chauffeur, Hogget Ambridge. The man was restraining a determined-looking child dressed in a miniature Controller's uniform that could only be Rodyard LaKarn, her son. It was the first time Brim had laid eyes on the boy. Five women—clearly Margot's retinue—had posted themselves at the door with drawn blasters. Forcing aside strong feelings of unreality, the Carescrian enabled TRANSMIT on his number-two COMM channel. "What in the name of Phil Storey's gray beard are you doing *there*?" he demanded.

"Wilf!" she cried. "Thank the Universe—I knew you'd answer. They've held me hostage here in the fort for nearly a month, knowing full well you would someday lead an attack."

Brim scowled. "Oh. A hostage, eh?" he said sarcastically. "After that little episode at the Palmerston, do you *really* think I'm going to believe that?"

"I know what you must think of me, Wilf," she said, a desperate look passing her eyes, "but you have to trust me now, or the fort will destroy you and all your ships." She started in fright as distant explosions shook the floor and their COMM link was broken several times. "We escaped when your first attack ruptured the deck in our suite. It sprung the door and—"

"If you were being held hostage," Brim interrupted, "how'd you get into their COMM room—and where did you get those blasters for that matter?"

Margot's eyes hardened for a moment. "We *took* the blasters," she answered. "In spite of what I have become, Wilf Brim, don't ever forget my years as an agent." She closed her eyes for a moment. "I am no more a stranger to killing than you are. And this COMM room is a very special one—reserved for the private affairs of visiting ministers and high-level officers. It has its own power and transmission systems. Rogan used it when he brought me here."

Brim closed his eyes for a moment. "I understand," he said.

"You had better understand," she replied, "and quickly. Because if you continue to whittle away at this fort, long before you can silence its disruptors, all of your ships will have been destroyed. You must already suspect that yourself."

Brim nodded. "I do," he admitted.

"Then listen and listen well, Wilf Brim," Margot said, "for I shall have time to tell you this once, then we must take to a lifeglobe." She paused and glanced at Ambridge.

The man nodded. "But you *will* have to be quick, my Princess," he added.

Margot returned her gaze to Brim. "The fort's one weak spot—if such a thing exists at all—are the doors to the hangar deck. You'll easily recognize them five levels above the bottommost disruptor gallery. There are three of them, and the whole assembly has oversize Bilmes beacons at all four corners—you know, the ones with the big ruby globes."

"I think I can find it," Brim replied, suddenly beside himself with turmoil. *Could* he trust this woman?

"Good," Margot said, "because the designers centrally located the power chambers directly behind the hangar deck. You will need to blow the doors away first with your disruptors, then send in torpedoes so they can traverse the hangar to the power chambers. Get Barbousse to fire them," she said excitedly. "It's your only hope. Disruptor fire dissipates rapidly within a closed space—as you well remember from the Battle of Atalanta."

"Your Highness," Ambridge interrupted, "we *must* leave now. Either they will capture us again or we will be caught in the explosion!"

Margot nodded. "I'm coming, Ambridge," she said, then turned once more to face Brim. "Good-bye for now, Wilf," she said, "the Universe speed your flight." Suddenly her retainers began to fire their blasters at something along the hallway, and young LaKarn attempted an escape by kicking the old chauffeur in the shins. "Try to remember that I have loved you always," she added, starting for the door, "even when I had no control of my mind."

Then, before Brim had a chance to reply, the little party was gone, and the display presented only an empty room. Shortly thereafter, three armed Controllers burst through the door shouting at each other in their guttural dialect. Immediately, one of the Controllers seemed to point at Brim. "*Sondghast vellersahn vonell gannist!*" he shouted in the Leaguers' language of Vertrucht: The machine is transmitting! Angrily, he smashed his hand somewhere behind the pickup lens, and the display went blank.

Totally spellbound by the incident, Brim had to force himself back to some sort of reality. If he decided *not* to trust Margot, there was a better-than-even chance that all five remaining starships would be lost while failing to destroy the fort at all. And even if he were successful in "whittling" the fort away, the odds were overwhelming that he would *still* lose two or even three more Starfuries—perhaps *Starfury* herself—in the process. On the other hand, if he did trust Margot and made a run for the hangar doors, he had at least some chance that he would indeed destroy the fort with no further IVG casualties at all. "Toby," he exclaimed, his mind working furiously, "here's what we're going to do."

"I say, old bean," Moulding said caustically, "you promised to tell me that at least five cycles ago. And I'm still waiting."

"Sorry," Brim replied, "I've just been talking to Margot on another display. She's in the fort."

"How *nice*, Wilf," Moulding continued, raising his eyebrows theatrically. "You two certainly *do* find the oddest places for renewing that little friendship of yours. . . ."

"No! Wait, Toby. This has nothing to do with friendship— she was a prisoner there." He shook his head—that wasn't going to do it. "I'll have to explain later," he said. "Just trust me that she may have given us the ticket to blowing that fort."

Wilf!" Moulding objected, "she *is* the same Margot who tried to have you killed a while back, isn't she?"

"She is," Brim admitted, "but, well, I have this feeling that this time she's telling the truth."

"And so do I," Tissaurd interrupted, leaning over to talk with Moulding's aristocratic visage in the global display. "Sorry, Skipper," she said out of the side of her mouth, "but I've been eavesdropping. Toby," she called, "I watched the whole thing, and unless Effer'wyck's better able to pull the wool over my eyes than she was a few months back, I think she's on the level."

Moulding's image stared at Tissaurd for a long time, but finally he shrugged. "I suppose there's only one way to find out, then," he acquiesced, his lopsided smile back in place. "Now, my old racing friend," he said, returning his gaze to Brim, "how about telling me what it is you want us to do. . . ."

Brim came in fast along one bank of the shoal with *Starterror* and *Starspirit* above and behind him. *Starsovereign* and *Stardemon* were speeding in from the other direction, attempting to split the Leaguers' defensive fire before it began. The tactic might help a little, but Brim knew it wouldn't be enough.

"Maybe the zukeeds won't shoot quite so fast now that we've taken out some of their disruptors," Tissaurd observed hopefully over the whine and thunder of *Starfury*'s big Admiralty generators.

Brim could only grunt out similar hopes as he concentrated on flying the ship; he was so close to the shoal now that its huge asteroids appeared to be rushing past only a few irals from *Starfury*'s belly. He could well imagine what the Leaguers must be thinking while they watched the five Starfuries home in on them. The remaining IVG ships were still a major threat, and the Leaguers knew it—but not so much as when there were eight of them. *Both* sides knew that.

"Coming up on their maximum range now, Captain," Meesha warned.

"Very well, Meesha," Brim said, sideslipping into his first jink. The fort had a few moments' advantage before the Starfuries' shorter-range disruptors could focus in. And the Leaguers took advantage of every one as space went wild with massive barrages of detonations that blasted *Starfury* in every direction with near misses. Many of the near misses blasted in huge fountains of rock and debris as they hit the shoal. Then Meesha opened up with his own disruptors, bouncing the deck and every console on the bridge. "Ready, Chief?" Brim asked.

"Ready, Cap'm," Barbousse replied grimly. "I've got eight more torpedoes in the launcher, all of 'em enabled already. So if we get hit, it's good-bye *Starfury*."

"I'll try to avoid that if I can," Brim swore fervently. He took a deep breath. The hangar-deck doors were still out of sight, nearly a quarter of the way around the fort's circumference from *Starfury*'s apparent aiming zone. Moments from now, while *Starterror* and *Starspirit* continued on their firing run, he would bank out to port and dive nearly to the surface of the fort where he would hug the wall until, at a predetermined point, he would pull away to minimum firing distance, reverse course abruptly, and make a torpedo run on the hangar. It seemed a lot like ancient dive bombing—only sideways. "All right, Meesha," he shouted. "Give it all you've got!" Curving slightly to starboard, he headed for a quartet of big disruptors while Meesha directed his fire at the big turrets with a vengeance. So did the other two Starfuries, with deadly accuracy—and results. The area quickly erupted into an absolute hell of energy from the concentrated fire of thirty-six big disruptors. Huge chunks of hullmetal and wreckage (including an entire turret) hurtled off in every direction from the rapidly expanding fireball while a chorus of cheers broke out around Brim on the bridge—who used the momentary lull to roll *Starfury* inverted, bunt under the other two ships, and set off for the wall with all the power he could feed to the generators.

Long moments later, the graceful cruiser was speeding along only a few hundred irals from the gigantic hullmetal plates, many cratered and burning fiercely as he passed. This time, he jinked only when it was necessary to avoid hitting one of the big disruptor turrets. He was moving far too rapidly for them to aim at him—much less fire. Soon, he was coming up on the array of heat exchangers Meesha's firing computers had calculated as his optimum breakaway point. "Ten clicks till the pop, Chief," he warned.

"I'm ready, Cap'm," Barbousse replied. "So are the torpedoes. Soon as Lieutenant Meesha blasts those doors."

From aft, the firing had stopped. Evidently, *Starterror* and *Starspirit* had finished their firing runs. Just beyond the fort's "horizon" Brim could see Moulding's two ships streaking away from the fort—while they drew fire from the desperate maneuver he was about to attempt. "Here we go!" he yelled, hauling back on the controls until *Starfury*'s spaceframe began to creak in protest. As the fort receded in the distance, Brim caught himself holding his breath. In a moment the disruptors would spot them again, and then all hell would surely break loose. But there was a slightly better chance of planting the torpedoes each moment they ran in the clear—and every one of them seemed to last an eternity until at last he heard Barbousse's voice.

"Comin' up on minimum firin' distance in five, Cap'm," the big rating announced.

Brim counted an extra fifteen clicks, then hauled the controls over in a renversment, getting three red warning lights on his panel from the steering engines. He ignored them—the mechanism had better stand a little overload. Then he started toward the fort again.

And suddenly space aft burst forth in a truly colossal series of brilliant detonations. At least one—probably more—of the fort's great disruptors had picked them up and were blasting away as quickly as the big weapons could build new charges. But the Leaguer gunners had fired where they *expected* him to be, before he'd reversed course. He could only pray that they were too well trained to try that trick again; he was now holding a smooth precision track toward the three big hangar doors he'd centered on his Hyperscreens—and this time their trick might work! "All right, Meesha," he shouted over the roar of the generators, "blast those doors. NOW!"

The months that Meesha and his disruptor crews had spent battling Dampiers and Gorn-Hoffs had turned *Starfury*'s gunners into extraordinary marksmen, and it all paid off in the next fifteen clicks. Each of the ten remaining 406s thundered independently, and fully seven scored direct hits with eruptions of radiation fire and debris of all kinds. One of the doors flew off intact, spinning off at an angle that would eventually take it completely out of the galaxy.

Only a moment later, Barbousse fired his tight spread of torpedoes.

Brim watched for the eight deadly missiles to clear *Starfury*'s forward pontoons, then he hauled the cruiser around and took off for deep space, jinking as he had never jinked before through an unbelievable hail of fire with the generators at MILITARY OVERLOAD PLUS. The terrific barrage made sense. Every disruptor in the fort was shooting at him.

"Skipper," Tissaurd reported as she stared into a rearview display, "couple of lifeglobes just launched from the side of the fort."

In his own display, Brim caught two pearlescent bubbles speeding away toward the protection of the shoal, but he was far too much taken up with jinking to think about much of anything except the ship, her controls, and the hellish explosions that were knocking her about like a leaf caught in a storm.

"Hey look!" someone yelled.

"Holy Voot!" another yelled excitedly, "the Chief's torpedoes just hit the doors in a tight pack. Just like he was drivin' them himself!"

"By Universe, that's right," still another exclaimed. "All eight of 'em!"

"*Universe*, what a bunch of explosions!"

"Explosions don't count!" Barbousse roared. "They're the ones that *missed* and hit the door frame. If none of 'em got through clean, we'll have to do it again!"

Nobody seemed to hear the big rating's protest. Instead, the whole bridge continued in wild, insane cheering.

Except for Brim. Hit or miss, it was now up to him to get them out of there! He could scarcely hear anything above the thunder of six overtaxed Admiralty A876 gravity generators—and the deafening rumble of raw energy smashing against *Starfury*'s streamlined flanks from literally hundreds of near misses.

Simultaneously the firing—and the shouting—stopped, replaced by a great chorus of astonished gasps. For a moment, only the whine and thunder of *Starfury*'s generators sounded on the bridge. Then one solitary, awestruck female voice could be heard—later, no one would admit it was hers.

"Voot's most greasy, tangled beard," it said, "will ya' LOOK AT THAT!"

CHAPTER 11

The IVG Passes

Brim hauled the racing starship around into a vertical curve just in time to see every hatch and scuttle in the mighty Leaguer fort pulse and flash like a thousand gleaming eyes . . . again . . . and again . . . and again. . . . Then, as if the very fabric of the Universe itself had burst, the whole structure was engulfed—from the inside out—by a colossal reddish-violet fireball that pulsed and glimmered spasmodically as it expanded, peppered with stark clarity by gigantic chunks of wreckage: huge turret assemblies, KA'PPA towers, power generators, formless curved plates of hullmetal armor, all bobbing on a roiling globe of radiation flame.

The shock wave of raw energy that preceded it slammed first into the mottled wall of the shoal, scattering asteroid-size chunks of rock like toy balls. Suddenly a vision of Margot's fragile lifeglobe racing among the great boulders forced its way to Brim's mind, tearing at his very soul. Had she been able to work her lifeglobe far enough back among the protecting rocks to save herself? Or was she now ground to space dust among the surface asteroids? His stomach churned in horror. . . .

A moment later the energy wave hit *Starfury* like a physical presence. Her whole starframe bucked violently, pulsing the ship's gravity and throwing people against their mechanical restraints with force enough to snap bones and fling bodies around like broken toy dolls. Screams and groans filled the voice circuits; somebody vomited loudly in his helmet. Whole arrays of Hyperscreens on the port side of the bridge shattered behind a wave of explosive decompression, while debris cascaded across the decks in a rolling cloud of sparks and the nameless detritus of mortal habitation. And—accompanied by a whole panel of indicators changing to brilliant crimson—the big Admiralty gravity generators tripped out completely.

By sheer chance, the colossal fireball never quite reached *Starfury*'s hull, but despite protectively darkened Hyperscreens, its radiated heat alone was enough to turn the rubble-strewn bridge into a raging, airless oven that melted portions of a navigation table and baked everything that was not specially battle-protected. Then the boiling sphere of radiation fire began to subside, falling into itself as it had exploded outward, and in a few moments dissolved into a dappled array of glittering radiation clouds that eventually scattered to the eight corners of the Universe.

Now the ship glided along on momentum alone, quiet as the starscape itself. Off to starboard, no trace of the Leaguer fort remained at all. Only the distant, massive wreck of I.F.S. *Queen Elidean* remained in view against the shoal—blasted at least ten c'lenyts from her original position and drifting slowly through space like a great skeletal meteor, still glowing with the heat of her own demise.

And the massive, all-prevading stillness! For a moment Brim was certain the voice circuits had all been destroyed. But then a surprised voice rang out in his helmet like a trumpet on a still morning.

"U-Universe," someone said as if he didn't quite believe his own words, "we did it!"

"Yeah. We did, didn't we?"

"H-help!"

"Who's that?"

"Huugo. S-Sublieutenant Huugo."

"Anybody else alive here on the bridge?"

"I am—I think."

"So'm I."

"Sweet mother of. . . . He's bleedin' inside his battlesuit. Medics! On the double!"

"Yeah. Hurry. Poor zukeed didn't want to leave his family in the first place!"

"MEDICS!"

A damage-control team with armored mittens was cleaning up razer-sharp Hyperscreen splinters by the time Brim had a chance to check Tissaurd. Behind her face plate, she had what appeared to be a nasty cut on the forehead, but otherwise she wore her customary smile. Carefully, as if checking each bone for consistency, she raised her fist in a "thumbs-up" gesture and winked. "See, Skipper," she said, "I knew we could believe her this time."

"I won't ask how you knew, Number One," Brim replied, "but thanks for the trust. Something tells me it was the last thing she did. We'll have to go look for her before the Leaguers return."

"Skipper!" Meesha interrupted. "I've got six ships coming at us at a high rate of speed. And they *aren't* IVGs."

"Wonderful," Brim pronounced disgustedly. "Just thraggling wonderful! Who are they?"

Meesha bent over his debris-strewn console and frowned. "They're returning what appear to be Torond IFF codes, Captain," he said.

"Any sign of Moulding or the other two Starfuries?" Brim demanded. Somehow, he *had* to go search for Margot—but *how*?

"None, Captain. Sorry."

Brim forced his mind back to the ship and switched a display to Zaftrak's huge console. "Strana'," he demanded, "did the generators require a cold start?"

"Is so, Captain," the Bear replied with a serious look. "When generators go into overload like that, is shutting themselves down. But not all bad, that. Keeps from blowing up."

"How long before we can get under way again?"

"Chief Baranev says he can give you little less than half power right now, Captain," the Bear replied. "Perhaps more later, depending on damage. You should be able maneuver, at least."

Brim nodded. Cold starts were difficult. The Chief was producing an authentic miracle to restore any motive power at all.

"Set it up, Strana'."

"Aye, Captain," the Bear said. Moments later a number of indicators on his power panel returned to steady green.

"Number One," Brim asked, "can you take over the helm for a moment? She'll be a bit sluggish."

"I'm all right, Captain," the plucky little officer replied. "You didn't know I have a hullmetal cranium, did you?"

"I've *suspected* something like that for a long time," Brim said, "but I never thought I'd live to hear you admit it." As the ship began to gather way, he activated the blower. "Attention all hands," he broadcast. "Remain at your action stations. I repeat: remain at your action stations. Six unknowns are approaching at high speed, and we will probably have to defend the ship again." He closed his eyes for a moment. "I realize what each of you has been through since we lifted ship yesterday," he continued. "I also am tired, believe me. But we must carry on, no matter what. We're all integral parts of this ship, vitally needed for both flying and fighting—even existence. This mission is not over until I signal 'Finished with generators.' Be alert and prepare to engage." With that, he reclaimed the controls from Tissaurd and waited for whatever destiny Lady Fate had in store. *Starfury* was hurt badly, that was certain. The ship lumbered along, accelerating and decelerating with difficulty, and all he could do was coax the controls.

"Dampiers at Orange Apex," Meesha warned suddenly. "Bearing nine fifty-nine point five at forty-eight seventy-five and closing."

Brim peered up to the left of the nose. Six graviton plumes were coming on *fast*, vanguard of whole squadrons racing back to avenge the ruined fort. There would be no mercy, especially since *Starfury* was in no condition for an all-out fight. He shook his head angrily. At least he would give the order to attack. "Meesha," he said, "make certain we fire the first shots. We've got a little range on them."

"Aye, Cáptain," Meesha replied grimly, his gray eyes flashing with determination.

Brim called up all the thrust the badly damaged starship could muster. It hardly made any difference; she was still very slow and unresponsive. He watched the graviton plumes curve toward him in twos. Grinding his teeth with frustration, he could imagine Valentin gloating in one of them.

True to his promise, Meesha's big 406-mmi disruptors spoke first, and with remarkable accuracy. The leading left-hand Dampier erupted in a flashing cloud of flame, then went guttering off to one side while the remaining five continued their run-in. And suddenly space was again filled by concussion and blinding flashes of light—all the more felt on the bridge through the missing Hyperscreens. Brim jinked as much as he possibly could with the weak generators, but great hammer-blasts of concussion began to thunder against the hull as the Toronder's shots converged from all sides. Then—in rapid succession—*Starfury* took a near miss beside the starboard pontoon and a direct hit in the starboard generator bay, rattling and vibrating her spaceframe like a child's toy. Immediately, the ship lost the power to accelerate and a Dampier arrogantly pulled in on her tail, firing slowly as if it had all the time in the Universe, obviously operating on the assumption that *Starfury* had lost all her power. Moments later the mistake cost them dearly when Brim stopped jinking for a moment. Meesha's ten surviving turrets all whirled aft and simultaneously delivered a tremendous salvo from twenty 406s. The bridge suddenly broke out in cheering as the Dampier shuddered aside with its whole forward area reduced to a tangle of burning girders and crumpled hullmetal armor. But it was quickly replaced by two more, both unquestionably determined to make short work of their nettlesome enemy before it could use its teeth again.

With a last burst of power, Brim pulled the crippled starship into a vertical right angle and activated his gravity brakes.

The clearly untried Dampier crews hadn't expected anything like it, for they shot past like meteors and ended up out in front. Both tail sections flared up as their startled Helmsmen tried to escape from the trap, but they were far too late. Once more, Meesha's gunners swung their turrets, this time blasting both ships, which wobbled out of range trailing hullmetal plates and pulsing clouds of sparks.

"Three more unidentifieds approaching at high speed, Captain," the Gunnery Officer reported tensely.

"What kind of IFF are they sending?" Brim asked warily.

"Can't tell, this time," Meesha replied with a raised eyebrow. "Almost like the old privateer IDs I used to hear."

Brim nodded helplessly and found himself chuckling in what were probably the last moments of his life. "This is so xaxtdamned WON-der-ful I can't believe it," he growled to Tissaud. "Now, we've got thraggling pirates after us." Far in the distance, he could see three more graviton plumes, and these were *really* moving fast. He laughed in spite of himself. "Well, the zukeeds better damn well hurry," he grumbled darkly, "otherwise there won't be anything left of us to steal."

Aft, the two remaining Dampiers had warily closed in just beyond the range of *Starfury*'s disruptors. Brim watched in his aft-view display while the ships maneuvered carefully into formation for a textbook torpedo attack. Obviously, these also were crewed by rookies, like the first three so easily put out of action. This time, however, it looked as if the rookies were about to . . .

"*Great thraggling Universe!*" he gasped with astonishment.

Before his very eyes, one of the remaining Dampiers disintegrated in a blinding explosion, while the other skidded to starboard and lit out with all its generators at maximum military overload. Its sparkling wake was dogged by a large, curious-looking torpedo that crept inexorably closer until, with a terrible eruption, it found its target.

As the unfortunate Dampier dissolved into roiling clouds of energy, a rating from the COMM center interrupted Brim's bemused astonishment. "Incoming transmission for you, Captain," she announced with eyes wide as saucers, "from I.F.S. *Patriot*. Will you take it?"

Brim glanced through the shattered port Hyperscreens as Calhoun's iridescent white star yacht eased into formation off his port pontoon. This time, however, the Imperial comet insignia shone abaft her bridge Hyperscreens—and she was armed with at least ten of the Leaguers' superfocused 375-mmi disruptors from Theobold Interspace of Lixor. Two identical copies of the powerful little attack ship cruised in perfect echelon to her left. As he stared in fascination, the elegant head and shoulders of Eve Cartier materialized in a global display on his console. This time, however, she was dressed in a regulation Imperial Fleet Cloak. "I'll take it," he croaked before the COMM room could announce her. Moments later a green LINK ENABLED indicator came on beneath the display.

"Captain Brim," the woman said with clearly genuine concern, "thank the Universe we got here in time. You *are* all right, are you na?"

Brim grinned in spite of everything. The woman was *proud* of the same Carescrian accent he had worked so hard to lose! "What's left of me seems to be all right," he replied with a dizzy grin. "And when did *you* join the Fleet?"

Cartier winked. "Emperor Greyffin IV issued our commissions nearly three months ago, Captain," she said, "the very day the Governor . . . er, Commodore Calhoun . . . presented all three o'his ships to the Admiralty." She smiled proudly. "'Twas the same day I took over *Patriot* as Skipper." Then her face became sober. "Er, Captain," she started with a look of concern, "is *Starfury* in any shape to fly? From what we're pullin' in on the KA'PPA, just aboot every Leaguer and Toronder ship in the area is headin' this way. We'll have to get you people out o' here in the next metacycle, wi' or wi'out *Starfury*, I'm afraid."

"We're running a damage check right now," Brim replied, glancing at Tissaurd. "Better see if you can get an early report from Chief Baranev, Number One," he said with a sinking heart. He had to make *some* sort of effort for Margot. He simply couldn't just leave—she'd risked her life to help him nail the fort. Indeed, she may have *given* it.

"I'm saddened we didna' arrive sooner, sir," Cartier said, interrupting his thoughts. "The Governor and General Drummond got us released just six days ago—just as soon as they decided on the declaration. But we were in Avalon at the time, an' hae a wee tiff wi' a crowd o' CIGAs on our way to the ships.'' She shook her head sadly. "Made us mair than a day late gettin' started.''

"All that matters is that you did get here,'' Brim said with real feeling. "As you could see, we were pretty close to the end.'' He was about to suggest they search for Margot's lifeglobe when he frowned, remembering a word. . . . "Did you say something about a *declaration*?'' he asked.

"Aye, Captain Brim,'' Eve replied. "You've heard aboot it, haven't you, sir?'' Cartier asked.

"I haven't heard anything since we lost our KA'PPA mast early on,'' Brim replied. "What kind o' . . . er . . . *of* declaration?''

"A declaration o' war, sir,'' Cartier replied with a sober mien. "Avalon KA'PPAed it all over the Universe.''

"Great thraggling Universe, Eve,'' Brim exclaimed. "WHAT war? When?''

"The one we declared on the League and its allies this mornin', sir,'' Cartier explained, looking a bit taken aback. "By Imperial Privilege, noo less. It all happened very quickly—*lots* o'KA'PPA traffic—probably right aboot the time you lost your K-tower, I imagine.''

Embarrassed, Brim pulled in his horns. "Sorry, Eve,'' he said. "And you don't have to call me 'sir,' you know. We're both Commanders, after all.''

"Na anymore, Captain Brim,'' Cartier said with a little grin. "You've been promoted. Scuttlebutt has it that your certificate was the first thing Emperor Onrad signed after the declaration.''

Brim's mind took off spinning again. "*Emperor* Onrad?'' he demanded. "What's happened to Greyffin IV?''

"Abdicated, Captain,'' Cartier explained. "He said he'd already led the Empire through ane war, an' that was enough. It was time for a younger mon to step in. Oh, Greyffin's still around from wha' I gather, but *this* war's Onrad's show to run.''

Stunned, Brim shook his head while he stared out into the starry void, trying to corral his milling thoughts into some—any—aspect of rational order.

Mercifully, Cartier gave him time to recover, for the next voice that impinged on his conscious mind was Tissaurd's.

"Good news, Skipper," she said, touching his gloved hand gently. "Chief Baranev says he can give us half power to the gravs within three quarters of a metacycle."

Brim felt like someone waking from a deep sleep, but he came out of it alert as if he had slept the clock around. "That's enough power to get us near LightSpeed and start the Drive," he replied, "even though it'll take us a while to accelerate." Then he frowned. "Assuming the Drive is all right," he added quickly.

"Hardly damaged," Tissaurd assured him. "We weren't using it at the time, so the Chief had only warm-up power to the crystals when we hit overload."

Brim turned to face the display. "Did you hear all that, Eve?" he asked.

"Aye, Captain," Cartier said, "an' 'tis good news, too. 'Twould be a shame to lose *Starfury*—she's the first of the few." She glanced across at the other two attack craft. "We'll stand guard here till you're ready to fly, then escort you back to . . . where is it that the Governor has himself set up, noo, Captain?"

"Varnholm Hall," Brim said, "but I've an important favor to ask of you in the meantime."

"An' what's that, Captain?"

Brim explained as quickly as he could Margot's role in the destruction of the fort, then peered into the display in an attempt to touch the Carescrian woman's soul. "Eve," he said, "I need all three of you searching that area in case either of the lifeglobes survived. I need you there for as long as you can stay."

Cartier nodded. "I understand, Captain," she said directly. "An' in many ways I agree. But twa of us must stay here wi' you. After all the driftin' and runnin' you did, you've come a far piece from the fort. An' if worst comes to worst, one of us can take your crew aboard for the dash home while the other fights."

Brim nodded. "You're right," he admitted grimly. His—and their—first responsibility was toward *Starfury* and her crew. Calhoun would have things no other way. "Thanks," he added. He meant it, even though it made him no happier.

"If it's any comfort, Captain," Cartier said quietly, "I know this is very important to you, so I'll go do the searchin' myself in *Patriot*. *Loyalist* an' *Champion* will stand guard just in case. Trust me to do what I can in the time I've got.''

Brim smiled while in the corner of his eye he saw Tissaurd nodding vigorously. "Do it, Eve," he said thankfully. "When those globes launched, they headed straight for the shoal, so you'll have no trouble finding where to search. You'll find a big impress behind where the fort used to be. If anybody's able to answer your calls, they'll be somewhere nearby.''

In the end, Cartier found nothing. Somehow, Brim wasn't surprised—but he was still grateful she looked.

Starfury required three Standard Days on her return from Ordu. But significantly, the little squadron encountered no enemy star-ships at all during the long trip, in spite of massive Gorn-Hoff and Dampier concentrations that had to be drawn from the same sector of the galaxy only days previously. The Leaguer ships simply had not returned. By the time *Starfury* was again safely moored at Varnholm—beside Moulding's *Starglory* and Mac-Alda's *Starspite* (both of which had limped home with serious damage)—Cartier and her two consorts were on their way at high speed to another part of the galaxy. With the destruction of Zonga'ar, a sea change had begun to take place in the conflict. The Leaguers appeared to be abandoning the whole Fluvannian campaign, and it was increasingly clear that Triannic's planned invasion had been seriously delayed, perhaps even canceled.

As things turned out, however, the so-called IVG "victory" had been a costly one indeed. Only a few of the brave Fluvannians from Task Force CLEAVE ever managed to return their antique warships home safely. And without the four new Imperial Starfuries (that were finally released for unrestricted combat duty at Varnholm Hall), the IVG would no longer be able to put up a practical defense—at least until Commodore Tor restored a number of the original Starfuries to battleworthiness.

The situation could have become a disaster; miraculously, it didn't turn out that way. Even though media reports from Avalon indicated that CIGAs throughout the Empire were mounting a great hue and cry over Onrad's declaration of war—as well as his accession to the Imperial throne—those same CIGA protestors were repeatedly being shouted down by loyal Imperials in the Fleet who had been goaded far past fearing for their careers. Now, it was their own *Empire* they were worried about!

And little by little the once-proud Imperial Fleet was throwing off its shackles. Clearly, it would be only a shadow of its former potential. But fortified by powerful squadrons of Starfuries that continued to soar out from secret yards at Gimmas Haefdon and other secret construction sites, the Imperials were gaining strength every day.

However, one element that remained missing from the insane equation was the Leaguers themselves. It was almost as if the loss of their fort at Zonga'ar caused them to abandon the war altogether. For some reason, they now seemed unwilling, or unprepared, to attack—anywhere. Sodeskayan intelligence promptly reported that this was indeed the case. The Leaguers had been preparing a grand offensive against Avalon itself, and after the grave losses they sustained during their ill-fated Fluvannian campaign, they now required at least three more Standard Months to recoup before they were again ready to attack.

Thanks to Baxter Calhoun and his gallant IVG "mercenaries," Nergol Triannic and his bloody minions had failed to deprive the rejuvenating Imperial Fleet of its precious Drive-crystal supply. But nearly as important, at least the way Brim saw things, was the inability of the CIGAs to keep things tied up in Avalon. Clearly, they had caused a great deal of mischief, but in the end, neither Puvis Amherst nor his Leaguer masters had reckoned on Greyffin IV's brave decision to abdicate, nor Onrad V's iron resolve to face the truth, and then do something about it. Perhaps it was a herald of things to come.

Penard Bay was in one of its rare peaceful moods as Brim relaxed at the peak of *Starfury*'s forward Hyperscreens, dangling his feet over the expanse of crystal that sloped gradually to her snub-nosed prow. Overhead, a billion-odd stars blinked and twinkled in the night air. A spring breeze carried with it the smell of the sea as he peered out at ranks of gentle breakers just visible against the dark mat of the bay itself. He'd climbed to this special perch nearly each night while Commodore Tor's crews rebuilt the ship's propulsion section for a second time. That such major repairs were even possible—considering what the ship had been through during the past months—paid high tribute to Mark Valerian's magnificent design as well as the Sherrington Works' historic ability to build fine starships.

And though this particular night seemed peaceful enough, a galvanic change was in the air, he could feel it—both for the war and for himself. Immediately after destruction of the Leaguers' fort, the conflict had slewed off into a bogus stage. Ursis had named it the "Phony War," and urged everyone concerned to use each metacycle preparing for the coming onslaught. Things wouldn't last this way much longer; Brim was certain of that. The Leaguers simply couldn't allow it. Every moment of untroubled existence for Onrad's Imperial Fleet meant new ships, disruptors, better-trained crews—all pouring in an ever-widening stream from once-secret shipyards, arsenals, and training bases throughout the great expanse of Empire.

But unless Brim missed his guess, even the *victor* of this next war would sustain appalling damage. He shook his head as he looked down through the Hyperscreen panel into the bridge where Tissaurd was leading a party of engineers along the main corridor. They'd be hooking up the new generator controls tonight. Inside work. As old-fashioned as it might sound in an age of starships and HyperLight drives, blackouts still afforded considerable protection.

He leaned back on his hands and looked up at the shimmering array of stars. His life and his career were both in a state of considerable flux. Clearly, he was moving farther and faster in the Fleet than he had ever dreamed. Destruction of the Leaguer fort had advanced his reputation a hundredfold, even though he'd been quick to admit that his success was due in large part to an old lover. Moreover, in the past weeks, Tor had begun hinting about a new ship from the Sherrington yards, one so new and confidential that its mere existence was still regarded as a top state secret. And Calhoun had likewise indicated that the IVG would soon be absorbed back into the Imperial Fleet from which it came. A new posting with new, increased responsibilities was right around the corner; he was certain of it.

He was also due in Avalon to receive an unheard-of honor, his *second* Order of the Imperial Comet. The medal itself consisted of an eight-pointed starburst in silver and dark blue with a single word engraved in its center: VALOR. This was attached to an ivory sash embroidered in gold with the full title of the awarding Emperor. An even greater honor, at least for Brim, was that his sash would be the first to read: ONRAD V, GRAND GALACTIC EMPEROR and carry a serial number of "1." Over the history of the Empire, only forty-one had been awarded. Each was still in existence, preserved through the centuries in a collection that was considered to be one of the most important Imperial treasures. The Comet was an honor for all eternity— at least so long as the Empire existed.

As Brim mused, a gravity pool three ships distant from *Starfury* erupted with landing crews and glowing optical bollards. Overhead, Brim watched one of the billion visible stars execute a smooth curve down from the heavens, level out, and thunder to a landfall just off the strand, its passing marked only by sound and a long glowing trail on the bay. Later, he watched the cruiser rumble in, great white wakes creaming away on either side of her gravity footprints. In a few cycles more, the pool complex had returned to the quiet of evening, broken only by occasional shouts as the starship's crew debarked and maintenance crews prepared her for the next patrol.

He leaned back on his hands and stared again at the glittering farrago of stars. Somewhere out there was Margot Effer'wyck. She was either alive or reduced to atomic particles, but he stubbornly chose to believe the former. The fact that "LaKarn" was tacked to her family name had little meaning for him anymore. Perhaps they might never meet again—or love again—but he truly believed the bond between them existed as a two-way spiritual ligature that not even the Universe could sunder again. Ever.

Meanwhile, he thought, climbing to his feet and starting toward the hatch along a dark divider strip between two Hyperscreen panels, there was a war to win. It might be temporarily on hold, but it could—and would—begin again in earnest on a moment's notice.

Like everyone else, he had a responsibility to be ready for it. . . .

Baxter Calhoun's IVG came to an official end one morning when fifteen superbly outfitted new Starfuries made landfall at Varnholm Hall, arriving direct from the great Fleet base at Atalanta. The ships had been prepared and crewed there under the special supervision of one Claudia Valemont on the orders of Chief Commissioner Bosporus Gallsworthy himself.

Three days afterward, and precisely one Standard Year following Brim's arrival at Varnholm Hall, the IVG and its seven battered Starfury survivors were ordered back to Sherrington's for a refit and eventual reassignment. Because *Starfury* had clearly suffered the most damage, she was the first to depart, with a short stopover in Avalon.

Now, with Tissaurd at the controls, the ship was descending in and out of an indefinite overcast directly above the Imperial capital, trailing long contrails that whirled in the damp air like gray streamers of raveling cable. Through a chance break in the overcast, Brim momentarily glimpsed the Grand Terminal before all was swallowed up in clouds again. To port, Lake Mersin was completely lost to view, covered by a thick mass of gray—right down on minimums for the area.

They intersected the outer marker at two thousand irals in dense white nothingness while Brim cross-checked the altimeters to make certain nothing was missed. Clearly, Tissaurd would have to feel her way down to the water, and a normally "inconsequential" error of thirty or forty irals could have quite an impact—literally—near the surface. *Starfury* was now stabilized on speed, with gravity gradient and lift modifiers down and all checklists complete. Brim's only job now was to monitor. They'd left the landing lights off to improve the contrast outside. It was an old trick Brim had picked up during his youth in Carescria where the weather was *usually* unpleasant. Often, it meant the difference between seeing the welcome red glow of a landing vector or a cloaking reflection of white incandescence.

At a thousand irals, Brim verified that a small amber FLARE light in the forward panel had illuminated, indicating that the autohelm's self-test was complete. They could now continue their approach through the soft white haze to a fifty-iral decision height. By that time, if Tissaurd hadn't seen the landing vector, Brim—who was monitoring instruments—would take over controls and execute a missed-approach procedure. Busy Lake Mersin was simply too crowded with small shipping to risk a totally blind landing.

At five hundred irals, both sets of eyes were now looking for things that could go wrong as the soft white cloud lulled them closer to the bay. They double-checked the minimums and ran a second test of the autohelm, but as they passed through two hundred, the view outside the Hyperscreens continued to remain featureless, and brightened only slightly after another hundred irals of descent.

"Approaching minimums; going heads up," Tissaurd said, concentrating all her attention outside, as though she could drill a hole in the remaining few irals of fog. She was ready to follow through with the autohelm if she elected to land with it or disconnect and let Brim manually fly the starship on a go-around. "Hope there's some water down there by now," she added with a tight little laugh.

"That would make me happy," Brim joshed back gently. "I'm the one who signed for this battle-weary bus, you know." His hands were over his own controls now, poised for a go-around with the autohelm DISCONNECT under his right thumb and *Starfury*'s missed-approach procedure memorized by countless hours simulating blind landings at Varnholm Hall.

Slightly above the fifty-iral decision height—when Brim was just about to start a go-around—Tissaurd announced, "I have the landing vector," and took the controls. Brim's eyes remained glued to his flight panel while he called out radio-altitude increments every ten irals until the starship settled firmly onto her gravity gradient in towering cascades of spray. He chuckled as they slowed to taxiing speed amid happy shouts and cheers from all over the bridge. They were home! Now, all that remained was the hard part: finding their way to the military complex through approximately four c'lenyts of intermittent pea-soup fog. . . .

As Tissaurd eased *Starfury* onto a transient gravity pool and the last mooring beams flashed into place, a huge, late-model limousine skimmer—in Fluvannian scarlet—pulled up at the foot of the brow with diplomatic flags flying. The chauffeur and footman no sooner had the passenger doors open than Drummond and Beyazh popped out one side while a Blue Cape wearing the two and a half stripes of a Lieutenant Commander exited the other. The three strode to the brow as if they were in a hurry.

"Looks like big doin's down there, Skipper," Tissaurd observed, shutting down the propulsion controls.

"At least," Brim replied with a frown. "I think I'd better go meet them."

"You'll have to hurry"—she laughed—"they're liable to beat you here."

As it turned out, they met in the main corridor, just outside Brim's cabin. "Brim," Drummond said, somewhat out of breath, "meet Commander Ambrose Contrell. He's replacing Tissaurd, who's been reassigned as skipper of this clapped-out derelict." He offered both his hand and an official-looking envelope. "*These*, you will be glad to know," he continued with a chuckle, "are *your* reassignment orders and travel voucher. We pride ourselves in the advance notice we give people."

Only slightly taken aback, Brim laughed; he'd been expecting something like this since the ship lifted for the last time from Penard Bay. "That's good to know, sir," he said, gripping the General's hand. "If I ever need a little extra time for something, I'll be sure to come to you." Then he turned to Contrell. "He hasn't done you any favors in the ship-assignment department, Commander," he said. "We treat equipment *rough* in the IVG."

"Er, yes, Captain," Contrell replied, looking just the slightest bit bewildered. "I couldn't help notice the missing forequarter of your port pontoon—or the . . . ah . . . *excellent* patching that has been done in the field.'' He had a wispy blond mustache and slightly buck teeth with just enough superciliousness about him to indicate that *Starfury* would soon have still another First Lieutenant. Contrell was an administrator, not a Helmsman.

Brim clapped him on the shoulder. ''She's a good old bus,'' he said gently. ''She just needs a little bit of work.'' Then he offered his hand to Beyazh. ''Mr. Ambassador,'' he said with a smile, ''to what do I owe the honor of your presence?''

Beyazh grinned. ''I wanted to make certain you actually *were* still alive, Captain,'' he said. ''In my business, one learns never to trust word-of-mouth reports completely—and the General here knows how much importance Mustafa Eyren places in your person. Had you lost your life jousting with that Leaguer space fort, I might never have heard the truth about you.''

''Oh, we'd have had to admit it,'' Drummond laughed. ''We couldn't fake him if we wanted to.''

''I sincerely believe *that*,'' Beyazh said, then drew a red envelope from the folds of his robe. ''But I had a second reason for meeting the Captain, too.'' He handed the envelope to Brim. ''In spite of my best detective efforts, I have no idea what this envelope contains, only that Raddisma herself sealed it in my presence and commanded me to personally deliver it into your hands.'' He smiled. ''I have now obeyed her wishes.''

Brim frowned as familiar perfume teased his nostrils. ''Thank you, Mr. Ambassador,'' he said, placing the letter inside his white IVG Fleet Cloak (that would soon be traded for a version in Imperial blue). A small inner voice had warned him that it would be a good idea to put off reading its contents until he was alone.

''And now, Captain,'' Drummond intruded into his thoughts, ''you and I need a few moments of privacy. Commander, I assume you can find your way to the bridge with Commander Tissaurd's promotion and orders.''

''I can indeed, General,'' Contrell replied. He nodded to Brim. ''My best to you, Captain,'' he said. Then—to Brim's horror —he bowed to Beyazh and strode off down the corridor. True Imperials *never* bowed.

Drummond shook his head. "Ex CIGA lickspittle," he explained. "He's only here because Tissaurd's in charge. He'll merely fill out her crew complement on the way to Sherrington's for the refit."

Beyazh nodded approval. "It would be frightening to discover that your actual combat billets were filled with such persons." He laughed. "I have always rather admired the way you Imperials normally refuse to bow." He placed a hand on Brim's shoulder and smiled. "If we do not meet before you depart for your new assignment—which General Drummond refuses to divulge," he added, peering with mock displeasure over his eyeglasses, "then I shall wish you well until the next time." With that, he touched his forehead and lips in the Fluvannian gesture of fellowship and strode off down the corridor.

In Brim's cabin, Drummond waited impatiently while the Carescrian scanned his new orders.:

ASHF234812-19E GROUP 198BA 113/52011
[TOP SECRET]

PERSONNEL ACTION MEMORANDUM,
IMPERIAL FLEET,
PERSONAL COPY

FROM:
BU FLEET PERSONNEL;
ADMIRALTY, AVALON

TO:
W. A. BRIM, CAPTAIN, I.F.
AVALON
<0893BVC-12-K2134MV/573250>
SUBJECT: DUTY ASSIGNMENT

(1) YOU ARE DETACHED PRESENT IVG DUTY
AS OF 205/52012.
(2) PROCEED MOST EXPEDITIOUS TRANSPORT
GIMMAS STARBASE, HAEFDON. REPORT REAR

ADM B. GALLSWORTHY, 11 GROUP, CENTRAL COMPLEX AS SECTOR COMMANDER.
(3) EMPEROR'S AWARD CEREMONIES POSTPONED. IMPERIAL COMBT FORWARDED GIMMAS UNDER SEPARATE COVER.
(4) SUBMIT TRAVEL EXPENSE VOUCHERS DIRECT ADMIRALTY
C/O K. I. BARNETT, LTCMDR, IF @ FLEET PERSONNEL, ADMIRALTY, AVALON

FOR THE EMPEROR:
TANDOR K. KNORR, CAPTAIN, I.F.

[END TOP SECRET]
ASHF234812-19E

"Sector Commander," Brim yelped in horror, "under Bosporus Gallsworthy? General, I'm just a simple Helmsman!"

Drummond laughed. "A Helmsman, maybe," he allowed. "But simple? Not on your life! At least not the way *either* Gallsworthy or Calhoun look at things. Those old friends had a tremendous row over who got you. It took Prince . . . er . . . Emperor Onrad to settle things. And since Calhoun's new assignment will be in the arena of overall strategy, Gallsworthy got the nod."

"But he's a Commissioner, not an Admiral, General!"

"You didn't read the message carefully enough," Drummond said with a chuckle. "It says 'Rear Admiral,' not 'Commissioner.' "

"Yes, sir," Brim grumped. "I guess I saw it."

"Old Bosporus wanted back into the war," Drummond continued. "He'd had enough of fighting from a desk chair. So he yelled loud enough—and in the proper ears—to make the switch."

Brim nodded. "Somehow, I'm not surprised, General," he said. "He was the most superb Helmsman I've known."

"In that case," Drummond said, "I'll assume you've accepted

the assignment without an argument—as if that would do any good?''

Brim frowned. "General," he remonstrated, "I hardly even know what a wing *is* much less what commanding one entails. Will I still get my hands on the controls of a starship once in a while?"

"*Starfury*'s been in a foreign country too long for me to trust that she hasn't been bugged," Drummond replied, glancing around the cabin. "And the details of your new job are highly classified. So you'll have to learn about all that when you arrive at Gimmas. But I will promise you this: Eventually, you will be quartered just outside Avalon—and if my predictions are anywhere close to accurate, even *you* may put in more flying time than you want."

This time, it was Brim's turn to smile. "In that case, General," he said, "no argument."

"Good man," Drummond said. "I figured that you'd come through. That's why I'm in such a hurry this morning—and *also* why *Starfury*'s parked where she is. On the next gravity pool to starboard is I.F.S. *Jacques Schneider*, scheduled to lift off in just one metacycle—or as soon as you pack a light travel bag. My office already forwarded the Imperial uniforms you had in storage here, and I'll have Barbousse pack and send the rest of your shipboard gear with his own." He chuckled for a moment. "Onrad gave strict orders that the two of you are not to be separated. Says you're the worst thing that's happened to the League since we invented the 406-mmi disruptor. . . ."

Less than one hectic metacycle later, Brim scrubbed at vestiges of Tissaurd's lipstick on his cheek while he strapped himself into a jump seat on the destroyer's tiny bridge. He looked back through the clearing afternoon at his first command. Even patched as she was, *Starfury* remained one of the most naturally beautiful machines he'd ever encountered. He thought about the great Mitchell racers she claimed as direct ancestors, and smiled. Every iral a thoroughbred!

Then, abruptly, the whole waterfront of the military complex disappeared behind cascades of water as *Schneider* began her takeoff run and presently soared into the overcast. So much for vacation plans. . . .

In the excitement of his transfer, it wasn't until that evening in the wardroom that Brim remembered Raddisma's letter. Relaxed in a comfortable recliner, he crossed his legs and broke the elaborate crest that sealed the envelope, extracting an old-fashioned letter written on what felt like authentic parchment paper. Incredible! But then, so was Raddisma. . . .

Dearest Wilf:

A few days ago, I discovered to my utter joy that our splendid evening together had indeed produced much more than merely a night of fleeting pleasure. I do hope you will forgive me, but following our afternoon tour of the infirmary, I decided, precipitously perhaps, that I wanted to bear your child. It was the proper time for me. And so before we departed for the Officers Club, I prepared myself to conceive. Later on, you accomplished the remainder, in a *most* delightful manner, I might add.

In a few Standard Months, then, you will become the father of a baby girl. Sorry, my Captain: I realize that men normally desire sons. But *I* desired a girl. And since the task of bearing the child falls to me, it seemed only fair that the choice should be mine as well.

Please understand, Wilf, that you bear no responsibility for this child whatsoever, except for putting me in a rare mood to make love and babies in the same night. And, of course, supplying your own juices, which I carefully, and respectfully, retained. Because the Nabob believes that the baby is his, this letter is one of joyful proclamation only—not one of obligation. All things being equal, including a war that I count on *you* to win, our daughter will be raised to a life of high privilege, comfort, discipline, and education. It will be as if she were a princess, without the grinding duty that rides with the title. And, of course, I shall insure that she *never* becomes a courtesan.

Finally, my once-and-future lover, please also know that although you bear no responsibility for this child, you are *also* most welcome to share as much of her life as you might desire—with the exception, obviously, of a proclaimed fatherhood. The Nabob, bless his heart, is much disposed to male heirs, and although he will love her in his own way, he will rarely remember that she exists. Therefore, at your own discretion, you may take any role with her you wish, from "nonexistent" to "favorite uncle." Over the next years, Wilf Brim, it will be interesting to discover which you choose.

Clearly, I shall be in no shape, either literally or figuratively, to entertain you during the next few months. But please be assured of two things. First: believe that I shall notify you as soon as our child is born, and second: know that we shall have other nights together if you so desire. Aside from being the father of my only child, Wilf Brim, you are a very, very special man to me.

With sincere and respectful love,
Raddisma

As the destroyer thundered out across the galaxy, Brim sat stunned for the second time in a single day, staring blindly at the stars rushing past the small Hyperscreen scuttles. When he finally corraled his galloping thoughts, they resolved themselves into two personal crises that he would need to resolve in the reasonably near future. First, he had to somehow discover if Margot Effer'wyck was still alive, because, in spite of a thousand declarations to the contrary, he still loved her—no matter what had transpired in the last few troubling years. And now, a daughter! He had some pretty unsettling thoughts about his still-unborn child—especially considering the war in which she would start her life, but he vowed he would sidestep those issues until he could at least start to resolve the first.

He shook his head and looked around the *Schneider*'s tiny wardroom, considering such arcana as dull moments. There were times when he wished he might have a few, just so he could catch up on all the moments that *weren't*. And he hadn't even considered what was happening to him *personally*: his mysterious new assignment—and the added responsibilities that would come with that territory. Closing his eyes for a moment, he wondered seriously how well Onrad's CIGA-weakened capital would endure the savage attacks that would soon develop in the skies over Avalon.

Then he shrugged. Clearly, he would have little trouble seeing *all* of it firsthand—so long as he managed to stay alive. . . .